THE PENGUIN POETS

BAUDELAIRE

BAUDELAIRE

INTRODUCED AND EDITED BY
FRANCIS SCARFE

★

WITH PLAIN
PROSE TRANSLATIONS
OF EACH POEM

PENGUIN BOOKS

Penguin Books Ltd, Harmondsworth, Middlesex, England
Penguin Books Inc., 7110 Ambassador Road, Baltimore, Maryland 21207, U.S.A.
Penguin Books Australia Ltd, Ringwood, Victoria, Australia

—

First published 1961
Reprinted 1964, 1967, 1968, 1970

—

—

Made and printed in Great Britain
by Richard Clay (The Chaucer Press) Ltd, Bungay, Suffolk
Set in Monotype Bembo

Cover pattern by Stephen Russ

GENERAL EDITOR'S FOREWORD

THE purpose of these Penguin books of verse in the chief European languages is to make a fair selection of the world's finest poetry available to readers who could not, but for the translations at the foot of each page, approach it without dictionaries and a slow plodding from line to line. They offer, even to those with fair linguistic knowledge, the readiest introduction to each country's lyrical inheritance, and a sound base from which to make further explorations.

But these editions are not intended only for those with a command of languages. They should appeal also to the adventurous who, for sheer love of poetry, will attack a poem in a tongue almost unknown to them, guided only by their previous reading and some Latin or French. In this way, if they are willing to start with a careful word-for-word comparison, they will soon dispense with the English, and read a poem by Petrarch, Campanella, or Montale, by Garcilaso, Gongora, or Lorca, straight through. Even German poetry can be approached in this unorthodox way. Something will, of course, always be lost, but not so much as will be gained.

The selections in each book have been made by the various editors alone. But all alike reflect contemporary trends in taste, and include only poetry that can be read for pleasure. No specimens have been included merely for their historical interest, or to represent some particular school or phase of literary history.

J. M. COHEN

CONTENTS

INTRODUCTION

I

A POET whose work is so complex and diverse, though apparently so simple and unified, as Baudelaire's is not to be summarized in any convenient formula. Yet many attempts of this kind have been made; they are useful and have to be taken seriously. A modern Dante? This suggestion, first made in 1857 by Thierry, has been discussed and modified by T. S. Eliot who would be more satisfied with a comparison with Goethe. In spite of the 'ideal' poems in *Spleen et idéal*, Baudelaire could at most be described as a Dante without the *Paradiso*. He is also a Dante without a system. There is no consistent metaphysic in Baudelaire, and in spite of the arguments of Pommier and Ferran the theory of *correspondances* fails to provide one. Then, in spite of the arbitrarily imposed 'architecture' of *Les Fleurs du mal*, expounded by Benedetto and Ruff with a subtlety it does not merit, Baudelaire's work has more of the disorder and fragmentariness of a Leonardo than the powerful structure of a Dante. Yet he does meet Dante at many points: for instance in his 'High-seriousness', to use Matthew Arnold's expression, which leads him so often to take the most important end-problems for his themes. The grave, majestic cadence of his verse at its best, the athletic vigour of his mind, the deep insight he often shows into the nature of mankind, and his intuitive awareness of the mystery of the world – it is these qualities which entitle us to discuss his name with those of the great writers of the past. T. S. Eliot's comparison with Goethe was made in a restrictive sense, in a way that perhaps diminished both: he was thinking of them as being only representative of their own age. Putting aside the romantic apparatus that Baudelaire inherited and which certainly marred some of his work, he was much more than a representative of his own age. What he condemned in society and in the soul of man are evils that are still with us, and the energy with which he defined the human condition enables us to discount the occasional artistic fault because we at once feel ourselves in the presence of problems that are universal, and listening to a universal voice. Baudelaire belongs to that race of poets which includes Blake and Lawrence, fanatics with something to say, and who in order to say it sometimes maltreated language. The corrections Baudelaire made to his poems are generally directed towards truth and clarity, rather than smoothness.

'The Swift of poetry', Lytton Strachey neatly suggested: but they meet only in their disgust, wit, and gloom, and Baudelaire is the bigger of the two. If he is, as a man, 'the tragic sophist' so ably described by G. T. Clapton, it is debatable whether he is the 'Too Christian' or the 'Near-Jansenist' portrayed by Bénouville and Ruff. If Aldous Huxley slipped almost as badly as Arthur Symons in calling Baudelaire 'a bored satanist', the admirable phrase of Lionel Johnson, 'Baudelaire sings sermons', while stressing rightly the poet's great claims as a moralist, leaves out that important part of his work which is gratuitous and compels the mind by its supreme aesthetic qualities.

The terms applied to Baudelaire's life are often misleading. It is usually regarded as a tragic failure, whereas it was a triumphant success in the sense of being the kind of life required to produce a certain kind of work, the kind of life which, testing its bearer beyond endurance, led him in the end, as his poems from 1859 onwards show, to a level of heroism and almost saintliness denied to his contemporaries. In Dr René Laforgue's opinion it was psychologically and morally a defeat (*échec*). In Sartre's it was not only a defeat but a 'deliberate failure'. Here we seem to be on the lunatic fringe of moral philosophy: for how can a life be judged as a deliberate failure when it was so inseparable from a precious and beautiful work? According to the philosopher, Baudelaire willed his own misfortune, doomed himself in advance by his worship of the bourgeois values which he flouted, and deliberately failed to live the life for which he was destined by his gifts. Sartre's statements are so framed as to reverberate angrily in the reader's consciousness: 'Baudelaire deliberately isolated himself.' 'Baudelaire is a man who chose to see himself as if he were another man: his life is merely the story of that failure.' 'He is the man who, while most profoundly experiencing his human condition, the most passionately sought to conceal it from himself.' 'He adopted his stepfather's moral code without discussion.' 'He was not a revolutionary but a man in revolt.' 'He chose to have a bad conscience.' 'That exceptional soul lived in bad faith.' (For Sartre, bad faith is defined not as cheating others, but as the cheating of oneself.) 'Having chosen Evil, he also chose to feel guilty.' 'Baudelaire submitted to Good in order to violate it.' Sartre does not even spare the *poet* in this callous examination: 'All his life, Baudelaire sought sterility.'

Apart from the context of existential philosophy on which Sartre's analysis is based, it is a compliment to Baudelaire to credit him with having 'chosen' so much of his life. But there is no life without Others. Much of Baudelaire's misery came, as we shall see, from the sternness of General Aupick, the unimaginativeness of his mother, the twisted character of Jeanne Duval, the obtuseness of Ancelle, the meanness of Sainte-Beuve who never found a word of praise – in public – for the only poet of the younger generation who really cared for him. His elected master Gautier, in spite of his solid position as a critic on government newspapers, never wrote a line about Baudelaire before the fulsome biography he produced after the poet's death. Baudelaire's suffering did not come from nowhere, and it did not all come from himself. He complained all his life about his bad luck, his *guignon*; but if much of it might have been avoided, it was certainly not his fault if his merits were ignored by the great and fouled by the vulgar, or that the only publisher who really cared for his work was a bankrupt. The whole story of the publication of Baudelaire's works in his lifetime, while containing instances of underhand shifts on Baudelaire's part, was one of disgraceful extortion on the part of his publishers, and to suggest that Baudelaire willed this, that he willingly slaved in poverty to write critical works and translations that were grossly underpaid, is nonsense. Maybe Baudelaire was a *déclassé* and maybe he had an exaggerated grudge against society, but when we read that he told Catulle Mendès, only two years before his death, that he had earned by his pen, in the whole of his life, only *fifteen thousand, eight hundred and ninety-two francs, sixty centimes*, we begin to see the other side of the picture.

The weakness of Sartre's position lies in judging Baudelaire in a vacuum, or as though he were living in a noble state of society, surrounded only by saints. His own arguments are not taken to their proper conclusion. For every case of underhand behaviour on the poet's part it would be possible to quote instances of his generosity to others, but that is not the point, either. We are concerned with a Baudelaire who not only *chose* to suffer, as Sartre suggests, and who not only *chose* to be a misfit, if we can go so far with Sartre, but who also *chose* to write *Les Fleurs du mal* and a dozen books of prose which have stood the tests of time and taste. Perhaps it would be pressing the point too far to say that he chose, not only to be the poet of evil or of Paris, but to be a European poet (as Valéry described him) and beyond that to be a universal poet. The so-called failure of Baudelaire is, of course, a failure to live a happy and comfortable existence. But his success lies in an unique exchange between a life and a work, the capacity for making a synthesis of sensation and contemplation in an unusual degree, the transcendence from the tawdry details of daily life into the life of the spirit, the exchange between ordinary human disgrace and enduring art. It is an insult to a poet to describe him, as one might do on some official form, as an anti-social male suffering from syphilis and an overdraft at the bank. The answer to Sartre is that Baudelaire failed to be a failure.

But it is far from my intention to dismiss all predecessors and then propose a new thesis, equally imperfect. On the contrary, the views quoted above serve to show the complexity of the problem that Baudelaire offers, and the statements quoted need to be borne in mind in any just appreciation of the nature and importance of his life and work. To them we should add P. Mansell-Jones's overall interpretation of Baudelaire as one who sought justification for his life on the aesthetic plane: he also shows the negative side of Baudelaire in describing in some of the poems 'the intimations they give of a mind in fundamental error'. Dr Enid Starkie, whose most recent assessment of Baudelaire (1957) is to be read in conjunction with the works of Crépet and Ruff, concludes her book in these terms: 'Many of those in whom Baudelaire today finds an echo, see, in his passionate longing "pour trouver du nouveau", their own aspiration towards something beyond themselves and the pitiable quest for material comfort and happiness, something in which to lose themselves, a return to a spiritual philosophy of life, to a difficult region which will make demands on man for effort and sacrifice, and will not play him false.' Even here the terms are sometimes reversible, for it could also be said that many readers are likely to *find* rather than lose themselves in a proper study of the work of this great poet.

II

Charles Baudelaire was born in Paris (rue Hautefeuille) on 9 April 1821 and was thus of that second 'romantic' generation which included Banville, Leconte de Lisle and Flaubert, the Brontës, and Matthew Arnold. His father, François, was born in 1759, taught for a while at the Collège Sainte-Barbe, became a tutor in the house of the duc de Choiseul-Praslin, and after the Revolution was rewarded for his devotion to that family, which he helped to save from the guillotine, with a comfortable post in the offices of the Senate. It has been recently suggested that François Baudelaire was admitted to holy orders before the Revolution but was released from his vows under the Civil Constitution of the Clergy. His first marriage in 1803 left him with a son, Claude-Alphonse, who later became a lawyer and had only the coolest of relations with his half-brother Charles. At the age of sixty the widowed François remarried, his second wife, the poet's mother, being Caroline Archimbaut-Dufays (or Defayis) who was born in London in 1793. The daughter of a French officer, she was a refined person who communicated to her son something of her knowledge of the English language.

Baudelaire never forgot the elegant manners, artistic tastes, and Jansenist inclinations of his father, whose death in 1827 came as a blow to the sensitive boy. Then followed an idyllic period when the precocious child thrived in the closeness of his mother's undivided love, a happiness nostalgically evoked in such poems as *Je n'ai pas oublié, voisine de la ville* and *La servante au grand cœur*. A note recalling his childhood background reads: 'Childhood – old Louis XVI furniture, antiques, consulate, pastels, eighteenth-century society' – exactly that old-world atmosphere which is fleetingly suggested in such poems as *Spleen* ('J'ai plus de souvenirs ...'), *Recueillement*, and even *L'Invitation au voyage*.

Unfortunately for Baudelaire, this interlude was so acutely happy and so short as to become a source of pain in after life, and no doubt the sense of loss and guilt and exclusion, which marks so much of his work, sprang from the experience of being driven from the earthly paradise at an impressionable age. Within eighteen months of his father's death his mother married a Captain Aupick, an energetic officer of Irish descent who later rose to the rank of General and became ambassador to Turkey and Spain. Charles was only about ten years old when he was separated from his mother, becoming a boarder at the Pension Delorme in Lyons, then at the Collège Royal of the same city, to which his step-father had been posted. When the family regained Paris in 1836 he became a boarder at the Lycée Louis-le-Grand.

Although he was academically a good pupil, excelling in Greek and Latin and later obtaining his *baccalauréat* (or matriculation) with ease, Baudelaire's own comments on his education were unflattering: 'After 1830, the Collège de Lyon – blows, struggles with the teachers and pupils, overwhelming fits of melancholy' – and, in a letter to his mother towards the end of his life, he referred to the 'lamentable education' that Aupick had given him. He felt himself to be an outsider and wrote of 'The feeling of solitude ever since my childhood. In spite of my family – and especially when I was surrounded by my schoolfellows – the feeling of an eternally lonely destiny.' At about the age of fifteen he began devouring the works of the romantics, especially Chateaubriand and Sainte-Beuve (see the Epistle to Sainte-Beuve in the present collection), and showed an aggressive attitude to those in authority. His friend Hignard described him as being 'always a dare-devil ... sometimes full of the deepest mysticism and sometimes of the grossest immorality – but in conversation only, which often went beyond the bounds of moderation and good sense'.

The beginning of Baudelaire's life as a *déclassé* came with his sudden expulsion from the Lycée Louis-le-Grand in 1839. The reasons given by his headmaster for this humiliation read rather like a pretext, and it seems likely that the masters were glad to be rid of an awkward rather than a bad character. Baudelaire was ordered by the vice-principal to hand over a note which a friend had passed to him in class. In loyalty to his friend, Baudelaire tore up the note and swallowed it. The headmaster accused him of sneering and wrote to Aupick that though the boy was 'certainly endowed with outstanding abilities' he was being dismissed for his bad influence on school discipline.

Meanwhile, though he apparently enjoyed the trip to the Pyrenees with his step-father in 1837, which is commemorated in the poem *Incompatibilité* (q.v.), Baudelaire was nursing a dislike for the man who, as he thought, had supplanted him in his mother's affections. The boy already wanted to become a writer, but Aupick determined that he would follow an administrative career. Baudelaire was first sent as a boarder to a Monsieur Lasègue, a tutor at the Pension Bailly, to prepare for his '*bachot*', and later, when he was enrolled to study Law at the École de Droit (November 1839) he lived in the famous Pension Bailly, place de l'Estrapade, where he began to enjoy all the diversions of student life. Aupick took his responsibilities with puritanical seriousness and, no doubt in order to save his charge from bad company as well as to change his mind about his career, had him embarked on a ship which left Bordeaux for India in June 1841. For this purpose, 5,000 francs were taken out of Charles's estate. There is no evidence whatever that Baudelaire reached India, and Marcel Ruff is one of the few biographers who think that he did. All that we know is that he stayed for some time in Mauritius and the Île Bourbon, returned by a different ship from the one in which he set out, and was (according to his mother's evidence) back in Paris by February 1842. The voyage had not the desired effect. Baudelaire spent most of it in solitude, emerging from his introspection only on one occasion when he showed extraordinary courage in the face of danger and helped the crew to save the ship. The voyage left an indelible mark of exoticism and reverie on the poet's mind and work, as can be seen in poems of such different texture as *À une dame créole*, *À une Malabaraise*, *Le Voyage*, *Le Cygne*, *L'Albatros*, and many of those in which he relies heavily on marine imagery for his effects, such as *La Chevelure*, *L'Homme et la mer*, *Don Juan aux Enfers*. Perhaps it is not too fanciful to regard this last-named poem as the poet's self-portrait at that time. No doubt this odyssey also gave him his initiation to the 'Black Venus' and explains his profound attachment to the mulatress, Jeanne Duval, whom he met on his return.

Looking back on Baudelaire's youth up to this point, it cannot be said that he was treated by his parents with direct unkindness, though there was a lack of thoughtfulness and insight on their part. Only the combination of a tender sensibility and a streak of intellectual violence can explain the rankling animosity which, in later life, led him to over-dramatize his relationship with his mother, as in *Bénédiction*. But when we probe under the surface there is more to be said for him than the apologists of the Aupicks would have us believe. The poet's early letters to his mother show nothing but absolute tenderness and respect. When sent to live with M. Lasègue (who later became a mental specialist and was called in to see the poet at the end of his life) he began a letter to his mother in July 1839: 'My dear mother, my good mother, I hardly know what to say to you, yet I have all kinds of things to tell you. First of all I feel a great need to see you. How different it is, living with strangers – and it isn't exactly your caresses and our laughter that I miss, so much as something which makes our mother always seem the best of women, and her qualities suit us better than those of other women: there's such a harmony between a mother and her son; they live so well in each other's company, so that, God knows, since I came to M. Lasègue's I feel upset.' Such openness and analysis are unusual in a youth of eighteen. At the same time his friend Hignard speaks of him as being 'very religious', as can be seen in the moving poem beginning 'Hélas, qui n'a gémi sur autrui, sur soi-même!' Until 1842 there is no serious sign of revolt. Even when he was exiled to the East Mme Aupick wrote: 'He would have preferred to stay here, without the slightest doubt, but without showing any repugnance he gave in.' His stepfather wrote: 'He yielded to my arguments. When he was leaving Charles wrote us a nice letter which is the first guarantee we have of the good results we expect from this harsh trial.' We can well feel astonished at the hypocrisy of the words 'Harsh trial' (*rude épreuve*) since it is obvious that Aupick's policy ever since he married was to keep the boy out of sight as much as possible – five or six boarding establishments followed by a year at sea! The poet was justified in regarding this as selfish, but unfortunately he set a glaze of cynicism, which was to remain, over his wounded feelings.

After his return from Mauritius, Baudelaire was due to come into his inheritance (about 75,000 francs, which was a large sum in those days), but this does not seem to have been handed over to him outright. He lived in rooms in the rue Vaneau, the quai de Béthune, then finally in the Hôtel de Lauzun (Pimodan) on the Île Saint-Louis. He used to send his mother flowers and trinkets and invite her to meals with him. He wrote in one of his letters: 'You speak of making your home pleasant for me, but the simplest way is to invite me when you are alone rather than when you have company.' It was only in 1844, then more seriously in 1847 that his relations with his mother broke down, and till then his revolt was directed only against Aupick. Perhaps he was also in trouble with his half-brother, Claude. Biographers have been slow to note why, while Baudelaire was away on his trip to the Indies, Claude was toadying to the Aupicks and nourishing the fires of resentment. He wrote to Mme Aupick about 'Protecting some part of Charles's fortune' and 'other means which you will find as distasteful as I do'. As the two brothers owned adjoining pieces of land at Neuilly, it is not hard to guess why Claude was so anxious to 'protect' his brother's fortune. Be that as it may, the upshot was that Baudelaire's inheritance never came into his own hands: as early as 1843 he agreed that his mother should take care of it and give him remittances from the interest.

By the middle of 1844 all the elements of Baudelaire's future torment were assembled, and the web of circumstance woven round him by himself and his family was only broken with his death. For the past two years the poet had – openly enough – been leading a kind of double life. While entirely sincere in his devotion to his mother and busily educating himself as well as writing, with his bohemian friends he was smoking hashish and opium, frequenting prostitutes, and squandering money. In the company of members of the so-called 'Norman School', Prarond, Levavasseur, and Dozon (who published a book of poems in 1843 which some critics believe to contain unsigned works by Baudelaire) he savoured all the delights of the Latin Quarter. Expecting to come into the inheritance left by his father, he proceeded to spend it in advance: not for him the bourgeois idea that money is to be saved and multiplied. He imagined that a certain social status would enable him to impress editors and publishers. His friends all describe him as incredibly handsome, and so he was. A brilliant conversationalist, he had a grasp of all the arts, was writing impressive poems, and showed every sign of having a brilliant career before him. But he had expensive tastes and indulged them fully after returning from the East. He decorated his room in the Hôtel Pimodan in stripes of red and black, and filled it with rich carpets and hangings, porcelain, fine paintings, and antiques. To quote Dr Starkie, 'Hignard tells us that he sometimes looked like a Titian portrait come to life, in his black velvet tunic, pinched in at the waist by a golden belt, with his dark waving hair and his pointed beard. Sometimes again he wore plain black broadcloth, skin-tight trousers fastened under his patent-leather shoes, with white silk socks, a coat with narrow tails, a fine white shirt with broad turned-back cuffs, and a collar wide-open at the neck, tied loosely with a scarlet tie. Again, according to Nadar, he would wear pale pink gloves.' Dandyism, however, is not always a sign of lack of character: we have to recall Disraeli wearing rings outside his gloves. There is some truth, none the less, in Rimbaud's reproach that Baudelaire 'lived in too artistic a milieu'.

All this was nothing compared with the poet's ostentatious

sexual choice (which Nadar dates as early as 1839–40 but which the poet's letters prove to have been in 1842). Though in many respects a chaste man who sought aesthetic rather than sensual satisfaction (Nadar said he died a 'virgin') he had begun living with a mulatto woman, Jeanne Lemer or Duval, with whom he was to share a short period of happiness followed by many years of misery. Jeanne Duval is the crucible and the cross of his subsequent life. Though she offered him the poles of ecstasy and disgust which are plainly to be seen in the cycle of poems he wrote for her, though she was unfaithful to him almost from the beginning, cheated and robbed and deliberately hurt him, he never lost his sense of responsibility for her. Baudelaire's nobility of character is seen in his devotion to her needs whenever they separated. If she brought out the worst in him, she also brought out the best. To complete the picture at that time, he had probably contracted the venereal complaint which recurred at intervals for the rest of his life: but it is to be noted that his brother died of the same symptoms.

Such were the conditions when, already in debt to tailors, junk-dealers, and other tradesmen, Baudelaire was suddenly flung from an extravagant and elegant way of life into a poverty from which he was never to recover. The Aupicks suddenly had his fortune sequestrated, it was turned into a trust, and Baudelaire was treated as a minor for the rest of his life, under the guardianship of the lawyer, Ancelle, who made him small monthly payments, often arriving late, on which he was unable to live. His outstanding debts were not all paid at this time, and with accumulating interest they hung round his neck thereafter. He was never able to live in the same lodging for more than a few weeks or months at a time: he explained to his mother some years later how he was obliged to 'flit' on Lady Day to avoid his creditors. In his last years his escape to Belgium in the hope of restoring his fortunes by lecturing and fresh contracts was a flight from their clutches as well as from himself.

The dismay with which Baudelaire faced the prospect of earning his living by his pen and perhaps becoming a hack can be seen in such poems as *Le Mauvais Moine* and *La Muse vénale*. Anger and humilation were for years to override his first feelings of despair. A long letter to his mother in 1844 while the plans were being laid to treat him as a ward, shows much less concern for money, which he did not even discuss, than with the moral aspects of the situation. It came as a hard blow to his pride. 'For my misfortune I am not made as other men – what you regard as a necessity and a painful circumstance is something I cannot bear.' He stressed again and again the humiliation of being put into the hands of strangers: 'Is there not an incredible cruelty in submitting me to the arbitration of a handful of men who find it a nuisance and who do not know me?' Worst of all his mother had in some way let him down and failed to keep her promises, rushing the affair through without enabling him to prepare any defence (the arrangements were all completed between July and September 1844). The poet was most hurt by the impersonality now imposed on their relationship: 'I would rather have no fortune at all and abandon myself entirely to you, than submit to any other judgement – the first is still a free act: the second is an infringement of my liberty.'

From now on, till Aupick's death in 1857, after which they drew closer together again, relations between mother and son became cooler: there was a more bitter rupture in 1847, and after that some years in which he hardly saw her or wrote to her at all. In some of his letters we find Baudelaire describing how hungry he was or being unable to go out because he had no clothes, or how he had pawned books and manuscripts and could not carry on with his work. It was not until 1851 when Mme Aupick, returning from Constantinople, found her son living in such abject poverty (she called it *dénuement* or destitution) that her heart melted and she began helping him a little from her own purse – but in every transaction between them it is clear that the poet intended these sums to be set against his credit. Even when her husband was earning 40,000 francs a year as an ambassador, she was never able to give her son more than trifling sums which could only cover his most urgent and immediate needs.

By this time, according to his friends, Baudelaire is supposed to have written a large part of *Les Fleurs du mal*, but in fact only about thirty poems can be attributed with any certainty to the period 1837–45. He was now moving away from the 'Norman School' and numbered among his friends the future Parnassians, Banville and Louis Ménard, also Asselineau (who later wrote a little book about him), Gautier, and the painter Deroy. He had already established contact with Sainte-Beuve and Balzac. With his first published prose work, the *Salon* of 1845, he began laying the basis of his reputation as the greatest art critic of the century. Though this Salon is spoiled by a somewhat ambiguous flattery of the 'bourgeois' ('the bourgois is eminently to be respected, for one has to please those at whose expense one wants to live'), which might have been meant to please the Aupicks or to split the sides of the bohemians, it is notable for its praise of Delacroix, Daumier, and Corot when they were generally misunderstood, and for the coining of the expression 'the heroism of modern life', which remained one of his constant themes as an art critic and is one of the keys to the understanding of his own poetry. As yet he had published only one poem, *To a Creole Lady*.

Only two months after issuing the 1845 *Salon*, which was well received, Baudelaire, no doubt in financial straits and exasperated by his isolation from his mother, wrote a violent letter to the lawyer Ancelle (30 June) announcing that as he was 'useless to others and a danger to himself' he was about to commit suicide and wished to leave all his estate to his mistress Jeanne Duval. 'I am killing myself because I am immortal and because I hope,' he said; characteristically affirming his religious belief at the very moment of an irreligious act. He went on to say that whereas his mother had, in her husband, 'a human being, an affection, a friendship, I have only Jeanne Lemer. I have found peace only in her.' Though some biographers do not take this incident seriously, Baudelaire certainly inflicted a wound on himself. After a reconciliation with his family be stayed for a few months at their home in the aristocratic Place Vendôme. But very soon he wrote 'I have fallen into a terrifying mood of depression and apathy and need a long spell of solitude ... it's impossible for me to turn myself into what your husband would like me to be, so it would be cheating him to live any longer under his roof.' In the same year (1845) he published an anonymous skit on Balzac (whom he greatly admired) called *How to pay your debts when you're a genius.*

The following year, 1846, was one of great activity. He first published a short story, *Le Jeune Enchanteur*, which has since been shown to be an unacknowledged translation from an English work. He began contributing to the *avant-garde* magazine *Le Corsaire Satan* with some *Consoling Maxims on Love.* In recommending this article to his sister-in-law Mme Claude Baudelaire, with the words 'Be so kind, Madame, as to be my Providence in the career opening to me through the medium of love', he was already showing the tendency, repeated in the case of Marie Daubrun and Mme Sabatier, to seek some idealized person for whom he could write, thus offsetting his unintellectual attachment to Jeanne Duval, whom he was vainly trying to teach to read.

In the same year he published *Advice to young writers*, humorous and for the most part useless advice mingled with such anti-romantic wisdom as 'Orgy is not the sister of inspiration – Inspiration is definitely the sister of daily toil', which marks him off from the slovenly bohemians whose life he shared. The *Salon* of 1846 contains many points which were to become constants in his aesthetic. Much light is thrown on his place in the romantic tradition by such statements as: 'Romanticism, for me, is the most recent, the most up-to-date expression of the beautiful ... Romanticism will not consist of perfect execution but of a conception analogous to the morality of this century ... Whoever speaks of romanticism means modern art, that is to say intimacy, spirituality, colour, aspiration towards the infinite.' There is a strong intuition of the theories of Poe (which he did not yet know) in the following almost classical definition of art which anticipates Mallarmé and Valéry: 'There is no *chance* in art, any more than in mechanics ... A painting is a *machine*, all the systems of which are intelligible to the experienced eye.' The essay also shows the germ of the theory of *correspondances* in the tendency to relate colour to music, and in the statement 'For E. Delacroix, Nature is a vast dictionary'. In Section XVIII ('On the Heroism of Modern Life') he was really defining his own aim as a poet as well as what he was seeking in art: 'Parisian life is fertile in poetic and supernatural subjects. The supernatural (*merveilleux*) envelopes us and answers our needs like the atmosphere, but we do not see it.' His postulation of two types of Beauty – however old-fashioned any argument in terms of an abstract beauty may now appear – shows his particular talent for grafting his modernism on to a well-established tradition: 'All forms of beauty contain, like all possible phenomena, something eternal and something transitory – absolute and particular.' This generous and almost impregnable theory of beauty enabled him to graft on to the old rhetoric and aesthetic his own personal symbolism, his vision of the modern world, and indeed his own *anti-aesthetic* which make him the forerunner of Symbolism and even Surrealism. Baudelaire was now coming into possession of those few 'general ideas' which Henry James says are necessary to any serious writer. The year closed with the publication of *L'Impénitent* (later called *Don Juan aux Enfers*) and *À une Indienne* (otherwise known as *À une Malabaraise*).

Baudelaire referred several times from 1843 onwards, in letters to his mother, to a work over which he was taking great pains. This was the short novel *La Fanfarlo* which was printed in January 1847 in the *Bulletin de la société des gens de lettres*, a society to which Baudelaire was often to turn for financial aid in later years. In this highly artificial work Baudelaire was one of the first to create that *écriture artiste* which was to become so widespread towards the end of the century (Wilde, Gide, etc.). The story is told with great detachment and lightness of touch and has the kind of trivial theme of which Musset would have made a sparkling play. The hero, Samuel Cramer, author of a slim volume of poems, *Les Orfraies* (Ospreys), has creole blood in his veins and is very handsome; with 'a pure and noble brow, eyes as brilliant as drops of coffee, an arrogant, mocking nose, impudent, sensual lips, a square, domineering chin, and hair pretentiously arranged in the manner of a Raphael'. He suffers from being at once 'an enormous idler, distressingly ambitious, a distinguished misfit', with 'a gloomy nature streaked with brilliant flashes of light, lazy and enterprising, fertile in intricate schemes and ludicrous failures'. Obviously Samuel is at once directly related to Sainte-Beuve's Amaury (hero of the novel *Volupté*, which Baudelaire admired at school), and an ironical portrait of Baudelaire himself. Meeting a Mme de Cosmelly whom he had known in Lyon, who is unhappy because her husband is philandering with the actress La Fanfarlo, Cramer undertakes to lure the actress away from the husband. He achieves this by writing harsh criticism of her in the theatre columns: she yields to him, but much to his disgust Mme de Cosmelly goes away with her husband and La Fanfarlo wreaks her vengeance on the poet. One incident throws a strange light on the reputed sexual inhibition of the poet, for when La Fanfarlo offers herself naked to her lover, Cramer protests that he only wanted *Colombine* and insists that she wear her stage dress.

Baudelaire had little financial benefit from this work, though it was successful enough to be reprinted in 1849. The rest of 1847 was a time of defeat and procrastination, but perhaps it was the moment when he was reading Hoffmann, Swedenborg, Diderot, and others who were to have a decisive influence on his mind. Was he now elaborating his theory of *correspondances*? Swedenborg was already mentioned in *La Fanfarlo*, but though some critics attribute the famous sonnet to the years 1845–6 there is no convincing evidence for this. Now his poverty and sickness overcame him: at one stage he wrote that he had been *locked* in his room by his doctor. He even thought of returning to the Île Bourbon as a tutor. He was also planning a *History of Caricature* and a *History of Sculpture*, but though the first bore fruit in a long essay a few years later, sculpture was an art for which he had neither sympathy nor understanding – his comments on sculpture in the *Curiosités esthétiques* are mainly deplorable. It was in this year that he first met the actress Marie Daubrun for whom he later wrote the fine cycle of poems between 1850 and 1860 which includes the *Invitation au voyage* (and, I am inclined to believe, its pendant, *Le Jet d'eau*). Apparently he used to stare at her offensively while she was being painted – perhaps by his friend Deroy – but when she rebuffed him he went to the opposite extreme and offered her a purely platonic affection.

1847, that apparently idle year, was thus one which bore fruit later. In the same year, though he was frequenting the ragged bohemian set described by Murger, he was also moving in socialist circles, with Toubin, Proudhon, and the brilliant young painter Courbet. Courbet included a portrait of Baudelaire smoking a pipe in his famous *Atelier de l'artiste*, but in later years they drifted apart as Baudelaire turned against realism. Baudelaire had written mockingly in the last paragraph of *La Fanfarlo*, 'Poor singer of the *Ospreys* – he has fallen very low. I recently heard that he had founded a socialist newspaper and wanted to enter politics – a dishonest intellect, as honest M. Nisard would say.' The poet was now able to revel in the irony of living his fiction – he already believed that nature imitates art.

Baudelaire's activities in the revolutionary period 1848–51 were complicated and often mysterious, but in the main they arose from the emotional commitment, at the outset, which gripped all his generation, even Leconte de Lisle, and which soon faded into disillusionment with the socialist cause, followed by political apathy. Though Baudelaire was active in political journalism his writings cannot be identified with certainty. He was out with his friends Courbet and Toubin on the violent day of the 'banquets' (22 February 1848) and was shocked by the callous way the military treated unarmed civilians. Two days later he was at the barricades, gun in hand, but the statement that he was demanding the death of Aupick, then director of the École Polytechnique (military academy), was made by a witness who cannot be trusted. He is also known to have attended meetings of Blanqui's Central Republican Society. At the end of February he started a news-sheet (*Le Salut public*) which only ran into two numbers because of lack of funds: the poet sold the paper in the streets himself. In April he became Editorial Secretary of the socialist *La Tribune nationale*. By now he was losing faith in socialist policy. Like Chénier and many other poets he lacked patience for the day to day intrigues and compromises of politics, which he later described as 'a heartless science'. In his hands the paper turned conservative, though his friend Poulet-Malassis was in gaol and Ménard had to flee to Belgium. Towards the end of his life Baudelaire wrote that he understood 'how a man could desert one side to serve the other': this is the ironical fate of thwarted idealists.

With his mother away in Turkey, where Aupick was Ambassador, the poet was left to his own devices. He was in Dijon for a time (with Jeanne) presumably editing another paper, while it is probable that he also worked as an editor in Châteauroux. The influence of the revolutionary period does not show very directly in his poems, which contain few political references, but it helped to cure him of the art for art's sake of his early manner. During this period some of the great *Spleen* poems were composed, and twenty-six poems in all are known to have been grouped under the title *Les Limbes* (Limbo), a book which the poet announced as being published by Michel-Lévy '*and which is intended to trace the history of the spiritual agitations of modern youth*'. Thus the Revolution did, temporarily, give a social significance to poems which might originally have been written without that intention. His outlook as a poet had matured, for whereas in 1846 he was announcing a collection of poems to be called *Les Lesbiennes* there was no more talk of this. The first of the *Limbes* poems (*Le Vin de l'assassin*) appeared in 1848 in *L'Écho des marchands de vin*: two were printed in *Le Magasin des familles* in 1850 and eleven in the following year. The title *Limbo* is ambiguous, being used in both a religious and a social sense. Fourier had spoken of 'limbic periods' meaning those in which society is making a fresh start accompanied by industrial strife. There is enough stress on both the social and religious aspects for us to take the term in both senses. Such works as *Châtiment de l'orgueil* and the *Spleen* poems bear heavily on the idea of excommunication and lack of grace. Together with his rejection of art for art's sake Baudelaire turned against the idea of material progress, but if he abandoned political socialism and artistic realism this did not mean that he welcomed the new regime or ceased hating its materialistic, bourgeois values.

Yet he could not become a Liberal because French Liberalism implied atheism or at least agnosticism.

Baudelaire's only other important publication in 1851 was *Du vin et du haschisch*, a short book which appeared in four parts in *Le Messager de l'Assemblée*. This prepared the way for the famous *Les Paradis artificiels* published between 1858 and 1860. The section on *Le Vin* contains prose versions of *L'Âme du vin* and *Le Vin des chiffonniers*.

In the next five years Baudelaire made enormous progress on all fronts. His interest in Edgar Allan Poe, first stimulated in 1847, now crystallized and became one of his main enthusiasms as well as providing a regular source of income. Beginning with a short study of Poe's life and works – much of it at second-hand – in 1851, by 1856 he had completed the volume of *Histoires extraordinaires* which has remained the standard text in France. Altogether he issued five volumes of Poe's works, but unwisely sold his copyright in them for a sum of only 2,000 francs – a step which reveals his penury and lack of bent for business. In the domain of criticism he produced some good essays which he regarded as 'very Parisian', including those on Caricature and the *Exposition universelle* of 1855. Parallel with these went some articles which were collected later in his book on *L'Art romantique*, including *L'École païenne* (an attack on the Parnassians and on philosophical poetry, for he was opposed to what he called 'the heresy of teaching'), and the essay on the worker-poet Pierre Dupont.

Perhaps the most important event of all, as Baudelaire had been so slow in publishing his poems, was the appearance of a group of ighteen poems under the title *Fleurs du mal* in the highly respectble *Revue des deux mondes* in 1855. Baudelaire had abandoned e title *Les Limbes* after another poet used it in 1852, and the new e was suggested to him by Hippolyte Babou. Baudelaire threw y this chance of gaining a new and influential audience by ding some of the poems most calculated to shock the re- readers. He wrote to the editor describing an Epilogue he to include (but which was rejected) in which occurred the dour and goodness are disgusting', and added 'That, as you see, makes a nice firework-display of monstrosities.' Only a lack of social maturity could have led Baudelaire to think that such a display would be acceptable in a review of that kind, or to be disappointed when the editors printed nothing more of his.

This is a very important period for two other reasons: it was the time when he was assembling his volume *Les Fleurs du mal*, and when he was living intensely on the emotional plane. He left Jeanne Duval in 1852 after ten years of cohabitation, only to return to her again in 1855. He wrote a long letter to his mother about this in March 1852, saying 'Jeanne has become an obstacle not only to my happiness but also to the perfecting of my mind.' At the same time he made frantic efforts to provide for her financially.

The emotional picture of these years is extremely involved, because it contained at least three women. It was probably in 1850 or 1851 that Baudelaire wrote to Marie Daubrun: 'Through you, Marie, I shall be strong and great. Like Petrarch I shall immortalize my Laura. Be my guardian Angel, my Muse, and my Madonna, and lead me along the paths of the Beautiful.' There was certainly no other satisfaction to be had than this remote adoration, for already Marie was more interested in his friend, Banville. Nor was Baudelaire himself constant. After the separation from Jeanne in the spring of 1852 he began, at the end of the year, a mysterious course of behaviour towards Mme Sabatier, that beautiful and witty but perhaps unprincipled person whose salon, the expenses of which were paid by the banker Mosselmann, was attended by eminent men of letters of the period. Baudelaire had known her for many years, but only in 1851 began frequenting her salon. Having 'lost' both Jeanne and Marie, Baudelaire wrote anonymously to Mme Sabatier in December 1852, enclosing the poem *celle qui est trop gaie*. This was followed at intervals by other u signed letters containing poems. Though Feuillerat points out his overtures to Mme Sabatier coincide with absences of M Daubrun, I cannot believe, as the biographers do, that this se acts came entirely 'out of the blue' and had nothing to d feeling. Such a course of action amounted, on both sides, t understanding, a kind of emotional game, which could only be possible between two persons who knew and respected one another well enough to bear the truth. The poem *Confession*, which has been consistently underestimated, strikes me as one of the most beautiful poems in the love-cycles because of its psychological penetration, the stripping of the mask and laying bare the truth in a manner which still implies the greatest respect and compassion. For once, Baudelaire was entirely disinterested, and there is no sign, in spite of Feuillerat's insinuation, that Baudelaire was trying to exploit Mme Sabatier as soon as Marie was out of sight: he wanted nothing. In the course of 1854 his relationship with Marie became closer: he was even for a time hoping to set up house with her, writing to his mother 'I am going back to concubinage and if I am not living with Jeanne Lemer by 9 January (1855) I shall be with the *other* one.' His efforts to help Marie's theatre career failed, and she turned again to Banville. From March to September 1856 he again lived with Jeanne, but this time it was she who left him, much to his distress. At the end of the same year he was again writing to Mme Sabatier and in 1857 he threw off his anonymity (which her sister, 'Sisina', had long ago seen through). When in August 1857 Mme Sabatier, in a spontaneous gesture of compassion and admiration, offered herself to him, he rejected her. During 1858–9 Baudelaire again made every effort to help Marie and win her affection, but for the third and last time she went off with Banville, who was ill.

Of all these women Mme Sabatier stands out as the finest and the most profound in spite of her reputation for superficiality. For all her bohemian morals she was beautiful, generous, and sensitive, which the others were not. As for Marie Daubrun, she seems to have been selfish and calculating to a point, as well as pusillanimous. Feuillerat writes 'She bears a great share of responsibility for the crushing sadness that marks the last years of Baudelaire's life.' It can well be asked, however, if Baudelaire ever knew the full exchange of real love. There is no doubt that his relationship with Jeanne was stormy and passionate: that Marie moved him to a protective tenderness, and that between him and Mme Sabatier there was some bond of deep friendship, perhaps based on the idea that they were both in a sense outlaws living beneath the level which their sensibility demanded, and cloaking their wounds with the appearance of cynicism. He knew the enchantments of ecstasy and moments of emotional despair, but perhaps failed to love others because he could not love himself. From all three women he sought a kind of escape and transcendence, but never complete self-recognition or the deep discovery of the other. Love for him was another artificial paradise. Each of the cycles of love-poems is as heavily charged with disillusionment, violence, contempt, and pain as with compassion, tenderness, or delight.

1857 was one of the most active years of Baudelaire's life. During it he published not only the *Nouvelles histoires extraordinaires* by Poe, but his first group of prose-poems (under the title *Poèmes nocturnes*) as well as the famous *Les Fleurs du mal*. At the beginning of the year General Aupick died and after a time the poet drew closer to his mother, despite the interference of busybodies who surrounded her at Honfleur.

The contract for the *Fleurs* was signed with his friend Poulet-Malassis late in 1856, and in April 1857 the sheets came from the press; but owing to Malassis' delays it was not on sale until the end of June. Already in 1855 the group of *Fleurs du mal* printed in the *Revue des deux mondes* had provoked some strong attacks on the poet, and he now feared the worst. He wrote to his mother in July 1857: 'You know that I have never considered literature and the arts except as pursuing an end which is outside morality, and that beauty of conception and style are enough for me. But this book, whose title *Fleurs du mal* says everything, is clothed, as you shall see, in a sinister and cold beauty: it was composed in fury and patience. Besides, proof of its positive value can be seen in all the bad that's being said of it. The book enrages people. In any case, appalled myself at the horror I was going to inspire, I cut a third of the book out when it was in the proofs.' It is enough to read between the lines to see a fundamental contradiction in Baudelaire's outlook. While he might, theoretically, have thought that literature does not pursue a moral end, he clearly realized that his book raised moral problems. It is irrelevant to ask whether poetry pursues a moral end, for at whatever points it touches morality it must face the challenge of moral judgements. When he reacted some years later against Swinburne's remarks on the book's moral import he failed entirely to see that he was writing in the French moral tradition. Why, otherwise, did he print an epigraph from D'Aubigné which so pointedly raised the moral issue: 'But vice has not knowledge for its mother, and virtue is not the daughter of ignorance.' Further, in a prose dedication to Gautier (which Gautier persuaded him not to print) he had written 'I know that in the ethereal regions of true Poesy, there is no longer any evil, any more than good, and that this miserable dictionary of melancholy and crime can justify the reactions of morality, just as the blasphemer confirms religion.' Thus Baudelaire was fully aware of his book's moral significance, and he would have done well to prepare a moral defence instead of claiming that it was beyond good and evil.

Trouble was already brewing. The book was put on sale at the end of June and in July it was attacked by Gustave Bourdin (who had already denounced Baudelaire in 1855) in *Le Figaro*. Bourdin went so far as to doubt the poet's sanity. A further attack followed in a few days, while Baudelaire's faction did little or nothing to defend him. Sainte-Beuve proved to be lily-livered as usual. He had already failed to say a word in praise of the Poe translations in 1856, and now he asked Thierry to write a review in his place. Thierry had the courage and perception to compare Baudelaire with Dante, though it might well be asked how many would grasp the implications, since at that time Dante was just emerging from the eclipse into which he fell in the seventeenth century. The Ministry of Justice had already prosecuted Flaubert and his publisher for *Madame Bovary* in the same year, and was out for a conviction. All the sheets of *Les Fleurs du mal* were confiscated. Now Baudelaire, throwing off his anonymity, appealed to Mme Sabatier to use her influence, only two days before the trial. On 20 August after a half-hearted defence arguing that other poets such as Béranger had written more shocking things, both poet and publisher were fined and six of the poems were condemned as 'an offence against morality and decency' (*bonnes mœurs*). The fine was reduced after Baudelaire had written a letter of appeal to the Empress.

A final word is necessary at this stage on the additional pain that arose for Baudelaire at this time in his relationship with Mme Sabatier. I have already suggested that this was a valuable relationship: it was certainly so because it encouraged Baudelaire to write poems of exceptional beauty and insight, and because, whereas he wrote about both Jeanne and Marie as though they were animals or children, in this case he was, for the first time, writing for and about a mature person. Critics have asked whether Baudelaire was 'exploiting' Mme Sabatier when he wrote to her in August 1857 asking her to help him in the matter of the trial of *Les Fleurs du mal*. It might be said that there are certain things a man does not ask a woman to do for him. If his action was perhaps not entirely in good taste, it was surely a mark of confidence. What better interpretation can we put on it than that of Mme Sabatier herself? It was too late to help him, but she at once showed her admiration for his poems and her compassion for the poet. Never for a moment did she suggest that she had been asked anything out of the ordinary. Friendship often needs only such a small catalyst to be transformed into love. What happened now was that her spontaneous gesture was to offer herself and her love. In the state of anger and frustration through which he was passing at the time of the trial Baudelaire seems to have misunderstood this gesture, and, reproaching her for immodesty, he wrote 'A few days ago you were a divinity, now you are a woman.' He certainly did not love her in the proper sense of the term, but the sharpness of his reaction suggests that something valuable was lost. He had written in *Confession* 'Everything cracks – both love and beauty', and the would-be Petrarch and his idol whom he had used only as a source of poetic inspiration were both knocked off their pedestals together.

The first edition of *Les Fleurs du mal* contained a hundred poems, divided into five sections, as follows: (1) *Spleen et idéal*, 77 poems; (2) *Fleurs du mal*, 12 poems; (3) *Révolte*, 3 poems; (4) *Le Vin*,

5 poems, and (5) *La Mort*, 3 poems. It can be seen at a glance that although Baudelaire protested that his book was not an 'album' or casual collection as such books usually are, but a book with a plan, in spite of all that has been written about its 'architecture' the arrangement is loose and unconvincing. There is far too great a disproportion between the first group of seventy-seven poems and the other four with only twenty-three between them. The group of *Tableaux parisiens* was not created until the second edition (1861) when it was made up of eight poems taken from *Spleen et idéal* and ten new ones. It is also to be noted that the third group (*Révolte*) was miraculously spared by the tribunal, though it consisted of the aggressive trio *Le Reniement de Saint-Pierre*, *Abel et Caïn*, and *Les Litanies de Satan*. Baudelaire was at least free from the charge of an offence against religion.

Another point of interest is that in this as in all subsequent editions the three cycles of love-poems were printed in the first section (*Spleen et idéal*) in the order Jeanne Duval, Mme Sabatier, and Marie Daubrun. In a chronological arrangement (as in the present edition) the order would be different, if Feuillerat's thesis about the liaison with Marie Daubrun is accepted. The Sabatier cycle begins in 1852 and ends with *Semper Eadem* in 1860. The first poems for Marie were probably written as early as 1850 or 1851, though the dates of publication stretch only from 1855 to 1860, ending with the bitter denunciation of *L'Amour du mensonge* and *À une Madone*. (Critics have wondered whether the prose-poem *Laquelle est la vraie?* refers to Mme Sabatier. This prose-poem, in which the poet buries his beautiful Benedicta and is then faced with a miserable, vulgar replica of her, could just as well refer to Marie Daubrun. The relationship with Mme Sabatier did not end in disgust, but in friendship.) Feuillerat is on sure ground when he claims that Marie Daubrun wrenched the poet free from 'his enslavement to the Black Venus'. If Baudelaire placed Marie last in the series of cycles, perhaps it was because in 1857 he still had hopes of a permanent liaison with her, whereas he had never contemplated one with Mme Sabatier. It seems logical, then, in a selection which does not follow an order laid down for aesthetic or personal reasons by the poet, that the Daubrun cycle should follow that of Jeanne Duval.

It is hardly surprising if Baudelaire suffered for a long time from the excitement and bitterness of 1857, yet in the next four years he worked very hard and produced a second edition of *Les Fleurs du mal* containing thirty-two 'new' poems – not all of them really new, since he sometimes took years to finish a poem. For instance it has been suggested that *Le Cygne* (like *L'Albatros*, begun in 1842 and having the final stanza added to it in 1859) might have been started in the eighteen-forties, or consist of several poems or pieces of poems worked into one. 1858 saw the publication of the third Poe volume (*Adventures of Arthur Gordon Pym*) and the *Poème du haschisch* which formed the first part of the *Paradis artificiels* of 1860.

In November 1858 Baudelaire wrote an important letter to Calonne in which he said: 'I have begun the new *Fleurs du mal*... perhaps I shall make twenty. Protestants pedants (*professeurs*) will be pained to see that I'm an incorrigible Catholic. I shall take care to make myself thoroughly understood, sometimes very low, and then very high. Thanks to this method I'll be able to descend to the ignoble passions. Nobody but the absolutely dishonest will fail to understand the deliberate impersonality of my poems.'

Several important matters arise from this statement. As for 'incorrigible Catholic', those who are content to approach Baudelaire from a strictly orthodox Catholic position are as likely to be pained as the 'Protestant pedants'. No doubt he meant that his work would shock Protestants through its stress on evil, hell, and Satan, on the notion of excommunication, human vice, and weakness, the reality of sin, the 'Poverty of man without God', as Pascal put it. If so, he was underestimating the Protestant mind and perhaps confusing it with that lay puritanism – whether Catholic or Protestant – which refuses to look evil in the face and prefers to console itself with its diet of cups of tea and buns. It is relevant to note that in the period 1842–56 when Baudelaire was composing *Les Fleurs du mal* he was a lapsed Catholic. This amounts to saying that though the poet did not and could not cast off his Catholic formation, the book was not written (i.e. not all the poems were written) with a Catholic intention. Nor can the structure of the book, ending with death and, noticeably, in some hope for a kind of survival rather than a belief in it (the last three poems were *La Mort des amants, La Mort des pauvres, La Mort des artistes*), be regarded as what one would expect from an 'incorrigible Catholic'. Baudelaire's Catholicism will not bear analysis in detail, but became so generalized and laïcized as to amount to a prejudice rather than a faith, a disposition rather than a conviction. As an example of what I mean: in 1860 Flaubert read *Les Paradis artificiels* and commented: 'Here is my only objection. It seems to me that in a subject treated at such a high level, in a study which is the beginning of a natural science, in a work of observation and induction, you have (more than once) insisted too much(?) on the *Spirit of Evil*. One feels a leaven of Catholicism here and there. I would have preferred you not to have condemned hashish, opium, excess. Do you know what will emerge from them later?' Baudelaire's answer was non-committal in the sense that he did not directly quote doctrine in his defence; yet none but a man shaped by Catholicism could have replied quite as he did: 'I have always been obsessed by the impossibility of accounting for some of man's sudden acts and thoughts except by the hypothesis of the intervention of an evil force outside himself.' On another occasion he wrote to his mother, defending himself against a priest, that his book 'started out from a Catholic idea'. That may be so: but the book did not follow one. It is no condemnation of Baudelaire to point out that an integral Catholic could not have written *Les Fleurs du mal*, and would not have had the need or the courage to write it. The need for such a book arises from the absence of God, not his presence. It is a book which can make Catholics, and which perhaps in the end made Baudelaire into one; but it is not a book made *of* Catholicism, it is a rosary of pain and revolt. Perhaps the truest statement he ever made on the matter was the famous one to Ancelle in February 1866 when he was at the frontier of death: 'Need I tell you, you who haven't guessed it any more than the rest, that in this *atrocious book* I put all my heart, all my tenderness, all my religion (*travestied*), all my hate? It is true that I shall write the opposite, that I'll swear by everything holy that it's a book of pure art, of antics, of entertainment, and I'll be lying like a dentist.' Nothing can better illustrate the life of a work of art, and its relationship to the author's life, than the way it so often changed colour in the mind of its author. The reader will not so easily forget the early poems of revolt and nausea, or the projected book *Les Lesbiennes* and the ambiguous aims of *Les Limbes*. The fact that towards the end of his life when he had learnt to pray and was better disposed towards religion than ever before, he saw *Les Fleurs du mal* as his *travestied* religion does not justify those critics who seek in it his religion in a pure state. The irony of the work depends on our remembering the razor's edge on which its spirituality is poised, and the statement 'incorrigible Catholic' of 1858 is not to be taken at its face value. Baudelaire presents the first case (to be followed by Bloy, Mauriac, Jouhandeau, and Graham Greene) of the modern Catholic adventure towards and beyond the boundary of orthodoxy, the search for God in the nature of evil itself, and for salvation even by our sins. But if Baudelaire was avowedly seeking beauty in evil, it was perhaps by accident that he found something more? No: what fundamentally kept the work rooted in religion was the author's religious sensibility. He was not a modern, inasmuch as he obstinately believed that the world had an inherent meaning or meanings; that is the sense of *Correspondances* and it haunts *Les Fleurs du mal*, even in the *Spleen* poems when he is in despair because the world suddenly closes up and refuses those meanings. Mallarmé, on the other hand, was the very opposite of a mystic because he believed the material world to be meaningless, and it is this which separates Baudelaire from the Symbolists. In spite of all his talk about the gulf, the abyss, the void, nothingness, Baudelaire clung to the end to the meaningfulness of life and things, and the desperate poems of the last period, paralleled in our own language by Hopkins's 'terrible sonnets', represent a virile, muscular protest against the 'dark night of the soul'. Far from being an 'incorrigible Catholic', the saintliness of Baudelaire lies in the conquest of belief against all the odds, though it is likely that he died before the battle was completely won. I am not certain that the question, whether the poems are 'Catholic' or not, is a legitimate critical question: it is certainly one on which almost any opinion can be offered, and what has been said, in lightly touching on it, may well serve as a warning to the critical mind in its temptation to use the book as a torch to illuminate the life, or vice versa. Oddly enough, the old aesthetic tests are often more satisfactory than those of the biographer, the philosopher, or the theologian, where poetry is concerned. I would say that *Le Reniement de Saint-Pierre* and *Abel et Caïn* are aesthetic blunders of the first order, and the worst lapses of taste ever committed by Baudelaire, though some people might try to justify them on religious grounds. I see no such aesthetic failure in *Une Charogne* and *Les Litanies de Satan*, and their aesthetic probity is matched instinctively by their religious depth and pureness. A final word on this point: in view of my suggestion (p. xiii) that Baudelaire had no consistent metaphysic, how can I assert that he believed the world had a meaning? The answer is, I think, that Baudelaire fails, even in *Correspondances*, to give any idea of what that meaning is, beyond the idea of unity or what he calls elsewhere 'universal harmony'. He does not appear to me to attribute to the world the meaning that an 'incorrigible Catholic' would have given it. His religious sensibility was generalized and only began to focus in the last poems (1859 onwards).

A second point arising from the letter to Calonne is the description he gave of his work ('thanks to this *method*' ... 'deliberate *impersonality* of my poems'). In the tremendous period of creation on which he was now entering, and which is comparable with the last phase of Beethoven, when in one year, 1859, he produced *Le Cygne*, *Les Petites Vieilles*, *Le Voyage*, and so many other sustained and perfect works, Baudelaire was writing with a confidence of thought and a precision of art that he had never achieved before. It is in this period that without any loss of emotional intensity he became the *deliberate* artist, the *poète volontaire*, described in Poe's *Philosophy of Composition* and, later, in Valéry's critical works. He was writing, as Valéry would put it, 'with the maximum consciousness possible'. He was able to create what he willed and how he willed. The comparison with Beethoven is not accidental: there is nothing in literature comparable with the deliberate *discords* of *Les Petites Vieilles* where irony and compassion are mercilessly clashed together: nothing comparable with the rising from the simple recitative at the beginning of *Le Cygne* into the sublime compassion of the aria in the second part, followed by the absolute fall into prose, ending this fine poem on a single note, on a kind of *etcetera*, in 'bien d'autres encore'. The expression 'deliberate impersonality' also needs comment. It could mean that he was seeing good and evil from above, and that the evil that he described was not only that of his own existence. The great strength and value of all Baudelaire's poetry is that his theme is always the human being; his most characteristic imagery is always the imagery of the human body and its sensations, as in comparing a street lamp with 'un œil sanglant qui palpite et qui bouge' or the rustle of dawn 'comme un visage en pleurs que les brises essuient'. In the final period he certainly entered more deeply than ever into the lives of others, but perhaps he misjudged himself in a sense in speaking of his *impersonality* if it was meant to refer to the content of his work. No, it must be taken as referring to his manner of creating, making these superb poems by an act of reason, calculating the extent of his resources and his talent. He was to write in his Journals that he had been accused of all the crimes that he had described. But his poems were now being written according to a set plan, to fit into a framework which already existed but which had little meaning in the first edition. Had Baudelaire died in 1857 his claim on posterity would have remained in doubt. Had the injustice of the trial discouraged him he might have been a distinguished failure, like Musset. But in his remaining years he consolidated his position in every domain and demonstrated the range of his genius as never before.

In November 1858 Baudelaire again set up house with Jeanne Duval, but while he was away at his mother's in April 1859 Jeanne had a paralytic seizure and was taken to hospital. He at once raised money to pay her expenses, but it was characteristic of Jeanne to pretend that she had not received it, so that he had to borrow again. Now he looked after her 'like a father and a guardian'. He set up a home with her at Neuilly, with new furniture. This was a period of tenderness and remorse on his part: he was again insisting with his mother that Jeanne must inherit his estate. Very soon she installed a 'brother' in the apartment, who lived on Baudelaire and tyrannized her and ended by selling the furniture. Now the final parting came: from 1861 onwards Baudelaire was completely alone, fleeing restlessly from one hotel to another, still sending money to Jeanne but never seeing her again, and trying to scrape francs together to go and stay with his mother at Honfleur.

Meanwhile his position as an art critic was finally established by various actions and publications. The idea of the section of *Tableaux parisiens* in the second edition of *Les Fleurs du mal* arose from his efforts to help the eccentric, if not insane artist, Méryon. The poet's idea was to illustrate Méryon's engravings of Paris with poems and prose-poems of his own, but, far from appreciating this, Méryon thought he was being robbed. The poet had also become a friend of Boudin, then working in obscurity, and was the first to recognize the merits of Manet, who now became a firm friend. He also made Constantin Guys the exemplar of his own theory of the 'heroism of modern life' and celebrated his work in a fine essay which was not issued until 1863. The *Salon* of 1859 is one of his finest and most lucid statements on art, in which he brought Coleridge to his aid in his praise of Imagination which he called 'the queen of the faculties'. Baudelaire rightly saw the work of art as a synthesis and for that reason warned that the pursuit of Truth is not enough. Baudelaire's aesthetic was nearer to that of Croce than to the thinkers of his own time. The same year saw the publication of his fine essays on Wagner (whose work he was the first to evaluate and appreciate in France), and on Hugo, Gautier, and other writers. Unfortunately his critical works as well as *Le Spleen de Paris*, that highly original collection of poems in prose, were not collected into volumes until after his death.

Although 1861 was such a remarkable year, including as it did the issue of the famous second edition of *Les Fleurs du mal*, it was one in which Baudelaire was constantly tormented by the urge to commit suicide and by the obscure feeling that he would not live long enough, in any case, to complete all the projects he had undertaken. The frenzy with which he worked was a struggle against time, against solitude and sickness, and against himself. In this period he was writing the notebooks which show the terrible physical and moral struggle in which he was engaged. The point of terror was reached very soon, when he wrote in his journal: 'I am always in a state of vertigo, and today, 23 January 1862, I received a remarkable warning, I felt pass over me the wind from the wing of imbecility.' This mounting mental and physical stress explains the bleak intensity of the poems of this period, the fear of Time in *L'Horloge*, the obsession with the pit and the void in *Le Gouffre*, *Obsession*, and *Le Goût du néant*, the sense of guilt and discouragement in *La Fin de la journée*. The only two moments of calm occur in *La Voix* and *Recueillement*, in both of which there are references to the work of Pascal.

The new edition of the *Fleurs* in 1861 failed to receive quite the welcome Baudelaire had expected. He was now in an odd frame of mind, displeased at not being awarded the rosette of the Légion d'Honneur. Perhaps his candidature for the French Academy in that year was partly intended to draw attention to his work. He made the traditional calls on the Academicians and drew fresh humiliations on his head: Alfred de Vigny was almost the only one to recognize his genius yet did his best to dissuade him. Baudelaire withdrew, after Sainte-Beuve, forced at last to mention him in public, described his work as 'Baudelaire's *Folly*', thus dismissing him as an eccentric.

From now on his affairs went from bad to worse. His publisher Poulet-Malassis was imprisoned for debt and declared a bankrupt in 1862. Papers for which he was writing closed down. Charpentier, editor of the *Revue nationale*, had the effrontery to change his text after the proofs were passed. Negotiations with new publishers hung fire. His attacks of nausea and dizziness became more frequent. The few poems he was left to write, though his most powerful, touched the depths of despair: *Le Coucher du soleil romantique*, a condemnation of the literary world as it then was; *Plaintes d'un Icare*, a lament for his own destiny; *Le Couvercle*, *Le Gouffre*, and *Examen de minuit*, an intense brooding over the cruelty of existence. His last serious poem (for one cannot count the satirical poems about Belgium) was *l'Imprévu*, 1863, a reply to Barbey d'Aurevilly's statement that the author of *Les Fleurs du mal* could only be converted or blow his brains out. This poem, with its usual stress on evil and the power of Satan, gives a glimpse of salvation in the final lines, but the reader must judge for himself whether they refer to Baudelaire. The poet's seriousness can best be judged by looking into his private journal, *My Heart Laid Bare*:

Hygiene. Morality. Conduct. – Too late, perhaps! My mother and Jeanne. – My health, out of charity and duty. – Jeanne's illnesses. My mother's infirmities and solitude.

– Do one's duty every day and trust in God for tomorrow.

– The only way of earning money is to work in a disinterested manner.

– A short formula for wisdom – toilet, prayer, work.

– Prayer: charity, wisdom, and strength.

– Without charity I am but a tinkling cymbal.

– My humiliations have been God's graces.

– Is my period of egotism over?

– The faculty for responding to the needs of each minute, in a word exactness, must inevitably find its reward.

The last page of the journal reads as follows:

Hygiene, Conduct, Method. – I swear to myself to adopt, from now on, the following rules as the permanent rules of my life:

Make my prayer every morning to God, the reservoir of all strength and all justice, and to my father, to Mariette, and to Poe as intercessors; pray them to afford me the necessary strength to carry out all my duties, and to grant my mother a long enough life for her to enjoy the change in me; work all day long, or at least as much as my strength allows; trust in God, that is to say in Justice itself, for the success of my undertakings; every evening make a new prayer asking God for life and strength for my mother and me; divide my earnings into four shares, one for daily expenses, one for my creditors, one for my friends, and one for my mother; obey the principles of the strictest sobriety, the first of which is to suppress all stimulants, of whatever kind.

The last chapter of Baudelaire's life was as painful and pointless as can be imagined. To recoup his fortunes he went to Belgium in 1864, and though he made one or two almost furtive visits to France his active life was to end in exile. The lecture-tour was a failure, and with Swiftian scorn and hatred he began writing a fierce attack on *Poor Belgium* which was never completed. His projects for collected editions of his works went awry and he ended by selling his copyright to Michel-Lévy for a pittance. After collapsing (ironically enough, in a church) and losing his powers of speech, Baudelaire had little more before him than the living death of a paralytic before he died in his mother's arms on 31 August 1867. In the meantime, in his absence, the younger generation, Mendès, Mallarmé, Verlaine, and others, had been hailing him as the greatest of French poets, but he turned a deaf ear to them. His mother wrote, not long after his death, 'Had Charles let himself be guided by his step-father, his career would have been very different. It is true that he would not have left a name in literature, but all three of us would have been happier.' As a mother, she was right, but she never realized that the dove may be called on to cherish the phoenix. Maybe it could be argued that the romantic fallacy consists in the choice between art and life, which Mme Aupick was lamenting – yet the lives of Molière and Racine are in a sense as lamentable as that of Baudelaire. Yeats put the matter in a nutshell in his lines:

> The intellect of man is forced to choose
> Perfection of the life, or of the work,
> And if it take the second must refuse
> A heavenly mansion, raging in the dark.

But Baudelaire was not entirely the victim of the romantic fallacy: he knew too well that no human life or work can reach perfection.

III

Baudelaire, as we have seen, regarded *Les Fleurs du mal* as a complete work, a unit with its own internal structure. Anyone reprinting it is morally obliged to reproduce the 1857 or 1861 edition which the poet issued in his lifetime. Poems omitted in 1861 or written later are usually given in an appendix which includes *Les Nouvelles Fleurs du mal* and *Les Épaves*. The 1868 edition has long been discredited. A recent departure from the usual practice is in Marcel Ruff's centenary edition, in which the condemned poems and those printed after 1861 were assigned places within the 1861 plan.

In the present volume, which offers only a selection of poems, there would be no point in retaining the 1861 structure while leaving gaps. Why omit anything? A selection from a poet's work implies an act of criticism. Taken to its proper conclusions such an act would mean the sacrifice of more poems than are excluded here. Baudelaire is a poet of very uneven quality and texture. Though he was the first to state that the poet must contain a critic, he clung obstinately to many works whose interest is less aesthetic than autobiographical. There is such a thing as autobiography expressed through form, as Valéry has said: but this does not mean that we need many examples of this or that period, theme, or manner, especially when the theme or manner is bad or caricatural. Baudelaire too often imitated himself. The poems that have been omitted are for the most part those in which theme or style are better exemplified by some other poem which has been retained. It is not true that any poem can be redeemed by its place in the poet's original classification.

But some kind of order is required in a selection. The student of Baudelaire is often at a loss to trace the poet's evolution; or to reconstitute the different 'cycles'; or to relate the verse to the prose-poems. This demands close work, especially as critics and biographers disagree about basic facts. I have undertaken, therefore, to lighten the reader's task to some extent by placing these poems, for the first time, in a roughly chronological order while trying to preserve the 'cycles'; by putting the cycles in their proper grouping and sequence, while omitting some from the Jeanne Duval cycle; and by setting a selection of the prose-poems alongside the verse to which they are related. This is the first edition in which the *Limbes* poems of 1848–51 can be seen as a separate group, representing a critical stage in Baudelaire's career. The main loss in the present arrangement is the *Tableaux parisiens* established by the poet in the second edition, but there is a certain gain in being able to observe the poet's position in the first and final groups.

As Baudelaire did not usually date his poems it is not possible to establish an exact chronology. The main evidence available is: (*a*) statements by his friends, often made long after his death, concerning the early works. Prarond gave a list of sixteen poems which he claimed to have heard or read before the end of 1843. A few others may be dated by reference to such witnesses as Asselineau, Charles Cousin, Hignard, and Dozon; (*b*) dates of publication; (*c*) references, which are few, in the poet's letters or other works; (*d*) conjectures by critics and biographers. These have to be taken with caution. Some critics, for instance, would have us believe that *Correspondances* was written in 1845 or 1846, on the ground that the poet was reading Swedenborg at that time. It has also been suggested that *Le Cygne* might be an early poem because of a reference to an escaped swan, in *Le Corsaire Satan*, in 1846. But the reading of a book, or a historical incident, are not proofs of composition. Thus I have dated *Correspondances* 1846–57 while believing it to belong to the period 1852–7; and *Le Cygne* 1846–59 while believing it to belong to the period 1857–9. Other forms of conjecture based on biographical, psychological, or internal evidence, or on mere hunches, are too numerous and divergent to be accepted without reserve.

Group I. Early Poems, 1837–47

This group comprises: those given as such in the present edition, together with five poems in the Jeanne Duval cycle; ten poems here printed in the *Limbes* cycle, and thirteen poems which have been omitted. Thus a total of fifty-three poems can with reasonable cause be attributed to the first decade of Baudelaire's output, and of these forty are given here. The grouping 1837–47 has been adopted because of the change in the poet's outlook just before and during the revolutionary period 1848–51.

Among the salient aspects of this group it will be noticed that most of the poems written in Alexandrine couplets appear to be early works. This fact enables us to accept Prarond's surprising statement that the *Crépuscule du matin* was written by the end of 1843. My own inclination would have been to assign it to the *Limbes* period. It is astonishing that such a mature poem, with its striking synthesis of realism and imagination, pure poetry and common speech, highly modern anti-aesthetic imagery which is throughout based on the human body, should belong to this period. The poem illustrates perfectly the poet's characteristic shifting of tone: the great ascending spiral of rhetoric that suddenly falls into prose (*Les maisons ça et là commençaient à fumer*), only to rise again. Even if, while accepting Prarond's date, we may assume that it was rehandled later (it was first published in 1852), this poem throws a very sharp light on the nature of Baudelaire's genius. It is that so far as style is concerned he was not the kind of poet who matures slowly and painfully. He was one of those in whom poetry is a gift, and a very dangerous gift in the sense that however hard he worked his poems fluctuate in both depth and quality. He could write both brilliantly and badly at the age of thirty, just as he had done at twenty. If he was precocious it was not so much in discovering his own manner as in his natural fineness of ear, his sense of balance and construction, which is something that can never be learnt, and in the tragic view of life that all his work embodies.

To see these early poems together reveals, also, something important about his themes and range. Faults of over-emphasis in style, the use of second-hand literary imagery and clichés are to be observed not only in this group but in some of the poems of the very last period. Yet already at the age of 21 or 22 he could write, in *Don Juan aux Enfers*, with that exceptional clarity, trenchant directness, and 'hardness' (to use the term which Ezra Pound applied to Gautier) that reappeared at the end of his life in *Recueillement* and *Le Gouffre*.

At the same time this first group falls readily into patterns which show his lifelong preoccupations and obsessions, as well as his variations of manner. The few poems grouped round *À une dame créole* contain the exoticism and reverie which we find twenty years later in *Le Voyage* and *Le Cygne*. There are a few important poems about Parisian life which are already the nucleus of the *Tableaux parisiens* and the prose-poems. There is an 'aesthetic' group running from *La Muse malade* to *Correspondances* that contain the basis of Baudelaire's idea of poetry. The germ of what he called *Idéal* is already to be observed in *La Beauté* and *Élévation*, while the theme of *Spleen* is implicit in *La Muse malade* and the rather pretentiously-written Epistle to Sainte-Beuve. Though Baudelaire only sent this epistle to the critic in 1844, its involved and fussy style bears the stamp of immaturity. In addition to all this the reader cannot fail to see the foundation of the poet's uneasy religious position: it was the period not only of *Hélas, qui n'a gémi* but of the powerful *Litanies de Satan*, *Abel et Caïn*, and *Le Reniement de Saint-Pierre*. Let it be noted at once that the term 'satanism' cannot satisfactorily be applied to Baudelaire. It is a pejorative term which can at most be used to describe a literary and almost impersonal pose of the second romantic generation headed by Petrus Borel. Of course Baudelaire was influenced by it, but in his case there is ample evidence of a profoundly disturbed and disturbing religious sensibility underlying this '*religion travestie*'.

Group II. The Jeanne Duval Cycle, 1842–61

Baudelaire met Jeanne Duval in 1842 and finally separated from her twenty years later. Some critics assert that all the Duval cycle is early work but there is no evidence for this and much evidence to the contrary. The many separations and reconciliations between them are enough to explain the changes of tone to be observed in these poems.

Key-works in the early period are *Les Bijoux*, in which sensuality is offset by sadism, and *Je t'adore à l'égal de la voûte nocturne* in which eroticism is closely bound up with a religious sense of sin. *Une Charogne* shows a characteristic Renaissance theme modernized and taken to the limit of the grotesque. Here (as in *Un Voyage à Cythère*) the reader is faced with the insoluble aesthetic problem that Baudelaire's work presents as acutely as Sade's or Gide's: in such poems the incantational beauty of the language, raised to the same lofty plane as in the most gruesome passages of Elizabethan tragedy, is counterpointed against the utmost brutality of vision. Is it permissible to argue that this is all very well in the larger context of a dramatic situation, but not in lyric poetry?

If *La Béatrice* shows the poet's disgust with Jeanne Duval's promiscuity, *Le Balcon* strikes a note of profound tenderness and communion. There is little evidence for including *L'Héautontimorouménos* in this group. J.G.F., to whom it is dedicated, could be either Jeanne Duval (according to Pommier) or Juliette Gex-Fagon. Sadistic imagery is by no means confined to the poems written about Jeanne Duval, and this poem, conceived in 1855 when the poet was writing its pendant *L'Irrémédiable* is seen in better perspective in the 1852–7 group of poems.

The central poem of the last years of this relationship is certainly *Je te donne ces vers*. This is not only an exercise in the type of dedication commonly written by the sixteenth-century poets for their mistresses: it enables us to see beyond the documentary nature of the Duval cycle and to grasp that Baudelaire did not only write for personal reasons, even about Jeanne Duval. He was not merely writing 'the novel of Jeanne Duval' but aspiring to set his work and personal experience on the high aesthetic level of Petrarch and Ronsard. There is, perhaps, some concealed irony, which must have satisfied the poet, in the idea of setting the mulatress on a level with Scève's Délie, or Ronsard's Hélène. The transmutation of dross into gold he applied to his unsatisfactory love-affairs as well as to modern Paris. The *Fleurs du mal* contains not merely the history of his loves but a critique of modern love. We do not need to choose (as J.-D. Hubert suggests) between the biographical as against the aesthetic interpretation of Baudelaire's poetry. While it is only natural that, at first, the reader might begin by reading these poems as a biographical cycle, he must inevitably end by seeing them on an impersonal aesthetic level, as though the 'I' of Baudelaire meant not himself but *the poet* or *the lover*. Some poets do not demand this dual approach; but in the case of Baudelaire we are before the same kind of problem as with Yeats or any poet who makes his own daily life the basis of his writing. In the end we spontaneously forget the physical W. B. Yeats and listen simply to a tragic voice.

Group III. Les Limbes, 1848–51

This group of poems is made up from several sources.

In November 1848 Baudelaire printed *Le Vin de l'assassin* (not in the present collection) with the announcement: 'Michel-Lévy, publisher, rue Neuve Vivienne: *Les Limbes*, poems by Charles Baudelaire. This book will appear in Paris and Leipzig on 24 February 1849.' The promised work did not appear on the date announced. In June 1850 the *Magasin des familles* printed *Châtiment de l'orgueil* and *Le Vin des honnêtes gens* (subsequently called *Le Vin des pauvres*) with the note: 'These two unpublished pieces are taken from a book entitled *Les Limbes* which will appear shortly and which is intended to represent the aspirations and melancholy of modern youth.' In April 1851 the *Messager de l'Assemblée* printed a group of eleven poems (running in the present edition from *Spleen* (*Pluviôse ...*) to *Les Hiboux* with the comment: 'These poems are taken from the book *Les Limbes* by Charles Baudelaire which will be published soon by Michel-Lévy and which is intended to retrace the history of the spiritual agitations of modern youth.' The cycle is completed by a list known as *Douze Poèmes* which Baudelaire sent to Gautier in late 1851 or early 1852, and which were certainly written by 1851. To these, thanks to a variation in the list, may be added *La Musique*, which is no doubt the poem *Beethoven* mentioned by the poet.

Of the above poems, *La Béatrice* (*De profundis clamavi*) will be found in its proper place in the Jeanne Duval cycle. I have omitted

Le Tonneau de la haine, *La Fontaine de sang*, *La Métamorphose du vampire*, and *Le Reniement de Saint-Pierre*.

Although the central idea of *Les Limbes* (already discussed, see p. xxx) apparently occurred to Baudelaire just before or as a result of the 1848 upheaval, the series contains a large number of early poems. In spite of the combined religious and social significance of the title it contains such poems as *Les Chats*, *La Mort des amants*, and *La Musique* which seem to have nothing to do with the title's meaning. *Les Limbes* would have had nothing like the unity suggested by its title and the advertisements made for it.

This cycle as a whole offers an interesting cross-section of the poet's various manners. It shows, also, that he was not yet fully conscious of the polarity Spleen-Idéal which was to form the very basis of *Les Fleurs du mal*. There is a strong emphasis on the religious theme in such poems as *Châtiment de l'orgueil*, *Le Mauvais moine*, and *Le Reniement de Saint-Pierre*. As for the poems *L'Idéa* and *Bohémiens en voyage* I am not at all convinced by the dates (1842 and 1845) given by Ruff and Starkie.

Although *Un Voyage à Cythère*, one of the most significant poems in this group, was not published until 1855 when it inspired Hugo's *Cérigo*, it was based on an item of the same title published by Baudelaire's friend, Gérard de Nerval, as early as 1844. The fact that there is a manuscript of the poem dated 1852 does not necessarily prove that it was written in that year: it would be wise to date it 1844–52. The *Voyage à Cythère* with its strong moral lesson which Nerval condemned in the line 'Silently you endured these insults in expiation of your infamous practices (*cultes*)' together with its underlying personal note, shows Baudelaire parting company with the romantic idealization of love. He finds in classical allegory a perfect objective-correlative for his own experience. The poem makes, indirectly, a sardonic pun on 'Venus' and 'venereal'. The poem shows at a high level the ironical construction, in the massive contrast between what the poet called 'supernaturalism and irony', which is typical of Baudelaire's most ambitious poems (cf. *Le Cygne* and *Le Voyage*) and which is one of the qualities that maintains his place among the moderns.

Group IV. The Marie Daubrun Cycle, 1850–60

The ten poems in this group are not presented in the order suggested by Feuillerat. As the exact dates of composition are not certain I have preferred to follow the order of publication. *L'Invitation au voyage* may be dated 1854. It would be tempting to print alongside it, in the same cycle, its pendant *Le Jet d'eau*, which is known to have been written by 1853. The two poems have strong affinities but I can find no evidence that the latter was written for Marie Daubrun.

Group V. The Sabatier Cycle, 1852–61

The first seven of these poems may be dated approximately, by reference to the covering letters with which Baudelaire sent them to Mme Sabatier. There is some disagreement about *Que diras-tu ce soir ...* and *Le Flambeau vivant*, which might well have been inspired by Marie Daubrun before being sent to Mme Sabatier. However, the poet himself included them in the Sabatier group in *Les Fleurs du mal*.

In the case of *Hymne*, Baudelaire wrote anonymously to Mme Sabatier saying 'These lines were written a long time ago' – he never pretended that they had been written expressly for her. In approaching these love-cycles we have to consider the person to whom they were offered, rather than the person for whom they might feasibly have been composed. A love-poem might well be written for its own sake and only subsequently offered to someone. Nor can the poems in the cycles be redistributed on psychological or critical grounds. Those who seek to idealize the unsatisfactory love-relationship between the poet and Marie Daubrun, for instance, seeing in it the tenderness of a much older man for a 'strip of a girl', seem to forget that Baudelaire was only twenty-nine in 1850 when the affair began. They must also be closing their eyes to the fact that all the love-cycles are permeated by violent and negative emotions. The hard truth is that *L'Irréparable* and *Le Poison* were addressed to Marie, just as much as the tender *Invitation au voyage*. Mme Sabatier, on the other hand, is just as much the recipient of the exquisite *Harmonie du soir* as of *À celle qui est trop gaie* or *Confession*. Baudelaire was too clairvoyant, too much imbued with the 'horror of being duped' to set any woman on a pedestal for long. Each of the cycles is impure, containing those extremes of feeling which reflect the poet's alternating idealization and contempt.

The only poem in this group which may be seriously questioned is *Moesta et errabunda*, for whose attribution I have accepted the view of L. Legras who notes the resemblance between the poem's third stanza and *Confession*. This is not evidence: but poets do not necessarily use the names of the people for whom they write, and the name Agathe is perhaps of no more significance than Laura or Beatrice. Mme Sabatier's names were Aglaë-Apollonie.

Group VI. Poems, 1852–7

At first sight this appears to be the least satisfactory of the groups, but the reader who has followed the previous groups can gain some idea of what the poet had to hand by the time he came to put *Les Fleurs du mal* together. By 1856 Baudelaire had published only fifty poems but had written more than twice as many. The 1857 edition contained 101 poems (including *Au Lecteur*). A number of early works (including *L'Albatros*, which was not finished until 1859) were omitted. Several poems (*Paysage*, *Hymne*, *Une Gravure fantastique*, and *La Rançon*) were not ready in time for the book but were published in the same year.

Baudelaire dropped the idea of *Les Limbes* in 1852, when another poet used the title, and from then on spoke of his poems as *Les Fleurs du mal*, a title suggested to him by Hippolyte Babou. He used the new rubric for the twenty poems printed in the *Revue des deux mondes* in 1855. The only alternative to printing *Les Limbes* as a group would have been to retain the *Revue des deux mondes* group, but this would have involved too much interference with the other sections.

It might be thought that some of the poems in this group could have been better placed elsewhere. For instance, Baudelaire obviously had the idea of writing a series of 'Spleen' poems some years earlier, for in *Les Limbes* of 1851 he included three poems (*Pluviôse ...*, *La Cloche fêlée*, and *Le Mort joyeux*) under the title *Le Spleen*. Only the first of these retained that title in the 1857 edition. Then in the *Revue des deux mondes* in 1855 he gave the title *Spleen* to *De profundis clamavi*, a poem which he subsequently classified in the Jeanne Duval cycle. This does not prove, however, that all the 'Spleen' poems should be moved back to *Les Limbes*, or dated 1855 for that matter. The same argument arises about the poems on wine. Baudelaire began this series with *Le Vin de l'assassin* as early as 1848, and published *L'Âme du vin* in 1851. *Le Vin des amants* and *Le Vin du solitaire*, published for the first time in the *Fleurs*, could have been written at any time between 1848 and 1857.

On the whole the poems in the present group show a marked and unpleasant hardening of both thought and style. *L'Irrémédiable* shows Baudelaire's challenge to the world in its most daring form: here he formulates the notion of 'consciousness in evil' (certainly a problem arising from the christian doctrine of free-will) which is developed perversely in *L'Héautontimorouménos* of the same year, 1855. This group also contains new major poems in which Baudelaire advances a neo-romantic conception of the poet as outcast and hero, in *Bénédiction* and *Les Phares*. *Au Lecteur*, a poem specially written for the series in the *Revue des deux mondes* is, to my mind, typical of Baudelaire's rhetoric at its worst. The poem is written at the top of the poet's voice and is none the better for that. The emphasis on boredom in the *Spleen* poems, where it achieved some gravity and dignity, now takes on an almost pathological significance. If we set this poem alongside *Les Phares*, of the same period, we have instances of the best and worst of Baudelaire being composed almost simultaneously.

Group VII. Last Poems, 1859–63

Baudelaire published only two poems in 1858 (*Que diras-tu ce soir* and *Duellum*, which are given in the Sabatier and Duval groups). These *Last Poems*, though their publication ostensibly stretches from 1859 to 1868, were all written between 1859 and 1863.

(i) 1859 was a year of great publishing activity on Baudelaire's part. He gave twelve new poems to reviews in this year.

The poet was now more aware than ever of struggling against time, but he was fully conscious of his powers and had a definite end in view, which was to produce a definitive edition of *Les Fleurs* that would establish his fame. Though *Le Goût du néant* prefigures the despair of *Obsession* and *Alchimie de la douleur* of the following year, the poet was none the less fertile in new ideas. With *Les Sept Vieillards* and *Les Petites Vieilles* he began writing a series of 'Parisian Ghosts' in which he was consciously pitting himself against the genius of Victor Hugo. These were intended for the group *Tableaux parisiens*, partly inspired by the work of Méryon, but in reality arising from the poet's long preoccupation with both the city and what he called 'the heroism of modern life' – which were to take an important place in the 1861 edition of the *Fleurs*. At the same time he wrote the crowning piece of the second edition, *Le Voyage*, in which so many of the vital and perennial themes of his work came together in a superb synthesis.

(ii) 1860 saw the publication of sixteen new poems. The emphasis is increasingly on the pain of existence, but now the imagination, 'the queen of the faculties' as he now described it, was in full control, and as he noted in *Le Cygne*, which is perhaps the most perfectly constructed and composed of all his poems, 'everything for me turns to allegory'. If the imaginative vision sometimes has a rather gaudy aspect as in *Rêve parisien*, the nightmare quality is grave and profound in such poems as *Alchimie de la douleur* and *L'Horloge*.

The *Hymne à la Beauté*, the poet's last word on this unsatisfactory and un-modern theme, has nothing to do with the fashionable 'art for art's sake' doctrines of the period. It is not enough to say that the poet placed beauty beyond good and evil. On the contrary, though the poet declares that it does not matter whether beauty springs from good or evil, he never more clearly raised the problem of its moral import, while leaning to the darker side. For Baudelaire, Beauty was bound up with the supernatural and was another 'artificial paradise' through which man can cheat his destiny. This obviously takes him far beyond the conventional notion of 'elevating the soul' advanced by Poe. Baudelaire's aestheticism is a kind of dilemma set in a significant moral context. Poetic creation alone can defeat both Time and Tedium, man's two vast enemies which can inflict on him a kind of spiritual excommunication.

(iii) 1861. Only *one* of the poems published in this year appeared in the 1861 edition of *Les Fleurs du mal*. This is *La Fin de la journée*, which reflects Baudelaire's renewed habit of self-examination and anticipates *Examen de minuit*.

La Voix is based not only on childhood memories but, like so many of the late poems, on a thought of Pascal's: it is perhaps not fanciful to suggest that, as so many poems in this group are based on Pascal, Baudelaire's intention was to write a kind of verse-commentary on the *Pensées*. *Le Rebelle* was listed by Prarond as one of the very early poems; but I am convinced that he was confusing it with *L'Impénitent* (subsequently renamed *Don Juan aux Enfers*), and it is therefore placed here according to its date of publication.

The *Épigraphe pour un livre condamné* either was not finished in time or was not thought good enough for inclusion in the 1861 edition. *Recueillement*, in spite of the harsh (Pascalian) outburst in the second quatrain, is one of the few moments of calm in the poet's later life. It shows him, as in a lucid interval, rising above himself and his sufferings and facing the thought of death with heroic resignation. It is interesting to note with what art the sweetening of an otherwise melancholy poem is achieved: the 'moribund' Sun falls asleep 'under an arch', that is to say like some old *clochard* under one of the Paris bridges: he speaks of 'le Regret *souriant*', evoking perhaps some fountain of Niobe, as well as an echo of Shakespeare ('smiling at grief'): the morbid image of the winding-sheet at the end is softened by the epithet, 'la *douce* nuit'. None of this, however, arose from pure artifice, for Baudelaire's letters to his mother at the time show beyond doubt that he would have welcomed death.

(iv) 1862. *Le Couvercle*, one of Baudelaire's darkest poems, looks back in tone and imagery to the *Spleen* group. With *Le Gouffre* a window is flung open into the poet's nihilism: the poem raises doubts as to the exact nature of the poet's return to his faith.

La Lune offensée has in recent years been the source of unnecessary controversy. Some critics suggest that he tried to 'hide' this poem from his mother because of an offensive reference to her in the final tercet. Others try to date this as an early poem in order to excuse that reference. My own belief is that the poem had nothing to do with his mother; that he did not try to hide it, but on the contrary drew her attention to it in a letter; and that it was intended as a general attack on the manners of the period.

Plaintes d'un Icare is one of Baudelaire's last personal statements. It sums up the physical and spiritual isolation in which he spent his last years. This is the Baudelaire bereft of Jeanne, Marie, and Mme Sabatier, and in a sense exiled from his mother; the poet who having felt 'the wings of madness' was alarmed at the idea that he would be unable to finish his life's work, and who was now abandoning France to start anew.

(v) Baudelaire published only three new poems of consequence after 1863. As for *Les Yeux de Berthe* (1864), some critics have identified Berthe with Jeanne Duval. Crépet has shown that, at any rate, Berthe was not a person he met in Belgium. In this case I have followed Prarond's list and classified it as an early poem (Group I). *Bien loin d'ici*, also published in 1864, was written in 1859, as can be seen from a letter from the poet to Poulet-Malassis. *Le Jet d'eau*, published in 1865, was written before 1853, as is proved by the Vandérem list.

Thus we are left with only two poems. Of these, *L'Examen de minuit*, published in February 1863, was written in 1861–2 and is a restatement of *La Fin de la journée* in more christian terms. Baudelaire's last important poem was *L'Imprévu*, 1863. In spite of the characteristic stress on the supernatural power of evil, there is a slight gleam of hope or salvation at the end. The poem shows in a remarkable way the final maturity of the poet's style. Despite its inspired violence it is at moments very close to common speech and has the sharp edge which all his best work achieves. The few poems he wrote afterwards in Belgium have none of the high-seriousness of this devastating comment on human existence.

*

In translating these poems of Baudelaire's into prose, I have tried to compromise as well as possible between the necessity, in this popular series, of giving word-for-word equivalents for the original, and a desire to render them into something like a prose-poem. The result in many cases is uneven. I should like to thank Dr and Mrs Basil Jackson for their admirable advice, and my friends Dr Enid Starkie and Dr Felix Leakey, whom I regret not having been able to consult more thoroughly, for encouraging me in this project.

FRANCIS SCARFE

READING LIST

WORKS IN ENGLISH ONLY

ANON. Review of Baudelaire's Collected Works. *Fraser's Magazine*, December 1869

BANDY, W. T. *Baudelaire Judged by his Contemporaries*. Columbia, N.Y., 1933

'New light on Baudelaire and Poe.' *Yale French Studies*, 1953

BENNET, J. D. *Baudelaire, a Criticism*. Oxford, 1944

CLAPTON, G. T. *Baudelaire, the Tragic Sophist*. London, 1934

ELIOT, T. S. 'Baudelaire.' *Selected Essays*. London, 1934

'Baudelaire in our time.' *Essays Ancient and Modern*. London, 1936

GILMAN, M. *Baudelaire the Critic*. New York, 1943

HUBERT, J. D. 'Baudelaire's Revolutionary Poetics.' *Romanic Review*, 1955

HUXLEY, ALDOUS. 'Baudelaire.' *Do What you Will*. Thinkers Library, London, 1936

HYSLOP, L. B. and F. E. *Baudelaire, a Self-Portrait*. Oxford, 1957

JAMES, HENRY. 'Baudelaire.' *French Poets and Novelists*. London, 1884

JOHNSON, LIONEL. 'Poets of the 19th Century.' *Daily Chronicle*, 27 December 1900

JONES, P. MANSELL. *Baudelaire*. Cambridge (Bowes & Bowes), 1952

LAFORGUE, RENÉ. *The Defeat of Baudelaire*. London (Hogarth Press), 1932

LEAKEY, F. W. 'Two poems of Baudelaire' (*La Lune offensée* and *Le Chat*). *Letterature Moderne*, 1956

MURRY, J. M. 'Baudelaire.' *Countries of the Mind*. London, 1922

NICOLSON, H. *Swinburne and Baudelaire*. Oxford, 1930

PARMEE, D. *Selected Critical Studies of Baudelaire*. Cambridge, 1949

PATTY, J. S. 'Baudelaire's knowledge of Dante.' *Studies in Philology*. October, 1956

QUENNELL, P. *Baudelaire and the Symbolists*. London, 1955 (revised)

RHODES, S. *The Cult of Beauty in Baudelaire*. New York, 1929

SAINTSBURY, G. 'Baudelaire.' *Miscellaneous Essays*. London, 1892. (Reprinted from *Fortnightly Review*, 1875)

SARTRE, J.-P. *Baudelaire*. (Trans. by M. Turnell.) London, 1940

SCOTT, J. A. 'Petrarch and Baudelaire.' *Revue de litt. comparée*, xxxi, 4, 1957

SIMCOX, H. Review of Baudelaire's Collected Works, in *The Academy*, I, 1869–70
STARKIE, ENID. *Baudelaire*. London (Faber), 1957
SWINBURNE, A. C. 'Les Fleurs du Mal.' *Spectator*, 6 September 1862. (Reprinted by Edmund Gosse, London, 1913)
TURNELL, M. *Baudelaire: a Study of his Poetry*. London, 1953
'The School of Baudelaire.' Blackfriars, 1934

I

Early Poems

1837–47

N'EST-ce pas qu'il est doux, maintenant que nous sommes
Fatigués et flétris comme les autres hommes,
De chercher quelquefois à l'Orient lointain
Si nous voyons encor les rougeurs du matin,
Et, quand nous avançons dans la rude carrière,
D'écouter les échos qui chantent en arrière
Et les chuchotements de ces jeunes amours
Que le Seigneur a mis au début de nos jours? ..

IL aimait à la voir, avec ses jupes blanches,
Courir tout au travers du feuillage et des branches
Gauche et pleine de grâce, alors qu'elle cachait
Sa jambe, si la robe aux buissons s'accrochait ...

Is it not pleasant, now that we are tired and tarnished like other men, sometimes to try and see, in the distant East, whether we can yet discern the glow of morning, and, as we press forward in life's rough arena, to listen to the echoes that sing behind us, and the whisperings of those young loves that the Lord has ordained at the outset of our days? ...

[1837. Published 1864]

HE loved to watch her, in her white skirts, running right through the leafage and branches, awkward yet full of grace, while she hid her leg when her dress rived on the briars ...

[1837. Published 1864]

INCOMPATIBILITÉ

TOUT là-haut, tout là-haut, loin de la route sûre,
Des fermes, des vallons, par delà les coteaux,
Par delà les forêts, les tapis de verdure,
Loin des derniers gazons foulés par les troupeaux,

On rencontre un lac sombre encaissé dans l'abîme
Que forment quelques pics désolés et neigeux;
L'eau, nuit et jour, y dort dans un repos sublime,
Et n'interrompt jamais son silence orageux.

Dans ce morne désert, à l'oreille incertaine
Arrivent par moments des bruits faibles et longs,
Et des échos plus morts que la cloche lointaine
D'une vache qui paît aux penchants des vallons.

Sur ces monts où le vent efface tout vestige,
Ces glaciers pailletés qu'allume le soleil,
Sur ces rochers altiers où guette le vertige,
Dans ce lac où le soir mire son teint vermeil,

Incompatibility

HIGH up, high up there, far from the beaten track, far from the farms and valleys, beyond the hills, beyond the forests, the carpets of green, far from the last meadows trampled by flocks, you find a dark lake sunk in the hollow between a few lonely, snowy peaks; night and day the water slumbers there in a sublime repose, and never breaks its stormy silence.

In that dour desert, to the uncertain ear there come, from time to time, faint prolonged sounds, and echoes more muffled than the far-off bell of a cow browsing on the dellside. On those mountains, where the wind sweeps every trace away, on those spangled glaciers, fired by the sun, on those lofty rocks where giddiness threatens, in that lake where evening mirrors its rosy hue, beneath

Sous mes pieds, sur ma tête et partout, le silence,
Le silence qui fait qu'on voudrait se sauver,
Le silence éternel de la montagne immense,
Car l'air est immobile et tout semble rêver.

On dirait que le ciel, en cette solitude,
Se contemple dans l'onde et que ces monts, là-bas,
Écoutent, recueillis, dans leur grave attitude,
Un mystère divin que l'homme n'entend pas.

Et lorsque par hasard une nuée errante
Assombrit dans son vol le lac silencieux,
On croirait voir la robe ou l'ombre transparente
D'un esprit qui voyage et passe dans les cieux.

À UNE DAME CRÉOLE

Au pays parfumé que le soleil caresse,
J'ai connu, sous un dais d'arbres tout empourprés
Et de palmiers d'où pleut sur les yeux la paresse,
Une dame créole aux charmes ignorés.

my feet, above my head, everywhere, is silence, a silence that makes you long to escape, the eternal silence of the vast mountain, for the air is still and everything seems to be dreaming.

It's as though the sky, in this solitude, were contemplating itself in the water, and yonder mountains listening, in their grave attitude, to a divine mystery which man cannot hear. And when, perchance, a wandering cloud overcasts in its flight the silent lake, you might think you saw the robe or the transparent shadow of some spirit, voyaging and vanishing across the heavens.

[1838–9. Published 1872]

To a Creole Lady

In that perfumed land, fondled by the sun, I knew – beneath a canopy of trees aglow with crimson, and palms from which languor pours upon your eyes – a creole lady whose charms are unknown to the world.

Son teint est pâle et chaud; la brune enchanteresse
A dans le cou des airs noblement maniérés;
Grande et svelte en marchant comme une chasseresse,
Son sourire est tranquille et ses yeux assurés.

Si vous alliez, Madame, au vrai pays de gloire,
Sur les bords de la Seine ou de la verte Loire,
Belle digne d'orner les antiques manoirs,

Vous feriez, à l'abri des ombreuses retraites,
Germer mille sonnets dans le cœur des poëtes,
Que vos grands yeux rendraient plus soumis que vos noirs.

À UNE MALABARAISE

TES pieds sont aussi fins que tes mains et ta hanche
Est large à faire envie à la plus belle blanche;
À l'artiste pensif ton corps est doux et cher;
Tes grands yeux de velours sont plus noirs que ta chair.
Aux pays chauds et bleus où ton Dieu t'a fait naître,

Her complexion is pale and warm; that dark enchantress has, in the poise of her head, poses of aristocratic grace; tall and slender, as she walks like a huntress, her smile is peaceful and her eyes assured.

Should you go, Lady, to the true home of fame, to the banks of the Seine or of the verdant Loire, your beauty might well grace some ancient manor-house,

and in many a shady arbour, you would inspire a thousand sonnets in the hearts of poets, whom your wide eyes would make more submissive than your black slaves.

[1841. Published 1845]

To a Malabar Woman

YOUR feet are as slender as your hands, and your hips are broad enough to fill the loveliest white woman with envy. To the thoughtful artist your body is suave and endearing; your great eyes of velvet are blacker than your flesh. In the hot, blue climes where your God caused you to be born, your task is to light your master's

Ta tâche est d'allumer la pipe de ton maître,
De pourvoir les flacons d'eaux fraîches et d'odeurs,
De chasser loin du lit les moustiques rôdeurs,
Et, dès que le matin fait chanter les platanes,
D'acheter au bazar ananas et bananes.
Tout le jour, où tu veux, tu mènes tes pieds nus,
Et fredonnes tout bas de vieux airs inconnus;
Et quand descend le soir au manteau d'écarlate,
Tu poses doucement ton corps sur une natte,
Où tes rêves flottants sont pleins de colibris,
Et toujours, comme toi, gracieux et fleuris.

Pourquoi, l'heureuse enfant, veux-tu voir notre France,
Ce pays trop peuplé que fauche la souffrance,
Et, confiant ta vie aux bras forts des marins,
Faire de grands adieux à tes chers tamarins?
Toi, vêtue à moitié de mousselines frêles,
Frissonnante là-bas sous la neige et les grêles,
Comme tu pleurerais tes loisirs doux et francs,
Si, le corset brutal emprisonnant tes flancs,

pipe, to fill the vessels with cool water and perfumes, to drive marauding mosquitoes far from his couch, and as soon as morning sets the plane-trees singing, to buy pineapples and bananas at the bazaar. All day long you may take your naked feet wherever you list, humming forgotten old melodies beneath your breath; and when evening descends in its scarlet cloak, you lay your body gently down on a straw mat, where your floating dreams are full of humming-birds and always, like yourself, full of grace and flowers.

Why, happy child, do you want to see our France, that over-peopled land ridden with suffering, and, entrusting your life to the care of sailors' arms, bid final farewells to your beloved tamarinds? Under-clad in flimsy muslins, shivering there in snow and hail, how you would pine for your sweet, innocent leisure, if, with a cruel corset imprisoning your flanks, you had to glean your supper in our

Il te fallait glaner ton souper dans nos fanges
Et vendre le parfum de tes charmes étranges,
L'œil pensif, et suivant, dans nos sales brouillards,
Des cocotiers absents les fantômes épars!

L'ALBATROS

Souvent, pour s'amuser, les hommes d'équipage
Prennent des albatros, vastes oiseaux des mers,
Qui suivent, indolents compagnons de voyage,
Le navire glissant sur les gouffres amers.

À peine les ont-ils déposés sur les planches,
Que ces rois de l'azur, maladroits et honteux,
Laissent piteusement leurs grandes ailes blanches
Comme des avirons traîner à côté d'eux.

Ce voyageur ailé, comme il est gauche et veule!
Lui, naguère si beau, qu'il est comique et laid!
L'un agace son bec avec un brûle-gueule,
L'autre mime, en boitant, l'infirme qui volait!

mire, and sell the perfume of your unusual charms, your eyes grown thoughtful, pursuing in our grimy fogs the vanished phantoms of your absent coconut-trees!

[1841? Published 1845]

The Albatross

Often, for their amusement, sailors catch albatross, those vast birds of the seas, indolent companions of their voyages, that follow the ship gliding across the bitter depths.

No sooner have the sailors stretched them out on the deck than those kings of the azure, awkward and ashamed, let their long white wings trail painfully by their side, like oars.

How ungainly, how contemptible the winged traveller becomes, how laughable and graceless, he who but a moment ago was so full of beauty. A sailor teases his beak with a pipe; another drags his foot to mimic the cripple who once soared through the air.

Le Poëte est semblable au prince des nuées
Qui hante la tempête et se rit de l'archer;
Exilé sur le sol au milieu des huées,
Ses ailes de géant l'empêchent de marcher.

LES YEUX DE BERTHE

VOUS pouvez mépriser les yeux les plus célèbres,
Beaux yeux de mon enfant, par où filtre et s'enfuit
Je ne sais quoi de bon, de doux comme la Nuit!
Beaux yeux, versez sur moi vos charmantes ténèbres!

Grands yeux de mon enfant, arcanes adorés,
Vous ressemblez beaucoup à ces grottes magiques
Où, derrière l'amas des ombres léthargiques,
Scintillent vaguement des trésors ignorés!

Mon enfant a des yeux obscurs, profonds et vastes,
Comme toi, Nuit immense, éclairés comme toi!
Leurs feux sont ces pensers d'Amour, mêlés de Foi,
Qui pétillent au fond, voluptueux ou chastes.

The Poet shares the fate of this prince of the clouds, who rejoices in the tempest, mocking the archer below; exiled on earth, an object of scorn, his giant wings impede him as he walks.

[1842–59. Published 1859. The final quatrain was added in 1859]

Bertha's Eyes

YOU may scorn the most illustrious eyes, o beautiful eyes of my child, through which distils and vanishes something as good, as gentle as the Night. Beautiful eyes, pour on me your enchanting darknesses!

Great eyes of my child, adored enigmas, you strongly resemble those magic grottoes in which, behind the mass of drowsy shadows, undiscovered treasures vaguely glint.

My child has dusky eyes, profound and vast as thou, immense Night, and like thee illuminated. Their lights are those thoughts of love, mingled with trust, that sparkle in their depths, voluptuous or chaste.

[1843? (Prarond). Published 1864]

JE n'ai pas oublié, voisine de la ville,
Notre blanche maison, petite mais tranquille;
Sa Pomone de plâtre et sa vieille Vénus
Dans un bosquet chétif cachant leurs membres nus,
Et le soleil, le soir, ruisselant et superbe,
Qui, derrière la vitre où se brisait sa gerbe,
Semblait, grand œil ouvert dans le ciel curieux,
Contempler nos dîners longs et silencieux,
Répandant largement ses beaux reflets de cierge
Sur la nappe frugale et les rideaux de serge.

LA servante au grand cœur dont vous étiez jalouse,
Et qui dort son sommeil sous une humble pelouse,
Nous devrions pourtant lui porter quelques fleurs.
Les morts, les pauvres morts, ont de grandes douleurs,
Et quand octobre souffle, émondeur des vieux arbres,
Son vent mélancolique à l'entour de leurs marbres,
Certe, ils doivent trouver les vivants bien ingrats,
À dormir, comme ils font, chaudement dans leurs draps,
Tandis que, dévorés de noires songeries,

I HAVE not forgotten our white house, near the city, small but quiet, with its Pomona in plaster, and its old statue of Venus, hiding their naked limbs in the meagre grove; and the sun, of an evening, streaming down superbly, that through the window-pane on which its sheaf of light broke, like a huge open eye in the curious sky, seemed to be watching over our long, silent dinners, generously spreading its lovely candle-glimmers on the frugal table-cloth and the serge curtains.

[Pre-1844 (Prarond). Published in *Les Fleurs du mal*, 1857]

THE great-hearted servant of whom you were jealous – and who is sleeping her last sleep under a humble grassy mound – we really ought to take her some flowers. The dead, the poor dead, have great griefs, and when October, that pruner of old trees, blows its doleful winds round their marble graves, they must surely think the living most ungrateful, sleeping so snugly in their sheets; whereas, de-

Sans compagnon de lit, sans bonnes causeries,
Vieux squelettes gelés travaillés par le ver,
Ils sentent s'égoutter les neiges de l'hiver
Et le siècle couler, sans qu'amis ni famille
Remplacent les lambeaux qui pendent à leur grille.

Lorsque la bûche siffle et chante, si le soir,
Calme, dans le fauteuil, je la voyais s'asseoir,
Si, par une nuit bleue et froide de décembre,
Je la trouvais tapie en un coin de ma chambre,
Grave, et venant du fond de son lit éternel
Couver l'enfant grandi de son œil maternel,
Que pourrais-je répondre à cette âme pieuse,
Voyant tomber des pleurs de sa paupière creuse?

PAYSAGE

JE veux, pour composer chastement mes églogues,
Coucher auprès du ciel, comme les astrologues,
Et, voisin des clochers, écouter en rêvant
Leurs hymnes solennels emportés par le vent.

voured by gloomy reflections, with no bedfellow, with no pleasant chats, frozen old skeletons riddled with worms, they feel the winter snows drip down, and the century flowing on, without friends or relatives replacing the scraps of wreaths that hang on their railings.

When the log whistles and sings, if, some evening, calm in the armchair where I used to watch her sit – if on some cold blue December night I could find her nestling in the corner of my room, solemn-faced and rising from the depths of her eternal bed in order to watch with her motherly eye over the grown child – what could I answer that pious soul, as I saw the tears fall from her hollow lids?

[Pre-1844 (Prarond). Published in *Les Fleurs du mal*, 1857]

Landscape

CHASTELY to compose my eclogues, I want to have my bed near the sky, as astrologers do, I want to live beside the belfries and dreamily listen to their solemn hymns being borne away on the

Les deux mains au menton, du haut de ma mansarde,
Je verrai l'atelier qui chante et qui bavarde;
Les tuyaux, les clochers, ces mâts de la cité,
Et les grands ciels qui font rêver d'éternité.

Il est doux, à travers les brumes, de voir naître
L'étoile dans l'azur, la lampe à la fenêtre,
Les fleuves de charbon monter au firmament
Et la lune verser son pâle enchantement.
Je verrai les printemps, les étés, les automnes,
Et quand viendra l'hiver aux neiges monotones,
Je fermerai partout portières et volets
Pour bâtir dans la nuit mes féeriques palais.
Alors je rêverai des horizons bleuâtres,
Des jardins, des jets d'eau pleurant dans les albâtres,
Des baisers, des oiseaux chantant soir et matin,
Et tout ce que l'Idylle a de plus enfantin.
L'Émeute, tempêtant vainement à ma vitre,
Ne fera pas lever mon front de mon pupitre;

wind. With my chin cupped in my hands, from my lofty attic I'll watch the workshop full of singing and gossip, and the rone-pipes and steeples, the city's masts, and the great skies that make you dream of eternity.

It is pleasant, through the mists, to watch the stars being born in the blue sky, or the lamp appearing at a window, or the rivers of coal-smoke flowing heavenwards, and the moon pouring her pale magic out. I shall see the springs and summers and autumns, and when winter comes with its monotonous snows, I shall close all my doors and shutters to build my faery palaces in the night.

Then I shall dream of blue-tinted horizons, and gardens, and fountains weeping on to alabaster forms. I'll dream of kisses, of birds in song at twilight or at dawn, and of all that is most unsophisticated in the Idyll. The clamour of the mob, vainly beating on my window-pane, will not make me lift my head from my desk;

Car je serai plongé dans cette volupté
D'évoquer le Printemps avec ma volonté,
De tirer un soleil de mon cœur, et de faire
De mes pensers brûlants une tiède atmosphère.

LE SOLEIL

Le long du vieux faubourg, où pendent aux masures
Les persiennes, abri des secrètes luxures,
Quand le soleil cruel frappe à traits redoublés
Sur la ville et les champs, sur les toits et les blés,
Je vais m'exercer seul à ma fantasque escrime,
Flairant dans tous les coins les hasards de la rime,
Trébuchant sur les mots comme sur les pavés,
Heurtant parfois des vers depuis longtemps rêvés.

Ce père nourricier, ennemi des chloroses,
Éveille dans les champs les vers comme les roses;
Il fait s'évaporer les soucis vers le ciel,
Et remplit les cerveaux et les ruches de miel.

for I'll be deep in the sensuous pleasure of evoking spring-time with my will, drawing a sun out of my own heart, making a genial atmosphere with my burning thoughts.

[This poem, the first of the *Parisian Pictures* in *Les Fleurs du mal* 1861, shows the influence of Chénier and is probably an early work. Crépet and Blin suggest 1848, taking the word *émeute* to refer to the revolution. First published in *Les Fleurs du mal*, 1857]

The Sun

Through the old suburb, where the persian blinds hang at the windows of tumbledown houses, hiding furtive pleasures; when the cruel sun strikes blow upon blow on the city and the meadows, the roofs and the cornfields, I go practising my fantastic fencing all alone, scenting a chance rhyme in every corner, stumbling against words as against cobblestones, sometimes striking on verses I had long dreamt of.

The providing father, enemy of anaemia, wakens both worms and roses in the fields; he makes our cares vanish into the sky, he fills our brains and all the hives with honey. It is he who gives youth

C'est lui qui rajeunit les porteurs de béquilles
Et les rend gais et doux comme des jeunes filles,
Et commande aux moissons de croître et de mûrir
Dans le cœur immortel qui toujours veut fleurir!

Quand, ainsi qu'un poëte, il descend dans les villes,
Il ennoblit le sort des choses les plus viles,
Et s'introduit en roi, sans bruit et sans valets,
Dans tous les hôpitaux et dans tous les palais.

TRISTESSES DE LA LUNE

Ce soir, la lune rêve avec plus de paresse;
Ainsi qu'une beauté, sur de nombreux coussins,
Qui d'une main discrète et légère caresse
Avant de s'endormir le contour de ses seins,

Sur le dos satiné des molles avalanches,
Mourante, elle se livre aux longues pâmoisons,
Et promène ses yeux sur les visions blanches
Qui montent dans l'azur comme des floraisons.

to those who go on crutches, and makes them as gay and gentle as girls; he bids the crops to grow and ripen in the immortal heart that ever longs to flower again.

When, like a poet, he comes down into cities, he ennobles the lot of even the meanest things, and, like a monarch, silent and unattended, he enters workhouses and palaces.

[Early (Crépet, Blin). Published in *Les Fleurs du mal*, 1857]

The Sorrows of the Moon

Tonight, the Moon is more languidly dreaming; like some beautiful woman reclining on her pile of cushions, who caresses the curve of her breast with her light, discreet hand before she sleeps, on the satined pillow of soft drifts of cloud, she dies away into deep swoons, and her eyes sweep the white visions which are rising like flowers into the azure sky.

Quand parfois sur ce globe, en sa langueur oisive,
Elle laisse filer une larme furtive,
Un poëte pieux, ennemi du sommeil,

Dans le creux de sa main prend cette larme pâle,
Aux reflets irisés comme un fragment d'opale,
Et la met dans son cœur loin des yeux du soleil.

HÉLAS! qui n'a gémi sur autrui, sur soi-même?
Et qui n'a dit à Dieu: «Pardonnez-moi, Seigneur,
Si personne ne m'aime et si nul n'a mon cœur?
Ils m'ont tous corrompu; personne ne vous aime!»

Alors, lassé du monde et de ses vains discours,
Il faut lever les yeux aux voûtes sans nuages
Et ne plus s'adresser qu'aux muettes images
De ceux qui n'aiment rien, consolantes amours.

Alors, alors, il faut s'entourer de mystère,
Se fermer aux regards, et, sans morgue et sans fiel,
Sans dire à vos voisins: «Je n'aime que le ciel»,
Dire à Dieu: «Consolez mon âme de la terre!»

When sometimes she lets fall a furtive tear upon our globe, a pious poet, the enemy of sleep, takes in the hollow of his hand that pale tear, veined with glinting hues like a chip of opal, and treasures it in his heart, far from the sun's eyes.

[Mentioned in a letter from C.B. to Ancelle, Jan. 1850, Published in *Les Fleurs du mal*, 1857]

ALAS, who has not groaned for others and for himself? Who has not said to God, 'Forgive me, Lord, if no one loves me and if no one has my heart. They have all corrupted me: no one loves you!'

Then, weary of the world and its idle talk, a man must raise his eyes towards the cloudless vaults, and address himself only to the mute images of those who love nothing – consoling loves.

Then, he must gird himself about with mystery, make himself inscrutable, and without pride and without bitterness, without saying to his fellows: 'I care only for heaven', yet say to God: 'Comfort my soul for earthly things.'

Tel, fermé par son prêtre, un pieux monument,
Quand sur nos sombres toits la nuit est descendue,
Quand la foule a laissé le pavé de la rue,
Se remplit de silence et de recueillement.

DON JUAN AUX ENFERS

QUAND don Juan descendit vers l'onde souterraine
Et lorsqu'il eut donné son obole à Charon,
Un sombre mendiant, l'œil fier comme Antisthène,
D'un bras vengeur et fort saisit chaque aviron.

Montrant leurs seins pendants et leurs robes ouvertes,
Des femmes se tordaient sous le noir firmament,
Et, comme un grand troupeau de victimes offertes,
Derrière lui traînaient un long mugissement.

Sganarelle en riant lui réclamait ses gages,
Tandis que don Luis avec un doigt tremblant
Montrait à tous les morts errant sur les rivages
Le fils audacieux qui railla son front blanc.

–Just as a holy building, when its priest has closed it, when night has fallen on our dark roof-tops, when the crowd has gone from the street, fills with silence and composure.

[An early poem, given by C.B. to Hignard between 1843 and 1846, and published posthumously]

Don Juan in the Underworld

WHEN Don Juan went down to the underworld stream and paid his ferriage to Charon, a swarthy beggar, with an eye as haughty as Antisthenes', laid hold on the oars with avenging, powerful arms.

Their open gowns showing their drooping breasts, the womenfolk writhed this way and that under the black firmament, and behind him, like a great herd of sacrificial victims, broke into endless keening.

Chuckling, Sganarelle demanded his hire; while with trembling finger Don Luis pointed out, to all those dead astray on Lethe's shores, the insolent son who had jeered at his hoary head.

Frissonnant sous son deuil, la chaste et maigre Elvire,
Près de l'époux perfide et qui fut son amant,
Semblait lui réclamer un suprême sourire
Où brillât la douceur de son premier serment.

Tout droit dans son armure, un grand homme de pierre
Se tenait à la barre et coupait le flot noir;
Mais le calme héros, courbé sur sa rapière,
Regardait le sillage et ne daignait rien voir.

SUR *LE TASSE EN PRISON*

D'EUGÈNE DELACROIX

LE poëte au cachot, débraillé, maladif,
Roulant un manuscrit sous son pied convulsif,
Mesure d'un regard que la terreur enflamme
L'escalier de vertige où s'abîme son âme.

Les rires enivrants dont s'emplit la prison
Vers l'étrange et l'absurde invitent sa raison;
Le Doute l'environne, et la Peur ridicule,
Hideuse et multiforme, autour de lui circule.

The lean and chaste Elvira stood shivering in her mourning weeds, nearby the treacherous spouse who had been her lover, as one awaiting the alms of his final smile in which glowed all the tenderness of his first vow.

Erect in armour, a giant man of stone stood gripping the helm, slicing the black wave: but unmoved, the hero, leaning on his sword, watched only the wake's foam, disdaining other sights.

[Pre-1844 (Prarond). Published 1846 as *L'Impénitent*]

On Tasso in Prison. (*A painting by Delacroix*).

THE poet in his cell, unkempt and ailing, trampling a manuscript beneath his feverish foot, measures with terror-inflamed gaze the stair of madness in which his soul is being undone. The intoxicating bursts of laughter that fill the gaol lure his reason into oddness and absurdity. Doubt encompasses him, and foolish Fear, hideous and multiform, prowls round him.

Ce génie enfermé dans un taudis malsain,
Ces grimaces, ces cris, ces spectres dont l'essaim
Tourbillonne, ameuté derrière son oreille,

Ce rêveur que l'horreur de son logis réveille,
Voilà bien ton emblème, Âme aux songes obscurs,
Que le Réel étouffe entre ses quatre murs!

FEMMES DAMNÉES

COMME un bétail pensif sur le sable couchées,
Elles tournent leurs yeux vers l'horizon des mers,
Et leurs pieds se cherchant et leurs mains rapprochées
Ont de douces langueurs et des frissons amers.

Les unes, cœurs épris de longues confidences,
Dans le fond des bosquets où jasent les ruisseaux,
Vont épelant l'amour des craintives enfances
Et creusent le bois vert des jeunes arbrisseaux;

D'autres, comme des sœurs, marchent lentes et graves
À travers les rochers pleins d'apparitions,

That man of genius caged in a noisome hovel, those grimaces, those shrieks, those ghosts that whirl in frenzied swarm behind his ear, that dreamer startled from his sleep by his lodging's horror – such is your true emblem, Soul, you with your darkling dreams, whom Reality suffocates between its four walls.

[MS. dated 1844. Published 1864]

Doomed Women

RECLINING like musing cattle on the sand, they turn their eyes towards the sea's horizon, and their feet seeking each other's, and their hands drawing more close, feel sweet languors and agonizing thrills. Some of them, hearts given to long intimate talks, deep in groves full of purling streams, go spelling out their shy girlhood loves and carving their names on the green wood of saplings. Others, like nuns, tread slow and grave among vision-haunted

Où saint Antoine a vu surgir comme des laves
Les seins nus et pourprés de ses tentations;

Il en est, aux lueurs des résines croulantes,
Qui dans le creux muet des vieux antres païens
T'appellent au secours de leurs fièvres hurlantes,
Ô Bacchus, endormeur des remords anciens!

Et d'autres, dont la gorge aime les scapulaires,
Qui, recélant un fouet sous leurs longs vêtements,
Mêlent, dans le bois sombre et les nuits solitaires,
L'écume du plaisir aux larmes des tourments.

Ô vierges, ô démons, ô monstres, ô martyres,
De la réalité grands esprits contempteurs,
Chercheuses d'infini, dévotes et satyres,
Tantôt pleines de cris, tantôt pleines de pleurs,

Vous que dans votre enfer mon âme a poursuivies,
Pauvres sœurs, je vous aime autant que je vous plains,
Pour vos mornes douleurs, vos soifs inassouvies,
Et les urnes d'amour dont vos grands cœurs sont pleins!

rocks where Saint Anthony saw the bare ruby breasts of his temptations surging like lava. There are others who, in the melting resin's glimmer in the silent hollow of pagan caves, implore you to assuage their shrieking fevers, O Bacchus, soother of many a long-standing remorse. And others whose throats' delight is to wear scapularies, and who, hiding a whip under their long robes, unite the sweat of pleasure and the tears of pain in the dark wood, on lonely nights. O virgins, demons, monsters, martyrs, great minds who despise reality, seekers after the Infinite, pious ones and lustful ones, you whom my soul has pursued into your inferno, poor sisters, I have as much love as compassion for your bleak sufferings and unquenchable thirsts, and the urns of love with which your great hearts brim.

[1846? Published in *Les Fleurs du mal*, 1857]

LES LITANIES DE SATAN

Ô TOI, le plus savant et le plus beau des Anges,
Dieu trahi par le sort et privé de louanges,

Ô Satan, prends pitié de ma longue misère!

Ô Prince de l'exil, à qui l'on a fait tort,
Et qui, vaincu, toujours te redresses plus fort,

Ô Satan, prends pitié de ma longue misère!

Toi qui sais tout, grand roi des choses souterraines,
Guérisseur familier des angoisses humaines,

Ô Satan, prends pitié de ma longue misère!

Toi qui, même aux lépreux, aux parias maudits,
Enseignes par l'amour le goût du Paradis,

Ô Satan, prends pitié de ma longue misère!

The Litanies of Satan

O YOU, the most omniscient and most beautiful of angels, a god betrayed by Fate and bereft of praises; O Satan, have pity on my long misery!

O Prince of exile, to whom injustice has been done, and who in defeat stand ever more firm; O Satan, have pity on my long misery!

You who know all, great king of underworld things, familiar healer of human anguishes; O Satan, have pity on my long misery!

You who, even to lepers and to outcasts under ban, teach us through love the taste for Paradise; O Satan, have pity on my long misery!

Ô toi qui de la Mort, ta vieille et forte amante,
Engendras l'Espérance – une folle charmante!

Ô Satan, prends pitié de ma longue misère!

Toi qui fais au proscrit ce regard calme et haut
Qui damne tout un peuple autour d'un échafaud,

Ô Satan, prends pitié de ma longue misère!

Toi qui sais en quels coins des terres envieuses
Le Dieu jaloux cacha les pierres précieuses,

Ô Satan, prends pitié de ma longue misère!

Toi dont l'œil clair connaît les profonds arsenaux
Où dort enseveli le peuple des métaux,

Ô Satan, prends pitié de ma longue misère!

Toi dont la large main cache les précipices
Au somnambule errant au bord des édifices,

Ô Satan, prends pitié de ma longue misère!

O you who through your old and powerful consort, Death, begot that charming madcap, Hope; O Satan, have pity on my long misery!

You who give the outlaw that serene and haughty smile that damns an entire nation thronging round the scaffold; O Satan have pity on my long misery!

You who know in what recesses of envious lands the jealous God hid precious stones; O Satan, have pity on my long misery!

You whose bright eye knows the deep arsenals where the buried race of metals slumbers; O Satan, have pity on my long misery!

You whose vast hand hides the precipice from the sleepwalker, as he strays on the brink of lofty buildings; O Satan, have pity on my long misery!

Toi qui, magiquement, assouplis les vieux os
De l'ivrogne attardé foulé par les chevaux,

Ô Satan, prends pitié de ma longue misère!

Toi qui, pour consoler l'homme frêle qui souffre,
Nous appris à mêler le salpêtre et le soufre,

Ô Satan, prends pitié de ma longue misère!

Toi qui poses ta marque, ô complice subtil,
Sur le front du Crésus impitoyable et vil,

Ô Satan, prends pitié de ma longue misère!

Toi qui mets dans les yeux et dans le cœur des filles
Le culte de la plaie et l'amour des guenilles,

Ô Satan, prends pitié de ma longue misère!

Bâton des exilés, lampe des inventeurs,
Confesseur des pendus et des conspirateurs,

Ô Satan, prends pitié de ma longue misère!

You who, by magic, make supple the old bones of the belated drunkard, trampled beneath hooves of horses; O Satan, have pity on my long misery!

You who, to console frail man in his suffering, taught us to mix saltpetre and sulphur; O Satan, have pity on my long misery!

You who set your mark, O subtle accomplice, on the brow of the pitiless, vile millionaire; O Satan, have pity on my long misery!

You who implant in women's eyes and hearts the cult of the wound and the love of rags; O Satan, have pity on my long misery!

Staff of the exiled, lamp of inventors, confessor of the hanged and of conspirators; O Satan, have pity on my long misery!

Père adoptif de ceux qu'en sa noire colère
Du paradis terrestre a chassés Dieu le Père,

Ô Satan, prends pitié de ma longue misère!

PRIÈRE

Gloire et louange à toi, Satan, dans les hauteurs
Du Ciel, où tu régnas, et dans les profondeurs
De l'Enfer, où, vaincu, tu rêves en silence!
Fais que mon âme un jour, sous l'Arbre de Science,
Près de toi se repose, à l'heure où sur ton front,
Comme un Temple nouveau ses rameaux s'épandront!

LA MUSE MALADE

MA pauvre muse, hélas! qu'as-tu donc ce matin?
Tes yeux creux sont peuplés de visions nocturnes,
Et je vois tour à tour réfléchis sur ton teint
La folie et l'horreur, froides et taciturnes.

Adoptive father of those whom, in his black anger, God the Father drove from the earthly Paradise; O Satan, have pity on my long misery!

PRAYER

Glory and praise to you, Satan, in the heights of heaven where once you reigned, and in the depths of hell where, vanquished, you dream in silence.

Grant that my soul, some day, may rest beside you, under the Tree of Knowledge, at the hour when on your brow, like a new Temple, its branches [will] spread!

[1846? (F. Caussy). Published in *Les Fleurs du mal*, 1857]

The Sick Muse

MY poor Muse, alas, what ails you this morning? Your sunken eyes are haunted by nocturnal visions, and I see madness and horror, cold and speechless, reflected each in turn in your complexion.

Le succube verdâtre et le rose lutin
T'ont-ils versé la peur et l'amour de leurs urnes?
Le cauchemar, d'un poing despotique et mutin,
T'a-t-il noyée au fond d'un fabuleux Minturnes?

Je voudrais qu'exhalant l'odeur de la santé
Ton sein de pensers forts fût toujours fréquenté,
Et que ton sang chrétien coulât à flots rythmiques,

Comme les sons nombreux des syllabes antiques,
Où règnent tour à tour le père des chansons,
Phœbus, et le grand Pan, le seigneur des moissons.

LA MUSE VÉNALE

Ô MUSE de mon cœur, amante des palais,
Auras-tu, quand Janvier lâchera ses Borées,
Durant les noirs ennuis des neigeuses soirées,
Un tison pour chauffer tes deux pieds violets?

Have the green succubus and pink goblin poured you a draught of fear and love from their urns? Has nightmare's bullying, wilful hand drowned you in the depths of some legendary Minturnae?

I would fain that, redolent of health, your breast were ever visited by powerful thoughts, and that your Christian blood would ever flow in cadenced waves, like the harmonious numbers of classical verse, in which reign turn by turn Phoebus, the father of songs, and mighty Pan, the lord of harvests.

[The influence of Sainte-Beuve and Chénier suggests that this was a relatively early poem. Published in *Les Fleurs du mal*, 1857]

The Venal Muse

O MUSE of my heart, lover of palaces, when January unleashes its icy blasts, through the dark tedium of snowy twilights, will you have embers enough to warm your feet, purple with cold?

Ranimeras-tu donc tes épaules marbrées
Aux nocturnes rayons qui percent les volets?
Sentant ta bourse à sec autant que ton palais,
Récolteras-tu l'or des voûtes azurées?

Il te faut, pour gagner ton pain de chaque soir,
Comme un enfant de chœur, jouer de l'encensoir,
Chanter des *Te Deum* auxquels tu ne crois guère,

Ou, saltimbanque à jeun, étaler tes appas
Et ton rire trempé de pleurs qu'on ne voit pas,
Pour faire épanouir la rate du vulgaire.

LA GÉANTE

Du temps que la Nature en sa verve puissante
Concevait chaque jour des enfants monstrueux,
J'eusse aimé vivre auprès d'une jeune géante,
Comme aux pieds d'une reine un chat voluptueux.

Can you revive your mottled shoulders with nothing but the beams of night that peep through the shutters? When both your purse and your mouth are dry, will you harvest the gold of heaven's azure vaults?

To sing for your supper, then you will have to swing the censer like a choir-boy, and chant Te Deums in which you scarce believe,

or like a starving acrobat, show off your points, and laugh while you hide your tears, to make the mob split their sides.

[First published in *Les Fleurs du mal*, 1857. Crépet and Blin compare line 11 with a poem by Banville (1853), and Ferran with Leconte de Lisle's *Les Montreurs* of 1862. But the poem is probably an early one, dating from 1844–5, when Baudelaire was faced with having to earn his living by his pen.]

The Giantess

In olden days when Nature, in her lusty exuberance, daily conceived monstrous offspring, I would fain have lived with some young giantess, like a voluptuous cat at the feet of a queen.

J'eusse aimé voir son corps fleurir avec son âme
Et grandir librement dans ses terribles jeux;
Deviner si son cœur couve une sombre flamme
Aux humides brouillards qui nagent dans ses yeux;

Parcourir à loisir ses magnifiques formes;
Ramper sur le versant de ses genoux énormes,
Et parfois en été, quand les soleils malsains,

Lasse, la font s'étendre à travers la campagne,
Dormir nonchalamment à l'ombre de ses seins,
Comme un hameau paisible au pied d'une montagne.

LA BEAUTÉ

JE suis belle, ô mortels! comme un rêve de pierre,
Et mon sein, où chacun s'est meurtri tour à tour,
Est fait pour inspirer au poète un amour
Éternel et muet ainsi que la matière.

I would have loved to watch her body flowering with her soul, and developing freely in her frightening games, and to speculate whether she was nourishing some tragic flame in her heart, as I saw the liquid mists float in her eyes. I would have loved to explore her limbs at my leisure; to climb the slope of her tremendous knees, and sometimes when the sickly suns of summer made her stretch wearily across the fields, to fall trustfully asleep in the shadow of her breasts, like a quiet hamlet at some mountain's foot.

[Pre-1844 (Prarond). Published 1857]

Beauty

I AM beautiful, O mortals, as a dream in stone, and my breast, on which every man has bruised himself in his turn, is formed to inspire in poets a love as eternal and as silent as matter itself.

Je trône dans l'azur comme un sphinx incompris;
J'unis un cœur de neige à la blancheur des cygnes;
Je hais le mouvement qui déplace les lignes,
Et jamais je ne pleure et jamais je ne ris.

Les poètes, devant mes grandes attitudes,
Que j'ai l'air d'emprunter aux plus fiers monuments,
Consumeront leurs jours en d'austères études;

Car j'ai, pour fasciner ces dociles amants,
De purs miroirs qui font toutes choses plus belles:
Mes yeux, mes larges yeux aux clartés éternelles!

LE FOU ET LA VÉNUS

QUELLE admirable journée! Le vaste parc se pâme sous l'œil brûlant du soleil, comme la jeunesse sous la domination de l'Amour.

I reign in the azure like a sphinx, beyond all understanding; my heart of snow matches my swan's whiteness; movement I hate, that disturbs the ideal line, and never do I weep, nor ever smile.

Before the grandeur of my poses – seemingly inspired by the noblest monuments – poets will consume their days in austere research;

since, to hypnotize my enslaved lovers, I have pure mirrors that magnify the beauty of all things – my eyes, my vast eyes filled with eternal light!

[An early work? (Crépet and Blin). Published 1857 and in *Les Fleurs du mal*, 1857]

The Jester and the Statue of Venus

WHAT an admirable day! The great park is languishing under the sun's burning eye, like youth under love's dominion.

L'extase universelle des choses ne s'exprime par aucun bruit; les eaux elles-mêmes sont comme endormies. Bien différente des fêtes humaines, c'est ici une orgie silencieuse.

On dirait qu'une lumière toujours croissante fait de plus en plus étinceler les objets; que les fleurs excitées brûlent du désir de rivaliser avec l'azur du ciel par l'énergie de leurs couleurs, et que la chaleur, rendant visibles les parfums, les fait monter vers l'astre comme des fumées.

Cependant, dans cette jouissance universelle, j'ai aperçu un être affligé.

Aux pieds d'une colossale Vénus, un de ces fous artificiels, un de ces bouffons volontaires chargés de faire rire les rois quand le Remords ou l'Ennui les obsède, affublé d'un costume éclatant et ridicule, coiffé de cornes et de sonnettes, tout ramassé contre le piédestal, lève des yeux pleins de larmes vers l'immortelle Déesse.

Et ses yeux disent: «Je suis le dernier et le plus solitaire des humains, privé d'amour et d'amitié, et bien inférieur en cela au plus imparfait des animaux. Cependant je suis fait,

The universal ecstasy of things is not expressed through any noise; the very fountains are as though asleep. Unlike human holidays, this is a silent orgy.

It's as though a constantly increasing light is making things glitter more and more; as though the impassioned flowers are burning with a desire to rival the sky's azure with the vividness of their hues; as though the heat, making the perfumes visible, sets them floating towards the sun like mists.

And yet, in the midst of that universal rejoicing, I saw one person in distress.

At the feet of a colossal Venus, one of those artificial madmen, one of those self-appointed jesters whose task is to make Kings laugh when remorse or boredom obsesses them, decked in a gaudy, comical outfit, wearing horns and bells on his head, was huddled against the pedestal, raising his tear-filled eyes towards the immortal goddess.

And his eyes were saying: 'I am the lowest and loneliest of human beings, deprived of love and friendship, and in this respect lowlier

moi aussi, pour comprendre et sentir l'immortelle Beauté! Ah! Déesse! ayez pitié de ma tristesse et de mon délire!»

Mais l'implacable Vénus regarde au loin je ne sais quoi avec ses yeux de marbre.

J'AIME le souvenir de ces époques nues,
Dont Phœbus se plaisait à dorer les statues.
Alors l'homme et la femme en leur agilité
Jouissaient sans mensonge et sans anxiété,
Et, le ciel amoureux leur caressant l'échine,
Exerçaient la santé de leur noble machine.
Cybèle alors, fertile en produits généreux,
Ne trouvait point ses fils un poids trop onéreux,
Mais, louve au cœur gonflé de tendresses communes,
Abreuvait l'univers à ses tétines brunes.
L'homme, élégant, robuste et fort, avait le droit

than the most imperfect of animals. Yet I, also, am capable of understanding and feeling immortal Beauty! Ah, goddess, have pity on my sorrow and delirium!'

But the inexorable Venus gazes far beyond him, at something else, with her eyes of marble.

[Published 1862]

I LOVE the memory of those ancient times of nakedness, epochs whose statues Phoebus gladly gilded. In those days, men and women rejoiced in their lithe bodies without deceit or shame, and with the fond sky caressing their backs, gave free play to their noble organism's health. In those days Cybele, teeming with bountiful harvests, did not regard her sons as too onerous a burden, but, [like] a she-wolf whose heart swelled with tenderness for all things, gave suck to the universe from her tawny breasts.

Elegant, stalwart, and strong, Man was rightly proud of the

D'être fier des beautés qui le nommaient leur roi;
Fruits purs de tout outrage et vierges de gerçures,
Dont la chair lisse et ferme appelait les morsures!

Le Poëte aujourd'hui, quand il veut concevoir
Ces natives grandeurs, aux lieux où se font voir
La nudité de l'homme et celle de la femme,
Sent un froid ténébreux envelopper son âme
Devant ce noir tableau plein d'épouvantement.
Ô monstruosités pleurant leur vêtement!
Ô ridicules troncs! torses dignes des masques!
Ô pauvres corps tordus, maigres, ventrus ou flasques,
Que le dieu de l'Utile, implacable et serein,
Enfants, emmaillota dans ses langes d'airain!
Et vous, femmes, hélas! pâles comme des cierges,
Que ronge et que nourrit la débauche, et vous, vierges,
Du vice maternel traînant l'hérédité
Et toutes les hideurs de la fécondité!

Nous avons, il est vrai, nations corrompues,
Aux peuples anciens des beautés inconnues:

beautiful women who hailed him as their lord – fruits pure of all assault, innocent of all taint, whose smooth, firm flesh was an invitation to bite!

Nowadays, when the poet seeks to visualize those native grandeurs in places where men's and women's nudity may be observed, he feels a dismal chill envelope his soul, at that sombre and dreadful sight. O freaks, bewailing their clothes! what ridiculous trunks, what torsoes fit for masks, what feeble twisted bodies, skinny, pot-bellied, and flabby, which the pitiless and unmoved god of Utility wrapped in his bronze swaddling-clothes when they were babies! And you, women, alas, as waxen-pale as candles, gnawed away or fattened up by debauchery! and you, virgins, dragging with you the inheritance of your mothers' viciousness and all the hideous stigmata of fertility!

True, we decadent nations have beauties unknown to the peoples

Des visages rongés par les chancres du cœur,
Et comme qui dirait des beautés de langueur;
Mais ces inventions de nos muses tardives
N'empêcheront jamais les races maladives
De rendre à la jeunesse un hommage profond,
– À la sainte jeunesse, à l'air simple, au doux front,
À l'œil limpide et clair ainsi qu'une eau courante,
Et qui va répandant sur tout, insouciante
Comme l'azur du ciel, les oiseaux et les fleurs,
Ses parfums, ses chansons et ses douces chaleurs!

ÉPÎTRE À SAINTE-BEUVE

Tous imberbes alors, sur les vieux bancs de chêne,
Plus polis et luisants que des anneaux de chaîne,
Que, jour à jour, la peau des hommes a fourbis,
Nous traînions tristement nos ennuis, accroupis
Et voûtés sous le ciel carré des solitudes
Où l'enfant boit dix ans l'âpre lait des études.
C'était dans ce vieux temps, mémorable et marquant,
Où, forcés d'élargir le classique carcan,

of old – faces gnawed by the cankers of the heart, and, so to speak, beauties of sickliness: but these inventions of our latter-day muses will never prevent the diseased peoples from paying a profound tribute to Youth – to saintly Youth with its unaffected mien, its untroubled brow, its eye limpid and clear as running water, and which goes spreading over all things – as carefree as the sky's azure, or birds or flowers – its perfumes, its songs, and its gentle ardours.

[Early (Starkie). Published in *Les Fleurs du mal*, 1857]

Epistle to Sainte-Beuve

As yet beardless, we all, on the old oaken benches, more polished and glossy than the links of a chain furbished day after day by men's skins, sadly endured our cares, huddled and round-shouldered under the square sky of solitudes beneath which, for ten years, a boy imbibes the bitter milk of lessons. It was in those far-off days, memorable and important, that, forced to loosen the classical yoke,

Les professeurs, encor rebelles à vos rimes,
Succombaient sous l'effort de nos folles escrimes
Et laissaient l'écolier, triomphant et mutin,
Faire à l'aise hurler Triboulet en latin. –
Qui de nous, en ces temps d'adolescences pâles,
N'a connu la torpeur des fatigues claustrales,
– L'œil perdu dans l'azur morne d'un ciel d'été
Ou l'éblouissement de la neige, – guetté,
L'oreille avide et droite, – et bu comme une meute
L'écho lointain d'un livre ou le cri d'une émeute?

C'était surtout l'été, quand les plombs se fondaient,
Que ces grands murs noircis en tristesse abondaient,
Lorsque la canicule ou le fumeux automne
Irradiait les cieux de son feu monotone
Et faisait sommeiller, dans les sveltes donjons,
Les tiercelets criards, effroi des blancs pigeons;
Saison de rêveries où la Muse s'accroche
Pendant un jour entier au battant d'une cloche;
Où la Mélancolie, à midi, quand tout dort,
Le menton dans la main, au fond du corridor, –

the teachers, still hostile to your rhymes, gave way to the thrust of our wild skirmishing, and allowed the triumphant and mischievous schoolboy to make Triboulet bellow in Latin to his heart's content. Which of us, in those days of pale adolescence, did not know the sluggish boredom of confinement, his eye lost in the depressing azure of a summer sky or the dazzlement of snow, and awaited, with hungry ears pricked, then drank like a pack of hounds the distant echo of a book or the shouts of a riot?

It was particularly in summer that, when the leads melted, those high, blackened walls were full of sadness, when the heat-wave or the hazy autumn made the skies radiant with its monotonous blaze, and made the shrill falcons, the white pigeons' terror, drowse in the narrow turrets; the season of daydreams when the Muse clings the livelong day to the tolling of a bell; when Melancholy, at noon when all is sleeping, chin in hand, at the end of the corridor, and

L'œil plus noir et plus bleu que la Religieuse
Dont chacun sait l'histoire obscène et douloureuse,
– Traîne un pied alourdi de précoces ennuis
Et son front moite encor des langueurs des ses nuits.
– Et puis, venaient les soirs malsains, les nuits fiévreuses
Qui rendent de leur corps les filles amoureuses
Et les font, aux miroirs, – stérile volupté –
Contempler les fruits mûrs de leur nubilité; –
Les soirs italiens, de molle insouciance,
Qui des plaisirs menteurs révèlent la science
Quand la sombre Vénus, du haut des balcons noirs,
Verse des flots de musc de ses frais encensoirs.

Ce fut dans ce conflit de molles circonstances,
Mûri par vos sonnets, préparé par vos stances,
Qu'un soir, ayant flairé le livre et son esprit,
J'emportai sur mon cœur l'histoire d'Amaury.
Tout abîme mystique est à deux pas du doute. –
Le breuvage infiltré lentement, goutte à goutte,
En moi qui, dès quinze ans, vers le gouffre entraîné,
Déchiffrais couramment les soupirs de René
Et que de l'inconnu la soif bizarre altère,

with an eye darker and more blue than Diderot's *Religieuse* (whose lewd and painful story is known to all) drags a foot heavy with precocious worries, its brow still moist with the languors of its nights. And then came the troubled evenings, those feverish nights which make girls love their own bodies, and (sterile pleasure) make them observe the ripened fruits of their nubility in the mirror; Italian evenings of indolent casualness, which reveal knowledge of false pleasures, when the dark Venus, from high black balconies, pours waves of musk from her cool censers.

It was in this clash of enervating circumstances, when I was matured by your sonnets and prepared by your stanzas, that one evening, having sensed your book's meaning and spirit, I bore the story of Amaury on my heart. Every abyss of mysticism is but two steps removed from doubt. The potion slowly filtered drop by drop into me, who from the age of fifteen, swept away towards the bottomless pit, readily deciphered René's sighs – I who am parched

A travaillé le fond de la plus mince artère.
J'en ai tout absorbé, les miasmes, les parfums,
Le doux chuchotement des souvenirs défunts,
Les longs enlacements des phrases symboliques,
Chapelets murmurants de madrigaux mystiques,
– Livre voluptueux, si jamais il en fut.

Et depuis, soit au fond d'un asile touffu,
Soit que, sous les soleils des zones différentes,
L'éternel bercement des houles enivrantes
Et l'aspect renaissant des horizons sans fin
Ramenassent ce cœur vers le songe divin,
Soit dans les lourds loisirs d'un jour caniculaire,
Ou dans l'oisiveté frileuse de frimaire,
Sous les flots du tabac qui masquent le plafond,
J'ai partout feuilleté le mystère profond
De ce livre si cher aux âmes engourdies
Que leur destin marqua des mêmes maladies,
Et, devant le miroir, j'ai perfectionné
L'art cruel qu'un démon, en naissant, m'a donné,
– De la douleur pour faire une volupté vraie, –
D'ensanglanter son mal et de gratter sa plaie.

with the thirst for the unknown – and it worked upon my slightest arteries. I absorbed all of it, the miasmas, the perfumes, the dulcet whispering of dead memories, the long intertwining of symbolic phrases, murmurous rosaries of mystic madrigals – a voluptuous book if ever there was one!

And since then, whether in some leafy sanctuary or beneath the suns of other hemispheres, the eternal swaying of the hypnotic sea-swell and the oft-reborn view of endless horizons bring back my heart to divine dreaming, whether in the heavy leisure hours of a midsummer day or in the chilly idleness of early winter, under waves of tobacco-smoke that hide the ceiling, I have everywhere perused the profound mystery of this book, so dear to those numbed souls whose fate has stamped them with the same disorders, and before the mirror I have practised the cruel art which a demon bestowed on me at birth – the need for pain, to create true voluptuousness – the need to draw blood from one's suffering, and scratch the wound.

Poète, est-ce une injure ou bien un compliment?
Car je suis vis-à-vis de vous comme un amant
En face du fantôme, au geste plein d'amorces,
Dont la main et dont l'œil ont, pour pomper les forces,
Des charmes inconnus. – Tous les êtres aimés
Sont des vases de fiel qu'on boit les yeux fermés,
Et le cœur transpercé, que la douleur allèche,
Expire chaque jour en bénissant sa flèche.

ÉLÉVATION

AU-DESSUS des étangs, au-dessus des vallées,
Des montagnes, des bois, des nuages, des mers,
Par delà le soleil, par delà les éthers,
Par delà les confins des sphères étoilées,

Mon esprit, tu te meus avec agilité,
Et, comme un bon nageur qui se pâme dans l'onde,
Tu sillonnes gaîment l'immensité profonde
Avec une indicible et mâle volupté.

Poet, is it an insult or a compliment? For towards you I am as a lover towards a ghost, whose gestures are full of caresses, whose hand and eye have hidden charms with which to drain strength away. All beloved beings are vessels of gall which we drink with closed eyes, and the pierced heart, attracted by pain, dies every day blessing its arrow.

[Baudelaire sent this poem to Sainte-Beuve in 1844. It is in a tortuous, clumsy style unusual for the poet. The references are to Diderot's *La Religieuse*; *Volupté*, of which the hero is Amaury, a novel by Sainte-Beuve; *René*, by Chateaubriand.]

Elevation

ABOVE the pools, above the valleys, the mountains, woods, clouds, and seas, beyond the Sun, beyond the expanses of ether, beyond the frontiers of the starry spheres,

agile you move, O my mind, and as a strong swimmer swoons on the wavy sea, gaily you cleave the unfathomable vastness with ineffable, male, voluptuous joy.

Envole-toi bien loin de ces miasmes morbides;
Va te purifier dans l'air supérieur,
Et bois, comme une pure et divine liqueur,
Le feu clair qui remplit les espaces limpides.

Derrière les ennuis et les vastes chagrins
Qui chargent de leur poids l'existence brumeuse,
Heureux celui qui peut d'une aile vigoureuse
S'élancer vers les champs lumineux et sereins!

Celui dont les pensers, comme des alouettes,
Vers les cieux le matin prennent un libre essor,
– Qui plane sur la vie, et comprend sans effort
Le langage des fleurs et des choses muettes!

CORRESPONDANCES

LA Nature est un temple où de vivants piliers
Laissent parfois sortir de confuses paroles;
L'homme y passe à travers des forêts de symboles
Qui l'observent avec des regards familiers.

Fly far away from this deadly slough; go, cleanse yourself in the upper air, and drink undiluted the nectar of the gods, that lucid fire that brims the limpid realms of space!

Behind all cares and vast chagrins that weigh upon our fogged existence, happy is he whose dauntless wing lifts him towards the luminous fields of peace;

he whose lark-like thoughts soar free towards the morning skies, who rides high above life, swift to interpret the speech of flowers and inarticulate things.

[Published in *Les Fleurs du mal*, 1857]

Correlatives

NATURE is a temple, in which living pillars sometimes utter a babel of words; man traverses it through forests of symbols, that watch him with knowing eyes.

Comme de longs échos qui de loin se confondent
Dans une ténébreuse et profonde unité,
Vaste comme la nuit et comme la clarté,
Les parfums, les couleurs et les sons se répondent.

Il est des parfums frais comme des chairs d'enfants,
Doux comme les hautbois, verts comme les prairies,
– Et d'autres, corrompus, riches et triomphants,

Ayant l'expansion des choses infinies,
Comme l'ambre, le musc, le benjoin et l'encens,
Qui chantent les transports de l'esprit et des sens.

Like prolonged echoes which merge far away in an opaque, deep oneness, as vast as darkness, as vast as light, perfumes, sounds, and colours answer each to each.

There are perfumes fresh and cool as the bodies of children, mellow as oboes, green as fields; and others that are perverse, rich, and triumphant,

that have the infinite expansion of infinite things – such as amber, musk, benjamin, and incense, which chant the ecstasies of the mind and senses.

[1845 (Ruff). 1846?? (Pommier). Post-1851 (Starkie). Published in *Les Fleurs du mal*, 1857]

II

The Jeanne Duval Cycle

1842–60

LES BIJOUX

LA très-chère était nue, et, connaissant mon cœur,
Elle n'avait gardé que ses bijoux sonores,
Dont le riche attirail lui donnait l'air vainqueur
Qu'ont dans leurs jours heureux les esclaves des Mores.

Quand il jette en dansant son bruit vif et moqueur,
Ce monde rayonnant de métal et de pierre
Me ravit en extase, et j'aime à la fureur
Les choses où le son se mêle à la lumière.

Elle était donc couchée et se laissait aimer,
Et du haut du divan elle souriait d'aise
À mon amour profond et doux comme la mer,
Qui vers elle montait comme vers sa falaise.

Les yeux fixés sur moi, comme un tigre dompté,
D'un air vague et rêveur elle essayait des poses,
Et la candeur unie à la lubricité
Donnait un charme neuf à ses métamorphoses;

The Jewels

MY darling was naked, and, knowing my heart, was clad only in her sonorous jewellery, whose rich splendour gave her the triumphant air that Moorish slave-women have in their days of happiness.

When, as it dances, it throws out its sharp, mocking noise, that glittering world of metal and stone thrills me to ecstasy, and I madly love those things in which sound and light commingle.

So she reclined and let herself be loved, and high on the divan she smiled for joy upon my love, as deep and gentle as the sea, which rose towards her as to a cliff. With her eyes intent on me, like a tame tigress, with a vague, dreamy look she tried this pose and that, and candidness and wantonness together gave a novel

Et son bras et sa jambe, et sa cuisse et ses reins,
Polis comme de l'huile, onduleux comme un cygne,
Passaient devant mes yeux clairvoyants et sereins;
Et son ventre et ses seins, ces grappes de ma vigne,

S'avançaient, plus câlins que les Anges du mal,
Pour troubler le repos où mon âme était mise,
Et pour la déranger du rocher de cristal
Où, calme et solitaire, elle s'était assise.

Je croyais voir unis par un nouveau dessin
Les hanches de l'Antiope au buste d'un imberbe,
Tant sa taille faisait ressortir son bassin.
Sur ce teint fauve et brun le fard était superbe!

– Et la lampe s'étant résignée à mourir,
Comme le foyer seul illuminait la chambre,
Chaque fois qu'il poussait un flamboyant soupir,
Il inondait de sang cette peau couleur d'ambre!

charm to her variations. Her arms and legs, her thighs and loins, glistening like oil, rippling swanlike, passed before my clairvoyant and serene eyes; and her belly and her breasts, those clusters of my vine, thrust themselves forward, more alluring than the angels of evil, to trouble the rest my soul had found, and cast it down from the crystal rock whereon it had settled, calm and solitary.

I thought I saw before me, united in a new pattern, Antiope's hips and a stripling's bust, so strongly did her narrow waist accentuate her pelvis. The rouge was superb on that wild, tawny complexion. And as the lamp had resigned itself to die, and the hearth alone lit up the room, each time it gave a fiery sigh it flowed like blood over that amber skin.

[Published in *Les Fleurs du mal*, 1857]

SED NON SATIATA

BIZARRE déité, brune comme les nuits,
Au parfum mélangé de musc et de havane,
Œuvre de quelque obi, le Faust de la savane,
Sorcière au flanc d'ébène, enfant des noirs minuits,

Je préfère au constance, à l'opium, au nuits,
L'élixir de ta bouche où l'amour se pavane;
Quand vers toi mes désirs partent en caravane,
Tes yeux sont la citerne où boivent mes ennuis.

Par ces deux grands yeux noirs, soupiraux de ton âme
Ô démon sans pitié! verse-moi moins de flamme;
Je ne suis pas le Styx pour t'embrasser neuf fois,

Hélas! et je ne puis, Mégère libertine,
Pour briser ton courage et te mettre aux abois,
Dans l'enfer de ton lit devenir Proserpine!

Never Satisfied

OUTLANDISH goddess, swarthy as the nights, with your perfume a blend of musk and Havana tobacco; creation of some Obi, some Faust of the savannah; ebony-flanked witch, daughter of black midnights,

I prefer above Constantia wine,* opium, and Nuits-Saint-Georges,† the elixir of your love-flaunting lips. When the caravan of my desires sets out on its pilgrimage towards you, your eyes are the reservoir where my cares may drink.

From those two vast, dark eyes, those skylights of your soul, O pitiless demon, pour me less flame! I am no Styx to embrace you ninefold, alas;

and, O lecherous Megaera, I cannot, in order to break your courage and set you at bay, become Proserpine in the underworld of your bed.

[1842–3? (C. Cousin). Published in *Les Fleurs du mal*, 1857]

* Constantia, a South African wine.
† Burgundy.

AVEC ses vêtements ondoyants et nacrés,
Même quand elle marche on croirait qu'elle danse,
Comme ces longs serpents que les jongleurs sacrés
Au bout de leurs bâtons agitent en cadence.

Comme le sable morne et l'azur des déserts,
Insensibles tous deux à l'humaine souffrance,
Comme les longs réseaux de la houle des mers,
Elle se développe avec indifférence.

Ses yeux polis sont faits de minéraux charmants,
Et dans cette nature étrange et symbolique
Où l'ange inviolé se mêle au sphinx antique,

Où tout n'est qu'or, acier, lumière et diamants,
Resplendit à jamais, comme un astre inutile,
La froide majesté de la femme stérile.

WITH her swinging, mother-of-pearl finery, even when she walks you would think she was dancing, like those long snakes which holy fakirs sway in rhythm at the end of their sticks.

Like the forlorn sand and azure of the deserts, both equally insensitive to human suffering, or like the sea-surge's endless webs, she glides along in her indifference.

Her polished eyes are wrought of hypnotic minerals, and in that strange symbolic nature in which unviolated angel and sphinx of old unite,

made all of gold and steel and light and diamonds, forever glitters, like a useless star, the frigid majesty of the sterile woman.

[Published April 1857 and in *Les Fleurs du mal*, 1857]

LE SERPENT QUI DANSE

QUE j'aime voir, chère indolente,
De ton corps si beau,
Comme une étoffe vacillante,
Miroiter la peau!

Sur ta chevelure profonde
Aux âcres parfums,
Mer odorante et vagabonde
Aux flots bleus et bruns,

Comme un navire qui s'éveille
Au vent du matin,
Mon âme rêveuse appareille
Pour un ciel lointain.

Tes yeux, où rien ne se révèle
De doux ni d'amer,
Sont deux bijoux froids où se mêle
L'or avec le fer.

À te voir marcher en cadence,
Belle d'abandon,
On dirait un serpent qui danse
Au bout d'un bâton.

The Dancing Snake

HOW I love watching, my indolent darling, the skin of your so beautiful body glisten like shimmering raiment. On your unfathomable, bitter-tanged hair, that odorous, restless sea with waves of blue and brown, like a ship awakening in the morning wind my dreamy soul sets sail for a far-off heaven. Your eyes in which nothing bitter or sweet can be seen, are two cold gems in which gold blends with steel. Watching you walk in cadence, lovely in your carefreeness, one would say you were a snake dancing at the end of

Sous le fardeau de ta paresse
    Ta tête d'enfant
Se balance avec la mollesse
    D'un jeune éléphant,

Et ton corps se penche et s'allonge
    Comme un fin vaisseau
Qui roule bord sur bord et plonge
    Ses vergues dans l'eau.

Comme un flot grossi par la fonte
    Des glaciers grondants,
Quand l'eau de ta bouche remonte
    Au bord de tes dents,

Je crois boire un vin de Bohême,
    Amer et vainqueur,
Un ciel liquide qui parsème
    D'étoiles mon cœur!

a stick. Under the burden of your own languidness, your childish head sways to and fro, with the gentle rhythm of a baby elephant's, and your body heels and stretches like a trim ship rolling from side to side and dipping its yards in the brine. Like a stream swollen by the melting of roaring glaciers, when the saliva in your mouth brims to the tips of your teeth, I fancy I am sipping a Bohemian wine, sharp and overpowering, a liquid sky that flecks my heart with stars.

[Published in *Les Fleurs du mal*, 1857]

JE t'adore à l'égal de la voûte nocturne,
Ô vase de tristesse, ô grande taciturne,
Et t'aime d'autant plus, belle, que tu me fuis,
Et que tu me parais, ornement de mes nuits,
Plus ironiquement accumuler les lieues
Qui séparent mes bras des immensités bleues.

Je m'avance à l'attaque, et je grimpe aux assauts,
Comme après un cadavre un chœur de vermisseaux,
Et je chéris, ô bête implacable et cruelle!
Jusqu'à cette froideur par où tu m'es plus belle!

UNE CHAROGNE

RAPPELEZ-VOUS l'objet que nous vîmes, mon âme,
  Ce beau matin d'été si doux:
Au détour d'un sentier une charogne infâme
  Sur un lit semé de cailloux,

I ADORE you as I adore the vault of night, O urn of sadness, you who are so silent; and I love you the more, beautiful one, the more you elude me, the more, O grace of my nights, you seem ironically to multiply the leagues that stretch between my arms and heaven's immensities.

I press to the attack, I climb to the assault, like a choir of worms upon a corpse, and I cherish, O implacable, cruel creature, even the frigidness that makes you more beautiful in my eyes.

[1843 (Prarond). Published 1845]

Carrion

REMEMBER, O my soul, that thing we saw on that fine summer's morning, so mild: there where the path turned, a disgusting corpse

Les jambes en l'air, comme une femme lubrique,
 Brûlante et suant les poisons,
Ouvrait d'une façon nonchalante et cynique
 Son ventre plein d'exhalaisons.

Le soleil rayonnait sur cette pourriture,
 Comme afin de la cuire à point,
Et de rendre au centuple à la grande Nature
 Tout ce qu'ensemble elle avait joint;

Et le ciel regardait la carcasse superbe
 Comme une fleur s'épanouir.
La puanteur était si forte, que sur l'herbe
 Vous crûtes vous évanouir.

Les mouches bourdonnaient sur ce ventre putride,
 D'où sortaient de noirs bataillons
De larves, qui coulaient comme un épais liquide
 Le long de ces vivants haillons.

Tout cela descendait, montait comme une vague,
 Ou s'élançait en pétillant;
On eût dit que le corps, enflé d'un souffle vague,
 Vivait en se multipliant.

on a bed of shingle, with its legs in the air like a lewd woman, burning and oozing poisons, nonchalantly and cynically opened its stinking belly.

The sun was shining on that rotten meat as if to roast it to a turn, and to render a hundredfold to Nature all that she had brought together; while the sky looked down on that proud carcass, watching it blossom like a flower, and the stench was so strong that you all but fainted on the grass.

The flies were humming on its putrid belly, from which black battalions of larvae crawled, flowing like a turgid fluid along those living rags of flesh. It was all rising and falling like a wave, and seething and sparkling, as if the body, swollen with a faint breathing, was alive and multiplying.

Et ce monde rendait une étrange musique,
  Comme l'eau courante et le vent,
Ou le grain qu'un vanneur d'un mouvement rythmique
  Agite et tourne dans son van.

Les formes s'effaçaient et n'étaient plus qu'un rêve,
  Une ébauche lente à venir,
Sur la toile oubliée, et que l'artiste achève
  Seulement par le souvenir.

Derrière les rochers une chienne inquiète
  Nous regardait d'un œil fâché,
Épiant le moment de reprendre au squelette
  Le morceau qu'elle avait lâché.

– Et pourtant vous serez semblable à cette ordure,
  À cette horrible infection,
Étoile de mes yeux, soleil de ma nature,
  Vous, mon ange et ma passion!

Oui! telle vous serez, ô la reine des grâces,
  Après les derniers sacrements,
Quand vous irez, sous l'herbe et les floraisons grasses,
  Moisir parmi les ossements.

And that microcosm gave out an eerie music like a flow of water or wind, or the sighing of the grain that the winnower's cadenced swing tosses and turns in his basket. Its forms were blurring as in a dream, nothing but a slowly-shaping sketch forgotten on the canvas, which the artist perfects from memory alone.

From behind the rocks a fretful bitch was glaring at us with angry eye, judging the moment to snatch from the skeleton the morsel of flesh it had left.

– And yet, you will come to resemble that offal, that loathsome corruption, O star of my eyes, O sun of my nature, my angel and my passion! Yes, such will you be, O queen of graces, after the last sacraments, when you will go down beneath the grass and unctuous

Alors, ô ma beauté! dites à la vermine
   Qui vous mangera de baisers,
Que j'ai gardé la forme et l'essence divine
   De mes amours décomposés!

LE CHAT

VIENS, mon beau chat, sur mon cœur amoureux;
   Retiens les griffes de ta patte,
Et laisse-moi plonger dans tes beaux yeux,
   Mêlés de métal et d'agate.

Lorsque mes doigts caressent à loisir
   Ta tête et ton dos élastique,
Et que ma main s'enivre du plaisir
   De palper ton corps électrique,

Je vois ma femme en esprit. Son regard,
   Comme le tien, aimable bête,
Profond et froid, coupe et fend comme un dard,

flowers to turn green among the bones. Then, O my beauty, tell the vermin which will devour you with kisses, how I have immortalized the form and divine essence of my decayed loves.

[1843? (Prarond). Published in *Les Fleurs du mal*, 1857]

The Cat

COME, handsome cat, stretch on my loving heart; disarm your paws, and let me lose myself in your lovely eyes of agate and metal.

When leisurely my fingers stroke your head, your elastic back, and my hand thrills from the feel of your electric body,

the image of the woman I love rises before me: her gaze, like yours, dear animal, is profound and cold, as sharp and penetrating as a sting,

Et, des pieds jusques à la tête,
Un air subtil, un dangereux parfum
Nagent autour de son corps brun.

DE PROFUNDIS CLAMAVI

J'IMPLORE ta pitié, Toi, l'unique que j'aime,
Du fond du gouffre obscur où mon cœur est tombé.
C'est un univers morne à l'horizon plombé,
Où nagent dans la nuit l'horreur et le blasphème;

Un soleil sans chaleur plane au-dessus six mois,
Et les six autres mois la nuit couvre la terre;
C'est un pays plus nu que la terre polaire;
– Ni bêtes, ni ruisseaux, ni verdure, ni bois!

Or il n'est pas d'horreur au monde qui surpasse
La froide cruauté de ce soleil de glace
Et cette immense nuit semblable au vieux Chaos;

and from head to foot an elusive atmosphere, a threatening perfume, swirls round her dusky limbs.

[Pre-1844 (Prarond). Published in *Les Fleurs du mal*, 1857]

De Profundis Clamavi

I IMPLORE your pity, you whom alone I love, from the depths of the black pit into which my soul has sunk, this forlorn world with leaden-grey horizon, in which horror and blasphemy swim through the dark.

For six months of the year a heatless sun hangs over it, then for six months night lies on the earth; this land is barer than the Arctic desert, with never an animal or stream, no wood or anything that is green.

No horror in the world can outdo the chill cruelty of this sun of ice, and this vast dark like the Chaos of old,

Je jalouse le sort des plus vils animaux
Qui peuvent se plonger dans un sommeil stupide,
Tant l'écheveau du temps lentement se dévide!

LA BÉATRICE

DANS des terrains cendreux, calcinés, sans verdure,
Comme je me plaignais un jour à la nature,
Et que de ma pensée, en vaguant au hasard,
J'aiguisais lentement sur mon cœur le poignard,
Je vis en plein midi descendre sur ma tête
Un nuage funèbre et gros d'une tempête,
Qui portait un troupeau de démons vicieux,
Semblables à des nains cruels et curieux.
À me considérer froidement ils se mirent,
Et, comme des passants sur un fou qu'ils admirent,
Je les entendis rire et chuchoter entre eux,
En échangeant maint signe et maint clignement d'yeux:

and so slowly does the skein of time unwind, that I envy the lot of the lowliest of creatures, which can plunge into their stupid winter sleep.

[First titles: *La Béatrix* and *Spleen*. Published 1851 in *Les Limbes*; 1855; in *Les Fleurs du mal*, 1857]

The Poet's Beatrice

THROUGH ashen fields, burnt to a cinder, where no green thing grew, while one day I was lamenting to Nature and, aimlessly wandering, was sharpening the dagger of my thought upon my heart, I saw, though it was high noon, a sinister, storm-heavy cloud descend upon my head, bearing with it a horde of depraved demons like cruel, inquisitive dwarfs. They began to examine me coldly and, like street-idlers gaping at a lunatic, I heard them chuckling and whispering to each other, exchanging many a nudge and many a wink.

– «Contemplons à loisir cette caricature
Et cette ombre d'Hamlet imitant sa posture,
Le regard indécis et les cheveux au vent.
N'est-ce pas grand'pitié de voir ce bon vivant,
Ce gueux, cet histrion en vacances, ce drôle,
Parce qu'il sait jouer artistement son rôle,
Vouloir intéresser au chant de ses douleurs
Les aigles, les grillons, les ruisseaux et les fleurs,
Et même à nous, auteurs de ces vieilles rubriques,
Réciter en hurlant ses tirades publiques?»

J'aurais pu (mon orgueil aussi haut que les monts
Domine la nuée et le cri des démons)
Détourner simplement ma tête souveraine,
Si je n'eusse pas vu parmi leur troupe obscène,
Crime qui n'a pas fait chanceler le soleil!
La reine de mon cœur au regard nonpareil,
Qui riait avec eux de ma sombre détresse
Et leur versait parfois quelque sale caresse.

'Let us gaze our fill on this mockery of a man, this Hamlet's understudy, imitating his poses, with his distraught gaze and unkempt hair. Isn't it an awful shame to see this epicure. this pauper, this unemployed actor, this oddfellow, just because he knows how to play his part like a professional, trying to interest the eagles, crickets, streams, and flowers in his song of woe, and even bellowing his public tirades at us, who invented all that mumbo-jumbo ourselves?'

As my pride, as lofty as mountains, stands far above the clouds and the cries of demons, I could simply have turned my sovereign head the other way, had I not seen among that obscene mob (O crime which failed to rock the Sun!) the queen of my heart, whose eyes are beyond compare, laughing with them at my dire affliction, and giving them now and then a foul caress.

[Published in *Les Fleurs du mal*, 1857. As *De profundis clamavi* and *Le Vampire* were both, originally, entitled *La Béatrix*, this poem no doubt belongs to the Jeanne Duval cycle.]

LE BALCON

Mère des souvenirs, maîtresse des maîtresses,
Ô toi, tous mes plaisirs! ô toi, tous mes devoirs!
Tu te rappelleras la beauté des caresses,
La douceur du foyer et le charme des soirs,
Mère des souvenirs, maîtresse des maîtresses!

Les soirs illuminés par l'ardeur du charbon,
Et les soirs au balcon, voilés de vapeurs roses,
Que ton sein m'était doux! que ton cœur m'était bon!
Nous avons dit souvent d'impérissables choses
Les soirs illuminés par l'ardeur du charbon.

Que les soleils sont beaux dans les chaudes soirées!
Que l'espace est profond! Que le cœur est puissant!
En me penchant vers toi, reine des adorées,
Je croyais respirer le parfum de ton sang.
Que les soleils sont beaux dans les chaudes soirées!

The Balcony

Mother of memories, mistress of mistresses, you who are all my pleasures, you who are all my duties; you will remember the beauty of caresses, the bliss of home, the charm of evenings, mother of memories, mistress of mistresses.

Evenings illumined by the glowing coal, evenings on the balcony, veiled with rosy mists, how gentle I found your breast, how kind your heart was to me: we often said things that never will perish, on those evenings illumined by the glowing coal.

How beautiful are the suns of sultry evenings; how space grows deep; how the heart compels! As I leaned towards you, my beloved queen, I seemed to breathe the bouquet of your blood. How beautiful are the suns of sultry evenings!

La nuit s'épaississait ainsi qu'une cloison,
Et mes yeux dans le noir devinaient tes prunelles,
Et je buvais ton souffle, ô douceur! ô poison!
Et tes pieds s'endormaient dans mes mains fraternelles.
La nuit s'épaississait ainsi qu'une cloison.

Je sais l'art d'évoquer les minutes heureuses,
Et revis mon passé blotti dans tes genoux.
Car à quoi bon chercher tes beautés langoureuses
Ailleurs qu'en ton cher corps et qu'en ton cœur si doux?
Je sais l'art d'évoquer les minutes heureuses!

Ces serments, ces parfums, ces baisers infinis,
Renaîtront-ils d'un gouffre interdit à nos sondes,
Comme montent au ciel les soleils rajeunis
Après s'être lavés au fond des mers profondes?
– Ô serments! ô parfums! ô baisers infinis!

The night was thickening round us like a wall, and in the dark my eyes were divining yours, and I drank the nectar, the poison of your breath, and your feet fell asleep in my fraternal hands, while the night was thickening round us like a wall.

I know the art of evoking happy moments, and live my past again as I nestle at your knees; for what would it avail to seek your drowsy beauties save in your beloved body and so tender heart? I know the art of evoking happy moments.

Those vows, those perfumes and infinite kisses – will they ever relive in a fathomless underworld, like suns reborn returning to the sky, after their cleansing in the depths of seas? O vows, O perfumes, O infinite kisses!

[1856? (Crépet, Blin). Published in *Le Fleurs du mal*, 1857]

PARFUM EXOTIQUE

QUAND, les deux yeux fermés, en un soir chaud
d'automne,
Je respire l'odeur de ton sein chaleureux,
Je vois se dérouler des rivages heureux
Qu'éblouissent les feux d'un soleil monotone;

Une île paresseuse où la nature donne
Des arbres singuliers et des fruits savoureux;
Des hommes dont le corps est mince et vigoureux,
Et des femmes dont l'œil par sa franchise étonne.

Guidé par ton odeur vers de charmants climats,
Je vois un port rempli de voiles et de mâts
Encor tout fatigués par la vague marine,

Pendant que le parfum des verts tamariniers,
Qui circule dans l'air et m'enfle la narine,
Se mêle dans mon âme au chant des mariniers.

Exotic Perfume

WHEN I lie with both eyes closed on a warm autumn evening, and breathe the fragrance of your sultry breast, I see a panorama of blissful shores, a-dazzle with the sun's monotonous blaze,

a languid island where Nature lavishes rare trees and luscious fruits, and men who are lean and virile of body, and women's eyes of astonishing candidness.

Led by your odour to enchanted climes, I see a port filled with sails and masts, still aching from the briny wave,

while the scent of the green tamarind-trees, that wafts through the air and fills my nostrils, mingles in my soul with the sailors' song.

[Published in *Les Fleurs du mal*, 1857]

LA CHEVELURE

Ô TOISON, moutonnant jusque sur l'encolure!
Ô boucles! Ô parfum chargé de nonchaloir!
Extase! Pour peupler ce soir l'alcôve obscure
Des souvenirs dormant dans cette chevelure,
Je la veux agiter dans l'air comme un mouchoir!

La langoureuse Asie et la brûlante Afrique,
Tout un monde lointain, absent, presque défunt,
Vit dans tes profondeurs, forêt aromatique!
Comme d'autres esprits voguent sur la musique,
Le mien, ô mon amour! nage sur ton parfum.

J'irai là-bas où l'arbre et l'homme, pleins de sève,
Se pâment longuement sous l'ardeur des climats;
Fortes tresses, soyez la houle qui m'enlève!
Tu contiens, mer d'ébène, un éblouissant rêve
De voiles, de rameurs, de flammes et de mâts:

Un port retentissant où mon âme peut boire
À grands flots le parfum, le son et la couleur;

Hair

O FLEECE, billowing down to the neck, O locks, O fragrance laden with languidness! O ecstasy! This night, to people the dark alcove of our love with all the memories that slumber in your hair, I long to wave it in the air as one waves a handkerchief.

All languid Asia, blazing Africa, a whole faraway world that is absent, almost dead, survives in the depths of this forest of aromas; and as other spirits transcend through music, so mine, O my beloved, shall float away upon your perfume.

I shall go there where men and trees, full of the sap of life, swoon in the ardent heats; dense tresses, be the swell that carries me away, for you contain, O sea of ebony, a dazzling dream of sails and oarsmen, flames, and masts;

an echoing port where my soul may drink long waves of perfume, sound, and colour; in which the ships that glide in gold and

Où les vaisseaux, glissant dans l'or et dans la moire,
Ouvrent leurs vastes bras pour embrasser la gloire
D'un ciel pur où frémit l'éternelle chaleur.

Je plongerai ma tête amoureuse d'ivresse
Dans ce noir océan où l'autre est enfermé;
Et mon esprit subtil que le roulis caresse
Saura vous retrouver, ô féconde paresse!
Infinis bercements du loisir embaumé!

Cheveux bleus, pavillon de ténèbres tendues,
Vous me rendez l'azur du ciel immense et rond;
Sur les bords duvetés de vos mèches tordues
Je m'enivre ardemment des senteurs confondues
De l'huile de coco, du musc et du goudron.

Longtemps! toujours! ma main dans ta crinière lourde
Sèmera le rubis, la perle et le saphir,
Afin qu'à mon désir tu ne sois jamais sourde!
N'es-tu pas l'oasis où je rêve, et la gourde
Où je hume à longs traits le vin du souvenir?

multicoloured silk, open wide their arms to embrace the splendour of an immaculate sky that shimmers with everlasting heat;

I shall plunge my head, never weary of its rapture, into the jet-black ocean that contains the other sea; and my subtle mind, caressed by the rolling swell, will know how to find you there, O fertile indolence, infinite lullaby of sweet-scented leisure!

Blue hair, tent hung with shadows, you bring me the azure of the great round sky, and on the downy shores of your plaited locks I grow drunk with the mingled scents of coconut-oil, and musk, and tar.

O long, O forever, my hand in your ponderous mane will sow rubies and pearls and sapphires, so that you will ever hearken to my desire: for you are the oasis of my dreaming, the gourd from which I drink long draughts of the wine of memory.

[Published 1859]

UN HÉMISPHÈRE DANS UNE CHEVELURE

LAISSE-MOI respirer longtemps, longtemps, l'odeur de tes cheveux, y plonger tout mon visage, comme un homme altéré dans l'eau d'une source, et les agiter avec ma main comme un mouchoir odorant, pour secouer des souvenirs dans l'air.

Si tu pouvais savoir tout ce que je vois! tout ce que je sens! tout ce que j'entends dans tes cheveux! Mon âme voyage sur le parfum comme l'âme des autres hommes sur la musique.

Tes cheveux contiennent tout un rêve, plein de voilures et de mâtures; ils contiennent de grandes mers dont les moussons me portent vers de charmants climats, où l'espace est plus bleu et plus profond, où l'atmosphère est parfumée par les fruits, par les feuilles et par la peau humaine.

A Hemisphere in a Woman's Hair

LET me breathe long and long the odour of your hair, and dip my whole face in it, as a parched man does in the water of a spring, and shake it in my hand like a perfumed handkerchief, so that I might wave memories in the air.

If you could but know all that I see, all that I can smell and hear in your hair! My soul floats away on perfume as other men's on music.

Your hair contains an entire dream, full of shrouds and rigging; it contains vast seas whose monsoons bear me away to enchanting climes, where space is more blue and more profound, where the air is redolent of the smell of fruits and leaves and the skin of human beings.

Dans l'océan de ta chevelure, j'entrevois un port fourmillant de chants mélancoliques, d'hommes vigoureux de toutes nations et de navires de toutes formes découpant leurs architectures fines et compliquées sur un ciel immense où se prélasse l'éternelle chaleur.

Dans les caresses de ta chevelure, je retrouve les langueurs des longues heures passées sur un divan, dans la chambre d'un beau navire, bercées par le roulis imperceptible du port, entre les pots de fleurs et les gargoulettes rafraîchissantes.

Dans l'ardent foyer de ta chevelure, je respire l'odeur du tabac mêlée à l'opium et au sucre; dans la nuit de ta chevelure, je m'enivre des odeurs combinées du goudron, du musc et de l'huile de coco.

Laisse-moi mordre longtemps tes tresses lourdes et noires. Quand je mordille tes cheveux élastiques et rebelles, il me semble que je mange des souvenirs.

In the ocean of your hair I glimpse a harbour alive with sad sea-songs, with hardy men of every race, and with ships of every trim outlining their delicate, complex structures on a huge sky in which the everlasting heat reposes.

In your hair's caresses I find again the languor of long hours whiled away on a divan in a fine ship's berth, rocked to and fro by the harbour's gentle swell, between the pots of flowers and the refreshing decanters.

In your hair's burning hearth I breathe the fragrance of tobacco together with opium and sugar; in your hair's night I see the glittering infinitude of tropical azure; on your hair's downy shores I am exalted by the confused aromas of tar and musk and coconut-oil.

Let me bite, a while, your ponderous black tresses: when I take your elastic, rebellious hair between my teeth, it's as though I were eating memories.

[Published 1862]

JE te donne ces vers afin que si mon nom
Aborde heureusement aux époques lointaines,
Et fait rêver un soir les cervelles humaines,
Vaisseau favorisé par un grand aquilon,

Ta mémoire, pareille aux fables incertaines,
Fatigue le lecteur ainsi qu'un tympanon,
Et par un fraternel et mystique chaînon
Reste comme pendue à mes rimes hautaines;

Être maudit à qui, de l'abîme profond
Jusqu'au plus haut du ciel, rien, hors moi, ne répond!
– Ô toi qui, comme une ombre à la trace éphémère,

Foules d'un pied léger et d'un regard serein
Les stupides mortels qui t'ont jugée amère,
Statue aux yeux de jais, grand ange au front d'airain!

I GIVE you these lines so that if, by good fortune, my name reaches the shores of future times, like a ship favoured by a good north wind, and of an evening causes men's minds to muse, your memory, like those vague legends handed down, will tease the reader like a dulcimer, and, by some mystical, fraternal bond, remain suspended from my arrogant rhymes;

O cursed being, to whom from the lowest depths to the highest heavens of the world, nothing but I responds, you who like the shade that leaves but a fleeting trace, tread under your light foot, with indifferent gaze, those foolish mortals who take you for a shrew, my statue with jet eyes, great angel of the bronze brow!

[Published 1857 and in *Les Fleurs du mal*, 1857]

DUELLUM

Deux guerriers ont couru l'un sur l'autre; leurs armes
Ont éclaboussé l'air de lueurs et de sang.
Ces jeux, ces cliquetis du fer sont les vacarmes
D'une jeunesse en proie à l'amour vagissant.

Les glaives sont brisés! comme notre jeunesse,
Ma chère! Mais les dents, les ongles acérés,
Vengent bientôt l'épée et la dague traîtresse.
– Ô fureur des cœurs mûrs par l'amour ulcérés!

Dans le ravin hanté des chats-pards et des onces
Nos héros, s'étreignant méchamment, ont roulé,
Et leur peau fleurira l'aridité des ronces.

– Ce gouffre, c'est l'enfer, de nos amis peuplé!
Roulons-y sans remords, amazone inhumaine,
Afin d'éterniser l'ardeur de notre haine!

The Duel

Two fighters fell upon each other; their weapons splashed the air with glints and blood. Those contests, those clashes of steel, are the tumults of youth in the throes of calf-love.

The blades are snapped, like our youth, my darling! But teeth and sharpened fingernails soon avenge the sword and treacherous dirk – O frenzy of grown-up hearts, by love embittered!

In the ravine haunted by lynxes and leopards, our heroes, wickedly grappling, have rolled, and their hide will flower the brambles' barrenness.

That pit is hell, peopled with our friends! Let us wallow there without remorse, inhuman Amazon, so as to perpetuate our hatred's ardour.

[Published 1858]

LE POSSÉDÉ

Le soleil s'est couvert d'un crêpe. Comme lui,
Ô Lune de ma vie! emmitoufle-toi d'ombre;
Dors ou fume à ton gré; sois muette, sois sombre,
Et plonge tout entière au gouffre de l'Ennui;

Je t'aime ainsi! Pourtant, si tu veux aujourd'hui,
Comme un astre éclipsé qui sort de la pénombre,
Te pavaner aux lieux que la Folie encombre,
C'est bien! Charmant poignard, jaillis de ton étui!

Allume ta prunelle à la flamme des lustres!
Allume le désir dans les regards des rustres!
Tout de toi m'est plaisir, morbide ou pétulant;

Sois ce que tu voudras, nuit noire, rouge aurore;
Il n'est pas une fibre en tout mon corps tremblant
Qui ne crie: *Ô mon cher Belzébuth, je t'adore!*

The Possessed

The sun has shrouded himself in crape. Like him, O Moon of my existence, wrap yourself in shadow; sleep or smoke as you desire, be taciturn or morose, and plunge yourself entire into the depths of tedium.

I love you, when you are like that. But if, today, like an eclipsed star emerging from its penumbra, you want to parade yourself in those haunts that Madness frequents – all right! – charming dagger, shoot from your sheath!

Kindle your pupils from the lustres' flame! kindle desire in the eyes of oafs! Morbid or petulant, all that is you is my delight. Be whatever you wish, dun night or red daybreak: there is not a fibre in my whole trembling body but cries out: *'O my beloved Beelzebub, I worship you!'*

[Published 1859]

UN FANTÔME

I
LES TÉNÈBRES

DANS les caveaux d'insondable tristesse
Où le Destin m'a déjà relégué;
Où jamais n'entre un rayon rose et gai;
Où, seul avec la Nuit, maussade hôtesse,

Je suis comme un peintre qu'un Dieu moqueur
Condamne à peindre, hélas! sur les ténèbres;
Où, cuisinier aux appétits funèbres,
Je fais bouillir et je mange mon cœur,

Par instants brille, et s'allonge et s'étale
Un spectre fait de grâce et de splendeur.
À sa rêveuse allure orientale,

Quand il atteint sa totale grandeur,
Je reconnais ma belle visiteuse:
C'est Elle! noire et pourtant lumineuse.

An Apparition

I. THE SHADOWS

IN the burial-vault of unfathomable sadness to which Fate has already consigned me, into which no rosy, cheerful beam ever enters, and in which, alone with Night, that dour landlady, I am as a painter doomed by a jeering God to paint, alas, upon the shadows; in which, like some cook with morbid tastes I boil and eat my own heart,

sometimes there shines, and lengthens and spreads, a ghost that's made of grace and splendour. From its dreamy, oriental figure, when it reaches its full height I recognize my beautiful visitor: it is She herself, black, yet luminous.

II

LE PARFUM

Lecteur, as-tu quelquefois respiré
Avec ivresse et lente gourmandise
Ce grain d'encens qui remplit une église,
Ou d'un sachet le musc invétéré?

Charme profond, magique, dont nous grise
Dans le présent le passé restauré!
Ainsi l'amant sur un corps adoré
Du souvenir cueille la fleur exquise.

De ses cheveux élastiques et lourds,
Vivant sachet, encensoir de l'alcôve,
Une senteur montait, sauvage et fauve,

Et des habits, mousseline ou velours,
Tout imprégnés de sa jeunesse pure,
Se dégageait un parfum de fourrure.

II. THE PERFUME

Reader, have you ever inhaled with rapture and slow relish the grain of incense that saturates a church, or the enduring musk in a sachet? A profound magic spell, with which the past, restored in the present, intoxicates us. Thus does a lover, on an adored body, pluck the exquisite flower of memory.

From her elastic and heavy hair, a living sachet, the censer of the alcove, a perfume rose savage and wild, and from her muslin or velvet garments, fraught with her pure youthfulness, there came a smell of fur.

III
LE CADRE

Comme un beau cadre ajoute à la peinture,
Bien qu'elle soit d'un pinceau très-vanté,
Je ne sais quoi d'étrange et d'enchanté
En l'isolant de l'immense nature,

Ainsi bijoux, meubles, métaux, dorure,
S'adaptaient juste à sa rare beauté;
Rien n'offusquait sa parfaite clarté,
Et tout semblait lui servir de bordure.

Même on eût dit parfois qu'elle croyait
Que tout voulait l'aimer; elle noyait
Sa nudité voluptueusement

Dans les baisers du satin et du linge,
Et, lente ou brusque, à chaque mouvement
Montrait la grâce enfantine du singe.

III. THE FRAME

As a beautiful frame adds to a painting, though it be the work of a master's brush, something strange and bewitched, isolating it from immense Nature, thus jewels, furniture, metals, gilding, adapted themselves even to her rare beauty; nothing detracted from her perfect radiance, and everything seemed to serve as a frame to her.

Sometimes, one might even have said that she thought everything wanted to love her – sensually she drowned her nakedness in the kisses of satin and lingerie, and, slow or abrupt, in every movement she showed a monkey's childlike grace.

IV

LE PORTRAIT

La Maladie et la Mort font des cendres
De tout le feu qui pour nous flamboya.
De ces grands yeux si fervents et si tendres,
De cette bouche où mon cœur se noya,

De ces baisers puissants comme un dictame,
De ces transports plus vifs que des rayons,
Que reste-t-il? C'est affreux, ô mon âme!
Rien qu'un dessin fort pâle, aux trois crayons,

Qui, comme moi, meurt dans la solitude,
Et que le Temps, injurieux vieillard,
Chaque jour frotte avec son aile rude ...

Noir assassin de la Vie et de l'Art,
Tu ne tueras jamais dans ma mémoire
Celle qui fut mon plaisir et ma gloire!

IV. THE PORTRAIT

Sickness and death reduce to ashes all the fire that flamed for us. Of those great eyes, so fervent and so tender; of those kisses powerful as balm; of those ecstasies swifter than sunbeams – what remains? It is lamentable, O my soul! Nought but a faded drawing, in three colours, which like myself is dying in loneliness, and which that insulting greybeard, Time, rubs every day with his rough wing. Black murderer of life and art, you will never kill, in my memory, she who was my pleasure and my glory!

[1858–60. Published 1860]

CHANSON D'APRÈS-MIDI

QUOIQUE tes sourcils méchants
Te donnent un air étrange
Qui n'est pas celui d'un ange,
Sorcière aux yeux alléchants,

Je t'adore ô ma frivole,
Ma terrible passion!
Avec la dévotion
Du prêtre pour son idole.

Le désert et la forêt
Embaument tes tresses rudes:
Ta tête a les attitudes
De l'énigme et du secret.

Sur ta chair le parfum rôde
Comme autour d'un encensoir;
Tu charmes comme le soir,
Nymphe ténébreuse et chaude.

Ah! les philtres les plus forts
Ne valent pas ta paresse,
Et tu connais la caresse
Qui fait revivre les morts!

Afternoon Song

ALTHOUGH your frowning eyebrows give you an unusual appearance – which is no angel's – witch with alluring eyes, I adore you, O my frivolous one, my terrible passion – with a priest's devotion to his idol.

Desert and forest perfume your primitive tresses; your head has poises of mystery and secrecy. The perfume swirls round your flesh as round a censer; you bewitch like eventide, O darkling, sultry nymph. Ah, the strongest potions are no match for your indolence, and you know the caress that resurrects the dead.

Tes hanches sont amoureuses
De ton dos et de tes seins,
Et tu ravis les coussins
Par tes poses langoureuses.

Quelquefois, pour apaiser
Ta rage mystérieuse,
Tu prodigues, sérieuse,
La morsure et le baiser;

Tu me déchires, ma brune,
Avec un rire moqueur,
Et puis tu mets sur mon cœur
Ton œil doux comme la lune.

Sous tes souliers de satin,
Sous tes charmants pieds de soie,
Moi, je mets ma grande joie,
Mon génie et mon destin,

Mon âme par toi guérie,
Par toi, lumière et couleur!
Explosion de chaleur
Dans ma noire Sibérie!

Your hips are enamoured of your back and breasts, and you delight the cushions with your languid poses. Sometimes, to appease your mysterious rage, gravely you lavish bites and kisses. You rend me, O dark-haired one, with mocking laughter – then on my heart you lay your eye, as gentle as the Moon.

Under your satin slippers, under your charming silky feet, I lay down my great joy, my genius, and my destiny, my soul restored to health by you, who are all light and colour, an explosion of warmth in my black Siberia.

[Published 1860]

MADRIGAL TRISTE

I

QUE m'importe que tu sois sage?
Sois belle! et sois triste! Les pleurs
Ajoutent un charme au visage,
Comme le fleuve au paysage;
L'orage rajeunit les fleurs.

Je t'aime surtout quand la joie
S'enfuit de ton front terrassé;
Quand ton cœur dans l'horreur se noie;
Quand sur ton présent se déploie
Le nuage affreux du passé.

Je t'aime quand ton grand œil verse
Une eau chaude comme le sang;
Quand, malgré ma main qui te berce,
Ton angoisse, trop lourde, perce
Comme un râle d'agonisant.

Sad Madrigal

I

WHY should I care if you're as good as gold? Be beautiful, and be sad. Tears add a charm to the face, as a river to a landscape; the storm makes the flowers young again. I love you especially when happiness vanishes from your dismayed brow; when your heart drowns in horror; when your Present is covered by the fearful cloud of the Past. I love you when your wide eye sheds water hot as blood; when despite my lulling hand your over-heavy anguish breaks through like the death-rattle of a man in his last throes. I

J'aspire, volupté divine!
Hymne profond, délicieux!
Tous les sanglots de ta poitrine,
Et crois que ton cœur s'illumine
Des perles que versent tes yeux!

II

Je sais que ton cœur, qui regorge
De vieux amours déracinés,
Flamboie encor comme une forge,
Et que tu couves sous ta gorge
Un peu de l'orgueil des damnés;

Mais tant, ma chère, que tes rêves
N'auront pas reflété l'Enfer,
Et qu'en un cauchemar sans trêves,
Songeant de poisons et de glaives,
Éprise de poudre et de fer,

breathe in – O divine voluptuousness – O profound and delicious hymn – all the sobs of your breast, and I do believe that your heart grows brighter from the pearls which well from your eyes.

II

I know that your heart, which is choked with old uprooted loves, still flames like a forge, and that in your breast you still nourish something like the pride of the damned. But so long, my dear, as your dreams have not mirrored the image of Hell, so long as in a treacherous nightmare – dreaming of poisons and daggers, infatuated with gunpowder and steel, full of dread as you open the

N'ouvrant à chacun qu'avec crainte,
Déchiffrant le malheur partout,
Te convulsant quand l'heure tinte,
Tu n'auras pas senti l'étreinte
De l'irrésistible Dégoût,

Tu ne pourras, esclave reine
Qui ne m'aimes qu'avec effroi,
Dans l'horreur de la nuit malsaine
Me dire, l'âme de cris pleine:
«Je suis ton égale, ô mon Roi!»

door to visitors, reading disaster into everything, falling into a fit when the clock strikes the hour – so long as you have never felt the clasp of irresistible Disgust, then you will not be able, enslaved queen, who love me from fear alone, to say in the horror of the queasy night, your soul full of shrieking: 'I am your equal, O my King!'

[Published 1867. The attribution of this poem to the Duval cycle is by no means certain, though Crépet and Blin suggest that it might have been inspired by Jeanne Duval.]

III

The Limbo Cycle

1848–51

CHÂTIMENT DE L'ORGUEIL

En ces temps merveilleux où la Théologie
Fleurit avec le plus de sève et d'énergie,
On raconte qu'un jour un docteur des plus grands,
– Après avoir forcé les cœurs indifférents;
Les avoir remués dans leurs profondeurs noires;
Après avoir franchi vers les célestes gloires
Des chemins singuliers à lui-même inconnus,
Où les purs Esprits seuls peut-être étaient venus, –
Comme un homme monté trop haut, pris de panique,
«Jésus, petit Jésus! Je t'ai poussé bien haut!
Mais, si j'avais voulu t'attaquer au défaut
De l'armure, ta honte égalerait ta gloire,
Et tu ne serais plus qu'un fœtus dérisoire!»

Immédiatement sa raison s'en alla.
L'éclat de ce soleil d'un crêpe se voila;
Tout le chaos roula dans cette intelligence,

Pride's Punishment

In those marvellous times when Theology flourished with most sap and vitality, the story goes that, one day, one of the greatest Doctors of the Church – after converting lukewarm hearts, after stirring them to their murky depths, after progressing towards heavenly glories along strange paths unknown even to himself – like someone who has climbed too high, seized with panic, carried away by satanic pride, cried out: 'Jesus, tiny Jesus, I have exalted you to great heights! But had I chosen to attack you through the chink in your armour, your shame would match your glory, and you would be no more than a ridiculous foetus!'

At once his reason left him: the light of that sun was veiled with crape, all chaos swirled into that intelligence, once a living temple

Temple autrefois vivant, plein d'ordre et d'opulence,
Sous les plafonds duquel tant de pompe avait lui.
Le silence et la nuit s'installèrent en lui,
Comme dans un caveau dont la clef est perdue.
Dès lors il fut semblable aux bêtes de la rue,
Et, quand il s'en allait sans rien voir, à travers
Les champs, sans distinguer les étés des hivers,
Sale, inutile et laid comme une chose usée,
Il faisait des enfants la joie et la risée.

L'ÂME DU VIN

[LE VIN DES HONNÊTES GENS]

UN soir, l'âme du vin chantait dans les bouteilles:
«Homme, vers toi je pousse, ô cher déshérité,
Sous ma prison de verre et mes cires vermeilles,
Un chant plein de lumière et de fraternité!

«Je sais combien il faut, sur la colline en flamme,
De peine, de sueur et de soleil cuisant

filled with order and plenty, under whose vaults so much pomp had glittered.

Silence and darkness lodged in him as in a burial-vault of which the key is lost. Thereafter he was like to the beasts of the street, and when he wandered through the fields, seeing nothing, unable to tell the summers from winters, as filthy, useless, and ugly as some cast-off thing, he was the sport and laughing-stock of children.

[Published 1850]

The Wine's Soul

ONE evening the wine's soul sang inside the bottles: 'Man, towards you I send, O dear disinherited one, from under my prison of glass and my crimson waxen seals, a song that is full of light and brotherhood.

'I know how much labour, sweat, and scorching sunshine are needed on the flaming hillside, to engender my life and give me a

Pour engendrer ma vie et pour me donner l'âme;
Mais je ne serai point ingrat ni malfaisant,

«Car j'éprouve une joie immense quand je tombe
Dans le gosier d'un homme usé par ses travaux,
Et sa chaude poitrine est une douce tombe
Où je me plais bien mieux que dans mes froids caveaux.

«Entends-tu retentir les refrains des dimanches
Et l'espoir qui gazouille en mon sein palpitant?
Les coudes sur la table et retroussant tes manches,
Tu me glorifieras et tu seras content;

«J'allumerai les yeux de ta femme ravie;
À ton fils je rendrai sa force et ses couleurs
Et serai pour ce frêle athlète de la vie
L'huile qui raffermit les muscles des lutteurs.

«En toi je tomberai, végétale ambroisie,
Grain précieux jeté par l'éternel Semeur,
Pour que de notre amour naisse la poésie
Qui jaillira vers Dieu comme une rare fleur!»

soul; but I shall never be ungrateful or unkind, for I feel a tremendous joy when I tumble down the throat of a man worn out by his toil, and his hot breast is a snug tomb where I am happier than in my chilly cellars.

'Can you hear the Sunday choruses echoing, and the hope that babbles in my throbbing breast? With your elbows on the table and your sleeves rolled up, you will glorify me and feel happy; I shall set a light in the eyes of your delighted wife; to your son I shall restore his strength and colour, and I shall be, for that frail athlete of existence, the oil that strengthens wrestlers' muscles.

'Into you I shall fall, a vegetable ambrosia, a precious seed cast by the everlasting Sower, so that from our love poetry may be born that shall leap upwards to God like a rare flower.'

[Pre-1843 (Prarond). Published 1850]

LE SPLEEN

PLUVIÔSE, irrité contre la ville entière,
De son urne à grands flots verse un froid ténébreux
Aux pâles habitants du voisin cimetière
Et la mortalité sur les faubourgs brumeux.

Mon chat sur le carreau cherchant une litière
Agite sans repos son corps maigre et galeux;
L'âme d'un vieux poëte erre dans la gouttière
Avec la triste voix d'un fantôme frileux.

Le bourdon se lamente, et la bûche enfumée
Accompagne en fausset la pendule enrhumée,
Cependant qu'en un jeu plein de sales parfums,

Héritage fatal d'une vieille hydropique,
Le beau valet de cœur et la dame de pique
Causent sinistrement de leurs amours défunts.

Spleen

PLUVIOSUS, god of rain, vexed with the whole city, is pouring great waves of stygian cold on the pale inmates of the nearby cemetery, and pouring the essence of Death on the fogbound suburbs.

My cat, trying to bed down on the floor, is feverishly jerking its skinny, mange-ridden body. An old poet's soul is walking the tiles, lifting a voice as miserable as a shivering ghost's.

The great bell is groaning, and the smoking log's falsetto keeps time with the rheumy, wheezing clock, while, in a smelly pack of cards (the deadly heirloom of a dropsical old hag), the dapper Knave of Hearts and the Queen of Spades chat sinisterly about their perished loves.

[This and ten other poems were published in *Le Messager de l'Assemblée* under the title *Les Limbes* on 9 April 1851.]

LE MAUVAIS MOINE

LES cloîtres anciens sur leurs grandes murailles
Étalaient en tableaux la sainte Vérité,
Dont l'effet, réchauffant les pieuses entrailles,
Tempérait la froideur de leur austérité.

En ces temps où du Christ florissaient les semailles,
Plus d'un illustre moine, aujourd'hui peu cité,
Prenant pour atelier le champ des funérailles,
Glorifiait la Mort avec simplicité.

– Mon âme est un tombeau que, mauvais cénobite,
Depuis l'éternité je parcours et j'habite;
Rien n'embellit les murs de ce cloître odieux.

Ô moine fainéant! quand saurai-je donc faire
Du spectacle vivant de ma triste misère
Le travail de mes mains et l'amour de mes yeux?

The Bad Monk

THE lofty walls of ancient cloisters once displayed holy Truth, in paintings that warmed the bowels of the faithful, with the effect of tempering the chill of their austerity.

In those olden days when the seed of Christ's word used to flourish, many a famed monk, now rarely spoken of, made the graveyard his studio and glorified Death in his simple art.

My soul is a tomb in which for centuries I have moved and lived, an evil monk; for no work of art embellishes my hateful close.

Faint-hearted monk! When shall I learn to turn the daily scene of my sad misery, into my hands' labour and my eyes' love?

[MS. 1842 or 1843. Dozon, pre-1843. Published 1851]

L'IDÉAL

CE ne seront jamais ces beautés de vignettes,
Produits avariés, nés d'un siècle vaurien,
Ces pieds à brodequins, ces doigts à castagnettes,
Qui sauront satisfaire un cœur comme le mien.

Je laisse à Gavarni, poëte des chloroses,
Son troupeau gazouillant de beautés d'hôpital,
Car je ne puis trouver parmi ces pâles roses
Une fleur qui ressemble à mon rouge idéal.

Ce qu'il faut à ce cœur profond comme un abîme,
C'est vous, Lady Macbeth, âme puissante au crime,
Rêve d'Eschyle éclos au climat des autans;

Ou bien toi, grande Nuit, fille de Michel-Ange,
Qui tords paisiblement dans une pose étrange
Tes appas façonnés aux bouches des Titans!

The Ideal

THOSE beauties with high laced boots and bony fingers like castanets, whom one sees in vignettes, debased products of a worthless age, will never appeal to such a heart as mine.

I leave to Gavarni, the poet of anaemia, his simpering bevy of decaying belles, for among those colourless roses I find no flower that recalls my ideal red.

What my chasm-deep heart is seeking is you, Lady Macbeth, O soul mighty in crime, O dream of Aeschylus unfolding in the storm-swept North!

Or you, great Night, daughter of Michelangelo, calmly displaying, in your unusual pose, those charms shaped for the Titans' kisses.

[Published 1851 and in *Les Fleurs du mal*, 1857. One of C.B.'s irregular sonnets (with seven rhymes). Probably an early poem, 1843–4 (Crépet and Blin). Compare with *La Géante*, *J'aime le souvenir de ces époques nues*, though it denies Baudelaire's youthful pretence of preferring the diseased and sickly.]

LE MORT JOYEUX
[LE SPLEEN]

DANS une terre grasse et pleine d'escargots
Je veux creuser moi-même une fosse profonde,
Où je puisse à loisir étaler mes vieux os
Et dormir dans l'oubli comme un requin dans l'onde.

Je hais les testaments et je hais les tombeaux;
Plutôt que d'implorer une larme du monde,
Vivant, j'aimerais mieux inviter les corbeaux
À saigner tous les bouts de ma carcasse immonde.

Ô vers! noirs compagnons sans oreille et sans yeux,
Voyez venir à vous un mort libre et joyeux;
Philosophes viveurs, fils de la pourriture,

À travers ma ruine allez donc sans remords,
Et dites-moi s'il est encor quelque torture
Pour ce vieux corps sans âme et mort parmi les morts!

Dead but Happy

IN a rich soil full of snails I want to dig myself a deep ditch, where I can stretch my old bones at leisure and sleep in oblivion like a shark in the sea. I hate last wills and testaments, and I hate graves. Rather than beg a tear from the world and be alive, I'd prefer to invite the crows to draw blood from every tatter of my loathsome carcass.

O worms, black companions without ears or eyes, behold: a free and happy dead man is coming to you, you philosophers who make the best of life, sons of putrefaction: pass through my ruins, then, without remorse, and tell me if there's still some other torment left for this old soulless body, dead among the dead.

[Published 1851 under the title *Le Spleen*]

LES CHATS

Les amoureux fervents et les savants austères
Aiment également, dans leur mûre saison,
Les chats puissants et doux, orgueil de la maison,
Qui comme eux sont frileux et comme eux sédentaires.

Amis de la science et de la volupté,
Ils cherchent le silence et l'horreur des ténèbres;
L'Érèbe les eût pris pour ses coursiers funèbres,
S'ils pouvaient au servage incliner leur fierté.

Ils prennent en songeant les nobles attitudes
Des grands sphinx allongés au fond des solitudes,
Qui semblent s'endormir dans un rêve sans fin;

Leurs reins féconds sont pleins d'étincelles magiques,
Et des parcelles d'or, ainsi qu'un sable fin,
Étoilent vaguement leurs prunelles mystiques.

Cats

Fervent lovers and austere scholars share the same love, in their riper years, for powerful but gentle cats, the pride of the household, who like themselves are sedentary and sensitive to draughts.

Friends of learning and sensuality, cats ever seek silence and dreadful night; Erebus would have employed them as messengers of gloom, could they lower their pride to slavery.

They assume, when their minds wander, the majestic poses of those colossal sphinxes who stretch their limbs in the realms of solitude, and who seem to be sleeping in an endless dream.

Magical sparks teem in their fertile loins, and particles of gold, like delicate grains of sand, vaguely fleck their mystic pupils with stars.

[1842 (Champfleury). Published 1847]

LA MORT DES ARTISTES

COMBIEN faut-il de fois secouer mes grelots
Et baiser ton front bas, morne caricature?
Pour piquer dans le but, de mystique nature,
Combien, ô mon carquois, perdre de javelots?

Nous userons notre âme en de subtils complots,
Et nous démolirons mainte lourde armature,
Avant de contempler la grande Créature
Dont l'infernal désir nous remplit de sanglots!

Il en est qui jamais n'ont connu leur Idole,
Et ces sculpteurs damnés et marqués d'un affront,
Qui vont se martelant la poitrine et le front,

N'ont qu'un espoir, étrange et sombre Capitole!
C'est que la Mort, planant comme un soleil nouveau,
Fera s'épanouir les fleurs de leur cerveau!

The Death of Artists

HOW often must I rattle my bells and kiss your beetling brow, dour caricature? To score a bull's-eye on that metaphysical target, how many arrows must I lose, O my quiver?

We shall wear out our souls in cunning stratagems, and demolish many a massy suit of armour, before being able to set eyes on that giant creature whose infernal desire fills us with sobs.

There are some who have never known their Idol, and those sculptors who are damned and branded with humiliation, who turn the hammer against their own breast and brow, have but one hope, one strange, dark Capitol: the hope that Death, soaring aloft like a new Sun, will cause the flowers of their minds to bloom.

[Published April 1851]

LA MORT DES AMANTS

NOUS aurons des lits pleins d'odeurs légères,
Des divans profonds comme des tombeaux,
Et d'étranges fleurs sur des étagères,
Écloses pour nous sous des cieux plus beaux.

Usant à l'envi leurs chaleurs dernières,
Nos deux cœurs seront deux vastes flambeaux,
Qui réfléchiront leurs doubles lumières
Dans nos deux esprits, ces miroirs jumeaux.

Un soir fait de rose et de bleu mystique,
Nous échangerons un éclair unique,
Comme un long sanglot, tout chargé d'adieux;

Et plus tard un Ange, entr'ouvrant les portes,
Viendra ranimer, fidèle et joyeux,
Les miroirs ternis et les flammes mortes.

The Death of Lovers

WE shall have beds full of lightsome perfumes, divans as deep as graves, and wondrous flowers displayed on shelves, blooming for us beneath more lovely skies.

Vying each with each to exhaust their final fires, our two hearts will be two enormous torches, reflecting their twin lights in both our minds, which are twin mirrors.

On an evening all rosiness and mystic blue, we shall exchange a single flash of light, like a prolonged sob heavy with farewells,

and afterwards an Angel, discreetly opening the doors, faithful and full of joy, will come to revive the lustreless mirrors and the lifeless flames.

[Published April 1851]

LA CLOCHE FÊLÉE
[LE SPLEEN]

Il est amer et doux, pendant les nuits d'hiver,
D'écouter, près du feu qui palpite et qui fume,
Les souvenirs lointains lentement s'élever
Au bruit des carillons qui chantent dans la brume.

Bienheureuse la cloche au gosier vigoureux
Qui, malgré sa vieillesse, alerte et bien portante,
Jette fidèlement son cri religieux,
Ainsi qu'un vieux soldat qui veille sous la tente!

Moi, mon âme est fêlée, et lorsqu'en ses ennuis
Elle veut de ses chants peupler l'air froid des nuits,
Il arrive souvent que sa voix affaiblie

Semble le râle épais d'un blessé qu'on oublie
Au bord d'un lac de sang, sous un grand tas de morts,
Et qui meurt, sans bouger, dans d'immenses efforts.

The Cracked Bell

It is bitter-sweet, of a winter's night, sitting by the crackling, smoking fire, to listen to distant memories slowly rising to the sound of the chiming angelus singing through the fog.

Happy is the strong-throated bell which despite its great age is still alert and hale, and faithfully voices its pious call, like some old veteran keeping watch in his tent.

But, as for me, my soul is flawed, and when, with all its cares, it would fain fill the night's chill air with its hymns, most often its faded voice sounds like the thick death-rattle of a wounded soldier, who lies there forgotten near a pool of blood, beneath a great pile of dead, and who dies, without stirring, despite his tremendous efforts.

[Published April 1851 under the title *Le Spleen*]

LES HIBOUX

Sous les ifs noirs qui les abritent,
Les hiboux se tiennent rangés,
Ainsi que les dieux étrangers,
Dardant leur œil rouge. Ils méditent.

Sans remuer ils se tiendront
Jusqu'à l'heure mélancolique
Où, poussant le soleil oblique,
Les ténèbres s'établiront.

Leur attitude au sage enseigne
Qu'il faut en ce monde qu'il craigne
Le tumulte et le mouvement;

L'homme ivre d'une ombre qui passe
Porte toujours le châtiment
D'avoir voulu changer de place.

Owls

In the shelter of the black yews, the owls stand in a row like alien gods, their red eyes darting. They are meditating.

They will stand there motionless until the melancholy hour when, pushing down the slanting sun, the shadows settle into place.

Their attitude teaches wise men that in this world of ours all tumult and movement are to be feared, for man, intoxicated by every fleeting shadow, is always punished for his desire to roam.

[Published April 1851]

À UNE MENDIANTE ROUSSE

BLANCHE fille aux cheveux roux,
Dont la robe par ses trous
Laisse voir la pauvreté
    Et la beauté,

Pour moi, poëte chétif,
Ton jeune corps maladif,
Plein de taches de rousseur,
    A sa douceur.

Tu portes plus galamment
Qu'une reine de roman
Ses cothurnes de velours
    Tes sabots lourds.

Au lieu d'un haillon trop court,
Qu'un superbe habit de cour
Traîne à plis bruyants et longs
    Sur tes talons;

To a Red-haired Beggar-girl

WHITE girl with ginger hair, whose frock, through its rents, gives glimpses of poverty and beauty, for me, wretched poet that I am, your seedy young body, all over freckles, has its attractions.

Your wear your heavy clogs more stylishly than a novelette-queen her velvet buskins.

Instead of your brief tatters, may a splendid courtly robe trail in long swishing folds down to your heels; instead of your undarned

En place de bas troués,
Que pour les yeux des roués
Sur ta jambe un poignard d'or
Reluise encor;

Que des nœuds mal attachés
Dévoilent pour nos péchés
Tes deux beaux seins, radieux
Comme des yeux;

Que pour te déshabiller
Tes bras se fassent prier
Et chassent à coups mutins
Les doigts lutins,

Perles de la plus belle eau,
Sonnets de maître Belleau
Par tes galants mis aux fers
Sans cesse offerts.

Valetaille de rimeurs
Te dédiant leurs primeurs
Et contemplant ton soulier
Sous l'escalier,

stockings may a golden dagger shine and shine again down your leg, for the eyes of the men-about-town. May casually-tied ribbons unveil, for our sins, your lovely twin breasts, as radiant as eyes; may your arms coquettishly refuse to undress you, and with arch blows discourage teasing fingers, pearls of the finest water, sonnets of Master Belleau ceaselessly offered by your admirers – cast into chains!

The rabble of rhymers dedicating to you the first fruits – or, rather, vegetables – of their Muse, and studying your shoe from below stairs; many a page-boy with an eye to the main chance,

Maint page épris du hasard,
Maint seigneur et maint Ronsard
Épieraient pour le déduit
Ton frais réduit!

Tu compterais dans tes lits
Plus de baisers que de lis
Et rangerais sous tes lois
Plus d'un Valois!

– Cependant tu vas gueusant
Quelque vieux débris gisant
Au seuil de quelque Véfour
De carrefour;

Tu vas lorgnant en dessous
Des bijoux de vingt-neuf sous
Dont je ne puis, oh! pardon!
Te faire don.

Va donc, sans autre ornement,
Parfum, perles, diamant,
Que ta maigre nudité
Ô ma beauté!

many a squire and many a Ronsard would spy, for their own excitement, on your cool lodging! You would count more kisses than lilies in your beds, and subject more than one Valois to your laws.

Meanwhile you go cadging for any old scraps at the door of some shabby cornerhouse; you go about goggling, from a distance, at elevenpence-halfpenny beads which – forgive me – I am unable to offer you for nothing. Go, then, with no adornment – whether scent, pearls, or diamonds – but your skinny nakedness, O my beauty!

[1842 (C. Cousin). Published in *Les Fleurs du mal*, 1857]

BOHÉMIENS EN VOYAGE

LA tribu prophétique aux prunelles ardentes
Hier s'est mise en route, emportant ses petits
Sur son dos, ou livrant à leurs fiers appétits
Le trésor toujours prêt des mamelles pendantes.

Les hommes vont à pied sous leurs armes luisantes
Le long des chariots où les leurs sont blottis,
Promenant sur le ciel des yeux appesantis
Par le morne regret des chimères absentes.

Du fond de son réduit sablonneux, le grillon,
Les regardant passer, redouble sa chanson;
Cybèle, qui les aime, augmente ses verdures,

Fait couler le rocher et fleurir le désert
Devant ces voyageurs, pour lesquels est ouvert
L'empire familier des ténèbres futures.

Wandering Gipsies

THE tribe of prophets with fiery eyes yesterday took to the road, carrying their little ones on their backs, or offering, for their proud hunger, the ever-flowing treasure of their ripe breasts.

Bearing their glittering weapons, the men are striding alongside their caravans, where their folk huddle together, their eyes sweeping the sky, heavy with mournful regret for absent dreams.

From the shelter of his sandy nook, the cricket, watching them go by, redoubles his song, while for love of them Cybele puts out more leaves, makes the rocks gush water and the desert blossom before these wanderers, for whom uncloses the familiar realm of shades to come.

[MS. 1852. Published in *Les Fleurs du mal*, 1857]

LE GUIGNON

POUR soulever un poids si lourd,
Sisyphe, il faudrait ton courage!
Bien qu'on ait du cœur à l'ouvrage,
L'Art est long et le Temps est court.

Loin des sépultures célèbres,
Vers un cimetière isolé,
Mon cœur, comme un tambour voilé,
Va battant des marches funèbres.

– Maint joyau dort enseveli
Dans les ténèbres et l'oubli,
Bien loin des pioches et des sondes;

Mainte fleur épanche à regret
Son parfum doux comme un secret
Dans les solitudes profondes.

Unluck

TO raise such a heavy burden your courage would be needed, O Sisyphus! However eagerly one works, Art is long and Time is short. Far from the graves of the famed, my heart like a muffled drum beats out its dead-march towards some lonely graveyard.

Many a gem sleeps buried in darkness and oblivion, far beyond the reach of spade or sounding-rod; many a flower grudgingly spills its perfume, its perfume sweet as a secret, in the depths of solitude.

[Written probably in 1849 or 1850 (Crépet and Blin). One of the twelve poems sent to Gautier in 1852. Published 1855 and in *Les Fleurs du mal*, 1857. The two quatrains are adapted from Longfellow (*A Psalm of Life*) and the tercets from Gray's *Elegy in a Country Churchyard.*]

LA MORT DES PAUVRES

C'EST la Mort qui console, hélas! et qui fait vivre;
C'est le but de la vie, et c'est le seul espoir
Qui, comme un élixir, nous monte et nous enivre,
Et nous donne le cœur de marcher jusqu'au soir;

À travers la tempête, et la neige, et le givre,
C'est la clarté vibrante à notre horizon noir;
C'est l'auberge fameuse inscrite sur le livre,*
Où l'on pourra manger, et dormir, et s'asseoir;

C'est un Ange qui tient dans ses doigts magnétiques
Le sommeil et le don des rêves extatiques,
Et qui refait le lit des gens pauvres et nus;

The Death of the Poor

IT is Death, alas, which consoles us and makes us keep on living. Death is the aim of life, and is the only hope which, like some elixir, rouses and intoxicates us and gives us courage to fare on till evening.

Through tempest, snow, and frost, it is the lamp that twinkles on our black horizon, the marvellous Inn inscribed in the Book,* where a man can eat and sleep, and sit himself down.

It is an Angel who holds, in his magnetic fingers, sleep and the gift of ecstatic dreams, and who makes the bed of poor and naked folk.

---

* Crépet and Blin relate this to the parable of the Good Samaritan (Luke, x. 30–35). However, if Baudelaire intended *le livre* to mean the Gospel, it is surprising that he did not use capitals. It is also possible that the allusion is to the Koran, or to Gautier's *Comédie de la Mort* in which the same image of the Inn is used. Cf. also *L'Irréparable* and *L'Horloge.*]

C'est la gloire des Dieux, c'est le grenier mystique,
C'est la bourse du pauvre et sa patrie antique,
C'est le portique ouvert sur les Cieux inconnus!

LA MUSIQUE

BEETHOVEN

LA musique souvent me prend comme une mer!
Vers ma pâle étoile,
Sous un plafond de brume ou dans un vaste éther,
Je mets à la voile;

La poitrine en avant et les poumons gonflés
Comme de la toile,
J'escalade le dos des flots amoncelés
Que la nuit me voile;

It is the glory of the gods, the mystic granary, the poor man's purse, his historic motherland: it is the gate which opens on to unknown skies.

[One of the twelve poems sent to Gautier by C.B. in 1852. Published in *Les Fleurs du mal*, 1857]

Music

MUSIC often carries me away like a sea, and under a canopy of mist or through the vast ether, I set sail for my faint star.

Breasting the swell, with my lungs dilated like a ship's canvas, I ride up the backs of the piled waves which the darkness veils from me;

Je sens vibrer en moi toutes les passions
D'un vaisseau qui souffre;
Le bon vent, la tempête et ses convulsions

Sur l'immense gouffre
Me bercent. D'autres fois, calme plat, grand miroir
De mon désespoir!

LA RANÇON

L'HOMME a, pour payer sa rançon,
Deux champs au tuf profond et riche,
Qu'il faut qu'il remue et défriche
Avec le fer de la raison;

Pour obtenir la moindre rose,
Pour extorquer quelques épis,
Des pleurs salés de son front gris
Sans cesse il faut qu'il les arrose.

I feel all the passions of a groaning ship vibrate within me; the fair wind and the tempest's rage cradle me on the fathomless deep – or else there is a flat calm, the giant mirror of my despair.

[One of the twelve poems sent to Gautier by C.B. in 1852. Published in *Les Fleurs du mal*, 1857. It has been suggested (Crépet and Blin) that the original title of the poem was *Beethoven*. Note the unusual variation on the sonnet form.]

The Ransom

MAN has, with which to pay his ransom, two fields of deep, rich growth, which he must dig and cultivate with the blade of Reason.

To nurse the smallest rose, to wring a few ears of corn from the earth, he must water them ceaselessly with the salt tears of his grey brow.

L'un est l'Art, et l'autre l'Amour.
– Pour rendre le juge propice,
Lorsque de la stricte justice
Paraîtra le terrible jour,

Il faudra lui montrer des granges
Pleines de moissons, et des fleurs
Dont les formes et les couleurs
Gagnent le suffrage des Anges.

LE VIN DES CHIFFONNIERS

SOUVENT, à la clarté rouge d'un réverbère
Dont le vent bat la flamme et tourmente le verre,
Au cœur d'un vieux faubourg, labyrinthe fangeux
Où l'humanité grouille en ferments orageux,

On voit un chiffonnier qui vient, hochant la tête,
Buttant, et se cognant aux murs comme un poëte,
Et, sans prendre souci des mouchards, ses sujets,
Épanche tout son cœur en glorieux projets.

One is Art, and the other is Love. In order to propitiate the judge when the terrible day of strict justice comes, he will have to show him barns full of harvested crops, and flowers whose shapes and colours win the Angels' approval.

[One of the twelve poems sent to Gautier by C.B. in 1852. Published November 1857 (after *Les Fleurs du mal*). The Laffont MS. contains the note *Socialisme mitigé* (modified socialism), which is a reference to C.B.'s temporary interest in Proudhon (1847–8).]

The Ragpickers' Wine

OFTEN, in the red glare of a streetlamp, with the wind flailing its flame and racking the glass panes, in the heart of some old suburb, a slimy labyrinth in which mankind seethes in tempestuous ferments, you'll see a ragpicker coming along, wagging his head, stumbling and banging himself against the walls like a poet, and, heedless of the stool-pigeons, his thralls, unburden his heart of his world-shaking intentions.

Il prête des serments, dicte des lois sublimes,
Terrasse les méchants, relève les victimes,
Et sous le firmament comme un dais suspendu
S'enivre des splendeurs de sa propre vertu.

Oui, ces gens harcelés de chagrins de ménage,
Moulus par le travail et tourmentés par l'âge,
Éreintés et pliant sous un tas de débris,
Vomissement confus de l'énorme Paris,

Reviennent, parfumés d'une odeur de futailles,
Suivis de compagnons, blanchis dans les batailles,
Dont la moustache pend comme les vieux drapeaux.
Les bannières, les fleurs et les arcs triomphaux

Se dressent devant eux, solennelle magie!
Et dans l'étourdissante et lumineuse orgie
Des clairons, du soleil, des cris et du tambour,
Ils apportent la gloire au peuple ivre d'amour!

He takes oaths, decrees sublime laws, lays low the wicked, and exalts the oppressed, and under the sky, like a suspended dais, waxes drunk on the splendours of his own virtuousness.

Yes, these folk, harassed by domestic sorrows, ground down by toil and racked by encroaching age, fagged out and bent double beneath a heap of scrap, the haphazard vomit of enormous Paris, return perfumed with the reek of wine-casks, followed by their comrades, white-haired from their battles, whose moustaches droop like old flags. Banners, garlands, triumphal arches loom before their eyes, by a solemn magic. And in the ear-splitting, luminous orgy of trumpet-calls, sunshine, shouts, and drums, they bring glory to the people, drunk with love.

C'est ainsi qu'à travers l'Humanité frivole
Le vin roule de l'or, éblouissant Pactole;
Par le gosier de l'homme il chante ses exploits
Et règne par ses dons ainsi que les vrais rois.

Pour noyer la rancœur et bercer l'indolence
De tous ces vieux maudits qui meurent en silence,
Dieu, touché de remords, avait fait le sommeil;
L'Homme ajouta le Vin, fils sacré du Soleil!

UN VOYAGE À CYTHÈRE

MON cœur, comme un oiseau, voltigeait tout joyeux
Et planait librement à l'entour des cordages;
Le navire roulait sous un ciel sans nuages,
Comme un ange enivré d'un soleil radieux.

Quelle est cette île triste et noire? – C'est Cythère,
Nous dit-on, un pays fameux dans les chansons,
Eldorado banal de tous les vieux garçons.
Regardez, après tout, c'est une pauvre terre.

Thus it is that among frivolous mankind, wine sets flowing a blinding Eldorado of gold: through the throat of man it sings its exploits and reigns through its bounty, as true monarchs do. To drown the rancour and comfort the idleness of all those old outcasts who die in silence, God, touched with remorse, created Sleep: Man added Wine, the sacred Son of the Sun.

[Pre-1843 (Prarond). Published in *Les Fleurs du mal*, 1857]

A Voyage to Cytherea

MY heart was soaring gaily as a bird and hovering untrammelled round the rigging; the ship sailed on beneath a cloudless sky, like an angel enraptured by the dazzling sun. 'But what can that drab, dark island be?' – 'It's Cytherea,' they told us, 'a place much famed in song, the tame Eldorado of all old bachelors – as you see, after all, it's not much of a place!'

– Île des doux secrets et des fêtes du cœur!
De l'antique Vénus le superbe fantôme
Au-dessus de tes mers plane comme un arome,
Et charge les esprits d'amour et de langueur.

Belle île aux myrtes verts, pleine de fleurs écloses,
Vénérée à jamais par toute nation,
Où les soupirs des cœurs en adoration
Roulent comme l'encens sur un jardin de roses

Ou le roucoulement éternel d'un ramier!
– Cythère n'était plus qu'un terrain des plus maigres,
Un désert rocailleux troublé par des cris aigres.
J'entrevoyais pourtant un objet singulier!

Ce n'était pas un temple aux ombres bocagères,
Où la jeune prêtresse, amoureuse des fleurs,
Allait, le corps brûlé de secrètes chaleurs,
Entre-bâillant sa robe aux brises passagères;

Mais voilà qu'en rasant la côte d'assez près
Pour troubler les oiseaux avec nos voiles blanches,
Nous vîmes que c'était un gibet à trois branches,
Du ciel se détachant en noir, comme un cyprès.

– Isle of the heart's sweet secrets and rejoicings! The majestic shade of the Venus of ancient times wafts like a perfume over the seas about you, and fills men's minds with love and languidness. Fair isle of the green myrtle-glades, covered with flowers in full bloom, revered for all time and by all peoples, where the sighs of adoring hearts breathe like incense through a garden of roses, or like the endless cooing of the dove!

– But Cytherea was now but the barrenest of lands, a rocky desert haunted by piercing cries. However, I glimpsed a strange thing there. It was not a temple with shady groves wherein the flower-loving young priestess walked, her body aflame with secret desires, loosening her robes to catch the passing breeze. No: as we passed close enough to the shore for our white sails to disturb the birds, we saw it was a three-branched gibbet looming black against

De féroces oiseaux perchés sur leur pâture
Détruisaient avec rage un pendu déjà mûr,
Chacun plantant, comme un outil, son bec impur
Dans tous les coins saignants de cette pourriture;

Les yeux étaient deux trous, et du ventre effondré
Les intestins pesants lui coulaient sur les cuisses,
Et ses bourreaux, gorgés de hideuses délices,
L'avaient à coups de bec absolument châtré.

Sous les pieds, un troupeau de jaloux quadrupèdes,
Le museau relevé, tournoyait et rôdait;
Une plus grande bête au milieu s'agitait
Comme un exécuteur entouré de ses aides.

Habitant de Cythère, enfant d'un ciel si beau,
Silencieusement tu souffrais ces insultes
En expiation de tes infâmes cultes
Et des péchés qui t'ont interdit le tombeau.

Ridicule pendu, tes douleurs sont les miennes!
Je sentis, à l'aspect de tes membres flottants,
Comme un vomissement, remonter vers mes dents
Le long fleuve de fiel des douleurs anciennes;

the sky, like a cypress-tree. Fierce birds, perched on their prey, were savagely rending the ripened corpse of a hanged man, each plunging its filthy beak like a scalpel into the carcass's bleeding wounds. His eyes were already two empty sockets, and from his caved-in belly the heavy intestines were rolling down his thighs, and his torturers, gorged on hideous tit-bits, had thoroughly castrated him with their beaks.

At his feet a pack of jealous beasts were circling and prowling to and fro with uplifted maws, while one bigger than the rest was leaping high in their midst, like an executioner surrounded by his henchmen.

– Child of Cytherea, son of that lovely sky, silently you suffered those affronts in expiation of your infamous practices and for sins which denied you a grave. O grotesque gallow-bird, your sufferings are mine! I felt, as I saw your swinging limbs, the long stream

Devant toi, pauvre diable au souvenir si cher,
J'ai senti tous les becs et toutes les mâchoires
Des corbeaux lancinants et des panthères noires
Qui jadis aimaient tant à triturer ma chair.

– Le ciel était charmant, la mer était unie;
Pour moi tout était noir et sanglant désormais,
Hélas! et j'avais, comme en un suaire épais,
Le cœur enseveli dans cette allégorie.

Dans ton île, ô Vénus! je n'ai trouvé debout
Qu'un gibet symbolique où pendait mon image ...
– Ah! Seigneur! donnez-moi la force et le courage
De contempler mon cœur et mon corps sans dégoût!

of gall of my past sufferings rising like vomit to my teeth. At the sight of you, poor devil whose memory I hold dear, I felt all the beaks and fangs of swooping ravens and black panthers which were once so fond of gobbling my own flesh.

– The sky was entrancing, the sea was calm, but for me all was now dark and smeared with blood. Alas, my heart lay buried in that allegory as in a winding-sheet. O Venus, in your isle I found nothing standing but a symbolic gallows, with my own image hanged upon it.

– O heavenly Father, give me strength and courage to contemplate my heart and body without disgust!

[One of the twelve poems sent to Gautier in 1852. Published 1855 and in *Les Fleurs du mal*, 1857. The poem was suggested to Baudelaire by a description of the island of Cerigo, the island of Venus, published by Nerval in 1844. Nerval died in 1855: it is perhaps for this reason that the original dedication was omitted.]

LE CRÉPUSCULE DU SOIR

VOICI le soir charmant, ami du criminel;
Il vient comme un complice, à pas de loup; le ciel
Se ferme lentement comme une grande alcôve,
Et l'homme impatient se change en bête fauve.

Ô soir, aimable soir, désiré par celui
Dont les bras, sans mentir, peuvent dire: Aujourd'hui
Nous avons travaillé! – C'est le soir qui soulage
Les esprits que dévore une douleur sauvage,
Le savant obstiné dont le front s'alourdit,
Et l'ouvrier courbé qui regagne son lit.
Cependant des démons malsains dans l'atmosphère
S'éveillent lourdement, comme des gens d'affaire,
Et cognent en volant les volets et l'auvent.
À travers les lueurs que tourmente le vent
La Prostitution s'allume dans les rues;
Comme une fourmilière elle ouvre ses issues;
Partout elle se fraye un occulte chemin,
Ainsi que l'ennemi qui tente un coup de main;
Elle remue au sein de la cité de fange

Evening Twilight

HERE's the delightful evening, the criminal's friend. It comes like an accomplice, with slinking wolf-like strides. The sky shuts slowly like a great alcove, and restless man turns into a wild beast.

O evening, pleasant evening, desired by him whose arms can truly say: 'Today we have toiled!' – Evening refreshes minds devoured by savage grief, or the poring scholar whose head begins to nod, or the back-bent workman returning home to bed. But now mischievous demons rouse lumpishly in the air, like men intent on business, and flounder in their flight against shutters and sheds.

Through glimmering gas-jets wincing in the wind, Prostitution lights up in the streets, like an ant-heap opening all its entrances and exits; it weaves its furtive passage everywhere, like an enemy planning a surprise attack; it burrows through the city's slime like a

Comme un ver qui dérobe à l'Homme ce qu'il mange.
On entend çà et là les cuisines siffler,
Les théâtres glapir, les orchestres ronfler;
Les tables d'hôte, dont le jeu fait les délices,
S'emplissent de catins et d'escrocs, leurs complices,
Et les voleurs, qui n'ont ni trêve ni merci,
Vont bientôt commencer leur travail, eux aussi,
Et forcer doucement les portes et les caisses
Pour vivre quelques jours et vêtir leurs maîtresses.

Recueille-toi, mon âme, en ce grave moment,
Et ferme ton oreille à ce rugissement.
C'est l'heure où les douleurs des malades s'aigrissent!
La sombre Nuit les prend à la gorge; ils finissent
Leur destinée et vont vers le gouffre commun;
L'hôpital se remplit de leurs soupirs. – Plus d'un
Ne viendra plus chercher la soupe parfumée,
Au coin du feu, le soir, auprès d'une âme aimée.

Encore la plupart n'ont-ils jamais connu
La douceur du foyer et n'ont jamais vécu!

worm filching away men's food. Here and there you hear the whistling from kitchens, yapping of theatres, droning of orchestras; the cheap joints whose main attraction is gambling are filling with whores and their crony crooks, and the thieves, as well, who show no signs of idleness or mercy, will soon be setting to work, tenderly forcing doors and safes, so as to keep themselves for a few days and buy togs for their molls.

O my soul, withdraw into yourself at this grave hour, and stop your ears against this roaring din. It is the hour when the pangs of the sick grow sharper. Cheerless Night clutches them by the throat, they reach their destiny's end and draw nigh to the universal pit: the hospital is brimming with their sighs. – More than one will never again return to take the fragrant soup at the fireside, of an evening, beside the one he loves. And besides, most of them have never known the solace of a home and have never lived!

[Published 1852 and in *Les Fleurs du mal*, 1857. See also the prose-poem of the same name, in this edition set beside *Recueillement.*]

LE CRÉPUSCULE DU MATIN

LA diane chantait dans les cours des casernes,
Et le vent du matin soufflait sur les lanternes.

C'était l'heure où l'essaim des rêves malfaisants
Tord sur leurs oreillers les bruns adolescents;
Où, comme un œil sanglant qui palpite et qui bouge,
La lampe sur le jour fait une tache rouge;
Où l'âme, sous le poids du corps revêche et lourd,
Imite les combats de la lampe et du jour.
Comme un visage en pleurs que les brises essuient,
L'air est plein du frisson des choses qui s'enfuient,
Et l'homme est las d'écrire et la femme d'aimer.

Les maison çà et là commençaient à fumer.
Les femmes de plaisir, la paupière livide,
Bouche ouverte, dormaient de leur sommeil stupide;
Les pauvresses, traînant leurs seins maigres et froids,
Soufflaient sur leurs tisons et soufflaient sur leurs doigts.

Morning Twilight

BUGLES were sounding the reveille in the barrack-squares, and the morning wind was blowing on the streetlamps.

It was the hour when a swarm of evil dreams twists swarthy adolescents on their pillows; when like a bloodshot eye that throbs and jerks, the lamp makes a red stain on the daylight; when the soul, beneath the sullen, leaden body's weight, enacts the struggle between lamp and day. Like a face in tears which the wind wipes dry, the air is full of the tremble of fleeting things, and man wearies of writing, woman wearies of love.

The houses here and there began to puff forth smoke. The women of pleasure, with bleary eyelids and gaping mouths, were sleeping their stupid sleep, while poor old women, trailing their scraggy, frozen breasts, blew now upon the embers, now on their own fingers. It was the hour when in bleakness and scraping

C'était l'heure où parmi le froid et la lésine
S'aggravent les douleurs des femmes en gésine;
Comme un sanglot coupé par un sang écumeux
Le chant du coq au loin déchirait l'air brumeux;
Une mer de brouillards baignait les édifices,
Et les agonisants dans le fond des hospices
Poussaient leur dernier râle en hoquets inégaux.
Les débauchés rentraient, brisés par leurs travaux.

L'aurore grelottante en robe rose et verte
S'avançait lentement sur la Seine déserte,
Et le sombre Paris, en se frottant les yeux,
Empoignait ses outils, vieillard laborieux.

poverty, the pangs of women in childbirth grew more sharp; and like a sob cut short by frothing blood, the cock-crow from afar tore through the hazy air; a sea of fog was swirling round the buildings, and dying men, in the workhouses, groaned their last death-rattle in heaving gasps. The debauched made their way home, broken by their labours.

The shuddering dawn, in her pink and green dress, wended her way slowly along the deserted Seine, and gloomy Paris, rubbing his eyes, laid hold of his tools, an old man doomed to toil.

[According to Prarond, written by 1843. Published 1852, 1855, and in *Les Fleurs du mal*, 1857]

IV

The Marie Daubrun Cycle

1850–60

L'INVITATION AU VOYAGE

Mon enfant, ma sœur,
Songe à la douceur
D'aller là-bas vivre ensemble!
Aimer à loisir,
Aimer et mourir
Au pays qui te ressemble!
Les soleils mouillés
De ces ciels brouillés
Pour mon esprit ont les charmes
Si mystérieux
De tes traîtres yeux,
Brillant à travers leurs larmes.

Là, tout n'est qu'ordre et beauté,
Luxe, calme et volupté.

Des meubles luisants,
Polis par les ans,
Décoreraient notre chambre;
Les plus rares fleurs
Mêlant leurs odeurs

The Invitation to the Voyage

My child, my sister, imagine the happiness of voyaging there to spend our lives together, to love to our hearts' content, to love and die in the land which is the image of you. The misty suns of those unsettled skies have, on my mind, the same mysterious hold as your fickle eyes, shining through their tears.

Everything there is harmony and beauty, luxury, tranquillity, and delight.

Furniture gleaming with the sheen of the years would grace our bedroom; the rarest of flowers, mingling their odours with the

Aux vagues senteurs de l'ambre,
    Les riches plafonds,
    Les miroirs profonds,
La splendeur orientale,
    Tout y parlerait
    À l'âme en secret
Sa douce langue natale.

Là, tout n'est qu'ordre et beauté,
Luxe, calme et volupté.

    Vois sur ces canaux
    Dormir ces vaisseaux
Dont l'humeur est vagabonde;
    C'est pour assouvir
    Ton moindre désir
Qu'ils viennent du bout du monde.
    – Les soleils couchants
    Revêtent les champs,
Les canaux, la ville entière,
    D'hyacinthe et d'or;
    Le monde s'endort
Dans une chaude lumière.

Là, tout n'est qu'ordre et beauté,
Luxe, calme et volupté.

vague fragrance of amber; the richly-painted ceilings, the fathomless mirrors, the splendour of the East, would all whisper in secret to our souls in their own gentle mother-tongue.

Everything there is harmony and beauty, luxury, tranquillity, and delight.

See how the craft, nomads by bent, are slumbering in the canals: it's to gratify your slightest desire that they come from the world's end. The westering suns enwrap the fields, the canals, and the entire city in hyacinth and gold, and the earth falls asleep in the warm gloaming.

Everything there is harmony and beauty, luxury, tranquillity, and delight.

[1854. Published 1855]

L'INVITATION AU VOYAGE

Il est un pays superbe, un pays de Cocagne, dit-on, que je rêve de visiter avec une vieille amie. Pays singulier, noyé dans les brumes de notre Nord, et qu'on pourrait appeler L'Orient de l'Occident, La Chine de l'Europe, tant la chaude et capricieuse fantaisie s'y est donné carrière, tant elle l'a patiemment et opiniâtrément illustré de ses savantes et luxuriantes végétations.

Un vrai pays de Cocagne, où tout est beau, riche, tranquille, honnête; où le luxe a plaisir à se mirer dans l'ordre; où la vie est grasse et douce à respirer; d'où le désordre, la turbulence et l'imprévu sont exclus; où le bonheur est marié au silence; où la cuisine elle-même est poétique, grasse et excitante à la fois; où tout vous ressemble, mon cher ange.

Tu connais cette maladie fiévreuse qui s'empare de nous dans les froides misères, cette nostalgie du pays qu'on ignore, cette angoisse de la curiosité? Il est une contrée qui te ressemble, où tout est beau, riche, tranquille et honnête, où la fantaisie a bâti et décoré une Chine occidentale, où la

The Invitation to the Voyage

There is a superb country, an earthly paradise, they say, that I dream of visiting with an old friend. A unique country, submerged in our northern mists, and which one might call the Orient of the West, the China of Europe, so freely has ardent and capricious Fancy expressed itself there, and so patiently and resolutely adorned it with meaningful, delicate plants.

A veritable earthly paradise, where everything is beautiful, sumptuous, quiet, authentic; where luxury is glad to reflect itself in orderliness; where life is full and sweet to breathe; from which disorder, turmoil, and the unexpected are banned; where the very cuisine is poetic, both rich and stimulating; where everything resembles you, my beloved angel.

Do you know that fever which grips us in moments of chill distress, that nostalgia for some land we have never seen, that anguish of curiosity? There is a land that resembles you, where everything is beautiful, sumptuous, quiet, and authentic, where Fancy has built and adorned a Cathay of the West, where life is sweet to breathe,

vie est douce à respirer, où le bonheur est marié au silence. C'est là qu'il faut aller vivre, c'est là qu'il faut aller mourir!

Oui, c'est là qu'il faut aller respirer, rêver et allonger les heures par l'infini des sensations. Un musicien a écrit *l'Invitation à la valse*; quel est celui qui composera *l'Invitation au voyage*, qu'on puisse offrir à la femme aimée, à la sœur d'élection?

Oui, c'est dans cette atmosphère qu'il ferait bon vivre, – là-bas, où les heures plus lentes contiennent plus de pensées, où les horloges sonnent le bonheur avec une plus profonde et plus significative solennité.

Sur des panneaux luisants, ou sur des cuirs dorés et d'une richesse sombre, vivent discrètement des peintures béates, calmes et profondes, comme les âmes des artistes qui les créèrent. Les soleils couchants, qui colorent si richement la salle à manger ou le salon, sont tamisés par de belles étoffes ou par ces hautes fenêtres ouvragées que le plomb divise en nombreux compartiments. Les meubles sont vastes, curieux, bizarres, armés de serrures et de secrets comme des âmes raffinées. Les miroirs, les métaux, les étoffes,

where happiness is wedded to silence. There we must go to live; there we must go to die.

Yes, it is there we must go in order to breathe and dream and prolong the hours with an infinity of sensations. A musician has composed the *Invitation to the Waltz*: who will compose the *Invitation to the Voyage*, that a man might offer to the woman he loves, the sister of his choice?

Yes, it is in that atmosphere that it would be good to be alive, yonder, where the slower hours contain more thoughts, where the clocks chime happiness with a deeper and more significant gravity.

On shining panels, or walls lined with darkly mellow gilded leathers, serene paintings pass their unassuming lives, as calm and full of depth as the souls of the artists who created them. The sunsets that so lavishly colour the dining-room or drawing-room, are filtered through fine fabrics or through those lofty latticed windows which the leads divide into many a section. The furniture is massive, quaint, strange, armed with locks and secrets, like exquisite souls. The mirrors, metals, draperies, the plate and ceramics there perform

l'orfévrerie et la faïence y jouent pour les yeux une symphonie muette et mystérieuse; et de toutes choses, de tous les coins, des fissures des tiroirs et des plis des étoffes s'échappe un parfum singulier, un *revenez-y* de Sumatra, qui est comme l'âme de l'appartement.

Un vrai pays de Cocagne, te dis-je, où tout est riche, propre et luisant, comme une belle conscience, comme une magnifique batterie de cuisine, comme une splendide orfévrerie, comme une bijouterie bariolée! Les trésors du monde y affluent, comme dans la maison d'un homme laborieux et qui a bien mérité du monde entier. Pays singulier, supérieur aux autres, comme l'art l'est à la Nature, où celle-ci est réformée par le rêve, où elle est corrigée, embellie, refondue.

Qu'ils cherchent, qu'ils cherchent encore, qu'ils reculent sans cesse les limites de leur bonheur, ces alchimistes de l'horticulture! Qu'ils proposent des prix de soixante et de cent mille florins pour qui résoudra leurs ambitieux problèmes! Moi, j'ai trouvé ma *tulipe noire* et mon *dahlia bleu*!

Fleur incomparable, tulipe retrouvée, allégorique dahlia,

for the eyes an unheard and mysterious symphony; and from every object, every corner, from the chinks in the drawers and the hangings' folds, there emanates an uncommon aroma, a whiff of Sumatra, which is like to the apartment's soul.

A veritable earthly paradise, believe me, where everything is sumptuous, clean, and bright, like a clear conscience, like a magnificent set of pots and pans, like a splendid specimen of the goldsmith's craft, like a multicoloured gem! The treasures of the earth abound there, as in the home of some hard-working man who has deserved well of the whole world. A unique land, superior to other lands, as art is superior to Nature, where nature is reshaped by reverie, where it is corrected, beautified, remoulded.

Let them seek and seek again, let them ceaselessly extend the frontiers of their bliss, the alchemists of the art of gardening! Let them offer rewards of sixty or a hundred thousand florins to whoever solves their ambitious problems. As for myself, I have found my *black tulip* and my *blue dahlia*.

Incomparable bloom, rediscovered tulip, allegorical dahlia, it is

c'est là, n'est-ce-pas, dans ce beau pays si calme et si rêveur, qu'il faudrait aller vivre et fleurir? Ne serais-tu pas encadrée dans ton analogie, et ne pourrais-tu pas te mirer, pour parler comme les mystiques, dans ta propre *correspondance*?

Des rêves! toujours des rêves! et plus l'âme est ambitieuse et délicate, plus les rêves s'éloignent du possible. Chaque homme porte en lui sa dose d'opium naturel, incessamment sécrétée et renouvelée, et, de la naissance à la mort, combien comptons-nous d'heures remplies par la jouissance positive, par l'action réussie et décidée? Vivrons-nous jamais, passerons-nous jamais dans ce tableau qu'a peint mon esprit, ce tableau qui te ressemble?

Ces trésors, ces meubles, ce luxe, cet ordre, ces parfums, ces fleurs miraculeuses, c'est toi. C'est encore toi, ces grands fleuves et ces canaux tranquilles. Ces énormes navires qu'ils charrient, tout chargés de richesses, et d'où montent les chants monotones de la manœuvre, ce sont mes pensées qui

there, is it not, in that beautiful land so calm and dreamful, that you should go to live and blossom? Would you not be surrounded by your own counterpart, and would you not be able to mirror yourself, as the mystics say, in your own correlative?

Dreams, forever dreams! And the more the soul is aspiring and fastidious, the more do dreams outdistance the possible. Every man bears within him his measure of natural opium, incessantly secreted and renewed; and, from birth till death, how many hours can we count that are filled with positive enjoyment, with successful and deliberate action? Shall we ever live?* will we never enter the picture my mind has painted, this picture which resembles you?

These treasures, this furniture, this luxury, this order, these perfumes, these miraculous flowers, are you yourself. You are also those great rivers and those peaceful canals. Those vast ships they bear along, all laden with riches and from which monotonous sea-shanties rise as they navigate, are my thoughts that sleep or glide

* *Shall we ever live*, etc. It is characteristic that even in this prose-poem Baudelaire echoes Pascal: '*Nous ne vivons jamais, mais nous espérons de vivre*' ('We never live, but we hope to live').

dorment ou qui roulent sur ton sein. Tu les conduis doucement vers la mer qui est l'Infini, tout en réfléchissant les profondeurs du ciel dans la limpidité de ta belle âme; – et quand, fatigués par la houle et gorgés des produits de l'Orient, ils rentrent au port natal, ce sont encore mes pensées enrichies qui reviennent de l'Infini vers toi.

L'IRRÉPARABLE

POUVONS-NOUS étouffer le vieux, le long Remords,
  Qui vit, s'agite et se tortille,
Et se nourrit de nous comme le ver des morts,
  Comme du chêne la chenille?
Pouvons-nous étouffer l'implacable Remords?

Dans quel philtre, dans quel vin, dans quelle tisane,
  Noierons-nous ce vieil ennemi,
Destructeur et gourmand comme la courtisane,
  Patient comme la fourmi?
Dans quel philtre? – dans quel vin? – dans quelle tisane?

upon your breast. You guide them gently towards that sea which is the Infinite, while you reflect the sky's depths in the limpidness of your lovely soul; and when, wearied by the swell and gorged with the wares of the East, they re-enter their home port, they are still my thoughts, enriched, returning from the Infinite to you.

[1857–61. Published September 1862]

The Irreparable

CAN we stifle the old and long Remorse which lives, heaves, coils, and feeds on us as the worm feeds on the dead, as the caterpillar battens on the oak? Can we stifle implacable Remorse?

In what potion, in what wine, in what brew shall we drown this ancient enemy, as destructive and greedy as a harlot, as patient as an ant? In what potion, in what wine, in what brew?

Dis-le, belle sorcière, oh! dis, si tu le sais,
  À cet esprit comblé d'angoisse
Et pareil au mourant qu'écrasent les blessés,
  Que le sabot du cheval froisse,
Dis-le, belle sorcière, oh! dis, si tu le sais,

À cet agonisant que le loup déjà flaire
  Et que surveille le corbeau,
À ce soldat brisé! s'il faut qu'il désespère
  D'avoir sa croix et son tombeau;
Ce pauvre agonisant que déjà le loup flaire!

Peut-on illuminer un ciel bourbeux et noir?
  Peut-on déchirer des ténèbres
Plus denses que la poix, sans matin et sans soir,
  Sans astres, sans éclairs funèbres?
Peut-on illuminer un ciel bourbeux et noir?

L'Espérance qui brille aux carreaux de l'Auberge
  Est soufflée, est morte à jamais!
Sans lune et sans rayons, trouver où l'on héberge
  Les martyrs d'un chemin mauvais!
Le Diable a tout éteint aux carreaux de l'Auberge!

Tell [us], lovely witch, Oh tell if you know what it is, to the anguish-laden mind which is like some dying man crushed under the wounded, bruised by the horse's hoof – tell it, lovely witch, if you know what it is, to the man in his death-throes, whom the wolf has already scented and over whom the raven is watching – tell the broken soldier whether he must despair of his medal and his tomb – the poor man in the throes of death, whom the wolf has already scented.

Can we illuminate a grimy, black sky? can we pierce shadows denser than pitch, with no morning or evening, with no stars, without even gloomy flashes of lightning? Can we illuminate a grimy, black sky?

The hope that shines in the windows of the Inn is snuffed, is dead for ever. Without moonlight, without beams, where find [a place] to shelter the martyrs of a painful journey? The devil has snuffed the light at the windows of the Inn.

Adorable sorcière, aimes-tu les damnés?
  Dis, connais-tu l'irrémissible?
Connais-tu le Remords, aux traits empoisonnés,
  À qui notre cœur sert de cible?
Adorable sorcière, aimes-tu les damnés?

L'Irréparable ronge, avec sa dent maudite
  Notre âme, piteux monument,
Et souvent il attaque, ainsi que le termite,
  Par la base le bâtiment.
L'Irréparable ronge avec sa dent maudite!

– J'ai vu parfois, au fond d'un théâtre banal
  Qu'enflammait l'orchestre sonore,
Une fée allumer dans un ciel infernal
  Une miraculeuse aurore;
J'ai vu parfois au fond d'un théâtre banal

Un être, qui n'était que lumière, or et gaze,
  Terrasser l'énorme Satan;
Mais mon cœur, que jamais ne visite l'extase,
  Est un théâtre où l'on attend
Toujours, toujours en vain, l'Être aux ailes de gaze!

Adorable witch, do you love the damned? Say, do you know the unforgivable? Do you know remorse with its poisoned barbs, for which our heart serves as target? Adorable witch, do you love the damned?

The Irreparable gnaws, with its accursed tooth, that pitiful monument, our soul, and like the white-ant it often attacks a building at its foundations. The Irreparable gnaws, with its accursed tooth.

Sometimes I have seen, in a third-rate theatre, lit up by the sonorous orchestra, a fairy kindle a miraculous dawn in an infernal sky: sometimes I have seen, in a third-rate theatre, a being who was naught but light and gold and gauze, overthrow the enormous Satan: but my heart, never visited by ecstasy, is a theatre in which the being with wings of gauze is for ever awaited in vain.

[Published in 1855 with a dedication to *La Belle aux Cheveux d'Or* (Goldenhair), viz. Marie Daubrun, who played that part.]

LE POISON

LE vin sait revêtir le plus sordide bouge
  D'un luxe miraculeux,
Et fait surgir plus d'un portique fabuleux
  Dans l'or de sa vapeur rouge,
Comme un soleil couchant dans un ciel nébuleux.

L'opium agrandit ce qui n'a pas de bornes,
  Allonge l'illimité,
Approfondit le temps, creuse la volupté,
  Et de plaisirs noirs et mornes
Remplit l'âme au-delà de sa capacité.

Tout cela ne vaut pas le poison qui découle
  De tes yeux, de tes yeux verts,
Lacs où mon âme tremble et se voit à l'envers …
  Mes songes viennent en foule
Pour se désaltérer à ces gouffres amers.

Tout cela ne vaut pas le terrible prodige
  De ta salive qui mord,
Qui plonge dans l'oubli mon âme sans remord,
  Et, charriant le vertige,
La roule défaillante aux rives de la mort!

Poison

WINE can clothe the most sordid hovel in miraculous luxury, and conjure up many a fabulous portico in its red vapour's gold, like a setting sun in a clouded sky.

Opium magnifies things that have no limits, it prolongs the boundless, makes Time more profound, deepens voluptuousness, and fills the soul to overbrimming with dark and gloomy pleasures.

None of these things equals the poison that flows from your eyes, from your green eyes – lakes wherein my soul trembles and sees its own image reversed. My dreams come flocking to quench their thirst in those bitter depths.

None of those things can equal the fearsome marvel of your acid saliva, which plunges my remorseless soul into oblivion and, bringing vertigo, swirls it in a swoon to the shores of death.

[Published April 1857]

CIEL BROUILLÉ

ON dirait ton regard d'une vapeur couvert;
Ton œil mystérieux (est-il bleu, gris ou vert?)
Alternativement tendre, rêveur, cruel,
Réfléchit l'indolence et la pâleur du ciel.

Tu rappelles ces jours blancs, tièdes et voilés,
Qui font se fondre en pleurs les cœurs ensorcelés,
Quand, agités d'un mal inconnu qui les tord,
Les nerfs trop éveillés raillent l'esprit qui dort.

Tu ressembles parfois à ces beaux horizons
Qu'allument les soleils des brumeuses saisons ...
Comme tu resplendis, paysage mouillé
Qu'enflamment les rayons tombant d'un ciel brouillé!

Ô femme dangereuse, ô séduisants climats!
Adorerai-je aussi ta neige et vos frimas,
Et saurai-je tirer de l'implacable hiver
Des plaisirs plus aigus que la glace et le fer?

Cloud-dappled Sky

YOUR gaze seems as though veiled with mist; your mysterious eyes – are they blue, grey, or green? – fitfully tender, dreamy, cruel, echo the indolence and paleness of the sky.

You make me think of those blank days, mild and hazy, which melt enamoured hearts into tears, when they fret with some vague, twisting pain, when the taut nerves mock the numbness of the mind.

Sometimes you recall delightful vistas lit by the misty seasons' suns; how splendid you are, a landscape all bedewed, yet aglow with the rays of a cloud-dappled sky.

O dangerous woman, with your seductive climes: perhaps some day I shall worship your snow and frost, and learn to draw from your pitiless winter, pleasures more sharply-edged than ice or steel?

[Published in *Les Fleurs du mal*, 1857]

LE CHAT

I

DANS ma cervelle se promène,
Ainsi qu'en son appartement,
Un beau chat, fort, doux et charmant.
Quand il miaule, on l'entend à peine,

Tant son timbre est tendre et discret;
Mais que sa voix s'apaise ou gronde,
Elle est toujours riche et profonde.
C'est là son charme et son secret.

Cette voix qui perle et qui filtre
Dans mon fonds le plus ténébreux,
Me remplit comme un vers nombreux
Et me réjouit comme un philtre.

Elle endort les plus cruels maux
Et contient toutes les extases;
Pour dire les plus longues phrases,
Elle n'a pas besoin de mots.

The Cat

I

A HANDSOME cat, strong and gentle and full of charm, prowls to and fro in my brain, as if in his own home. When he mews you can hardly hear him at all, so tender and discreet is his tone of voice. But whether his voice be mild or vexed it is always rich and deep. That is his special charm and secret. This voice which pearls and filters down to the darkest depths of my being, expands in me like a harmonious verse and delights me like a magic philtre.

It soothes my cruellest sufferings and is full of every ecstasy. To say the longest sentences it has no need of words.

Non, il n'est pas d'archet qui morde
Sur mon cœur, parfait instrument,
Et fasse plus royalement
Chanter sa plus vibrante corde,

Que ta voix, chat mystérieux,
Chat séraphique, chat étrange,
En qui tout est, comme en un ange,
Aussi subtil qu'harmonieux!

II

De sa fourrure blonde et brune
Sort un parfum si doux, qu'un soir
J'en fus embaumé, pour l'avoir
Caressée une fois, rien qu'une.

C'est l'esprit familier du lieu;
Il juge, il préside, il inspire
Toutes choses dans son empire;
Peut-être est-il fée, est-il dieu?

No, there is no violin-bow in the world that, biting on my heart, that most perfect of instruments, more richly draws song from even its most sensitive string, than does your voice, O most mysterious, seraphic, extraordinary cat, in whom everything, as in an Angel, is as subtle as it is harmonious.

II

From its blond and brown fur there rises such a sweet aroma that, one evening, I was impregnated with its perfume after caressing it but once – yes, only once.

It is the house's familiar spirit, judging, presiding, inspiring all things within its empire: is it a fairy, or a god?

Quand mes yeux, vers ce chat que j'aime
Tirés comme par un aimant,
Se retournent docilement
Et que je regarde en moi-même,

Je vois avec étonnement
Le feu de ses prunelles pâles,
Clairs fanaux, vivantes opales,
Qui me contemplent fixement.

LE BEAU NAVIRE

JE veux te raconter, ô molle enchanteresse!
Les diverses beautés qui parent ta jeunesse;
  Je veux te peindre ta beauté,
Où l'enfance s'allie à la maturité.

Quand tu vas balayant l'air de ta jupe large,
Tu fais l'effet d'un beau vaisseau qui prend le large,
  Chargé de toile, et va roulant
Suivant un rythme doux, et paresseux, et lent.

When my eyes are drawn as by a magnet towards my beloved cat, and obediently I turn them upon him, I look into myself, and am amazed to see the fire of his pale pupils, bright lamps, living opals, hypnotically fixed upon me.

[Published in *Les Fleurs du mal*, 1857]

The Beautiful Ship

I WANT to describe to you, O tender enchantress, the various beauties which adorn your youth: I want to depict your loveliness in which childhood and maturity combine.

When you walk, sweeping the air with your ample skirt, you give the impression of a handsome ship setting out to sea with all its canvas spread, and swinging away, keeping a gentle, languid, slow rhythm.

Sur ton cou large et rond, sur tes épaules grasses,
Ta tête se pavane avec d'étranges grâces;
 D'un air placide et triomphant
Tu passes ton chemin, majestueuse enfant.

Je veux te raconter, ô molle enchanteresse!
Les diverses beautés qui parent ta jeunesse;
 Je veux te peindre ta beauté,
Où l'enfance s'allie à la maturité.

Ta gorge qui s'avance et qui pousse la moire,
Ta gorge triomphante est une belle armoire
 Dont les panneaux bombés et clairs
Comme les boucliers accrochent des éclairs;

Boucliers provocants, armés de pointes roses!
Armoire à doux secrets, pleine de bonnes choses,
 De vins, de parfums, de liqueurs
Qui feraient délirer les cerveaux et les cœurs!

On your broad, round throat, on your plump shoulders, your head sways with many a strange grace; with a placid, conquering air you go your way, majestic child.

I want to describe to you, O tender enchantress, the various beauties which adorn your youth; I want to depict your loveliness in which childhood and maturity combine.

Your jutting breast which curves the watered-silk, your triumpant breast, is [like] some beautiful press, whose rounded, bright panels catch the light like shields: provoking shields, armed with rosy tips – a press full of delicious secrets, full of good things, with wines and perfumes and liqueurs that would fill men's minds and hearts with delirium.

Quand tu vas balayant l'air de ta jupe large,
Tu fais l'effet d'un beau vaisseau qui prend le large,
  Chargé de toile, et va roulant
Suivant un rythme doux, et paresseux, et lent.

Tes nobles jambes, sous les volants qu'elles chassent,
Tourmentent les désirs obscurs et les agacent,
  Comme deux sorcières qui font
Tourner un philtre noir dans un vase profond.

Tes bras, qui se joueraient des précoces hercules,
Sont des boas luisants les solides émules,
  Faits pour serrer obstinément,
Comme pour l'imprimer dans ton cœur, ton amant.

Sur ton cou large et rond, sur tes épaules grasses,
Ta tête se pavane avec d'étranges grâces;
  D'un air placide et triomphant
Tu passes ton chemin, majestueuse enfant.

When you walk, sweeping the air with your ample skirt, you give the impression of a handsome ship setting out to sea with all its canvas spread, and swinging away, keeping a gentle, languid, slow rhythm.

Your noble legs, under the flounces which they thrust before them, torment and tease obscure desires, like twin witches stirring a black potion in a deep vessel.

Your arms, which would be more than a match for an infant Hercules, are worthy rivals of glistening boas, fashioned for relentless embraces, as though to imprint your lover on your heart.

On your broad, round throat, on your plump shoulders, your head sways with many a strange grace; with a placid, conquering air you go your way, majestic child.

[Published in *Les Fleurs du mal*, 1857. This poem is attributed to the *Daubrun* cycle by Crépet, Blin, and Starkie; to the *Dorothée* group by Ruff, and to the *Jeanne Duval* cycle by Le Dantec.]

CAUSERIE

VOUS êtes un beau ciel d'automne, clair et rose!
Mais la tristesse en moi monte comme la mer,
Et laisse, en refluant, sur ma lèvre morose
Le souvenir cuisant de son limon amer.

– Ta main se glisse en vain sur mon sein qui se pâme;
Ce qu'elle cherche, amie, est un lieu saccagé
Par la griffe et la dent féroce de la femme.
Ne cherchez plus mon cœur; les bêtes l'ont mangé.

Mon cœur est un palais flétri par la cohue;
On s'y soûle, on s'y tue, on s'y prend aux cheveux!
– Un parfum nage autour de votre gorge nu! …

Ô Beauté, dur fléau des âmes, tu le veux!
Avec tes yeux de feu, brillants comme des fêtes,
Calcine ces lambeaux qu'ont épargnés les bêtes!

Monologue

YOU are a fine Autumn sky, clear and rosy – but sadness is rising in me like the sea, and leaves, as it withdraws, only the poignant after-taste of bitter lime on my sullen lip.

In vain your hand glides over my numb breast: what it seeks, my dear, is a place laid waste by women's claws and fangs – seek no more my heart; wild beasts have fed on it.

The rabble have defiled the palace of my heart, they swill and murder there, clutching each other's hair – but such a perfume hovers round your naked throat –

O Beauty, pitiless scourge of human souls, if it is your will, may your eyes of fire, dazzling as festivals, consume these mortal tatters, spared by the beasts!

[Published in *Les Fleurs du mal*, 1857]

CHANT D'AUTOMNE

I

BIENTÔT nous plongerons dans les froides ténèbres;
Adieu, vive clarté de nos étés trop courts!
J'entends déjà tomber avec des chocs funèbres
Le bois retentissant sur le pavé des cours.

Tout l'hiver va rentrer dans mon être: colère,
Haine, frissons, horreur, labeur dur et forcé,
Et, comme le soleil dans son enfer polaire,
Mon cœur ne sera plus qu'un bloc rouge et glacé.

J'écoute en frémissant chaque bûche qui tombe;
L'échafaud qu'on bâtit n'a pas d'écho plus sourd.
Mon esprit est pareil à la tour qui succombe
Sous les coups du bélier infatigable et lourd.

Il me semble, bercé par ce choc monotone,
Qu'on cloue en grande hâte un cercueil quelque part.
Pour qui? – C'était hier l'été; voici l'automne!
Ce bruit mystérieux sonne comme un départ.

Autumn-Song

I

SOON we shall plunge into the chill shadows. Farewell to the vivid sunlight of our summers, all too short! Already I hear falling the logs [of winter fuel], their forlorn thuds resounding in the courtyards.

The whole winter will lodge itself once more into my being: anger, hatred, ague, horror, hard, forced labour, and like the sun in its arctic hell, my heart will be no more than a block of scarlet ice.

I tremble as I hear the logs drop, one by one; the hammering of the scaffold makes no duller an echo than this; my mind is like a tower, crashing beneath the blows of the ponderous, tireless Ram.

As I am rocked this way and that by the monotonous thuds, I fancy that somewhere a coffin is being hastily nailed together – and for whom? Yesterday it was summer, but now Autumn is with us. The mysterious noise resounds, like a farewell.

II

J'aime de vos longs yeux la lumière verdâtre,
Douce beauté, mais tout aujourd'hui m'est amer,
Et rien, ni votre amour, ni le boudoir, ni l'âtre,
Ne me vaut le soleil rayonnant sur la mer.

Et pourtant aimez-moi, tendre cœur! soyez mère,
Même pour un ingrat, même pour un méchant;
Amante ou sœur, soyez la douceur éphémère
D'un glorieux automne ou d'un soleil couchant.

Courte tâche! La tombe attend; elle est avide!
Ah! laissez-moi, mon front posé sur vos genoux,
Goûter, en regrettant l'été blanc et torride,
De l'arrière-saison le rayon jaune et doux!

II

I love the emerald light of your long eyes, my gentle beauty; but today I find all things fraught with bitterness, and nothing, not even your love nor the boudoir nor the hearth, means as much to me as the sunlight glittering on the sea.

Yet love me still, O tender heart, and be as a mother, however ungrateful I am and however unworthy: whether as mistress or sister, be the short-lived bliss of a splendid Autumn or a westering Sun.

Your task will be short, for the famished grave is waiting. Ah, let me rest my brow upon your knees, regretting the white and torrid summer-time, and enjoying the yellow, gentle rays of autumntide.

[Published 1859. MS. dedicated to M.D.]

SONNET D'AUTOMNE

ILS me disent, tes yeux, clairs comme le cristal:
«Pour toi, bizarre amant, quel est donc mon mérite?»
– Sois charmante et tais-toi! Mon cœur, que tout irrite,
Excepté la candeur de l'antique animal,

Ne veut pas te montrer son secret infernal,
Berceuse dont la main aux longs sommeils m'invite,
Ni sa noire légende avec la flamme écrite.
Je hais la passion et l'esprit me fait mal!

Aimons-nous doucement. L'Amour dans sa guérite,
Ténébreux, embusqué, bande son arc fatal.
Je connais les engins de son vieil arsenal:

Crime, horreur et folie! – Ô pâle marguerite!
Comme moi n'es-tu pas un soleil automnal,
Ô ma si blanche, ô ma si froide Marguerite?

Autumn Sonnet

THEY say to me, your eyes, clear as crystal: 'Strange lover, what merit do you find in me?' – Be charming, and hold your tongue! My heart, on which everything jars save the candour of the primitive animal, is unwilling to reveal you its hellish secret, nor its black legend written in flame, O sleep-giver whose hand invites me to long slumbers. I hate passion, and wit irks me.

Let us love each other gently. Love, in his watch-tower, darkling and in ambush, is stretching his deadly bow. I know the weapons of his old arsenal – crime, horror, and madness! O my pale marguerite, are you not, like me, an autumn sun, O my so white, O my so cold Marguerite?

[Published 1859. Attributed by Crépet and Blin to the Daubrun cycle, on the grounds that Marie Daubrun played the part of *Margue* in *Le Sanglier des Ardennes*, in 1854. It could also be related to Mme Sabatier – see *Semper Eadem*.]

L'AMOUR DU MENSONGE

QUAND je te vois passer, ô ma chère indolente,
Au chant des instruments qui se brise au plafond
Suspendant ton allure harmonieuse et lente,
Et promenant l'ennui de ton regard profond;

Quand je contemple, aux feux du gaz qui le colore,
Ton front pâle, embelli par un morbide attrait,
Où les torches du soir allument une aurore,
Et tes yeux attirants comme ceux d'un portrait,

Je me dis: Qu'elle est belle! et bizarrement fraîche!
Le souvenir massif, royale et lourde tour,
La couronne, et son cœur, meurtri comme une pêche,
Est mûr, comme son corps, pour le savant amour.

The Love of Falsehood

WHEN I see you pass by, dear languid girl, to the band's tune refracted on the ceiling, pausing in your harmonious, unhurried progress and casting all around your deep gaze's boredom; when I contemplate your pallid brow, coloured by the gas-jets and the lovelier for its morbid charm, in which evening's torches light a dawn, and your eyes, magnetic as those of a painted portrait,

I say to myself: 'How beautiful she is, how curiously unspoiled! Massive memory [like] a royal, cumbrous tower, crowns her head, and her heart – bruised like a peach – is ripe, like her body, for the lore of love.'

Es-tu le fruit d'automne aux saveurs souveraines?
Es-tu vase funèbre attendant quelques pleurs,
Parfum qui fait rêver aux oasis lointaines,
Oreiller caressant, ou corbeille de fleurs?

Je sais qu'il est des yeux, des plus mélancoliques,
Qui ne recèlent point de secrets précieux;
Beaux écrins sans joyaux, médaillons sans reliques,
Plus vides, plus profonds que vous-mêmes, ô Cieux!

Mais ne suffit-il pas que tu sois l'apparence,
Pour réjouir un cœur qui fuit la vérité?
Qu'importe ta bêtise ou ton indifférence?
Masque ou décor, salut! J'adore ta beauté.

Are you Autumn's fruit, of supreme savours? Are you a funeral urn awaiting tears? a perfume that sets one dreaming of far oases? a pampering pillow? or a bed of flowers?

I know there are eyes, most melancholy, that hide no precious secrets; fine caskets empty of jewels, lockets without relics, emptier, deeper than even you, O Heavens!

But isn't it enough for you to be a semblance, in order to rejoice a heart that flees from truth? What matter your stupidity, your indifference? I hail you, whether mask or sham display – I worship your beauty.

[Attributed to the Daubrun cycle by Benedetto, Ruff, Crépet, Blin, and Starkie. Written 1859 or 1860; published May 1860]

V

The Sabatier Cycle

1852–60

À CELLE QUI EST TROP GAIE

TA tête, ton geste, ton air
Sont beaux comme un beau paysage;
Le rire joue en ton visage
Comme un vent frais dans un ciel clair.

Le passant chagrin que tu frôles
Est ébloui par la santé
Qui jaillit comme une clarté
De tes bras et de tes épaules.

Les retentissantes couleurs
Dont tu parsèmes tes toilettes
Jettent dans l'esprit des poëtes
L'image d'un ballet de fleurs.

Ces robes folles sont l'emblème
De ton esprit bariolé;
Folle dont je suis affolé,
Je te hais autant que je t'aime!

To She who is too Gay

YOUR head, your gesture, your bearing, are as beautiful as a beautiful landscape: laughter frolics in your face like a cool wind in a clear sky.

The glum passer-by, whom you brush against, is dazzled by the health that flashes like light from your arms and shoulders. The vivid colours that bedeck your clothes bring to poets' minds the image of a ballet of flowers. Those fantastic dresses are the emblem of your motley mind, O madcap for whom I am out of my wits! I hate you as much as I love you!

Quelquefois dans un beau jardin
Où je traînais mon atonie,
J'ai senti, comme une ironie,
Le soleil déchirer mon sein;

Et le printemps et la verdure
Ont tant humilié mon cœur,
Que j'ai puni sur une fleur
L'insolence de la Nature.

Ainsi je voudrais, une nuit,
Quand l'heure des voluptés sonne,
Vers les trésors de ta personne,
Comme un lâche, ramper sans bruit,

Pour châtier ta chair joyeuse,
Pour meurtrir ton sein pardonné,
Et faire à ton flanc étonné
Une blessure large et creuse,

Et, vertigineuse douceur!
À travers ces lèvres nouvelles,
Plus éclatantes et plus belles,
T'infuser mon venin, ma sœur!

Sometimes in a beautiful garden in which I dragged my listlessness, I have felt the sunshine sear my breast like an irony, and the springtime and the verdure so humiliated my heart, that on a flower I punished Nature's insolence.

Thus, some night, when the hour of sensuality strikes, I would like to slink noiselessly, like a coward, towards your body's riches, in order to chastise your happy flesh, to bruise your pardoned breast and open in your astonished side a wide, deep wound, and – O blinding rapture – through those new lips, more vivid and more beautiful, infuse my poison into you, my sister.

[Poem sent to Mme Sabatier, December 1852. Published in *Les Fleurs du mal*, 1857]

RÉVERSIBILITÉ

ANGE plein de gaîté, connaissez-vous l'angoisse,
La honte, les remords, les sanglots, les ennuis,
Et les vagues terreurs de ces affreuses nuits
Qui compriment le cœur comme un papier qu'on froisse?
Ange plein de gaîté, connaissez-vous l'angoisse?

Ange plein de bonté, connaissez-vous la haine,
Les poings crispés dans l'ombre et les larmes de fiel,
Quand la Vengeance bat son infernal rappel,
Et de nos facultés se fait le capitaine?
Ange plein de bonté, connaissez-vous la haine?

Ange plein de santé, connaissez-vous les Fièvres,
Qui, le long des grands murs de l'hospice blafard,
Comme des exilés, s'en vont d'un pied traînard,
Cherchant le soleil rare et remuant les lèvres?
Ange plein de santé, connaissez-vous les Fièvres?

Reversibility

ANGEL of gaiety, do you know that anguish, the shame and remorse, sobs, cares, the nameless terrors of those awful nights which tighten the heart like crushed paper? Angel of gaiety, do you know that anguish?

Angel of goodness, do you know that hate, the fists clenched in the dark, the tears of gall, when revenge drums its devilish tattoo and takes command of all our faculties? Angel of goodness, do you know that hate?

Angel of health, do you know those fevers, stalking between the high walls of dingy workhouses, like exiles dragging their feet in quest of the infrequent sun, moving their lips? Angel of health, do you know those fevers?

Ange plein de beauté, connaissez-vous les rides,
Et la peur de vieillir, et ce hideux tourment
De lire la secrète horreur du dévouement
Dans des yeux où longtemps burent nos yeux avides?
Ange plein de beauté, connaissez-vous les rides?

Ange plein de bonheur, de joie et de lumières,
David mourant aurait demandé la santé
Aux émanations de ton corps enchanté;
Mais de toi je n'implore, ange, que tes prières,
Ange plein de bonheur, de joie et de lumières!

CONFESSION

UNE fois, une seule, aimable et douce femme,
À mon bras votre bras poli
S'appuya (sur le fond ténébreux de mon âme
Ce souvenir n'est point pâli);

Angel of beauty, do you know those wrinkles, the fear of growing old, the hideous torture of reading, in eyes that our own thirsty eyes drank from for years, the secret horror of devotion? Angel of beauty, do you know those wrinkles?

Angel of happiness, of joy, and radiance, David at the hour of death would have sought health in the fragrance of your enchanted body: but all I ask of you, my angel, is your prayers, Angel of happiness, of joy and radiance!

[1853. Published 1855]

Confession

ONCE and once only, lovable and gentle woman, you leaned your smooth arm on mine: the memory of it has never faded from the dark background of my soul.

Il était tard; ainsi qu'une médaille neuve
  Le pleine lune s'étalait,
Et la solennité de la nuit, comme un fleuve,
  Sur Paris dormant ruisselait.

Et le long des maisons, sous les portes cochères,
  Des chats passaient furtivement,
L'oreille au guet, ou bien, comme des ombres chères,
  Nous accompagnaient lentement.

Tout à coup, au milieu de l'intimité libre
  Éclose à la pâle clarté,
De vous, riche et sonore instrument où ne vibre
  Que la radieuse gaieté,

De vous, claire et joyeuse ainsi qu'une fanfare
  Dans le matin étincelant,
Une note plaintive, une note bizarre
  S'échappa tout en chancelant

Comme une enfant chétive, horrible, sombre, immonde,
  Dont sa famille rougirait,

The hour was late, when like a freshly-minted medal the full moon was spread out, when the solemnness of night streamed like a river on sleeping Paris.

And along by the houses and under wide carriage-gates, cats crept furtively with pricking ears, or else slowly walked beside us like familiar shades.

Then suddenly, in the midst of our easy intimacy, grown frank and open in the dim light, there escaped from you – from you, who are such a rich, sonorous instrument, vibrating always with radiant cheer –

from you, as bright and lively as trumpets sounding through the glittering dawn – there came a strange, lamenting cry, a faltering note

(like some sickly, repulsive child, sullen and foul, whose ashamed

Et qu'elle aurait longtemps, pour la cacher au monde,
  Dans un caveau mise au secret.

Pauvre ange, elle chantait, votre note criarde:
  «Que rien ici-bas n'est certain,
Et que toujours, avec quelque soin qu'il se farde,
  Se trahit l'égoïsme humain;

«Que c'est un dur métier que d'être belle femme,
  Et que c'est le travail banal
De la danseuse folle et froide qui se pâme
  Dans un sourire machinal;

«Que bâtir sur les cœurs est une chose sotte;
  Que tout craque, amour et beauté,
Jusqu'à ce que l'Oubli les jette dans sa hotte
  Pour les rendre à l'Éternité!»

J'ai souvent évoqué cette lune enchantée,
  Ce silence et cette langueur,
Et cette confidence horrible chuchotée
  Au confessionnal du cœur.

family would hide it away for years, in a secret cellar, far from the eyes of the world).

My poor Angel, that harsh note of yours sang, saying: 'that nothing on earth is certain; that always in spite of every disguise human selfishness is forever breaking through:

'that it's a thankless occupation, being a beautiful woman, like the inane job of a crazy, cold dancing-girl, dancing till she drops with the same, mechanical smile:

'that it's foolish to build anything on human hearts, for everything cracks, yes, even love and beauty, till oblivion flings them into its hod and restores them to eternity ...'

I have often recalled that entrancing moon, that silence, that languor; that fearful secret, whispered in the heart's confessional.

[Poem sent to Mme Sabatier, 9 May 1853. Published 1855]

QUE diras-tu ce soir, pauvre âme solitaire,
Que diras-tu, mon cœur, cœur autrefois flétri,
À la très-belle, à la très-bonne, à la très-chère,
Dont le regard divin t'a soudain refleuri?

– Nous mettrons notre orgueil à chanter ses louanges:
Rien ne vaut la douceur de son autorité;
Sa chair spirituelle a le parfum des Anges,
Et son œil nous revêt d'un habit de clarté.

Que ce soit dans la nuit et dans la solitude,
Que ce soit dans la rue et dans la multitude,
Son fantôme dans l'air danse comme un flambeau.

Parfois il parle et dit: «Je suis belle, et j'ordonne
Que pour l'amour de moi vous n'aimiez que le Beau;
Je suis l'Ange gardien, la Muse et la Madone.»

WHAT will you say tonight, poor solitary soul: what will you say, my heart, my heart withered till now, to her who is most beautiful most good, most dear, whose divine gaze has suddenly made me flower again?

We shall set our pride in singing her praises; nothing can rival her gentle authority; her spiritual flesh has an angelic fragrance; her eye clothes us in garments of light.

Whether I am in darkness or solitude, or in the crowded street, her image hovers like a torch in the air.

Sometimes it speaks and says: 'I am beautiful, and bid you, for love of me, to love the Beautiful alone; for I am your guardian Angel, your Muse, and your Madonna.'

[Poem sent to Mme Sabatier, 16 February 1854. Published 1855]

LE FLAMBEAU VIVANT

Ils marchent devant moi, ces Yeux pleins de lumières,
Qu'un Ange très-savant a sans doute aimantés;
Ils marchent, ces divins frères qui sont mes frères,
Secouant dans mes yeux leurs feux diamantés.

Me sauvant de tout piège et de tout péché grave,
Ils conduisent mes pas dans la route du Beau;
Ils sont mes serviteurs et je suis leur esclave;
Tout mon être obéit à ce vivant flambeau.

Charmants Yeux, vous brillez de la clarté mystique
Qu'ont les cierges brûlant en plein jour; le soleil
Rougit, mais n'éteint pas leur flamme fantastique;

Ils célèbrent la Mort, vous chantez le Réveil;
Vous marchez en chantant le réveil de mon âme,
Astres dont nul soleil ne peut flétrir la flamme!

The Living Torch

They go before me, those eyes full of many lights, which must have been magnetized by some Angel's craft; they advance, those divine brothers, my own brothers, flashing in my eyes their diamond-lustred flames.

Preserving me from every snare and from every grievous sin, they lead my steps along the paths of Beauty: although they serve me I am their bondsman; my entire being obeys this living torch.

Entrancing eyes, you glitter with the mystic radiance of candles lit in the broad light of day: the sun glows red, but cannot dowse their eerie flame:

the candles honour Death; but you hymn the Resurrection: as you advance you sing my soul's awakening, O stars whose fire no Sun can ever dim!

[Poem sent to Mme Sabatier, February 1854. Published 1857]

HYMNE

À LA très-chère, à la très-belle
Qui remplit mon cœur de clarté,
À l'ange, à l'idole immortelle,
Salut en l'immortalité!

Elle se répand dans ma vie
Comme un air imprégné de sel,
Et dans mon âme inassouvie
Verse le goût de l'éternel.

Sachet toujours frais qui parfume
L'atmosphère d'un cher réduit,
Encensoir oublié qui fume
En secret à travers la nuit,

Comment, amour incorruptible,
T'exprimer avec vérité?
Grain de musc qui gis, invisible,
Au fond de mon éternité!

À la très-bonne, à la très-belle
Qui fait ma joie et ma santé,
À l'ange, à l'idole immortelle,
Salut en l'immortalité!

Hymn

To the very dear, to the very beautiful, who fills my heart with light; to the angel, the immortal idol, Hail, in immortality.

She spreads into my life like briny air, and into my hungry soul she pours the taste of the eternal. Ever-fresh sachet, perfuming the atmosphere of a beloved nook, forgotten censer smoking in secret through the night – O how, my incorruptible love, can I express you truthfully, grain of musk who lie unseen in the depths of my eternity?

To the very good, the very beautiful, who is my joy and my health, to the angel, to the immortal idol, Hail, in immortality!

[Poem sent to Mme Sabatier, 8 May 1854. Published 1855]

L'AUBE SPIRITUELLE

QUAND chez les débauchés l'aube blanche et vermeille
Entre en société de l'Idéal rongeur,
Par l'opération d'un mystère vengeur
Dans la brute assoupie un ange se réveille.

Des Cieux Spirituels l'inaccessible azur,
Pour l'homme terrassé qui rêve encore et souffre,
S'ouvre et s'enfonce avec l'attirance du gouffre.
Ainsi, chère Déesse, Être lucide et pur,

Sur les débris fumeux des stupides orgies
Ton souvenir plus clair, plus rose, plus charmant,
À mes yeux agrandis voltige incessamment.

Le soleil a noirci la flamme des bougies;
Ainsi, toujours vainqueur, ton fantôme est pareil,
Âme resplendissante, à l'immortel soleil!

The Spiritual Dawn

WHEN, into rakes' rooms, the white and ruby dawn enters, and with it the Ideal that frets the mind, some avenging mystery sets to work, and an angel wakens in the slothful beast.

The unattainable azure of the spiritual Heavens opens for the still dreaming, suffering, felled man, and floods down into his being as though drawn by a precipice.

Thus, my beloved goddess, O translucent and pure being, above the ruins of stupefying debauch, your memory, brighter, rosier, and more enchanting, ceaselessly hovers before my dilated eyes.

The Sun has blackened the candle-flames: thus, O radiant soul, your ever-triumphant image is sister to the immortal Sun.

[1854. Published 1855]

MOESTA ET ERRABUNDA

DIS-MOI, ton cœur parfois s'envole-t-il, Agathe,
Loin du noir océan de l'immonde cité,
Vers un autre océan où la splendeur éclate,
Bleu, clair, profond, ainsi que la virginité?
Dis-moi, ton cœur parfois s'envole-t-il, Agathe?

La mer, la vaste mer, console nos labeurs!
Quel démon a doté la mer, rauque chanteuse
Qu'accompagne l'immense orgue des vents grondeurs,
De cette fonction sublime de berceuse?
La mer, la vaste mer, console nos labeurs!

Emporte-moi, wagon! enlève-moi, frégate!
Loin, loin! ici la boue est faite de nos pleurs!
– Est-il vrai que parfois le triste cœur d'Agathe
Dise: Loin des remords, des crimes, des douleurs,
Emporte-moi, wagon, enlève-moi, frégate?

Sad and Restless

TELL me, Agatha, does your heart sometimes soar away from the black ocean of the ignoble city, towards another ocean where splendour blazes blue and bright and deep, like virginity itself? Tell me, Agatha, does your heart sometimes soar away?

The sea, the enormous sea, consoles us for our labours. What demon endowed the sea – that hoarse contralto accompanied by the immense organ of the roaring winds – with the sublime task of singing lullabies? The sea, the enormous sea, consoles us for our labours.

Would that some carriage would carry me away, some frigate kidnap me, far, far away! Here the city slime is made of human tears. Is it true that sometimes Agatha's mournful heart cries out: 'far from remorses, crimes and sufferings, carry me away, carriage, kidnap me, frigate?'

Comme vous êtes loin, paradis parfumé,
Où sous un clair azur tout n'est qu'amour et joie,
Où tout ce que l'on aime est digne d'être aimé,
Où dans la volupté pure le cœur se noie!
Comme vous êtes loin, paradis parfumé!

Mais le vert paradis des amours enfantines,
Les courses, les chansons, les baisers, les bouquets,
Les violons vibrant derrière les collines,
Avec les brocs de vin, le soir, dans les bosquets,
– Mais le vert paradis des amours enfantines,

L'innocent paradis, plein de plaisirs furtifs,
Est-il déjà plus loin que l'Inde et que la Chine?
Peut-on le rappeler avec des cris plaintifs,
Et l'animer encor d'une voix argentine,
L'innocent paradis plein de plaisirs furtifs?

How remote you are, O perfumed paradise, where under the lucid azure all is love and joy; where all that one loves is worthy to be loved; where the heart drowns in pure voluptuousness. – How remote you are, O perfumed paradise!

But the green paradise of childhood loves, with its romps and songs, its kisses and bouquets, the violins vibrating beyond the braes, and the jugs of wine at twilight in the groves – O the green paradise of childhood loves,

the innocent paradise, full of secret pleasures – is it really farther away than India or China? Can we never call it back with plaintive cries, make it alive again with silvery voices, that innocent paradise, full of furtive pleasures?

[Poem attributed by L. Legras to the Sabatier cycle. Published 1855]

HARMONIE DU SOIR

VOICI venir les temps où vibrant sur sa tige
Chaque fleur s'évapore ainsi qu'un encensoir;
Les sons et les parfums tournent dans l'air du soir;
Valse mélancolique et langoureux vertige!

Chaque fleur s'évapore ainsi qu'un encensoir;
Le violon frémit comme un cœur qu'on afflige;
Valse mélancolique et langoureux vertige!
Le ciel est triste et beau comme un grand reposoir.

Le violon frémit comme un cœur qu'on afflige,
Un cœur tendre, qui hait le néant vaste et noir!
Le ciel est triste et beau comme un grand reposoir;
Le soleil s'est noyé dans son sang qui se fige.

Un cœur tendre qui hait le néant vaste et noir,
Du passé lumineux recueille tout vestige!
Le soleil s'est noyé dans son sang qui se fige ...
Ton souvenir en moi luit comme un ostensoir!

Evening Harmony

NOW the days are coming when, throbbing on its stalk, each flower sheds its perfume like a censer; the sounds and perfumes spiral in the evening air, in a melancholy waltz, a slow, sensual gyre.

Each flower sheds its perfume like a censer; the violin trembles like a wounded heart, in a melancholy waltz, a slow, sensual gyre; the sky is sad and beautiful, like a vast altar.

The violin trembles like a wounded heart, a tender heart that hates the huge, black void; the sky is sad and beautiful like a vast altar; the sun has drowned in its congealing blood.

A tender heart that hates the huge, black void, is gathering to itself all traces of the luminous past; the Sun has drowned in its congealing blood, and like a monstrance your memory shines in me.

[Published April 1857 and in *Les Fleurs du mal*, 1857]

TOUT ENTIÈRE

LE Démon, dans ma chambre haute,
Ce matin est venu me voir,
Et, tâchant à me prendre en faute,
Me dit: «Je voudrais bien savoir,

«Parmi toutes les belles choses
Dont est fait son enchantement,
Parmi les objets noirs ou roses
Qui composent son corps charmant,

«Quel est le plus doux.» – Ô mon âme!
Tu répondis à l'Abhorré:
«Puisqu'en Elle tout est dictame,
Rien ne peut être préféré.

«Lorsque tout me ravit, j'ignore
Si quelque chose me séduit.
Elle éblouit comme l'Aurore
Et console comme la Nuit;

Entire

SATAN visited me this morning in my high attic, and said, in an effort to trick me: 'It would please me to know which is the loveliest of all the beautiful things that compose her magic, which is the loveliest of all those black or rosy features that make her charming person?'

And you, my soul, answered the hateful spirit: 'Since all her being is my solace, there is nothing to be preferred. When all delights me, I am not even aware whether one thing entrances me more than another. She dazzles me, like Dawn, and comforts me, like Night;

«Et l'harmonie est trop exquise,
Qui gouverne tout son beau corps,
Pour que l'impuissante analyse
En note les nombreux accords.

«Ô métamorphose mystique
De tous mes sens fondus en un!
Son haleine fait la musique,
Comme sa voix fait le parfum!»

LE FLACON

Il est de forts parfums pour qui toute matière
Est poreuse. On dirait qu'ils pénètrent le verre.
En ouvrant un coffret venu de l'Orient
Dont la serrure grince et rechigne en criant,

Ou dans une maison déserte quelque armoire
Pleine de l'âcre odeur des temps, poudreuse et noire,
Parfois on trouve un vieux flacon qui se souvient,
D'où jaillit toute vive une âme qui revient.

and the unison that governs all her beautiful form is too exquisite for sterile analysis to detail its countless harmonies.'

– O mystic transformation, whereby all my senses are fused into one: her breath is music, her voice is perfume.

[Published April 1857 and in *Les Fleurs du mal*, 1857]

The Scent-bottle

There are strong perfumes for which all matter is porous. They seem to penetrate through glass. Opening a casket from the East, with its lock grating, protesting, crying out; or in some empty house, when you open a wardrobe redolent of the acrid smell of the years, all dusty and dark, perhaps you will find an old scent-bottle which remembers everything, and from which a returning soul springs fully alive.

Mille pensers dormaient, chrysalides funèbres,
Frémissant doucement dans les lourdes ténèbres,
Qui dégagent leur aile et prennent leur essor,
Teintés d'azur, glacés de rose, lamés d'or.

Voilà le souvenir enivrant qui voltige
Dans l'air troublé; les yeux se ferment; le Vertige
Saisit l'âme vaincue et la pousse à deux mains
Vers un gouffre obscurci de miasmes humains;

Il la terrasse au bord d'un gouffre séculaire,
Où, Lazare odorant déchirant son suaire,
Se meut dans son réveil le cadavre spectral
D'un vieil amour ranci, charmant et sépulcral.

Ainsi, quand je serai perdu dans la mémoire
Des hommes, dans le coin d'une sinistre armoire
Quand on m'aura jeté, vieux flacon désolé,
Décrépit, poudreux, sale, abject, visqueux, fêlé,

A thousand thoughts lay slumbering there, chrysalids of death gently rustling in the thick shadows, but which now unfold their wings and take flight once more, tinged with azure and glazed with rosy hues, and spangled with gold.

And so memory spirals entrancing on the troubled air; your eyes close and the gyre grips the vanquished soul, thrusting it with both hands down to the Pit that is darkened with the foul vapours of mortal decay, striking down the soul on the very brim of the ancient pit, where like a stinking Lazarus rending his shroud, the spectral corpse of an old, rancid love, full of charm and death, writhes into wakefulness.

Thus, when I no longer live in the memories of men, when I am cast aside in the corner of some sinister cupboard like an old, neglected scent-bottle, decrepit and covered with dust, foul and

Je serai ton cercueil, aimable pestilence!
Le témoin de ta force et de ta virulence,
Cher poison préparé par les anges! liqueur
Qui me ronge, ô la vie et la mort de mon cœur!

SEMPER EADEM

«D'où vous vient, disiez-vous, cette tristesse étrange,
Montant comme la mer sur le roc noir et nu?»
– Quand notre cœur a fait une fois sa vendange,
Vivre est un mal. C'est un secret de tous connu,

Une douleur très-simple et non mystérieuse,
Et, comme votre joie, éclatante pour tous.
Cessez donc de chercher, ô belle curieuse!
Et, bien que votre voix soit douce, taisez-vous!

abject, slimy and cracked – then I shall be your coffin, attractive plague, proof of your strength and virulence, O poison brewed by angels, corroding ichor, O life and death of my heart!

[Published April 1857 and in *Les Fleurs du mal*, 1857]

Always the Same

'WHENCE comes', you asked, 'this strange sadness of yours, that wells like the sea over a bare, black rock?' – When once our heart has reaped its harvest and all the grapes are plucked, life is an evil. This is a secret known to all, the simplest of sorrows, by no means mysterious, and, like your joy, impossible to conceal. Ask no more questions, then, O inquisitive beauty, and though your voice be gentle, hold your tongue!

Taisez-vous, ignorante! âme toujours ravie!
Bouche au rire enfantin! Plus encor que la Vie,
La Mort nous tient souvent par des liens subtils.

Laissez, laissez mon cœur s'enivrer d'un *mensonge*,
Plonger dans vos beaux yeux comme dans un beau songe
Et sommeiller longtemps à l'ombre de vos cils!

Be quiet, ignorant woman, forever delighted soul, silence the childish laughter bubbling on your lips; for even more than Life itself, Death grapples us by many a subtle bond.

Leave, then, my heart to drink deep of a lie, to lose itself in your lovely eyes as in a perfect dream, to sleep without end in your eyelashes' shade.

[Published 1860, and in *Les Fleurs du mal*, 1861. This poem is a link between the Jeanne Duval and Sabatier cycles (Crépet et Blin) though Le Dantec would attribute it to Marie Daubrun. In spite of its position in *Les Fleurs du mal* at the head of the Sabatier cycle, my view is that it was composed after all these 'cycles' were completed: it comments on all the women concerned, but particularly on the aggressive curiosity of Mme Sabatier.]

VI

Poems

1852-7

L'HOMME ET LA MER

HOMME libre, toujours tu chériras la mer!
La mer est ton miroir; tu contemples ton âme
Dans le déroulement infini da sa lame,
Et ton esprit n'est pas un gouffre moins amer.

Tu te plais à plonger au sein de ton image;
Tu l'embrasses des yeux et des bras, et ton cœur
Se distrait quelquefois de sa propre rumeur
Au bruit de cette plainte indomptable et sauvage.

Vous êtes tous les deux ténébreux et discrets:
Homme, nul n'a sondé le fond de tes abîmes,
Ô mer, nul ne connaît tes richesses intimes,
Tant vous êtes jaloux de garder vos secrets!

Man and the Sea

O MAN, so long as you are free you will cherish the sea! The sea is your looking-glass; you contemplate your own soul in the infinite unfolding of its waves, while your mind is a no less bitter gulf.

You love to plunge into the depths of your own image; you clasp it into your eyes and arms; sometimes your heart forgets its own muffled throbbing, at the sound of that unconquerable and wild lament.

Both of you are brooding and secretive: none has ever plumbed the depths of your chasms, O Man; while no man knows what intimate riches you contain, O Sea, so jealously you guard your secrets.

Et cependant voilà des siècles innombrables
Que vous vous combattez sans pitié ni remord,
Tellement vous aimez le carnage et la mort,
Ô lutteurs éternels, ô frères implacables!

LE JET D'EAU

TES beaux yeux sont las, pauvre amante!
Reste longtemps, sans les rouvrir,
Dans cette pose nonchalante
Où t'a surprise le plaisir.
Dans la cour le jet d'eau qui jase
Et ne se tait ni nuit ni jour,
Entretient doucement l'extase
Où ce soir m'a plongé l'amour.

La gerbe épanouie
En mille fleurs,
Où Phœbé réjouie
Met ses couleurs,
Tombe comme une pluie
De larges pleurs.

And yet you have warred against each other for untold centuries, with neither mercy nor remorse, such is your love of slaughter and death, O eternal wrestlers, O implacable brothers!

[Published 1852]

The Fountain

YOUR beautiful eyes are weary, poor darling! Bide a while, without opening them, in that pose in which pleasure surprised you. In the courtyard the prattling fountain which is never quiet day or night, softly accompanies the ecstasy into which love has plunged me this evening.

The sheaf opening in a thousand flowers, in which gladdened Phoebe sets her colours, is falling like a shower of great tears.

Ainsi ton âme qu'incendie
L'éclair brûlant des voluptés
S'élance, rapide et hardie,
Vers les vastes cieux enchantés.
Puis, elle s'épanche, mourante,
En un flot de triste langueur,
Qui par une invisible pente
Descend jusqu'au fond de mon cœur.

La gerbe épanouie
En mille fleurs,
Où Phœbé réjouie
Met ses couleurs,
Tombe comme une pluie
De larges pleurs.

Ô toi, que la nuit rend si belle,
Qu'il m'est doux, penché vers tes seins,
D'écouter la plainte éternelle
Qui sanglote dans les bassins!
Lune, eau sonore, nuit bénie,
Arbres qui frissonnez autour,
Votre pure mélancolie
Est le miroir de mon amour.

Thus your soul fired by the searing flash of sensual pleasures, springs swift and bold towards the vast enchanted skies. Then it brims over, dying, in a wave of sad languor which, down some invisible slope, descends into the depths of my heart.

The sheaf opening in a thousand flowers, in which gladdened Phoebe sets her colours, is falling like a shower of great tears.

O you whom night so beautifies: how I love, as I bend towards your breasts, listening to the eternal lament that sobs in the founts. O Moon, O mellifluous waters, blest Night and trees that tremble all around, your pure melancholy is the mirror of my love.

La gerbe épanouie
En mille fleurs,
Où Phœbé réjouie
Met ses couleurs,
Tombe comme une pluie
De larges pleurs.

AU LECTEUR

LA sottise, l'erreur, le péché, la lésine,
Occupent nos esprits et travaillent nos corps,
Et nous alimentons nos aimables remords,
Comme les mendiants nourrissent leur vermine.

Nos péchés sont têtus, nos repentirs sont lâches;
Nous nous faisons payer grassement nos aveux,
Et nous rentrons gaîment dans le chemin bourbeux,
Croyant par de vils pleurs laver toutes nos taches.

Sur l'oreiller du mal c'est Satan Trismégiste
Qui berce longuement notre esprit enchanté,
Et le riche métal de notre volonté
Est tout vaporisé par ce savant chimiste.

The sheaf opening in a thousand flowers, in which gladdened Phoebe sets her colours, is falling like a shower of great tears.

[Pre-1853 (Crépet). Published 1865]

To the Reader

STUPIDITY, error, sin, and meanness possess our minds and work on our bodies, and we feed our fond remorses as beggars suckle their own lice.

Our sins are stubborn, our repentance cowardly. We make sure that our confessions are well rewarded; gaily we return down the slimy path, as if our paltry tears could wash the dirt from our souls.

Satan Trismegistes soothes our bewitched minds on the pillow of evil, and this expert alchemist dissolves our will's precious metal into vapour.

C'est le Diable qui tient les fils qui nous remuent!
Aux objets répugnants nous trouvons des appas;
Chaque jour vers l'Enfer nous descendons d'un pas,
Sans horreur, à travers des ténèbres qui puent.

Ainsi qu'un débauché pauvre qui baise et mange
Le sein martyrisé d'une antique catin,
Nous volons au passage un plaisir clandestin
Que nous pressons bien fort comme une vieille orange.

Serré, fourmillant, comme un million d'helminthes,
Dans nos cerveaux ribote un peuple de Démons,
Et, quand nous respirons, la Mort dans nos poumons
Descend, fleuve invisible, avec de sourdes plaintes.

Si le viol, le poison, le poignard, l'incendie,
N'ont pas encor brodé de leurs plaisants dessins
Le canevas banal de nos piteux destins,
C'est que notre âme, hélas! n'est pas assez hardie.

Mais parmi les chacals, les panthères, les lices,
Les singes, les scorpions, les vautours, les serpents,
Les monstres glapissants, hurlants, grognants, rampants,
Dans la ménagerie infâme de nos vices,

It's the Devil who pulls the strings that make us dance: we take delight in loathsome things; each day we take a further step to Hell, yet feel no horror as we descend through stinking gloom.

Like a penniless lecher kissing and nibbling an old strumpet's tortured breast, we thieve our furtive pleasure as we pass on, squeezing it to the last drop like a wizened orange.

A dense, seething host of Demons, like a million helminths, orgies in our brains; even as we breathe the invisible stream of Death flows down into our lungs, yet we hear not its groans.

If rape, poison, dagger, and fire have not yet woven all their ridiculous pattern on the dull canvas of our lamentable destinies, that is only, alas, because our souls lack daring.

But among the jackals, panthers, bitch-hounds, monkeys, scorpions, vultures, snakes, and monsters that scream and howl and grunt and crawl in the sordid menagerie of our vices,

Il en est un plus laid, plus méchant, plus immonde!
Quoiqu'il ne pousse ni grands gestes ni grands cris,
Il ferait volontiers de la terre un débris
Et dans un bâillement avalerait le monde;

C'est l'Ennui! – l'œil chargé d'un pleur involontaire,
Il rêve d'échafauds en fumant son houka.
Tu le connais, lecteur, ce monstre délicat,
– Hypocrite lecteur, – mon semblable, – mon frère!

L'IRRÉMÉDIABLE

I

UNE Idée, une Forme, un Être
Parti de l'azur et tombé
Dans un Styx bourbeux et plombé
Où nul œil du Ciel ne pénètre;

there is one even uglier and more wicked and filthier than all the rest! Although it makes no frenzied gestures and utters no savage cries, yet it would fain reduce the earth to ruin, it would gladly swallow the world in one gaping yawn:

it is Boredom, *Tedium vitae*, who with an unwilling tear in his eye dreams of gibbets as he smokes his pipe. You know him, Reader, you know that fastidious monster – O hypocritical Reader, my fellow-man and brother!

[Published 1855, and in *Les Fleurs du mal*, 1857]

The Irremediable

I

AN Idea, a Form, a Being, lapsed from the azure and fallen into the slough of a leaden Styx into which no eye of Heaven can penetrate;

Un Ange, imprudent voyageur
Qu'a tenté l'amour du difforme,
Au fond d'un cauchemar énorme
Se débattant comme un nageur,

Et luttant, angoisses funèbres!
Contre un gigantesque remous
Qui va chantant comme les fous
Et pirouettant dans les ténèbres;

Un malheureux ensorcelé
Dans ses tâtonnements futiles,
Pour fuir d'un lieu plein de reptiles,
Cherchant la lumière et la clé;

Un damné descendant sans lampe,
Au bord d'un gouffre dont l'odeur
Trahit l'humide profondeur,
D'éternels escaliers sans rampe,

Où veillent des monstres visqueux
Dont les larges yeux de phosphore
Font une nuit plus noire encore
Et ne rendent visibles qu'eux:

an Angel, unwary traveller, tempted by the love of ugliness, lashing out like a swimmer in the depths of a huge nightmare, and struggling – O heartrending anguishes – against a gigantic undertow which goes singing like a horde of madmen and pirouetting in the gloom;

an unfortunate man, bewitched in his futile gropings, seeking the light and the key to escape from a hole full of reptiles;

a damned man, going lampless down the brink of a pit whose stench hints at its watery depths, descending endless, banisterless stairs where slimy monsters glare with great phosphorescent eyes that deepen the darkness of the night and make nought but themselves visible;

Un navire pris dans le pôle,
Comme en un piège de cristal,
Cherchant par quel détroit fatal
Il est tombé dans cette geôle;

– Emblèmes nets, tableau parfait
D'une fortune irrémédiable,
Qui donne à penser que le Diable
Fait toujours bien tout ce qu'il fait!

II

Tête-à-tête sombre et limpide
Qu'un cœur devenu son miroir!
Puits de Vérité, clair et noir,
Où tremble une étoile livide,

Un phare ironique, infernal,
Flambeau des grâces sataniques,
Soulagement et gloires uniques,
– La conscience dans le Mal!

a ship seized as in a crystal trap at the Pole, seeking by what fatal passage it landed in that prison;

[All these are] plain emblems, a perfect picture of an unchangeable fate, which make you reflect that the Devil makes a thorough job of all he does!

II

What a sombre, lucid exchange [there is, in] a heart become its own mirror – a well of truth, clear though black, wherein trembles a livid star, an ironic, infernal beacon, a torch of satanic graces, [man's] sole relief and glory – consciousness in Evil.

[1855? A poem to be compared with *L'Héautontimorouménos* of that year. Published 10 May 1857, and in *Les Fleurs du mal*, 1857]

L'HÉAUTONTIMOROUMÉNOS

À J. G. F.

JE te frapperai sans colère
Et sans haine, comme un boucher,
Comme Moïse le rocher!
Et je ferai de ta paupière,

Pour abreuver mon Saharah,
Jaillir les eaux de la souffrance.
Mon désir gonflé d'espérance
Sur tes pleurs salés nagera

Comme un vaisseau qui prend le large,
Et dans mon cœur qu'ils soûleront
Tes chers sanglots retentiront
Comme un tambour qui bat la charge!

Ne suis-je pas un faux accord
Dans la divine symphonie,
Grâce à la vorace Ironie
Qui me secoue et qui me mord?

Elle est dans ma voix, la criarde!
C'est tout mon sang, ce poison noir!
Je suis le sinistre miroir
Où la mégère se regarde.

Heautontimoroumenos

I SHALL strike you without anger and without hate, like a butcher, as Moses struck the rock, and from your eyelids, to slake my Sahara's thirst, I shall make the waters of suffering gush forth. My desire, big with hope, will swim in your salt tears like a ship setting out to sea; while in my heart, elated by your weeping, your beloved sobs will reverberate like a drum sounding the attack.

Am I not a dissonant chord in the divine symphony, thanks to the insatiable irony that mauls and savages me? That spitfire is in my voice, all my blood has turned into her black poison; I am the sinister glass in which the shrew beholds herself.

Je suis la plaie et le couteau!
Je suis le soufflet et la joue!
Je suis les membres et la roue,
Et la victime et le bourreau!

Je suis de mon cœur le vampire,
– Un de ces grands abandonnés
Au rire éternel condamnés,
Et qui ne peuvent plus sourire!

LES PHARES

RUBENS, fleuve d'oubli, jardin de la paresse,
Oreiller de chair fraîche où l'on ne peut aimer,
Mais où la vie afflue et s'agite sans cesse,
Comme l'air dans le ciel et la mer dans la mer;

Léonard de Vinci, miroir profond et sombre,
Où des anges charmants, avec un doux souris
Tout chargé de mystère, apparaissent à l'ombre
Des glaciers et des pins qui ferment leur pays;

I am both the wound and the knife, both the blow and the cheek, the limbs and the rack, the victim and the torturer. I am my own heart's vampire, one of the thoroughly abandoned, condemned to eternal laughter, but who can never smile again.

[1855? Published 1857]

The Beacons

RUBENS, river of oblivion, garden of idleness, pillow of cool human flesh whereon we cannot love, but where life endlessly flows and heaves, like the air into the sky, and the sea within the sea;

Leonardo da Vinci, fathomless dark glass in which exquisite angels, their gentle smile all fraught with mystery, surge in the shadow of the glaciers and pines that mark the frontiers of their domain;

Rembrandt, triste hôpital tout rempli de murmures,
Et d'un grand crucifix décoré seulement,
Où la prière en pleurs s'exhale des ordures,
Et d'un rayon d'hiver traversé brusquement;

Michel-Ange, lieu vague où l'on voit des Hercules
Se mêler à des Christs, et se lever tout droits
Des fantômes puissants qui dans les crépuscules
Déchirent leur suaire en étirant leurs doigts;

Colères de boxeur, impudences de faune,
Toi qui sus ramasser la beauté des goujats,
Grand cœur gonflé d'orgueil, homme débile et jaune,
Puget, mélancolique empereur des forçats;

Watteau, ce carnaval où bien des cœurs illustres,
Comme des papillons, errent en flamboyant,
Décors frais et légers éclairés par des lustres
Qui versent la folie à ce bal tournoyant;

Rembrandt, drab hospital echoing whispered woes, furnished with nought but a vast crucifix, where a weeping prayer sighs out of the filth, and suddenly pierced by a winter sun;

Michelangelo, no-man's-land where one sees Hercules and Christs together, and, rising stark upright, powerful phantoms who, in the twilight, rend their winding-sheets and stretch their fingers out;

Puget, with boxer's fury and faun's immodesty, who could exalt the beauty of the scum of the earth, that great heart swollen with pride, that sickly, jaundiced man, Puget, dour emperor of jailbirds;

Watteau, that carnival in which so many illustrious hearts wander incandescent, like butterflies, in cool, frivolous settings, with chandeliers pouring the garish light of madness on the swirling dance;

Goya, cauchemar plein de choses inconnues,
De fœtus qu'on fait cuire au milieu des sabbats,
De vieilles au miroir et d'enfants toutes nues,
Pour tenter les démons ajustant bien leurs bas;

Delacroix, lac de sang hanté des mauvais anges,
Ombragé par un bois de sapins toujours vert,
Où, sous un ciel chagrin, des fanfares étranges
Passent, comme un soupir étouffé de Weber;

Ces malédictions, ces blasphèmes, ces plaintes,
Ces extases, ces cris, ces pleurs, ces *Te Deum*,
Sont un écho redit par mille labyrinthes;
C'est pour les cœurs mortels un divin opium!

C'est un cri répété par mille sentinelles,
Un ordre renvoyé par mille porte-voix;
C'est un phare allumé sur mille citadelles,
Un appel de chasseurs perdus dans les grands bois!

Goya, that nightmare full of the unknown, foetuses roasted at witches' sabbaths, old hags peering in their looking-glasses, immature girls naked but for their stockings which they stretch neat to tempt hell's demons;

Delacroix, that lake of blood haunted by fallen angels, with a dark fringe of fir-trees, evergreen, where under a glowering sky strange fanfares can be heard, like Weber's muted sigh;

– These curses, blasphemies, lamentations, ecstasies, cries and tears and Te Deums echo down a thousand labyrinths, a divine opium for the hearts of men!

Theirs is a cry repeated by a thousand sentinels, an order passed on by a thousand messengers, a beacon lit upon a thousand citadels, the call of the huntsmen lost in the wide woods;

Car c'est vraiment, Seigneur, le meilleur témoignage
Que nous puissions donner de notre dignité
Que cet ardent sanglot qui roule d'âge en âge
Et vient mourir au bord de votre éternité!

L'ENNEMI

MA jeunesse ne fut qu'un ténébreux orage,
Traversé ça et là par de brillants soleils;
Le tonnerre et la pluie ont fait un tel ravage,
Qu'il reste en mon jardin bien peu de fruits vermeils.

Voilà que j'ai touché l'automne des idées,
Et qu'il faut employer la pelle et les râteaux
Pour rassembler à neuf les terres inondées,
Où l'on creuse des trous grands comme des tombeaux.

Et qui sait si les fleurs nouvelles que je rêve
Trouveront dans ce sol lavé comme une grève
Le mystique aliment qui ferait leur vigueur?

For truly, Lord, this is the best witness we can give of our human dignity, this impassioned keening which endures down the ages, and which shall die only on thine eternal shore!

[1855? Quoted in the 'Exposition Universelle de 1855' Published in *Les Fleurs du mal*, 1857]

The Enemy

MY youth was but a glowering storm, pierced here and there by brilliant sunshines; thunder and rain have so ravaged my garden that very few rosy fruits survive.

Now I have reached the autumn of the mind, and now must toil with spade and rake to reclaim the flooded land where pits are being digged as deep as graves.

And who can tell, whether the new flowers of which I dream will ever find, in this soil as thoroughly washed as the sea-shore, the mystic manna that will bring them strength?

– Ô douleur! ô douleur! Le Temps mange la vie,
Et l'obscur Ennemi qui nous ronge le cœur
Du sang que nous perdons croît et se fortifie!

LA VIE ANTÉRIEURE

J'AI longtemps habité sous de vastes portiques
Que les soleils marins teignaient de mille feux,
Et que leurs grands piliers, droits et majestueux,
Rendaient pareils, le soir, aux grottes basaltiques.

Les houles, en roulant les images des cieux,
Mêlaient d'une façon solennelle et mystique
Les tout-puissants accords de leur riche musique
Aux couleurs du couchant reflété par mes yeux.

C'est là que j'ai vécu dans les voluptés calmes,
Au milieu de l'azur, des vagues, des splendeurs
Et des esclaves nus, tout imprégnés d'odeurs,

Qui me rafraîchissaient le front avec des palmes,
Et dont l'unique soin était d'approfondir
Le secret douloureux qui me faisait languir.

O sorrow, O sorrow! Time eats away all life: the unseen enemy who gnaws our hearts waxes and thrives on our wasted blood!

[Published 1855]

The Previous Life

LONG was my home among vast porticoes, which the suns of the sea tinged with a thousand fires, and whose great columns, straight and majestic, at evening made them look like basalt caves.

The sea-swell, heaving images of the skies, solemnly and mystically interwove the overwhelming harmonies of their rich music with the hues of sunset mirrored in my eyes.

And there I lived in calm voluptuousness, surrounded by the azure, the waves and splendours and naked perfume-laden slaves who refreshed my brow with [waving] palms, and whose only care was to make deep the secret grief wherefore I pined.

[Published 1855]

BÉNÉDICTION

LORSQUE, par un décret des puissances suprêmes,
Le Poëte apparaît en ce monde ennuyé,
Sa mère épouvantée et pleine de blasphèmes
Crispe ses poings vers Dieu, qui la prend en pitié:

– «Ah! que n'ai-je mis bas tout un nœud de vipères,
Plutôt que de nourrir cette dérision!
Maudite soit la nuit aux plaisirs éphémères
Où mon ventre a conçu mon expiation!

«Puisque tu m'as choisie entre toutes les femmes
Pour être le dégoût de mon triste mari,
Et que je ne puis pas rejeter dans les flammes,
Comme un billet d'amour, ce monstre rabougri,

«Je ferai rejaillir ta haine qui m'accable
Sur l'instrument maudit de tes méchancetés,
Et je tordrai si bien cet arbre misérable,
Qu'il ne pourra pousser ses boutons empestés!»

The Blessing

WHEN, by decree of the supreme Powers the poet enters this weary world, his horrified mother, full of blasphemies, clenches her fists against God, who takes pity on her:

'Ah,' she cries, 'I would rather have spawned a clutch of snakes than give suck to this mockery! Cursed be the night and all its short-lived pleasures, when my womb conceived this, my atonement!

'Since you have chosen me of all women, for my sad husband's loathing, and since I cannot cast this stunted freak like a love-letter into the flames,

'I shall pass the hatred you have heaped upon me, on to this cursed instrument of your spite; so thoroughly will I twist this miserable tree that he'll never put forth his evil-smelling buds!'

Elle ravale ainsi l'écume de sa haine,
Et, ne comprenant pas les desseins éternels,
Elle-même prépare au fond de la Géhenne
Les bûchers consacrés aux crimes maternels.

Pourtant, sous la tutelle invisible d'un Ange,
L'Enfant déshérité s'enivre de soleil,
Et dans tout ce qu'il boit et dans tout ce qu'il mange
Retrouve l'ambroisie et le nectar vermeil.

Il joue avec le vent, cause avec le nuage,
Et s'enivre en chantant du chemin de la croix;
Et l'Esprit qui le suit dans son pèlerinage
Pleure de le voir gai comme un oiseau des bois.

Tous ceux qu'il veut aimer l'observent avec crainte,
Ou bien, s'enhardissant de sa tranquillité,
Cherchent à qui saura lui tirer une plainte,
Et font sur lui l'essai de leur férocité.

Dans le pain et le vin destinés à sa bouche
Ils mêlent de la cendre avec d'impurs crachats;

Thus she swallows her foaming hatred, and, without the slightest understanding of eternal designs, she herself prepares those pyres in the depths of Gehenna, which await the crimes of motherhood.

And yet, under the unseen guidance of an Angel, the disinherited child drinks deep of the inebriating sun, discovering ambrosia and ruby nectar in all his food and drink.

He plays with the wind and prattles with the clouds; with rapture he sings the way of the Cross, while the Spirit who follows him on his pilgrimage weeps to see him happy as a woodland bird.

All those whom gladly he would love watch him with fear; or else, making bold of his calm bearing, vie with each other to draw a whine from him, abusing him with their cruelty.

They mix ash and filthy spit with the bread and wine destined for

Avec hypocrisie ils jettent ce qu'il touche,
Et s'accusent d'avoir mis leurs pieds dans ses pas.

Sa femme va criant sur les places publiques:
«Puisqu'il me trouve assez belle pour m'adorer,
Je ferai le métier des idoles antiques,
Et comme elles je veux me faire redorer;

«Et je me soûlerai de nard, d'encens, de myrrhe,
De génuflexions, de viandes et de vins,
Pour savoir si je puis dans un cœur qui m'admire
Usurper en riant les hommages divins!

«Et, quand je m'ennuierai de ces farces impies,
Je poserai sur lui ma frêle et forte main;
Et mes ongles, pareils aux ongles des harpies,
Sauront jusqu'à son cœur se frayer un chemin.

«Comme un tout jeune oiseau qui tremble et qui palpite,
J'arracherai ce cœur tout rouge de son sein,
Et, pour rassasier ma bête favorite,
Je le lui jetterai par terre avec dédain!»

his lips; hypocritically they cast down what his hands have touched; they falsely blame themselves for following where he led.

His wife goes out and cries in public places: 'Since he finds me beautiful enough to adore, I shall follow the trade of those idols of olden days, and, like them, have myself covered with leaf of gold:

'I will make myself drunk with nard, with incense and myrrh, with the bowing of knees before me, with flesh, and with wines, to find whether I can mockingly usurp the homage due to God alone, in whatever heart shall worship me:

'And when I tire of all these impious mockeries, I will lay my delicate but powerful hand upon him, and my nails, my harpy-like nails, will surely claw their way into his very heart;

'Yes, like a little bird that trembles and throbs I will tear the red heart out of his breast and throw it scornfully into the dust, to gorge my favourite beast!'

Vers le Ciel, où son œil voit un trône splendide,
Le Poëte serein lève ses bras pieux,
Et les vastes éclairs de son esprit lucide
Lui dérobent l'aspect des peuples furieux:

– «Soyez béni, mon Dieu, qui donnez la souffrance
Comme un divin remède à nos impuretés
Et comme la meilleure et la plus pure essence
Qui prépare les forts aux saintes voluptés!

«Je sais que vous gardez une place au Poëte
Dans les rangs bienheureux des saintes Légions,
Et que vous l'invitez à l'éternelle fête
Des Trônes, des Vertus, des Dominations.

«Je sais que la douleur est la noblesse unique
Où ne mordront jamais la terre et les enfers,
Et qu'il faut pour tresser ma couronne mystique
Imposer tous les temps et tous les univers.

«Mais les bijoux perdus de l'antique Palmyre,
Les métaux inconnus, les perles de la mer,

But towards heaven, where his gaze beholds a splendid throne, the serene Poet raises his pious arms, and the great lightning-flashes of his lucid mind shut out the sight of the frenzied hordes of mankind:

'Be blessed, O God,' he cries, 'who offer suffering as a divine balm for our impurities, suffering which is the best and purest essence for preparing the strong for those joys that only saints may know:

'I know that you set aside a place for the Poet in the happy ranks of the Holy Legions, and that you will invite him to share in the eternal feast of the Thrones, the Virtues, and the Dominations:

'I know that sorrow is the one nobility on which neither earth nor hell can lay its fangs, and that all ages and universes must be taxed for the tressing of my mystic crown:

'But the vanished jewels of ancient Palmyra, and metals as yet unknown to man, and all the pearls of the seas, even were they set

Par votre main montés, ne pourraient pas suffire
À ce beau diadème éblouissant et clair;

«Car il ne sera fait que de pure lumière,
Puisée au foyer saint des rayons primitifs,
Et dont les yeux mortels, dans leur splendeur entière,
Ne sont que des miroirs obscurcis et plaintifs!»

BRUMES ET PLUIES

Ô FINS d'automne, hivers, printemps trempés de boue,
Endormeuses saisons! je vous aime et vous loue
D'envelopper ainsi mon cœur et mon cerveau
D'un linceul vaporeux et d'un vague tombeau.

Dans cette grande plaine où l'autan froid se joue,
Où par les longues nuits la girouette s'enroue,
Mon âme mieux qu'au temps du tiède renouveau
Ouvrira largement ses ailes de corbeau.

Rien n'est plus doux au cœur plein de choses funèbres,
Et sur qui dès longtemps descendent les frimas,
Ô blafardes saisons, reines de nos climats,

together by your hand, would never be enough to complete this fair diadem, so dazzling, so bright:

'For it will be made of nought but pure Light drawn from the sacred source of the Sun's first rays, of which mortal eyes, even in all their splendour, are but dimmed and mournful mirrors.'

[Published in *Les Fleurs du mal*, 1857]

Mists and Rains

O LATE Autumns, Winters, Spring seasons steeped in mud, O drowsy seasons I love you and praise you for thus enfolding my heart and brain in a misty shroud, a cloudy tomb. In this great plain where the cold south wind plays, where through the long nights the weather-cock shrieks himself hoarse, my soul, far better than in the days of warm renewal, will stretch wide its raven's wings.

Nothing is dearer to my heart, full of gloomy things, and on which the hoar-frosts long ago began to fall, O sallow seasons,

Que l'aspect permanent de vos pâles ténèbres,
– Si ce n'est, par un soir sans lune, deux à deux,
D'endormir la douleur sur un lit hasardeux.

LE VIN DES AMANTS

AUJOURD'HUI l'espace est splendide!
Sans mors, sans éperons, sans bride,
Partons à cheval sur le vin
Pour un ciel féerique et divin!

Comme deux anges que torture
Une implacable calenture,
Dans le bleu cristal du matin
Suivons le mirage lointain!

Mollement balancés sur l'aile
Du tourbillon intelligent,
Dans un délire parallèle,

Ma sœur, côte à côte nageant,
Nous fuirons sans repos ni trêves
Vers le paradis de mes rêves!

queens of our climes, than the changeless aspect of your pale shadows – unless it be, on a moonless night, two by two, to lay our suffering to sleep on a perilous bed.

[This very irregular sonnet (couplets in first eight lines) was first published in *Les Fleurs du mal*, 1857]

Lovers' Wine

HOW splendid Space is today! Without bit or spurs or bridle, let us mount this wine like a horse, and ride away to a divine and faery heaven! Like two angels goaded by merciless sea-fever, let us pursue our distant mirage into the blue crystal of the morning.

Gently swaying on the wing of the wise whirlwind, in parallel desire, my sister, swimming side by side, we shall take flight, taking neither rest nor respite, towards the paradise of my dreams!

[Published in *Les Fleurs du mal*, 1857]

LE VIN DU SOLITAIRE

Le regard singulier d'une femme galante
Qui se glisse vers nous comme le rayon blanc
Que la lune onduleuse envoie au lac tremblant,
Quand elle y veut baigner sa beauté nonchalante;

Le dernier sac d'écus dans les doigts d'un joueur;
Un baiser libertin de la maigre Adeline;
Les sons d'une musique énervante et câline,
Semblable au cri lointain de l'humaine douleur,

Tout cela ne vaut pas, ô bouteille profonde,
Les baumes pénétrants que ta panse féconde
Garde au cœur altéré du poëte pieux;

Tu lui verses l'espoir, la jeunesse et la vie,
– Et l'orgueil, ce trésor de toute gueuserie,
Qui nous rend triomphants et semblables aux Dieux!

The Lonely Man's Wine

The uncommon look in the eyes of a woman bent on pleasure, as she glides towards you, like the white beam which the snaking Moon casts on the quivering lake where she would bathe her unblushing beauty; the last bag of sovereigns in the gambler's hand; a salty kiss from narrow Adeline; the notes of a disturbing, caressing piece of music like some distant cry of human pain: none of these things, O profound bottle, can equal the pungent balms that your bountiful belly reserves for the pious poet's thirsting heart. For him you pour out hope, youth, life – and pride, the treasure of the most poor, which fills us with triumph and sets us beside the gods.

[Published in *Les Fleurs du mal*, 1857]

LA PIPE

JE suis la pipe d'un auteur.
On voit, à contempler ma mine
D'Abyssinienne ou de Cafrine,
Que mon maître est un grand fumeur.

Quand il est comblé de douleur,
Je fume comme la chaumine
Où se prépare la cuisine
Pour le retour du laboureur.

J'enlace et je berce son âme
Dans le réseau mobile et bleu
Qui monte de ma bouche en feu,

Et je roule un puissant dictame
Qui charme son cœur et guérit
De ses fatigues son esprit.

The Pipe

I AM an author's pipe. You can see, by a glance at my complexion, as jet as any Abyssinian or Kaffir woman's, that my master is a heavy smoker.

When he is overcome with grief, then I puff smoke like a cottage in which supper is being cooked for the ploughman, home from his toil.

I entwine and lull his soul in the hovering net of blue that floats up from my fiery mouth,

and I make rings of pungent balm which gladdens his heart and cures his mind of every strain.

[Published in *Les Fleurs du mal*, 1857. A poem described by Marcel Proust as a '*chef-d'œuvre*']

LE JEU

DANS des fauteuils fanés des courtisanes vieilles,
Pâles, le sourcil peint, l'œil câlin et fatal,
Minaudant, et faisant de leurs maigres oreilles
Tomber un cliquetis de pierre et de métal;

Autour des verts tapis des visages sans lèvre,
Des lèvres sans couleur, des mâchoires sans dent,
Et des doigts convulsés d'une infernale fièvre,
Fouillant la poche vide ou le sein palpitant;

Sous de sales plafonds un rang de pâles lustres
Et d'énormes quinquets projetant leurs lueurs
Sur des fronts ténébreux de poëtes illustres
Qui viennent gaspiller leurs sanglantes sueurs;

Voilà le noir tableau qu'en un rêve nocturne
Je vis se dérouler sous mon œil clairvoyant.
Moi-même, dans un coin de l'antre taciturne,
Je me vis accoudé, froid, muet, enviant,

Gambling

IN faded armchairs senile harlots, sallow, with painted eyebrows, come-hither, compelling eyes, simpering, making their skinny ears give out a rattle of metal and stone; round the green baize, lipless faces, bloodless lips, toothless jaws, fingers convulsed by a devilish fever, rummaging in an empty pocket or a heaving bosom; under filthy ceilings, a row of anaemic lustres and enormous hanging lamps casting their dingy gleams on the glowering brows of poets of renown, who have come to squander the sweat and blood of their genius:

– such is the sombre picture that in a dream, one night, I saw unfold before my seer's gaze. I saw myself in a corner of that silent

Enviant de ces gens la passion tenace,
De ces vieilles putains la funèbre gaîté,
Et tous gaillardement trafiquant à ma face,
L'un de son vieil honneur, l'autre de sa beauté!

Et mon cœur s'effraya d'envier maint pauvre homme
Courant avec ferveur à l'abîme béant,
Et qui, soûl de son sang, préférerait en somme
La douleur à la mort et l'enfer au néant!

SPLEEN

J'AI plus de souvenirs que si j'avais mille ans.

Un gros meuble à tiroirs encombré de bilans,
De vers, de billets doux, de procès, de romances,
Avec de lourds cheveux roulés dans des quittances,
Cache moins de secrets que mon triste cerveau.
C'est une pyramide, un immense caveau,
Qui contient plus de morts que la fosse commune.

den, myself leaning there on my elbows, cold, speechless, and envying, yes, *envying* those people's intense passion, the old bawds' dismal sprightliness, and all of them as they cheerfully sold, under my very nose, one, his long-established honour, the other, her beauty. And my heart brimmed with fear that I should envy many a poor man hastening so eagerly towards the gaping pit, who, drunk with his own blood, would really prefer pain to death, and Hell to nothingness.

[Published in *Les Fleurs du mal*, 1857]

Spleen

I HAVE more memories than if I had lived a thousand years.

Even a huge chest of drawers stuffed with accounts and verses, love-letters and law-suits, drawing-room ballads, and heavy plaits of hair rolled up in receipts, has less secrets to hide than has my unhappy brain. It is a pyramid, a vast burial-vault, fuller of dead than a charnel-house.

– Je suis un cimetière abhorré de la lune,
Où comme des remords se traînent de longs vers
Qui s'acharnent toujours sur mes morts les plus chers.
Je suis un vieux boudoir plein de roses fanées,
Où gît tout un fouillis de modes surannées,
Où les pastels plaintifs et les pâles Boucher,
Seuls, respirent l'odeur d'un flacon débouché.

Rien n'égale en longueur les boiteuses journées,
Quand sous les lourds flocons des neigeuses années,
L'ennui, fruit de la morne incuriosité,
Prend les proportions de l'immortalité.
– Désormais tu n'es plus, ô matière vivante!
Qu'un granit entouré d'une vague épouvante,
Assoupi dans le fond d'un Saharah brumeux;
Un vieux sphinx ignoré du monde insoucieux,
Oublié sur la carte, et dont l'humeur farouche
Ne chante qu'aux rayons du soleil qui se couche.

I am a graveyard abhorred by the Moon, in which long worms crawl like Remorses, always battening on those dead whom I hold most dear. I am a bygone boudoir full of faded roses, in which a medley of old-fashioned dresses lie scattered everywhere, with only the plaintive pastels and the pale Boucher canvases to breathe the fragrance of an uncorked scent-bottle.

Nothing could be as long-drawn-out as the limping days, when under the heavy flakes of the snowy years, boredom, the fruit of sullen indifference, takes on the proportions of immortality.

Henceforth, O living matter, you are but a granite form shrouded in vague horror, listlessly sunken in the depths of a misty Sahara; an old Sphinx unknown to the careless world, forgotten on the map, whose grim humour it is to sing only in the rays of the setting Sun.

[Published in *Les Fleurs du mal*, 1857. Crépet and Blin suggest that *matière vivante* refers to the poet's own being. A more satisfactory interpretation may be reached by reference to the sonnet *Correspondances*: in the state of 'spleen' the poet's lack of grace is such that the world suddenly refuses him its meanings; he is excommunicated.]

SPLEEN

JE suis comme le roi d'un pays pluvieux,
Riche, mais impuissant, jeune et pourtant très-vieux,
Qui, de ses précepteurs méprisant les courbettes,
S'ennuie avec ses chiens comme avec d'autres bêtes.
Rien ne peut l'égayer, ni gibier, ni faucon,
Ni son peuple mourant en face du balcon.
Du bouffon favori la grotesque ballade
Ne distrait plus le front de ce cruel malade;
Son lit fleurdelisé se transforme en tombeau,
Et les dames d'atour, pour qui tout prince est beau,
Ne savent plus trouver d'impudique toilette
Pour tirer un souris de ce jeune squelette.
Le savant qui lui fait de l'or n'a jamais pu
De son être extirper l'élément corrompu,
Et dans ces bains de sang qui des Romains nous viennent,
Et dont sur leurs vieux jours les puissants se souviennent,
Il n'a su réchauffer ce cadavre hébété
Où coule au lieu de sang l'eau verte du Léthé.

Spleen

I AM like the monarch of some rainy kingdom, rich but impotent, young but senile, who, despising the bowing and scraping of his tutors, is bored with his hounds, as with all other creatures.

Nothing can cheer him, neither game nor falcon, nor his subjects who come to die beneath his balcony. His favorite jester's drollest ballad can no longer smooth the cruelly sick man's brow; his couch, adorned with fleur-de-lys, becomes his tomb, and the ladies-in-waiting, who find all princes handsome, can invent no new wanton costume to draw a smile from this youthful skeleton.

The alchemist who makes his gold has never managed to eliminate the corrupt element from his being, and in those blood-baths which we inherit from the Romans, and which men of power recall in their declining days, he has failed to rewarm that stupefied, living corpse, in which not blood but Lethe's green water flows.

[Published in *Les Fleurs du mal*, 1857]

SPLEEN

QUAND le ciel bas et lourd pèse comme un couvercle
Sur l'esprit gémissant en proie aux longs ennuis,
Et que de l'horizon embrassant tout le cercle
Il nous verse un jour noir plus triste que les nuits;

Quand la terre est changée en un cachot humide,
Où l'Espérance, comme une chauve-souris,
S'en va battant les murs de son aile timide
Et se cognant la tête à des plafonds pourris;

Quand la pluie étalant ses immenses traînées
D'une vaste prison imite les barreaux,
Et qu'un peuple muet d'infâmes araignées
Vient tendre ses filets au fond de nos cerveaux,

Spleen

WHEN the low, leaden sky weighs like a lid on the groaning mind tortured by long-felt cares, and when, embracing the whole ring of the horizon, it pours on us dark day which is sadder than any night;

when the earth is turned into a dripping prison-cell in which Hope, bat-like, goes bruising its timid wing against the walls and knocking its head against the rotted ceilings;

when the rain, fanning-out its long streaks of water, imitates the bars of an enormous gaol, and a silent horde of loathsome spiders come and weave their webs inside our brains,

Des cloches tout à coup sautent avec furie
Et lancent vers le ciel un affreux hurlement,
Ainsi que des esprits errants et sans patrie
Qui se mettent à geindre opiniâtrément.

– Et de longs corbillards, sans tambours ni musique,
Défilent lentement dans mon âme; l'Espoir,
Vaincu, pleure, et l'Angoisse atroce, despotique,
Sur mon crâne incliné plante son drapeau noir.

then suddenly the bells swing angrily and hurl their horrible howl into the sky, like wandering, homeless spirits beginning their relentless wailing.

And long hearses, with neither drums nor music, move slowly in procession through my soul, and defeated Hope bursts into tears, and the beastly tyrant, Anguish, sets his black flag on my bowed head.

[Published in *Les Fleurs du mal*, 1857]

VII

Last Poems

1859–63

LE GOÛT DU NÉANT

MORNE esprit, autrefois amoureux de la lutte,
L'Espoir, dont l'éperon attisait ton ardeur,
Ne veut plus t'enfourcher! Couche-toi sans pudeur,
Vieux cheval dont le pied à chaque obstacle butte.

Résigne-toi, mon cœur; dors ton sommeil de brute.

Esprit vaincu, fourbu! Pour toi, vieux maraudeur,
L'amour n'a plus de goût, non plus que la dispute;
Adieu donc, chants du cuivre et soupirs de la flûte!
Plaisirs, ne tentez plus un cœur sombre et boudeur!

Le Printemps adorable a perdu son odeur!

Et le Temps m'engloutit minute par minute,
Comme la neige immense un corps pris de roideur;
Je contemple d'en haut le globe en sa rondeur,
Et je n'y cherche plus l'abri d'une cahute.

Avalanche, veux-tu m'emporter dans ta chute?

The Longing for Nothingness

DISCONSOLATE mind, once so enamoured of the struggle, Hope, whose spur used to add fuel to your ardour, no longer desires to mount you. Lay you down without shame, old steed whose foot falters at every stile. Resign yourself, my heart, sleep the sleep of the brute.

O vanquished, worn-out mind! For you, old hack, there's no more pleasure in love than in argument. Farewell then, brassy cantos, farewell to the sighings of the flute! Pleasures, entice no more this sombre, brooding heart! The adorable Spring has lost its perfume.

Time is engulfing me, minute by minute, as the interminable snow swallows a stiffening body. I look down from on high on the roundness of the globe, and seek no hut for shelter. O avalanche, will you take me with you when you fall?

[Published January 1859]

LE VOYAGE

À Maxime du Camp.

I

POUR l'enfant, amoureux de cartes et d'estampes,
L'univers est égal à son vaste appétit.
Ah! que le monde est grand à la clarté des lampes!
Aux yeux du souvenir que le monde est petit!

Un matin nous partons, le cerveau plein de flamme,
Le cœur gros de rancune et de désirs amers,
Et nous allons, suivant le rythme de la lame,
Berçant notre infini sur le fini des mers:

Les uns, joyeux de fuir une patrie infâme;
D'autres, l'horreur de leurs berceaux, et quelques-uns,
Astrologues noyés dans les yeux d'une femme,
La Circé tyrannique aux dangereux parfums.

Pour n'être pas changés en bêtes, ils s'enivrent
D'espace et de lumière et de cieux embrasés;
La glace qui les mord, les soleils qui les cuivrent,
Effacent lentement la marque des baisers.

The Voyage

I

FOR the child in love with maps and prints, the universe matches his vast appetite. Ah, how big the world is, in the lamplight; but how small, viewed through the eyes of memory! One morning we set out, our minds aflame, our heart bursting with resentment and bitter longings, and we fare onwards in rhythm with the waves, soothing our infinity on the finite of the seas. Some are overjoyed to quit an infamous homeland; others, to leave the horror of their infancy behind; some are astrologers drowned in a woman's eyes, the tyrannical Circe, she of the dangerous perfumes. To avoid being changed into beasts they drug themselves with space and light and blazing skies, and the ice's sting, the suns that burn them bronze, gradually efface the kisses' scars.

Mais les vrais voyageurs sont ceux-là seuls qui partent
Pour partir; cœurs légers, semblables aux ballons,
De leur fatalité jamais ils ne s'écartent,
Et, sans savoir pourquoi, disent toujours: Allons!

Ceux-là dont les désirs ont la forme des nues,
Et qui rêvent, ainsi qu'un conscrit de canon,
De vastes voluptés, changeantes, inconnues,
Et dont l'esprit humain n'a jamais su le nom!

II

Nous imitons, horreur! la toupie et la boule
Dans leur valse et leurs bonds; même dans nos sommeils
La Curiosité nous tourmente et nous roule,
Comme un Ange cruel qui fouette des soleils.

Singulière fortune où le but se déplace,
Et, n'étant nulle part, peut être n'importe où!
Où l'Homme, dont jamais l'espérance n'est lasse,
Pour trouver le repos court toujours comme un fou!

But the true travellers are those, and those alone, who set out only for the journey's sake, and with light balloon-like hearts they never swerve from their destiny, but, without knowing why, keep saying 'Let us fare forward!' – those whose desires are shaped like the clouds, and who, like the conscript dreaming of his cannon, dream of boundless, ever-changing, unexplored sensualities which the human mind has never been able to name.

II

We imitate – O loathsome sight – the spinning-top's waltz and the bouncing ball. Even as we sleep, curiosity torments us and drives us on, like a cruel Angel whipping Suns. A strange destiny, this, in which the target is ever shifting, and which, being nowhere, can be anywhere; in which Man, with untiring hope, is always rushing like a madman in search of rest. Our soul is a three-master in quest

Notre âme est un trois-mâts cherchant son Icarie;
Une voix retentit sur le pont: «Ouvre l'œil!»
Une voix de la hune, ardente et folle, crie:
«Amour ... gloire ... bonheur!» Enfer! c'est un écueil!

Chaque îlot signalé par l'homme de vigie
Est un Eldorado promis par le Destin;
L'Imagination qui dresse son orgie
Ne trouve qu'un récif aux clartés du matin.

Ô le pauvre amoureux des pays chimériques!
Faut-il le metttre aux fers, le jeter à la mer,
Ce matelot ivrogne, inventeur d'Amériques
Dont le mirage rend le gouffre plus amer?

Tel le vieux vagabond, piétinant dans la boue,
Rêve, le nez en l'air, de brillants paradis;
Son œil ensorcelé découvre une Capoue
Partout où la chandelle illumine un taudis.

III

Étonnants voyageurs! quelles nobles histoires
Nous lisons dans vos yeux profonds comme les mers!

of its Icaria: a voice from the bridge booms 'Watch out!' but another from aloft, eager and demented, cries 'Love! Glory! Happiness!' – but no, it's hell let loose, we've struck a rock! Every island sighted by the man on watch is an Eldorado, promised by Destiny; our imagination conjures up an orgy in advance; but in the morning light it proves to be a barren reef. Poor lover of non-existent Utopias! – should he be cast in irons and hurled into the sea, this drunken sailor who invents Americas, whose mirage only adds more acid to the deep? Like some old tramp trudging in the mire and dreaming with his nose in the air of dazzling paradises, his bewitched eyes find a Capua in every candle-lit hovel!

III

Astounding travellers! what noble tales we can read in your sea-deep eyes! Show us the caskets that are your rich memories, those

Montrez-nous les écrins de vos riches mémoires,
Ces bijoux merveilleux, faits d'astres et d'éthers.

Nous voulons voyager sans vapeur et sans voile!
Faites, pour égayer l'ennui de nos prisons,
Passer sur nos esprits, tendus comme une toile,
Vos souvenirs avec leurs cadres d'horizons.

Dites, qu'avez-vous vu?

IV

«Nous avons vu des astres
Et des flots; nous avons vu des sables aussi;
Et, malgré bien des chocs et d'imprévus désastres,
Nous nous sommes souvent ennuyés, comme ici.

«La gloire du soleil sur la mer violette,
La gloire des cités dans le soleil couchant,
Allumaient dans nos cœurs une ardeur inquiète
De plonger dans un ciel au reflet alléchant.

«Les plus riches cités, les plus grands paysages,
Jamais ne contenaient l'attrait mystérieux

wondrous gems fashioned from stars and ethers! We would fain travel without steam or sail. To enliven the tedium of our prisons, project on to our minds, which are stretched tight like sails, your horizon-framed memories! Tell us, what have you seen?

IV

'We have seen stars and waves, and deserts also, and despite many an alarm and many an unforeseen disaster, we were often bored, just as we are here. The glory of the sunlight on the violet sea, the glory of cities in the setting sun, kindled an unquiet longing in our hearts, to plunge into the sky's alluring reflection.

'The richest of cities, the greatest of landscapes, never contained the mysterious magnetism of those which Chance makes from

De ceux que le hasard fait avec les nuages.
Et toujours le désir nous rendait soucieux!

«– La jouissance ajoute au désir de la force.
Désir, vieil arbre à qui le plaisir sert d'engrais,
Cependant que grossit et durcit ton écorce,
Tes branches veulent voir le soleil de plus près!

«Grandiras-tu toujours, grand arbre plus vivace
Que le cyprès? – Pourtant nous avons, avec soin,
Cueilli quelques croquis pour votre album vorace,
Frères qui trouvez beau tout ce qui vient de loin!

«Nous avons salué des idoles à trompe;
Des trônes constellés de joyaux lumineux;
Des palais ouvragés dont la féerique pompe
Serait pour vos banquiers un rêve ruineux;

«Des costumes qui sont pour les yeux une ivresse;
Des femmes dont les dents et les ongles sont teints,
Et des jongleurs savants que le serpent caresse.»

the clouds. Besides, we were always fretful with desire. Enjoyment adds strength to desire – O Desire, ancient tree whose muck is pleasure, while your bark thickens and hardens, your branches yearn to view the sky more near! Will you grow forever, mighty tree, deeper of root than any cypress? However, we carefully collected a few specimens for your greedy album, O brothers who find beauty in whatever comes from afar. We have hailed idols trunked like elephants; thrones bestarred with luminous gems; sculptured palaces whose faery splendour would be a ruinous dream for your bankers; clothes that would make you see double; women with painted teeth and finger-nails; fakirs full of lore, caressed by snakes ...'

V

Et puis, et puis encore?

VI

«O cerveaux enfantins!
Pour ne pas oublier la chose capitale,
Nous avons vu partout, et sans l'avoir cherché,
Du haut jusques en bas de l'échelle fatale,
Le spectacle ennuyeux de l'immortel péché:

«La femme, esclave vile, orgueilleuse et stupide,
Sans rire s'adorant et s'aimant sans dégoût;
L'homme, tyran goulu, paillard, dur et cupide,
Esclave de l'esclave et ruisseau dans l'égout;

«Le bourreau qui jouit, le martyr qui sanglote;
La fête qu'assaisonne et parfume le sang;
Le poison du pouvoir énervant le despote,
Et le peuple amoureux du fouet abrutissant;

«Plusieurs religions semblables à la nôtre,
Toutes escaladant le ciel; la Sainteté,

V

And then – what else?

VI

'O childish minds! Lest we forget the most important thing of all – everywhere, without even looking for it, from top to bottom of the deadly scale, we saw the tedious sight of immortal sin: woman, that vile slave, proud and stupid, seriously adoring herself and loving herself without disgust; and man, that greedy tyrant, lewd, merciless, and grasping, the slave of a slave, the tributary of a sewer; the torturer enjoying himself, the martyr sobbing; the banquet seasoned and perfumed with blood; the poison of power exasperating the despot; the people enamoured of the stupefying lash; several religions like our own, so many ladders to heaven;

Comme en un lit de plume un délicat se vautre,
Dans les clous et le crin cherchant la volupté;

«L'Humanité bavarde, ivre de son génie,
Et, folle maintenant comme elle était jadis,
Criant à Dieu, dans sa furibonde agonie:
Ô mon semblable, ô mon maître, je te maudis!

«Et les moins sots, hardis amants de la Démence,
Fuyant le grand troupeau parqué par le Destin,
Et se réfugiant dans l'opium immense!
– Tel est du globe entier l'éternel bulletin.»

VII

Amer savoir, celui qu'on tire du voyage!
Le monde, monotone et petit, aujourd'hui,
Hier, demain, toujours, nous fait voir notre image:
Une oasis d'horreur dans un désert d'ennui!

Faut-il partir? rester? Si tu peux rester, reste;
Pars, s'il le faut. L'un court, et l'autre se tapit
Pour tromper l'ennemi vigilant et funeste,
Le Temps! Il est, hélas! des coureurs sans répit,

saintliness finding a thrill in nails and hair-shirts, like an invalid snug in his feather-bed; chattering mankind drunk with its own wit, as crazy today as it was in the past, shrieking to God in its insane agony, "O Thou, my likeness, my master, I curse Thee!" – and, least stupid of all, the dauntless lovers of madness, fleeing the Fate-guarded herd and taking refuge in the infinity of opium ... Such is the eternal balance-sheet of the entire globe.'

VII

Bitter the knowledge we draw from voyaging! Monotonous and mean, today, yesterday, tomorrow, always, the world shows us our own image – an oasis of horror in a desert of tedium. Should we go, or stay? Stay, if you can stay: go, if you must. One man takes to his heels, and another crouches at home to outwit Time, that watchful, baneful enemy. Alas! there are runners who find no respite, like the

Comme le Juif errant et comme les apôtres,
À qui rien ne suffit, ni wagon ni vaisseau,
Pour fuir ce rétiaire infâme; il en est d'autres
Qui savent le tuer sans quitter leur berceau.

Lorsque enfin il mettra le pied sur notre échine,
Nous pourrons espérer et crier: En avant!
De même qu'autrefois nous partions pour la Chine,
Les yeux fixés au large et les cheveux au vent,

Nous nous embarquerons sur la mer des Ténèbres
Avec le cœur joyeux d'un jeune passager.
Entendez-vous ces voix, charmantes et funèbres,
Qui chantent: «Par ici! vous qui voulez manger

«Le Lotus parfumé! c'est ici qu'on vendange
Les fruits miraculeux dont votre cœur a faim;
Venez vous enivrer de la douceur étrange
De cette après-midi qui n'a jamais de fin?»

À l'accent familier nous devinons le spectre;
Nos Pylades là-bas tendent leurs bras vers nous.
«Pour rafraîchir ton cœur nage vers ton Électre!»
Dit celle dont jadis nous baisions les genoux.

Wandering Jew or the Apostles, those for whom nothing is enough, neither carriage nor ship, to outdistance the infamous slave-driver: there are others who can kill him without ever stirring from their cradle.

When at last he sets his foot on our spine, we can still hope and cry out, 'Fare forward!' – just as when we once set out for China, with our eyes fixed on the open sea, our hair streaming in the wind, we shall set sail across the sea of shadows with a young passenger's joyful heart. Can you hear those seductive, mournful voices chanting, 'Come this way, you who would eat of the scented Lotus: here we harvest the miraculous fruits for which your heart is longing! Come and drink the strange bliss of an afternoon without end!' But we scent the ghost behind those familiar tones. Yonder our Pylades are stretching their arms towards us: 'To cool your heart, swim towards your Electra!' calls she whose knees we once embraced.

VIII

Ô Mort, vieux capitaine, il est temps! levons l'ancre.
Ce pays nous ennuie, ô Mort! Appareillons!
Si le ciel et la mer sont noirs comme de l'encre,
Nos cœurs que tu connais sont remplis de rayons!

Verse-nous ton poison pour qu'il nous réconforte!
Nous voulons, tant ce feu nous brûle le cerveau,
Plonger au fond du gouffre, Enfer ou Ciel, qu'importe?
Au fond de l'Inconnu pour trouver du *nouveau*!

ANYWHERE OUT OF THE WORLD

CETTE vie est un hôpital où chaque malade est possédé du désir de changer de lit. Celui-ci voudrait souffrir en face du poêle, et celui-là croit qu'il guérirait à côté de la fenêtre.

Il me semble que je serais bien là où je ne suis pas, et cette question de déménagement en est une que je discute sans cesse avec mon âme.

VIII

O Death, old navigator, the hour has come! Let us weigh anchor! O Death, we are weary of this land, let us spread sail! Though sea and sky be black as ink, our hearts, which you know well, are full of shafts of light. Pour us the hemlock, for our comfort: its fire so burns our brains that we yearn to dive into the gulf's depths, and – what matter if it's heaven or hell? – into the depths of the Unknown, in quest of *something new*.

[Written and published 1859]

Anywhere out of the World

THIS life is a hospital, in which the sick are all obsessed with the desire for a change of bed. One would like to suffer in front of the stove; another imagines he would recover, were he near the window.

It seems to me that I would always feel well wherever I don't happen to be, and this question of a change of domicile is one which I am forever discussing with my soul.

«Dis-moi, mon âme, pauvre âme refroidie, que penserais-tu d'habiter Lisbonne? Il doit y faire chaud, et tu t'y regaillardirais comme un lézard. Cette ville est au bord de l'eau; on dit qu'elle est bâtie en marbre, et que le peuple y a une telle haine du végétal, qu'il arrache tous les arbres. Voilà un paysage selon ton goût; un paysage fait avec la lumière et le minéral, et le liquide pour les réfléchir!»

Mon âme ne répond pas.

«Puisque tu aimes tant le repos, avec le spectacle du mouvement, veux-tu venir habiter la Hollande, cette terre béatifiante? Peut-être te divertiras-tu dans cette contrée dont tu as souvent admiré l'image dans les musées. Que penserais-tu de Rotterdam, toi qui aimes les forêts de mâts, et les navires amarrés au pied des maisons?»

Mon âme reste muette.

«Batavia te sourirait peut-être davantage? Nous y trouverions d'ailleurs l'esprit de l'Europe marié à la beauté tropicale.»

'Tell me, my soul, my poor chilled soul, what would you think of living in Lisbon? It must be warm there, you would soon be as merry as a lizard. It's a town on the waterfront; they say it's built of marble, and that its inhabitants have such a horror of plants that they uproot all the trees. There's a landscape after your taste – a landscape made entirely of light and mineral, with water to reflect them.'

My soul offers no reply.

'Since you are so fond of rest and quiet, so long as you have some movement to watch, would you like to go and live in Holland, that land which fills one with bliss? Perhaps you will find plenty to interest you in that country whose image you have often admired in art-galleries. What about Rotterdam, you who love forests of masts, and ships berthed right beside the houses?'

My soul remains silent.

'Perhaps you would find Batavia more to your liking? There, incidentally, we would find the spirit of Europe wedded to tropical beauty.'

Pas un mot. – Mon âme serait-elle morte?

«En es-tu donc venue à ce point d'engourdissement que tu ne te plaises que dans ton mal? S'il en est ainsi, fuyons vers les pays qui sont les analogies de la mort. – Je tiens notre affaire, pauvre âme! Nous ferons nos malles pour Tornéo. Allons plus loin encore, à l'extrême bout de la Baltique; encore plus loin de la vie, si c'est possible; installons-nous au pôle. Là le soleil ne frise qu'obliquement la terre, et les lentes alternatives de la lumière et de la nuit suppriment la variété et augmentent la monotonie, cette moitié du néant. Là, nous pourrons prendre de longs bains de ténèbres, cependant que, pour nous divertir, les aurores boréales nous enverront de temps en temps leurs gerbes roses, comme des reflets d'un feu d'artifice de l'Enfer!»

Enfin, mon âme fait explosion, et sagement elle me crie: «N'importe où! pourvu que ce soit hors de ce monde!»

Not a word. – Can my soul be dead?

'Have you reached such a state of torpor that you enjoy your suffering? If so, then let us escape to those countries which are the counterparts of death. I have exactly what you are looking for, my poor soul! We'll pack our bags for Torneo. Let's go even farther – to the extreme end of the Baltic – or even farther from life, if you like – let's set up house at the North Pole! There the sun only obliquely skims the earth, and the slow alternation of light and dark cuts out variety and enhances the monotony, which is half of Nothingness itself. There, we can take long baths of darkness, while for our entertainment the Aurora Borealis will offer us its rosy sheaves from time to time, like reflections of a firework-display in Hell.'

At last my soul erupts and cries out, in its wisdom: 'Anywhere! – so long as it is out of this world!'

[Published September 1857. Paragraph 3 is to be related to *Rêve Parisien* and the theme as a whole to *Le Voyage*. The title is taken from Edgar Allan Poe.]

LES SEPT VIEILLARDS

À Victor Hugo

FOURMILLANTE cité, cité pleine de rêves,
Où le spectre, en plein jour, raccroche le passant!
Les mystères partout coulent comme des sèves
Dans les canaux étroits du colosse puissant.

Un matin, cependant que dans la triste rue
Les maisons, dont la brume allongeait la hauteur,
Simulaient les deux quais d'une rivière accrue,
Et que, décor semblable à l'âme de l'acteur,

Un brouillard sale et jaune inondait tout l'espace,
Je suivais, roidissant mes nerfs comme un héros
Et discutant avec mon âme déjà lasse,
Le faubourg secoué par les lourds tombereaux.

Tout à coup, un vieillard dont les guenilles jaunes
Imitaient la couleur de ce ciel pluvieux,
Et dont l'aspect aurait fait pleuvoir les aumônes,
Sans la méchanceté qui luisait dans ses yeux,

The Seven Old Men

O SWARMING city, city full of dreams, where the ghost accosts the passer-by in broad daylight! Mysteries flow everywhere like sap in the narrow veins of this mighty giant.

One morning, when in the dingy street the houses seemed to be stretched upwards by the mist and looked like the two banks of some swollen river, and when (a background comparable to an actor's soul) a dirty yellow fog was flooding the whole of space, I was making my way, steeling my nerves heroically and nagging my already weary soul, through the suburb shaken by heavy tumbrils.

Suddenly an old man whose yellow rags were the same colour as the rainy sky, and whose very appearance was enough to invite showers of alms, were it not for the wicked glint in his eyes, hove

M'apparut. On eût dit sa prunelle trempée
Dans le fiel; son regard aiguisait les frimas,
Et sa barbe à longs poils, roide comme une épée,
Se projetait, pareille à celle de Judas.

Il n'était pas voûté, mais cassé, son échine
Faisant avec sa jambe un parfait angle droit,
Si bien que son bâton, parachevant sa mine,
Lui donnait la tournure et le pas maladroit

D'un quadrupède infirme ou d'un juif à trois pattes.
Dans la neige et la boue il allait s'empêtrant,
Comme s'il écrasait des morts sous ses savates,
Hostile à l'univers plutôt qu'indifférent.

Son pareil le suivait: barbe, œil, dos, bâton, loques,
Nul trait ne distinguait, du même enfer venu,
Ce jumeau centenaire, et ces spectre baroques
Marchaient du même pas vers un but inconnu.

À quel complot infâme étais-je donc en butte,
Ou quel méchant hasard ainsi m'humiliait?

in sight. You would have thought his eyes were steeped in gall; his glance made the winter frost still more acute and his long beard, as stiff as any sword, jutted out like the beard of Judas himself. He was not so much bent, as broken, his backbone making a perfect right-angle with his legs, so that his walking-stick, adding the finishing touch to his appearance, gave him the ungainly shape and gait of some ailing quadruped or a three-legged Jew. He scuffled along, sinking into the mud and snow as if crushing the dead under his old boots, not merely indifferent to the world but hating it.

He was followed by his double – beard, eye, back, stick, rags – not a single feature distinguished this hell-bent centenarian twin from the other: and these two outlandish ghosts plodded at the same speed towards some unknown destination.

What infamous conspiracy was I the victim of? What evil chance was thus humiliating me? For, seven times, minute by

Car je comptai sept fois, de minute en minute,
Ce sinistre vieillard qui se multipliait!

Que celui-là qui rit de mon inquiétude,
Et qui n'est pas saisi d'un frisson fraternel,
Songe bien que malgré tant de décrépitude
Ces sept monstres hideux avaient l'air éternel!

Aurais-je, sans mourir, contemplé le huitième,
Sosie inexorable, ironique et fatal,
Dégoûtant Phénix, fils et père de lui-même?
– Mais je tournai le dos au cortège infernal.

Exaspéré comme un ivrogne qui voit double,
Je rentrai, je fermai ma porte, épouvanté,
Malade et morfondu, l'esprit fiévreux et trouble,
Blessé par le mystère et par l'absurdité!

Vainement ma raison voulait prendre la barre,
La tempête en jouant déroutait ses efforts,
Et mon âme dansait, dansait, vieille gabarre
Sans mâts, sur une mer monstrueuse et sans bords!

minute, I counted that same, sinister multiple old man! Whoever laughs at my uneasiness and does not feel a brotherly chill run down his spine, let him not forget that in spite of their senility these seven hideous freaks had a look of eternity about them! Could I, without being stricken dead, have looked on yet an eighth, a pitiless, ironical, deadly twin, a loathsome phoenix, his own son and his own father?

But I turned my back on that satanical procession, irritated beyond endurance like some drunkard seeing double. I went home and locked my door, terrified, nauseated, and depressed, my mind feverish and disturbed, hurt by this enigma, this absurdity. My reason tried to take over, but in vain; its efforts were all undone by the storm, and my soul danced and danced like some old mastless barge on a monstrous, shoreless sea.

[Written and published in 1859, one of a series of *Parisian Ghosts.*]

LES PETITES VIEILLES

À Victor Hugo

I

DANS les plis sinueux des vieilles capitales,
Où tout, même l'horreur, tourne aux enchantements,
Je guette, obéissant à mes humeurs fatales,
Des êtres singuliers, décrépits et charmants.

Ces monstres disloqués furent jadis des femmes,
Éponine ou Laïs! Monstres brisés, bossus
Ou tordus, aimons-les! ce sont encor des âmes.
Sous des jupons troués ou sous de froids tissus

Ils rampent, flagellés par les bises iniques,
Frémissant au fracas roulant des omnibus,
Et serrant sur leur flanc, ainsi que des reliques,
Un petit sac brodé de fleurs ou de rébus;

Ils trottent, tous pareils à des marionnettes;
Se traînent, comme font les animaux blessés,
Ou dansent, sans vouloir danser, pauvres sonnettes
Où se pend un Démon sans pitié! Tout cassés

Little Old Women

I

IN the twisting folds of old capital cities, where everything, even horror, turns into magic, obeying my irresistible impulses I spy on odd, decrepit, charming creatures.

Let us love these disjointed freaks who once were women – Eponine or Laïs – broken-down monsters, hunch-backed or bent double, for they are still human souls! Under their tattered skirts and skimpy garments, they crawl along, whipped by the malignant winds, trembling at the din of the buses thundering past, clutching against their ribs, like holy relics, their little handbags embroidered with flowers or puzzling patterns. They trot along like puppets, or hobble like lame animals, or, though they don't intend to, they do a kind of jig, like puny bells swung by a merciless demon. Though

Qu'ils sont, ils ont des yeux perçants comme une vrille,
Luisants comme ces trous où l'eau dort dans la nuit;
Ils ont les yeux divins de la petite fille
Qui s'étonne et qui rit à tout ce qui reluit.

– Avez-vous observé que maints cercueils de vieilles
Sont presque aussi petits que celui d'un enfant?
La Mort savante met dans ce bières pareilles
Un symbole d'un goût bizarre et captivant,

Et lorsque j'entrevois un fantôme débile
Traversant de Paris le fourmillant tableau,
Il me semble toujours que cet être fragile
S'en va tout doucement vers un nouveau berceau;

À moins que, méditant sur la géométrie,
Je ne cherche, à l'aspect de ces membres discords,
Combien de fois il faut que l'ouvrier varie
La forme de la boîte où l'on met tous ces corps.

– Ces yeux sont des puits faits d'un million de larmes,
Des creusets qu'un métal refroidi pailleta ...
Ces yeux mystérieux ont d'invincibles charmes
Pour celui que l'austère infortune allaita!

they are falling to pieces, their eyes are as piercing as drills, they glint like holes where water sleeps at night, they have the divine eyes of little girls, full of wonder and laughing at anything shiny.

Have you ever noticed that many old women's coffins are almost as small as little children's? Cunning old Death gives these similar coffins a strange and entrancing symbolism: when I catch a glimpse of a flimsy ghost passing through the swarming Parisian landscape, I always have the feeling that this frail creature is gently advancing towards her second cradle, unless, turning my thoughts to geometry as I see those incongruent limbs, I reflect on how often the carpenter has to vary the shape of the boxes in which all those bodies are laid ...

Those eyes are the wells of a million tears, crucibles spangled with cool metal. Those enigmatic eyes have compelling charms for whoever was suckled on the milk of austere misfortune.

II

De Frascati défunt Vestale enamourée;
Prêtresse de Thalie, hélas! dont le souffleur
Enterré sait le nom; célèbre évaporée
Que Tivoli jadis ombragea dans sa fleur,

Toutes m'enivrent! mais parmi ces êtres frêles
Il en est qui, faisant de la douleur un miel,
Ont dit au Dévouement qui leur prêtait ses ailes:
Hippogriffe puissant, mène-moi jusqu'au ciel!

L'une, par sa patrie au malheur exercée,
L'autre, que son époux surchargea de douleurs,
L'autre, par son enfant Madone transpercée,
Toutes auraient pu faire un fleuve avec leurs pleurs!

III

Ah! que j'en ai suivi de ces petites vieilles!
Une, entre autres, à l'heure où le soleil tombant
Ensanglante le ciel de blessures vermeilles,
Pensive s'asseyait à l'écart sur un banc,

II

Vestal enamoured of some dead Frascati; priestess of Thalia, alas, whose name is known only to the buried prompter; illustrious beauty whom Tivoli once sheltered in her bloom – they all intoxicate me! But among those fragile beings there are those who, turning their grief to honey, have implored the Devotion which lent them wings, saying 'O mighty hippogriff, bear me up to heaven!' One, whose homeland schooled her in misfortune; another, whom her husband overwhelmed with sufferings; or she who through her child became a Madonna, pierced to the heart – all could have made a river with their tears!

III

Ah, how many of these little old women I have followed! One of them, at the hour when the setting sun bloodens the sky with scarlet wounds, used to sit thoughtfully alone on a bench, listening to

Pour entendre un de ces concerts, riches de cuivre,
Dont les soldats parfois inondent nos jardins,
Et qui, dans ces soirs d'or où l'on se sent revivre,
Versent quelque héroïsme au cœur des citadins.

Celle-là, droite encor, fière et sentant la règle,
Humait avidement ce chant vif et guerrier;
Son œil parfois s'ouvrait comme l'œil d'un vieil aigle;
Son front de marbre avait l'air fait pour le laurier!

IV

Telles vous cheminez, stoïques et sans plaintes,
À travers le chaos des vivantes cités,
Mères au cœur saignant, courtisanes ou saintes,
Dont autrefois les noms par tous étaient cités.

Vous qui fûtes la grâce ou qui fûtes la gloire,
Nul ne vous reconnaît! un ivrogne incivil
Vous insulte en passant d'un amour dérisoire;
Sur vos talons gambade un enfant lâche et vil.

one of those recitals, full of brass, with which the military sometimes flood our parks, and which, on those golden evenings when you feel yourself coming to life again, pour a certain heroism into the hearts of city folk. This woman, still upright, full of pride, and radiating a sense of discipline, eagerly used to drink in that lively, warlike song; sometimes her eye would open like an old eagle's, and her marble brow looked as though shaped for a laurel crown.

IV

Thus you pass on, stoical and uncomplaining, through the chaos of our living cities, mothers whose hearts are bleeding; courtesans and saints whose names were once on everybody's lips! You who were grace itself, and you who were glory, nobody recognizes you now: a foul-mouthed drunkard insults you as he goes by, with his mock advances, or some cowardly, despicable urchin dances at your heels.

Honteuses d'exister, ombres ratatinées,
Peureuses, le dos bas, vous côtoyez les murs;
Et nul ne vous salue, étranges destinées!
Débris d'humanité pour l'éternité mûrs!

Mais moi, moi qui de loin tendrement vous surveille,
L'œil inquiet fixé sur vos pas incertains,
Tout comme si j'étais votre père, ô merveille!
Je goûte à votre insu des plaisirs clandestins:

Je vois s'épanouir vos passions novices;
Sombres ou lumineux, je vis vos jours perdus;
Mon cœur multiplié jouit de tous vos vices!
Mon âme resplendit de toutes vos vertus!

Ruines! ma famille! ô cerveaux congénères!
Je vous fais chaque soir un solennel adieu!
Où serez-vous demain, Èves octogénaires,
Sur qui pèse la griffe effroyable de Dieu?

Ashamed to be alive, shrivelled shadows, timorous and bent-backed, you hug the walls and nobody takes his hat off to you, O strangely-fated ones! O human wrecks, ripe for eternity! But I, who watch you tenderly from afar, with my uneasy eye fixed on your tottering steps, as though (what next!) I were your father – unknown to you I enjoy secret pleasures: I watch your untutored passions flower, and dark or bright, I relive your vanished days; my manifold heart delights in all your vices, and my soul resplends with all your virtues. O ruins, O you my flesh and blood, O you, like minds, I bid you every evening a grave farewell! Where will you be tomorrow, octogenarian Eves, on whom God's terrible claw is poised?

[Written and published 1859, one of the projected series of *Parisian Ghosts*. Cf. the prose-poems *The Old Woman's Despair* and *The Widows*. Though Baudelaire wrote that he was 'imitating Hugo's manner' in this poem, it goes far beyond that and has a combination of irony, tenderness, and dignity which shows Baudelaire's own manner and art at their highest point.]

LES VEUVES

VAUVENARGUES dit que dans les jardins publics il est des allées hantées principalement par l'ambition déçue, par les inventeurs malheureux, par les gloires avortées, par les cœurs brisés, par toutes ces âmes tumultueuses et fermées, en qui grondent encore les derniers soupirs d'un orage, et qui reculent loin du regard insolent des joyeux et des oisifs. Ces retraites ombreuses sont les rendez-vous des éclopés de la vie.

C'est surtout vers ces lieux que le poète et le philosophe aiment diriger leurs avides conjectures. Il y a là une pâture certaine. Car s'il est une place qu'ils dédaignent de visiter, comme je l'insinuais tout à l'heure, c'est surtout la joie des riches. Cette turbulence dans le vide n'a rien qui les attire. Au contraire, ils se sentent irrésistiblement entraînés vers tout ce qui est faible, ruiné, contristé, orphelin.

Un œil expérimenté ne s'y trompe jamais. Dans ces traits rigides ou abattus, dans ces yeux caves et ternes, ou brillants des derniers éclairs de la lutte, dans ces rides pro-

Widows

VAUVENARGUES says that in public parks there are pathways which are haunted mainly by disappointed ambition, by unhappy inventors, by those thwarted of fame, by broken hearts, by all those volcanic, inapproachable souls in whom the last sighs of storm still heave, and who withdraw far from the insolent stare of happy, idle folk. Those shady retreats are the place where life's maimed come together.

It is especially towards such spots that the poet and philosopher love to direct their eager speculations. There they are sure to find food for thought. For if there is any place which they disdain to visit, as I was suggesting a few moments ago, it is surely wherever the rich can be seen enjoying themselves. That uproar in a vacuum holds no attraction for them. On the contrary, they feel themselves irresistibly drawn towards all that is weak, ruined, saddened, orphaned.

The experienced eye never fails. In those set or dejected features, in those hollow, lack-lustre eyes, or eyes glinting with the last flashes of the struggle, in those deep and abundant furrows, in that

fondes et nombreuses, dans ces démarches si lentes ou si saccadées, il déchiffre tout de suite les innombrables légendes de l'amour trompé, du dévouement méconnu, des efforts non récompensés, de la faim et du froid humblement, silencieusement supportés.

Avez-vous quelquefois aperçu des veuves sur ces bancs solitaires, des veuves pauvres? Qu'elles soient en deuil ou non, il est facile de les reconnaître. D'ailleurs, il y a toujours dans le deuil du pauvre quelque chose qui manque, une absence d'harmonie qui le rend plus navrant. Il est contraint de lésiner sur sa douleur. Le riche porte la sienne au grand complet.

Quelle est la veuve la plus triste et la plus attristante, celle qui traîne à sa main un bambin avec qui elle ne peut pas partager sa rêverie, ou celle qui est tout à fait seule? Je ne sais ... Il m'est arrivé une fois de suivre pendant de longues heures une vieille affligée de cette espèce; celle-là roide, droite, sous un petit châle usé, portait dans tout son être une fierté de stoicienne.

Elle était évidemment condamnée, par une absolue solitude, à des habitudes de vieux célibataire, et le caractère

sluggish or jerky step, it at once deciphers innumerable histories of cheated love, unappreciated devotion, unrewarded effort, hunger, and cold borne in humility and silence.

Have you ever noticed widows, penniless widows, on those lonely benches? Whether they are in mourning or not, they are easily recognized. Incidentally, in the poor person's mourning there is always something missing, some lack of harmony which makes it the more distressing. The poor person is forced to be niggardly over his grief, while the rich sports his in all its glory.

Who is the saddest and most saddening of widows: she who trails with her a little child who is incapable of sharing her meditations, or she who is entirely alone? I am not sure. I once happened to follow, for several hours, an old bereaved woman of the latter sort: she held herself straight and upright beneath her little threadbare shawl, and in all her person she showed the pride of a stoic.

She was obviously condemned, by her complete solitude, to the habits of an old bachelor, and the masculine character of her ways

masculin de ses mœurs ajoutait un piquant mystérieux à leur austérité. Je ne sais dans quel misérable café et de quelle façon elle déjeuna. Je la suivis au cabinet de lecture; et je l'épiai longtemps pendant qu'elle cherchait dans les gazettes, avec des yeux actifs, jadis brûlés par les larmes, des nouvelles d'un intérêt puissant et personnel.

Enfin, dans l'après-midi, sous un ciel d'automne charmant, un de ces ciels d'où descendent en foule les regrets et les souvenirs, elle s'assit à l'écart dans un jardin, pour entendre, loin de la foule, un de ces concerts dont la musique des régiments gratifie le peuple parisien.

C'est sans doute là la petite débauche de cette vieille innocente (ou de cette vieille purifiée), la consolation bien gagnée d'une de ces lourdes journées sans ami, sans causerie, sans joie, sans confident, que Dieu laissait tomber sur elle, depuis bien des ans peut-être! trois cent soixante-cinq fois par an.

Une autre encore:

Je ne puis jamais m'empêcher de jeter un regard, sinon universellement sympathique, au moins curieux, sur la foule de parias qui se pressent autour de l'enceinte d'un concert

added a mysterious piquancy to their austereness. I don't know in what shabby café or in what manner she took her midday meal. I followed her into a public reading-room and watched her a long time as she searched in the gazettes, with quick eyes that must long ago have been burnt by tears, for news that must have had some powerful, personal meaning for her.

Finally, in the afternoon, under a charming autumn sky, one of those skies from which regrets and memories swarm down, she sat all by herself in a park, away from the crowd, to listen to one of those concerts which regimental bands bestow on the Parisian masses.

This was no doubt that innocent – or reformed – old lady's little orgy, the well-earned consolation for one of those dreary days spent without a friend or a chat, without a moment of joy or someone to confide in, which for many years past God made her lot for three hundred and sixty-five days a year.

Yet another of them. I can never resist casting a glance, if not always of sympathy, at least of curiosity, at the crowd of outcasts

public. L'orchestre jette à travers la nuit des chants de fête, de triomphe ou de volupté. Les robes traînent en miroitant; les regards se croisent; les oisifs, fatigués de n'avoir rien fait, se dandinent, feignant de déguster indolemment la musique. Ici rien que de riche, d'heureux; rien qui ne respire et n'inspire l'insouciance et le plaisir de se laisser vivre; rien, excepté l'aspect de cette tourbe qui s'appuie là-bas sur la barrière extérieure, attrapant gratis, au gré du vent, un lambeau de musique, et regardant l'étincelante fournaise intérieure.

C'est toujours chose intéressante que ce reflet de la joie du riche au fond de l'œil du pauvre. Mais ce jour-là, à travers ce peuple vêtu de blouses et d'indienne, j'aperçus un être dont la noblesse faisait un éclatant contraste avec toute la trivialité environnante.

C'était une femme grande, majestueuse, et si noble dans tout son air, que je n'ai pas souvenir d'avoir vu sa pareille dans les collections des aristocratiques beautés du passé. Un parfum de hautaine vertu émanait de toute sa personne. Son visage, triste et amaigri, était en parfaite accordance

thronging round the entrance to a concert-hall. The orchestra is pouring into the night its songs of festivity, triumph, or rapture. The shimmering dresses trail along the ground, the audience are exchanging glances, the idle men-about-town, tired out with doing nothing, loll in their seats in a languid pretence of savouring the music. There is nothing but wealth and happiness here, nothing but which gives out or inspires the unconcern and pleasure of living – nothing, that is, but the sight of that rabble leaning there on the rail outside, catching, at the wind's whim and free of charge, a whiff of music, and gaping at the glittering splendour within.

It is always interesting to see the reflection of the rich man's happiness in the eyes of the poor. But on that occasion, in the midst of those workaday folk clad in smocks and cheap cottons, I glimpsed a figure whose distinguished appearance was in sharp contrast with all the surrounding triviality.

It was a tall, majestic woman, of such a noble bearing that I cannot recall having seen her equal in the albums of the aristocratic beauties of the past. An atmosphere of the loftiest virtue emanated from her entire person. Her sad, emaciated face was in perfect har-

avec le grand deuil dont elle était revêtue. Elle aussi, comme la plèbe à laquelle elle s'était mêlée et qu'elle ne voyait pas, elle regardait le monde lumineux avec un œil profond, et elle écoutait en hochant doucement la tête.

Singulière vision! À coup sûr, me dis-je, cette pauvreté-là, si pauvreté il y a, ne doit pas admettre l'économie sordide; un si noble visage m'en répond. Pourquoi donc reste-t-elle volontairement dans un milieu où elle fait une tache si éclatante?

Mais en passant curieusement près d'elle, je crus en deviner la raison. La grande veuve tenait par la main un enfant comme elle vêtu de noir; si modique que fût le prix d'entrée, ce prix suffisait peut-être pour payer un des besoins du petit être, mieux encore, une superfluité, un jouet.

Et elle sera rentrée à pied, méditant et rêvant, seule, toujours seule; car l'enfant est turbulent, égoiste, sans douceur et sans patience; et il ne peut même pas, comme le pur animal, comme le chien ou le chat, servir de confident aux douleurs solitaires.

mony with the full mourning in which she was dressed. She also like the common folk she had joined, but of whom she was unaware, was gazing on that luminous world with her unfathomable eye, and swaying her head in time with the music as she listened.

What an unusual sight! Surely, I said to myself, that poverty of hers, if it is poverty, would not allow any sordid economy: such a noble face is proof of that. Why, then, does she voluntarily remain in a setting with which she is in such marked contrast?

But as I drew nearer, out of curiosity, I thought I could guess why. The tall widow was holding the hand of a little boy, dressed like herself in black. However modest the price of admission, that sum would no doubt be enough to provide for one of the little one's needs, or, better still, for some luxury, such as a toy.

And she will have returned home on foot, meditating and dreaming all by herself, always alone: for the child is wild and selfish, and neither gentle nor patient, and he cannot even, like something purely animal such as a dog or cat, serve as the confidant of solitary griefs.

[Written and published 1861]

LE SQUELETTE LABOUREUR

I

DANS les planches d'anatomie
Qui traînent sur ces quais poudreux
Où maint livre cadavéreux
Dort comme une antique momie,

Dessins auxquels la gravité
Et le savoir d'un vieil artiste,
Bien que le sujet en soit triste,
Ont communiqué la Beauté,

On voit, ce qui rend plus complètes
Ces mystérieuses horreurs,
Bêchant comme des laboureurs,
Des Écorchés et des Squelettes.

II

De ce terrain que vous fouillez,
Manants résignés et funèbres,
De tout l'effort de vos vertèbres,
Ou de vos muscles dépouillés,

The Digging Skeleton

I

ON the anatomical plates which languish [in the book-boxes] on the dusty quays [by the Seine], where many a shrivelled book sleeps like an ancient mummy, in drawings to which an artist of old, however depressing the theme, has communicated Beauty, you can see (to make these mysterious horrors more complete) flayed men and skeletons, digging like farm-hands.

II

Poor devils, resigned and full of gloom, say: what strange harvest do you draw from that soil you hack, from all the straining of your backbones, or from your skinned muscles: hard-labourers dragged

Dites, quelle moisson étrange,
Forçats arrachés au charnier,
Tirez-vous, et de quel fermier
Avez-vous à remplir la grange?

Voulez-vous (d'un destin trop dur
Épouvantable et clair emblème!)
Montrer que dans la fosse même
Le sommeil promis n'est pas sûr;

Qu'envers nous le Néant est traître;
Que tout, même la Mort, nous ment,
Et que sempiternellement,
Hélas, il nous faudra peut-être

Dans quelque pays inconnu
Écorcher la terre revêche
Et pousser une lourde bêche
Sous notre pied sanglant et nu?

BIEN LOIN D'ICI

C'EST ici la case sacrée
Où cette fille très-parée,
Tranquille et toujours préparée,

from the boneyard, what farmer's barn have you to fill? Do you want to show – O shocking and clear emblem of too harsh a fate – that even in the grave the promised sleep remains unsure; that even the Void cheats us; that all things, even Death, tell us lies; and that, for ever and ever, alas, perhaps in some land unknown to us we will have to scrape the sullen earth, and push a heavy spade beneath our bleeding, naked foot?

[Dated 15 December 1859]

Far from Here

THIS is the wooden sanctuary where the much-adorned young lady, unruffled and always ready, fanning her breasts with one

D'une main éventant ses seins,
Et son coude dans les coussins,
Écoute pleurer les bassins:

C'est la chambre de Dorothée.
– La brise et l'eau chantent au loin
Leur chanson de sanglots heurtée
Pour bercer cette enfant gâtée.

De haut en bas, avec grand soin,
Sa peau délicate est frottée
D'huile odorante et de benjoin.
– Des fleurs se pâment dans un coin.

hand and reclining with her elbow on the cushions, listens to the fountains weeping. It is Dorothy's boudoir. The wind and water are singing, in the distance, their song interspersed with sobs, to lull the spoiled child. From tip to toe, most thoroughly, her sensitive skin is anointed with aromatic oil and benjamin. Some flowers are swooning in the corner.

[Written in 1859, this poem was at first to have been called *Dorothée* and was described by C.B. as being a reminiscence of l'Île Bourbon (Mauritius). The prose-poem *La Belle Dorothée*, published 1863, describes the same person: 'Why has she left her little hut, so coquettishly arranged, where the flowers and straw mats make such a perfect boudoir for so little cost; where she finds such pleasure in combing her hair, smoking, fanning herself, or looking at her own reflection in the mirror of her great feather fans, while the sea, which pounds the beach near by, makes a powerful and monotonous accompaniment to her vague reveries, and the iron pan, in which a stew of crabs is cooking in rice and saffron, wafts its stimulating perfumes towards her from the other side of the courtyard?']

LE CYGNE

À Victor Hugo

I

ANDROMAQUE, je pense à vous! Ce petit fleuve,
Pauvre et triste miroir où jadis resplendit
L'immense majesté de vos douleurs de veuve,
Ce Simoïs menteur qui par vos pleurs grandit,

A fécondé soudain ma mémoire fertile,
Comme je traversais le nouveau Carrousel.
Le vieux Paris n'est plus (la forme d'une ville
Change plus vite, hélas! que le cœur d'un mortel);

Je ne vois qu'en esprit tout ce camp de baraques,
Ces tas de chapiteaux ébauchés et de fûts,
Les herbes, les gros blocs verdis par l'eau des flaques,
Et, brillant aux carreaux, le bric-à-brac confus.

Là s'étalait jadis une ménagerie;
Là je vis, un matin, à l'heure où sous les cieux

The Swan

To Victor Hugo

I

ANDROMACHE, my thoughts are turned to you. That narrow stream, that unworthy, sad mirror that long ago resplended with the immense majesty of your widow's grief, that second Simois that grew from your tears, has suddenly enriched my fertile memory, as I was crossing the new Carrousel bridge.

The Paris of old is no more – a city's pattern changes, alas, more swiftly than a human heart. Only in my mind's eye can I see those makeshift booths, those piles of rough-hewn capitals and pillars, the weeds, the massive blocks of stone stained green by the puddles, the jumble of bric-à-brac glittering in the shop-fronts.

A menagerie used to sprawl just here: there, one morning, at the hour when beneath the clear, chill sky Toil stirs from sleep, when

Froids et clairs le Travail s'éveille, où la voirie
Pousse un sombre ouragan dans l'air silencieux,

Un cygne qui s'était évadé de sa cage,
Et, de ses pieds palmés frottant le pavé sec,
Sur le sol raboteux traînait son blanc plumage.
Près d'un ruisseau sans eau la bête ouvrant le bec

Baignait nerveusement ses ailes dans la poudre,
Et disait, le cœur plein de son beau lac natal:
'Eau, quand donc pleuvras-tu? quand tonneras-tu, foudre?'
Je vois ce malheureux, mythe étrange et fatal,

Vers le ciel quelquefois, comme l'homme d'Ovide,
Vers le ciel ironique et cruellement bleu,
Sur son cou convulsif tendant sa tête avide,
Comme s'il adressait des reproches à Dieu!

II

Paris change! mais rien dans ma mélancolie
N'a bougé! palais neufs, échafaudages, blocs,
Vieux faubourgs, tout pour moi devient allégorie,
Et mes chers souvenirs sont plus lourds que des rocs.

the roadmenders send their dark uproar into the silent air, I saw a Swan who had just escaped from his cage. Rubbing the parched roadway with his webbed feet, he was trailing his white plumes on the raw ground. Beside a dried-up gutter the poor beast, with gaping beak, was frantically bathing his wings in the dust, and with his heart full of longing for his native land, cried out: 'O water, when will you rain down? O lightning, when will you rage?' I can see that unhappy bird, that strange symbol of doom, sometimes like the Man of Ovid lifting his eager head on his writhing neck, towards the ironical, cruelly blue sky, as though reproaching God.

II

Paris is changing, but nought in my melancholy has moved. These new palaces and scaffoldings, blocks of stone, old suburbs – everything for me becomes an allegory, and my memories are heavier than any rocks.

Aussi devant ce Louvre une image m'opprime:
Je pense à mon grand cygne, avec ses gestes fous,
Comme les exilés, ridicule et sublime,
Et rongé d'un désir sans trêve! et puis à vous,

Andromaque, des bras d'un grand époux tombée,
Vil bétail, sous la main du superbe Pyrrhus,
Auprès d'un tombeau vide en extase courbée;
Veuve d'Hector, hélas! et femme d'Hélénus!

Je pense à la négresse, amaigrie et phthisique,
Piétinant dans la boue, et cherchant, l'œil hagard,
Les cocotiers absents de la superbe Afrique
Derrière la muraille immense du brouillard;

À quiconque a perdu ce qui ne se retrouve
Jamais, jamais! à ceux qui s'abreuvent de pleurs
Et tettent la Douleur comme une bonne louve!
Aux maigres orphelins séchant comme des fleurs!

Ainsi dans la forêt où mon esprit s'exile
Un vieux Souvenir sonne à plein souffle du cor!
Je pense aux matelots oubliés dans une île,
Aux captifs, aux vaincus!... à bien d'autres encor!

Thus, before the Louvre I am oppressed by a vision: I think of my great Swan with his frenzied gestures, ridiculous and sublime like all exiles, gnawed by an unremitting desire: and then of you, O Andromache, fallen from the arms of an heroic spouse, become a vile chattel in the hands of overweening Pyrrhus; the widow of Hector, alas, then wife of Helenus! I think of the lean, consumptive negress trudging through the mud, with her haggard eyes peering in vain through the huge wall of fog for the absent palm-trees of her noble Africa. I think of all those who have lost what they can never, never hope to find again; of those who quench their thirst with tears, and suck the breast of Sorrow like a good mother-wolf. I think of the under-fed orphans withering like flowers. Thus, in the forest where my mind is exiled, an old memory winds its horn: I think of sailors forgotten on a desert isle, I think of those who are captive or defeated ... and of many another!

[1859. Published 1860]

RÊVE PARISIEN

À Constantin Guys

I

De ce terrible paysage,
Tel que jamais mortel n'en vit,
Ce matin encore l'image,
Vague et lointaine, me ravit.

Le sommeil est plein de miracles!
Par un caprice singulier,
J'avais banni de ces spectacles
Le végétal irrégulier,

Et, peintre fier de mon génie,
Je savourais dans mon tableau
L'enivrante monotonie
Du métal, du marbre et de l'eau.

Babel d'escaliers et d'arcades,
C'était un palais infini,
Plein de bassins et de cascades
Tombant dans l'or mat ou bruni;

Parisian Dream

I

The imprecise and distant image of this terrifying landscape, the like of which no mortal ever saw, entranced me again this morning. Sleep is full of miracles. By a strange caprice I had banished shapeless, organic forms from these scenes, and, proud of my genius, just like a painter I enjoyed, in my picture, the entrancing monotony of metal, marble, and water.

A babel of stairways and arcades, there was an infinite palace, full of fountains and waterfalls flowing into lustreless or burnished gold,

Et des cataractes pesantes,
Comme des rideaux de cristal,
Se suspendaient, éblouissantes,
A des murailles de métal.

Non d'arbres, mais de colonnades
Les étangs dormants s'entouraient,
Où de gigantesques naïades,
Comme des femmes, se miraient.

Des nappes d'eau s'épanchaient, bleues,
Entre des quais roses et verts,
Pendant des millions de lieues,
Vers les confins de l'univers;

C'étaient des pierres inouïes
Et des flots magiques; c'étaient
D'immenses glaces éblouies
Par tout ce qu'elles reflétaient!

Insouciants et taciturnes,
Des Ganges, dans le firmament,
Versaient le trésor de leurs urnes
Dans des gouffres de diamant.

and massy cataracts, like curtains of crystal, hung suspended, dazzling, from walls of metal.

Not trees but colonnades encircled the sleeping pools, in which colossal nymphs admired their reflections, like women. Expanses of water stretched blue between rosy and green embankments, for millions of leagues, towards the confines of the universe. There were fabulous stones and magic waves, there were enormous mirrors dazzled by all they reflected. Impassive, silent Ganges rivers in the sky poured down the treasures of their urns into diamond

Architecte de mes féeries,
Je faisais, à ma volonté,
Sous un tunnel de pierreries
Passer un océan dompté;

Et tout, même la couleur noire,
Semblait fourbi, clair, irisé;
Le liquide enchâssait sa gloire
Dans le rayon cristallisé.

Nul astre d'ailleurs, nuls vestiges
De soleil, même au bas du ciel,
Pour illuminer ces prodiges,
Qui brillaient d'un feu personnel!

Et sur ces mouvantes merveilles
Planait (terrible nouveauté!
Tout pour l'œil, rien pour les oreilles!)
Un silence d'éternité.

abysses. The architect of my wonderland, at will I caused a tamed ocean to pass through a tunnel of precious gems, and everything, even the colour black, seemed polished, pellucid, and iridescent; the liquid enshrined its glory like a gem in the crystallized light. Moreover there was not a single star, no trace of the sun even low in the sky, to illuminate these marvels, which shone with an intrinsic fire. And (terrible novelty, with all for the eye and nothing for the ear), over these moving wonders there hovered a silence of eternity.

II

En rouvrant mes yeux pleins de flamme
J'ai vu l'horreur de mon taudis,
Et senti, rentrant dans mon âme,
La pointe des soucis maudits;

La pendule aux accents funèbres
Sonnait brutalement midi,
Et le ciel versait des ténèbres
Sur le triste monde engourdi.

LE RÊVE D'UN CURIEUX

À F. N.

CONNAIS-TU, comme moi, la douleur savoureuse,
Et de toi fais-tu dire: «Oh! l'homme singulier!»
– J'allais mourir. C'était dans mon âme amoureuse,
Désir mêlé d'horreur, un mal particulier;

II

Opening my flame-filled eyes I beheld the horror of my wretched lodging, and felt the barb of cursed cares re-entering my soul. With mournful chimes the clock struck noon, and the sky poured darkness down on the sad and sluggish world.

[Written in 1860, published in 2nd edn of *Les Fleurs du mal*, 1861. See the prose-poem, *The Double Room*.]

An Inquisitive Man's Dream

[*To F. Nadar*]

Do you know, as I do, delicious pain, and do you make others say of you: 'Oh, what an odd man!'

Angoisse et vif espoir, sans humeur factieuse.
Plus allait se vidant le fatal sablier,
Plus ma torture était âpre et délicieuse;
Tout mon cœur s'arrachait au monde familier.

J'étais comme l'enfant avide du spectacle,
Haïssant le rideau comme on hait un obstacle...
Enfin la vérité froide se révéla:

J'étais mort sans surprise, et la terrible aurore
M'enveloppait. – Eh quoi! n'est-ce donc que cela?
La toile était levée et j'attendais encore.

OBSESSION

GRANDS bois, vous m'effrayez comme des cathédrales;
Vous hurlez comme l'orgue; et dans nos cœurs maudits,
Chambres d'éternel deuil où vibrent de vieux râles,
Répondent les échos de vos *De profundis*.

I was about to die. In my amorous soul there was desire mingled with horror, a peculiar queasiness, anguish, and keen hope, no fault-finding bile. The more the hour-glass of doom emptied, the more acute and exquisite was my torture: my entire heart was tearing itself away from the familiar world.

I was like a child agog for the show, loathing the curtain as one hates an obstacle. Then at last the naked truth became plain to me: I had died unsurprised, and the terrible dawn surrounded me. What, can that be all? The curtain was up, but I was still waiting.

[Written and published 1860]

Obsession

GREAT woods, you terrify me like cathedrals! You roar like an organ, and in our condemned hearts, those chambers of eternal mourning in which death-rattles vibrate from the past, the echoes of your *De profundis* repeat their responses.

Je te hais, Océan! tes bonds et tes tumultes,
Mon esprit les retrouve en lui; ce rire amer
De l'homme vaincu, plein de sanglots et d'insultes,
Je l'entends dans le rire énorme de la mer.

Comme tu me plairais, ô nuit! sans ces étoiles
Dont la lumière parle un langage connu!
Car je cherche le vide, et le noir, et le nu!

Mais les ténèbres sont elles-mêmes des toiles
Où vivent, jaillissant de mon œil par milliers,
Des êtres disparus aux regards familiers.

Ocean, I hate you: my mind is full of your leaping and pandemonium. In the enormous laughter of the sea I hear the bitter laughter of man defeated, full of sobs and blasphemies.

How you would please me, O Night, without those stars whose light speaks a language I understand! For my quest is for emptiness, blackness, and bareness.

But the very shadows are canvases in which – leaping in thousands from my eyes – live vanished beings with familiar gaze.

[Published 1860: a poem to be read in conjunction with *Alchimie de la Douleur* and *Le Goût du Néant*, as well as *Correspondances*. In 1851 Baudelaire wrote to F. Desnoyers, denying any belief in pantheism: 'I have, even, always thought there was in Nature, ever flowering and renewed, something impudent and distressing . . . In the depths of woods, enclosed by those vaults which resemble those of sacristies and cathedrals, I think of our astonishing cities, and the prodigious music which unfurls on the heights seems to me to be the translation of human lamentations.' This letter, which was accompanied by the two 'Twilights' (*Crépuscule du soir* and *Crépuscule du matin*) is undoubtedly the 'canvas' of *Obsession*, particularly stanzas 1 and 2.]

HORREUR SYMPATHIQUE

De ce ciel bizarre et livide,
Tourmenté comme ton destin,
Quels pensers dans ton âme vide
Descendent? Réponds, libertin.

– Insatiablement avide
De l'obscur et de l'incertain,
Je ne geindrai pas comme Ovide
Chassé du paradis latin.

Cieux déchirés comme des grèves,
En vous se mire mon orgueil;
Vos vastes nuages en deuil

Sont les corbillards de mes rêves,
Et vos lueurs sont le reflet
De l'Enfer où mon cœur se plaît.

Sympathetic Horror

From that outlandish, livid sky, as tormented as your destiny, what thoughts descend into your empty soul? Freethinker, reply!

– Insatiably hungering for whatever is obscure and uncertain, I shall not whimper like Ovid when he was cast out from the latin paradise!

Skies split asunder like sea-shores, my pride reflects itself in you; your vast clouds, clad in mourning weeds, are the hearses of my dreams, and your red gleams are the reflection of the Hell in which my heart rejoices.

[Published October 1860]

ALCHIMIE DE LA DOULEUR

L'UN t'éclaire avec son ardeur,
L'autre en toi met son deuil, Nature!
Ce qui dit à l'un: Sépulture!
Dit à l'autre: Vie et splendeur!

Hermès inconnu qui m'assistes
Et qui toujours m'intimidas,
Tu me rends l'égal de Midas,
Le plus triste des alchimistes;

Par toi je change l'or en fer
Et le paradis en enfer;
Dans le suaire des nuages

Je découvre un cadavre cher,
Et sur les célestes rivages
Je bâtis de grands sarcophages.

The Alchemy of Pain

ONE man illuminates you with his ardour; another sets in you his sorrow, O Nature. What spells the Grave to one, spells life and splendour to the other.

Unknown Hermes who are my helper, but of whom I ever went in fear, you make me the peer of Midas, the unhappiest of alchemists. Through you I transmute gold into iron, and Paradise into Hell; in the winding-sheet of the clouds I find the corpse of what I loved, and on the shores of heaven I build colossal tombs.

[Published 1860. G. T. Clapton (*Baudelaire and de Quincey*) shows that this poem has some relationship to the *Confessions of an English Opium-Eater*. De Quincey speaks of 'The faculty of shaping images in the distance out of slight elements, and grouping them after the yearnings of the heart ...']

LES AVEUGLES

CONTEMPLE-LES, mon âme; ils sont vraiment affreux!
Pareils aux mannequins; vaguement ridicules;
Terribles, singuliers comme les somnambules;
Dardant on ne sait où leurs globes ténébreux.

Leurs yeux, d'où la divine étincelle est partie,
Comme s'ils regardaient au loin, restent levés
Au ciel; on ne les voit jamais vers les pavés
Pencher rêveusement leur tête appesantie.

Ils traversent ainsi le noir illimité,
Ce frère du silence éternel. O cité!
Pendant qu'autour de nous tu chantes, ris et beugles,

Éprise du plaisir jusqu'à l'atrocité,
Vois! je me traîne aussi! mais, plus qu'eux hébété,
Je dis: Que cherchent-ils au Ciel, tous ces aveugles?

The Blind

OBSERVE them, O my soul – they are truly frightful, like tailors' dummies; faintly ridiculous, terrifying, and strange, like sleep-walkers, darting this way and that their lightless orbs.

Their eyes, from which the divine spark has departed, as though they were staring into the distance, remain lifted towards the sky: you never see them dreamily bow their weary heads towards the streets.

Thus they pass on through the boundless dark, that brother of eternal silence. O city, while you sing, laugh, and bellow around us, abominably bent on pleasure, behold, I also drag myself along; but even more stupefied than they, I ask myself – What are they looking for in the sky, all those blind men?

[Published 1860]

À UNE PASSANTE

LA rue assourdissante autour de moi hurlait.
Longue, mince, en grand deuil, douleur majestueuse,
Une femme passa, d'une main fastueuse
Soulevant, balançant le feston et l'ourlet;

Agile et noble, avec sa jambe de statue.
Moi, je buvais, crispé comme un extravagant,
Dans son œil, ciel livide où germe l'ouragan,
La douceur qui fascine et le plaisir qui tue.

Un éclair ... puis la nuit! – Fugitive beauté
Dont le regard m'a fait soudainement renaître,
Ne te verrai-je plus que dans l'éternité?

Ailleurs, bien loin d'ici! trop tard! *jamais* peut-être!
Car j'ignore où tu fuis, tu ne sais où je vais,
Ô toi que j'eusse aimée, ô toi qui le savais!

To a Woman Passing By

THE deafening street was howling round me, when a woman passed by, so tall, so slender, all in black, majestically mourning, with her stately hand lifting and swaying the scallop and hem; light-footed and noble, revealing a statuesque leg. And I, tense as a man out of his wits, drank from her eye, a pallid sky in which a tempest brews, that gentleness which bewitches and that pleasure which destroys.

A flash of lightning – then darkness. O fleeting beauty, whose glance brought me suddenly to life again in a second birth, shall I never see you again, except in eternity? Elsewhere, far away from here – too late, or perhaps never? For whither you flee I know not; nor do you know whither I am bound – O you whom I could have loved, O you who knew it!

[Published 1860. See the prose-poem, *Widows*.]

HYMNE À LA BEAUTÉ

VIENS-TU du ciel profond ou sors-tu de l'abîme,
Ô Beauté? ton regard, infernal et divin,
Verse confusément le bienfait et le crime,
Et l'on peut pour cela te comparer au vin.

Tu contiens dans ton œil le couchant et l'aurore;
Tu répands des parfums comme un soir orageux;
Tes baisers sont un philtre et ta bouche une amphore
Qui font le héros lâche et l'enfant courageux.

Sors-tu du gouffre noir ou descends-tu des astres?
Le Destin charmé suit tes jupons comme un chien;
Tu sèmes au hasard la joie et les désastres
Et tu gouvernes tout et ne réponds de rien.

Tu marches sur des morts, Beauté, dont tu te moques;
De tes bijoux l'Horreur n'est pas le moins charmant,
Et le Meurtre, parmi tes plus chères breloques,
Sur ton ventre orgueilleux danse amoureusement.

Hymn to Beauty

O BEAUTY, do you come from the deep heavens, or do you rise from the bottomless pit? Your gaze, daemonic and divine, deals out good deeds and crime together, and in this you resemble wine.

Your eye contains the sunset and the dawn, you spread perfumes about you like a stormy evening; your kisses are a potion, your mouth an amphora, they make heroes cowards, and children brave.

Do you issue from the infernal pit, or do you descend from the stars? Bewitched Destiny follows your skirts like a dog; without discrimination you sow the seed of joy and disasters; you govern all things but answer for none.

You walk upon the dead, O Beauty, scorning them. Horror is not the least fascinating of your jewels; murder, one of your most cherished trinkets, dances lustfully on your proud navel.

L'éphémère ébloui vole vers toi, chandelle,
Crépite, flambe et dit: Bénissons ce flambeau!
L'amoureux pantelant incliné sur sa belle
A l'air d'un moribond caressant son tombeau.

Que tu viennes du ciel ou de l'enfer, qu'importe,
Ô Beauté! monstre énorme, effrayant, ingénu!
Si ton œil, ton souris, ton pied, m'ouvrent la porte
D'un Infini que j'aime et n'ai jamais connu?

De Satan ou de Dieu, qu'importe? Ange ou Sirène,
Qu'importe, si tu rends, – fée aux yeux de velours,
Rythme, parfum, lueur, ô mon unique reine! –
L'univers moins hideux et les instants moins lourds?

L'HORLOGE

HORLOGE! dieu sinistre, effrayant, impassible,
Dont le doigt nous menace et nous dit: «*Souviens-toi!*
Les vibrantes Douleurs dans ton cœur plein d'effroi
Se planteront bientôt comme dans une cible;

The dazzled moth wings towards you, its candle, and sizzles and flames, yet cries, 'Blessed be this torch!' The quivering lover outstretched on his beloved looks like a dying man caressing his tomb.

Whether you come from heaven or hell, O Beauty, huge, frightening, ingenuous monster, what does it matter? What does it matter, so long as your eye, your smile, your foot, open to me the gate of an Infinite which I love and have never known?

What does it matter if you come from Satan or from God? – Angel or Siren, velvet-eyed fairy, all rhythm, perfume, and light, so long as you make the world less hideous and lighten the leaden hours?

[Published October 1860 and in *Les Fleurs du mal*, 1861]

The Clock

THE clock, a sinister, terrifying, inscrutable god, whose finger threatens us, crying '*Remember!* – throbbing pains will soon stab into your cringing heart, as into a target! Pleasure will vanish like a

«Le Plaisir vaporeux fuira vers l'horizon
Ainsi qu'une sylphide au fond de la coulisse;
Chaque instant te dévore un morceau du délice
À chaque homme accordé pour toute sa saison.

«Trois mille six cents fois par heure, la Seconde
Chuchote: *Souviens-toi!* – Rapide, avec sa voix
D'insecte, Maintenant dit: Je suis Autrefois,
Et j'ai pompé ta vie avec ma trompe immonde!

«*Remember! Souviens-toi*, prodigue! *Esto memor!*
(Mon gosier de métal parle toutes les langues.)
Les minutes, mortel folâtre, sont des gangues
Qu'il ne faut pas lâcher sans en extraire l'or!

«*Souviens-toi* que le Temps est un joueur avide
Qui gagne sans tricher, à tout coup! c'est la loi.
Le jour décroît; la nuit augmente; *souviens-toi!*
Le gouffre a toujours soif; la clepsydre se vide.

cloud over the horizon, as a sylph vanishes into the wings of a stage. Every moment is devouring some portion of that delight which is granted to every man for the season of his existence. Three thousand and six hundred times an hour, the Second whispers: "*Remember!*" Swift, with its insect-voice, *Now* says: "I am already your Past, and I have drained your life with my loathsome suckers! *Remember! Souviens-toi*, O prodigal, *Esto memor!*" (My metal throat can speak all languages!) The minutes, O playful mortal, are seams not to be abandoned before you extract their gold. Time is a greedy gambler who at every turn of the wheel wins without cheating. Such is the law! The Day declines, Night waxes fat, *do not forget*! The pit's thirst knows no end, the water-clock runs dry.

«Tantôt sonnera l'heure où le divin Hasard,
Où l'auguste Vertu, ton épouse encor vierge,
Où le Repentir même (oh! la dernière auberge!),
Où tout te dira: Meurs, vieux lâche! il est trop tard!»

LA CHAMBRE DOUBLE

UNE chambre qui ressemble à une rêverie, une chambre véritablement *spirituelle*, où l'atmosphère stagnante est légèrement teintée de rose et de bleu.

L'âme y prend un bain de paresse, aromatisé par le regret et le désir. – C'est quelque chose de crépusculaire, de bleuâtre et de rosâtre; un rêve de volupté pendant une éclipse.

Les meubles y ont des formes allongées, prostrées, alanguies. Les meubles ont l'air de rêver; on les dirait doués d'une vie somnambulique, comme le végétal et le minéral. Les étoffes parlent une langue muette, comme les fleurs, comme les ciels, comme les soleils couchants.

The hour will shortly strike, when divine Chance or austere Virtue (your still virgin spouse!) or even Repentance (the last tavern of all!), in fact everything, will tell you, "Die, you old coward, it's too late now!"'

[Published 1860, and in *Les Fleurs du mal*, 1861. See the prose-poem, *The Double Room*.]

The Double Room

A ROOM like to a daydream, a truly spiritual room, in which the unmoving air is faintly tinged with rosiness and blue.

In it, the soul enjoys a bath of idleness, a bath scented with regret and with desire. It has something of twilight about it, bluish and roseate, a sensuous dream during an eclipse.

The furniture is elongated, prostrate, languorous. The pieces of furniture look as though they were dreaming, as if they lived in a state of sleep, like the vegetable and mineral orders. The draperies speak an unheard language, like flowers, like skies, like setting suns.

Sur les murs nulle abomination artistique. Relativement au rêve pur, à l'impression non analysée, l'art défini, l'art positif est un blasphème. Ici, tout a la suffisante clarté et la délicieuse obscurité de l'harmonie.

Une senteur infinitésimale du choix le plus exquis, à laquelle se mêle une très-légère humidité, nage dans cette atmosphère, où l'esprit sommeillant est bercé par des sensations de serre chaude.

La mousseline pleut abondamment devant les fenêtres et devant le lit; elle s'épanche en cascades neigeuses. Sur ce lit est couchée l'Idole, la souveraine des rêves. Mais comment est-elle ici? Qui l'a amenée? quel pouvoir magique l'a installée sur ce trône de rêverie et de volupté? Qu'importe? la voilà! je la reconnais.

Voilà bien ces yeux dont la flamme traverse le crépuscule; ces subtiles et terribles *mirettes*, que je reconnais à leur effroyable malice! Elles attirent, elles subjuguent, elles dévorent le regard de l'imprudent qui les contemple. Je les ai souvent étudiées, ces étoiles noires qui commandent la curiosité et l'admiration.

There is no artistic abomination on the walls. Compared with the pure dream or the unanalysed impression, definitive or positive art is a blasphemy. Here, everything has the appropriate light and delicious dark of harmony.

An infinitely vague fragrance, most exquisitely chosen, to which is added a hint of moistness, floats in this atmosphere, in which the slumbering mind is lulled by such sensations as a hot-house stirs.

Muslin falls in a profuse shower over the window and the canopy of the bed, streaming in snowy cascades. On this bed reclines the Idol, queen of dreams. How came she there? Who brought her? What magic power set her on that palanquin of reverie and delight? What matter – she is there, I recognize her!

Certainly those are the eyes whose flame sears through the dusk, those subtle and terrifying, ogling eyes which I recognize by their blood-curdling malice. They draw and vanquish and devour the gaze of whatever unwary man contemplates them. I have often studied them, those sable stars which compel curiosity and admiration.

À quel démon bienveillant dois-je d'être ainsi entouré de mystère, de silence, de paix et de parfums? O béatitude! ce que nous nommons généralement la vie, même dans son expansion la plus heureuse, n'a rien de commun avec cette vie suprême dont j'ai maintenant connaissance et que je savoure minute par minute, seconde par seconde!

Non! il n'est plus de minutes, il n'est plus de secondes! Le temps a disparu; c'est l'Éternité qui règne, une éternité de délices!

Mais un coup terrible, lourd, a retenti à la porte, et, comme dans les rêves infernaux, il m'a semblé que je recevais un coup de pioche dans l'estomac.

Et puis un Spectre est entré. C'est un huissier qui vient me torturer au nom de la loi; une infâme concubine qui vient crier misère et ajouter les trivialités de sa vie aux douleurs de la mienne; ou bien le saute-ruisseau d'un directeur de journal qui réclame la suite du manuscrit.

La chambre paradisiaque, l'idole, la souveraine des rêves, la *Sylphide*, comme disait le grand René, toute cette magie a disparu au coup brutal frappé par le Spectre.

To what well-wishing demon am I indebted for being thus surrounded by mystery, silence, peace, and perfumes? O bliss! What we commonly call life, even in its happiest expansiveness, has nothing in common with this life of lives which I now know and savour minute by minute, second by second.

No, there are no more minutes, there are no more seconds. Time has vanished: Eternity reigns, an eternity of delights ...

– But a terrible, heavy thump resounded on the door, and as in hellish dreams, I felt as though I had just received a blow from a pick-axe, in the pit of my stomach ...

And then a ghost came in. It's a bailiff come to torment me in the name of the law, or a shameless concubine come to cry poverty and add the trifles of her existence to the sufferings of mine, or some newspaper-editor's pimp demanding the next instalment of copy.

The room which was heaven on earth, the Idol, the Queen of Dreams, the Sylphide as the great Chateaubriand used to say, – all that magic vanished at the ghost's brutal thumping.

Horreur! je me souviens! je me souviens! Oui! ce taudis, ce séjour de l'éternel ennui, est bien le mien. Voici les meubles sots, poudreux, écornés: la cheminée sans flamme et sans braise, souillée de crachats; les tristes fenêtres où la pluie a tracé des sillons dans la poussière; les manuscrits, raturés ou incomplets; l'almanach où le crayon a marqué les dates sinistres!

Et ce parfum d'un autre monde, dont je m'enivrais avec une sensibilité perfectionnée, hélas! il est remplacé par une fétide odeur de tabac mêlée à je ne sais quelle nauséabonde moisissure. On respire ici maintenant le ranci de la désolation.

Dans ce monde étroit, mais si plein de dégoût, un seul objet connu me sourit: la fiole de laudanum; une vieille et terrible amie; comme toutes les amies, hélas! féconde en caresses et en traîtrise.

Oh! oui! le Temps a reparu; le Temps règne en souverain

O horror, I remember, I remember. Yes, this hovel, this abode of everlasting boredom is indeed my own! See, there are the idiotic bits of furniture, dusty and chipped; the hearth with no flame or glowing ember, all fouled with spit; the dismal windows down which the rain has traced runnels in the grime; the manuscripts crossed out or unfinished; the calendar on which the sinister days are marked in pencil.

And that otherworld perfume on which I waxed exalted with ultra-perfect sensibility is replaced, alas, by a fetid stench of tobacco mingled with the nauseating stink of damp. Here there's a smell of rank desolation.

In this cramped world, so full of disgust, only one familiar thing gives me a smile – the phial of laudanum, an old and formidable girl-friend: like all female friends, alas, she is rich in caresses and treacheries.

Ah, yes, Time has returned: Time now governs like a sovereign,

maintenant, et avec le hideux vieillard est revenu tout son démoniaque cortège de Souvenirs, de Regrets, de Spasmes, de Peurs, d'Angoisses, de Cauchemars, de Colères et de Névroses.

Je vous assure que les secondes maintenant sont fortement et solennellement accentuées, et chacune, en jaillissant de la pendule, dit: – «Je suis la Vie, l'insupportable, l'implacable Vie!»

Il n'y a qu'une Seconde dans la vie humaine qui ait mission d'annoncer une bonne nouvelle, *la bonne nouvelle* qui cause à chacun une inexprimable peur.

Oui! le Temps règne; il a repris sa brutale dictature. Et il me pousse, comme si j'étais un bœuf, avec son double aiguillon. – «Et hue donc! bourrique! Sue donc, esclave! Vis donc, damné!»

and with that hideous old greybeard has returned the whole demoniacal rout of Memories, Regrets, Fits, Fears, Anguishes, Nightmares, Angers, and Neuroses.

I assure you that the Seconds are now strongly and solemnly stressed, and that each one as it jumps from the clock, says: 'I am Life; unbearable, unrelenting Life!'

There is only one Second in human existence whose mission is to announce good news, *the* good news, which arouses an inexplicable fear in every man.

Yes, Time reigns, he has reassumed his bullying dictatorship. And he drives me on, as if I were a bullock, with his double goad. – 'Along with you, you old hack! Sweat, you slave! Live, though you are damned!'

[Published 1862]

PROJET D'ÉPILOGUE

Pour la Seconde Edition des *Fleurs du mal*

TRANQUILLE comme un sage et doux comme un maudit,
...j'ai dit:
Je t'aime, ô ma très-belle, ô ma charmante ...
Que de fois ...
Tes débauches sans soif et tes amours sans âme,
Ton goût de l'infini
Qui partout, dans le mal lui-même, se proclame,

Tes bombes, tes poignards, tes victoires, tes fêtes,
Tes faubourgs mélancoliques,
Tes hôtels garnis,
Tes jardins pleins de soupirs et d'intrigues,
Tes temples vomissant la prière en musique,
Tes désespoirs d'enfant, tes jeux de vieille folle,
Tes découragements;

Et tes feux d'artifice, éruptions de joie,
Qui font rire le Ciel, muet et ténébreux.

Draft of an Epilogue

for the second edition of *Les Fleurs du mal*

CALM as a sage and gentle as one on whom the curse is laid, I said: I love you, O my Beauty, O my charmer. Many a time ... your debauches though you did not thirst, and your soulless love-affairs; your longing for the Infinite, which everywhere, even in Evil, is manifest,

your bombs, your daggers, your victories, your public holidays, your dismal suburbs, your hired furnished rooms, your parks alive with sighs and conspiracies, your chapels vomiting musical prayer, your childish despairs, your old madwife's games, your discouragements;

and your firework-displays, volcanic eruptions of joy, which cheer the dumb and gloomy sky.

Ton vice vénérable étalé dans la soie,
Et ta vertu risible, au regard malheureux,
Douce, s'extasiant au luxe qu'il déploie.

Tes principes sauvés et tes lois conspuées,
Tes monuments hautains où s'accrochent les brumes,
Tes dômes de métal qu'enflamme le soleil,
Tes reines de théâtre aux voix enchanteresses,
Tes tocsins, tes canons, orchestre assourdissant,
Tes magiques pavés dressés en forteresses,

Tes petits orateurs, aux enflures baroques,
Prêchant l'amour, et puis tes égoûts pleins de sang,
S'engouffrant dans l'Enfer comme des Orénoques,

Tes anges, tes bouffons neufs aux vieilles défroques.

Anges revêtus d'or, de pourpre et d'hyacinthe,
Ô vous, soyez témoins que j'ai fait mon devoir
Comme un parfait chimiste et comme une âme sainte.

Your venerable vice displayed in silk, and your laughable virtue with its sad gaze, gentle, delighting in the luxury it exhibits;

your rescued 'principles', your flouted laws, your haughty monuments on which the mists are caught, your domes of metal, fired by the sun, your theatre-queens with their enchanting voices, your tocsins, cannons, that deafening orchestra, your magic cobbles piled up for barricades,

your puny orators' baroque rhetoric, ranting of love while your sewers run with blood, swirling to Hell like Orinoco rivers, your angels, your latest clowns decked in old rags.

Angels clad in gold and purple and hyacinth, O you, bear witness that I've fulfilled my task like a perfect alchemist, like a saintly soul:

Car j'ai de chaque chose extrait la quintessence,

Tu m'as donné ta boue et j'en ai fait de l'or.

ÉPILOGUE

Le cœur content, je suis monté sur la montagne
D'où l'on peut contempler la ville en son ampleur,
Hôpital, lupanars, purgatoire, enfer, bagne,

Où toute énormité fleurit comme une fleur.
Tu sais bien, ô Satan, patron de ma détresse,
Que je n'allais pas là pour répandre un vain pleur;

Mais comme un vieux paillard d'une vieille maîtresse,
Je voulais m'enivrer de l'énorme catin
Dont le charme infernal me rajeunit sans cesse.

for from each thing I've extracted the quintessence. You gave me your mud and I've turned it into gold.

[This draft was written in 1860. Baudelaire wrote to Poulet-Malassis saying that it would be written in *terza rima*. Published posthumously in 1887. Perhaps the Epilogue to the prose-poems (q.v.) which is also unfinished, was intended originally to be the first lines of the above draft?]

Epilogue
[to the prose-poems]

With contented heart I went up the hill from which one can contemplate the city in all its completeness – hospital, brothels, purgatory, hell, penitentiary, in which every outrage blossoms like a flower. You know full well, O Satan, patron of my anguish, that I did not go there to shed a useless tear, but like an old rake with his senile mistress, I sought to intoxicate myself with the enormous bawd whose infernal charm never fails to make me young again.

Que tu dormes encor dans les draps du matin,
Lourde, obscure, enrhumée, ou que tu te pavanes
Dans les voiles du soir passementés d'or fin,

Je t'aime, ô capitale infâme! Courtisanes
Et bandits, tels souvent vous offrez des plaisirs
Que ne comprennent pas les vulgaires profanes.

LA FIN DE LA JOURNÉE

Sous une lumière blafarde
Court, danse et se tord sans raison
La Vie, impudente et criarde.
Aussi, sitôt qu'à l'horizon

La nuit voluptueuse monte,
Apaisant tout, même la faim,
Effaçant tout, même la honte,
Le Poëte se dit: «Enfin!

Whether you sleep still in your morning sheets, lumpish and dark and snivelling with a cold, or whether you strut abroad in your evening veils with fine gold trimmings, I love you, O infamous capital! Harlots and apaches, often you hold out pleasures such as the profane mob cannot understand.

[First published posthumously, 1869]

The End of the Day

In the anaemic sunlight, Life aimlessly rushes and dances and postures, shameless and shrill; so as soon as voluptuous Night looms on the horizon, appeasing all things, even hunger, effacing all things, even shame, the Poet says to himself: 'At last! My mind, like my

«Mon esprit, comme mes vertèbres,
Invoque ardemment le repos;
Le cœur plein de songes funèbres,

«Je vais me coucher sur le dos
Et me rouler dans vos rideaux,
Ô rafraîchissantes ténèbres!»

LA VOIX

MON berceau s'adossait à la bibliothèque,
Babel sombre, où roman, science, fabliau,
Tout, la cendre latine et la poussière grecque,
Se mêlaient. J'étais haut comme un in-folio.

Deux voix me parlaient. L'une, insidieuse et ferme,
Disait: «La Terre est un gâteau plein de douceur;
Je puis (et ton plaisir serait alors sans terme!)
Te faire un appétit d'une égale grosseur.»

Et l'autre: «Viens! oh! viens voyager dans les rêves,
Au delà du possible, au delà du connu!»

spine, is vehemently imploring for rest. With my heart full of disconsolate visions I shall lie on my back and roll myself in your curtains, O refreshing shadows!'

[Published in *Les Fleurs du mal*, 1861]

The Voice

MY cradle had its back to the book-case, a gloomy Babel in which novels, works of science, medieval tales, everything including Latin ash and Greek dust, was jumbled together. I was no taller than a folio.

Two voices used to talk to me. The first, sly and firm, said: 'The earth is a cake full of sweetness. I can give you (and then endless pleasure would be yours) an appetite equally big.' And the second said: 'Come, O come and travel in dreams, beyond the possible,

Et celle-là chantait comme le vent des grèves,
Fantôme vagissant, on ne sait d'où venu,

Qui caresse l'oreille et cependant l'effraie.
Je te répondis: «Oui! douce voix!» C'est d'alors
Que date ce qu'on peut, hélas! nommer ma plaie
Et ma fatalité. Derrière les décors

De l'existence immense, au plus noir de l'abîme,
Je vois distinctement des mondes singuliers,
Et, de ma clairvoyance extatique victime,
Je traîne des serpents qui mordent mes souliers.

Et c'est depuis ce temps que pareil aux prophètes,
J'aime si tendrement le désert et la mer;
Que je ris dans les deuils et pleure dans les fêtes,
Et trouve un goût suave au vin le plus amer;

Que je prends très-souvent les faits pour des mensonges,
Et que, les yeux au ciel, je tombe dans des trous.
Mais la Voix me console et dit: «Garde tes songes:
Les sages n'en ont pas d'aussi beaux que les fous!»

beyond the known!' And the voice sang like the wind on the sea-shores, a keening phantom from who knows where, caressing yet frightening the ear.

I answered you: 'Yes, gentle voice.' From then dates what, alas, may be called my wound and my calamity. For behind the scenes of immense existence, in the pit's deepest dark, I distinctly see strange worlds, and, the entranced victim of my own insight, I am attended by snakes which snap at my shoes. And it is since then that, like the prophets, I so tenderly love the desert and the sea; that I laugh when others are grieving, and weep when they make merry; that I find a smooth flavour in the tartest wine; that I often take facts for lies; and that, with my eyes upon the sky, I tumble into holes. But the Voice consoles me, saying: 'Keep your dreams! – the wise have not such beautiful ones as madmen have!'

[Published February 1861. Cf. *Alchimie de la douleur*, and Pascal: 'Imagination ... has its wise men and its madmen. ... Those gifted with imagination are more at home with themselves than the prudent. ... It cannot make madmen wise, but it makes them happy.']

LA PRIÈRE D'UN PAÏEN

AH! ne ralentis pas tes flammes;
Réchauffe mon cœur engourdi,
Volupté, torture des âmes!
Diva! supplicem exaudi!

Déesse dans l'air répandue,
Flamme dans notre souterrain!
Exauce une âme morfondue,
Qui te consacre un chant d'airain.

Volupté, sois toujours ma reine!
Prends le masque d'une sirène
Faite de chair et de velours,

Ou verse-moi tes sommeils lourds
Dans le vin informe et mystique,
Volupté, fantôme élastique!

A Pagan's Prayer

AH, slow not thy flames; warm my numbed heart again, voluptuousness, tormentor of souls: O goddess, grant my prayer! Goddess who, spread through the air, art a torch in our dark cellar, grant the prayer of a downcast soul who offers thee a hymn of bronze.

Voluptuousness, be thou ever my queen: assume the Siren's mask of flesh and velvet, or pour me thy heavy slumbers in formless, mystic wine, O voluptuousness, elastic Shade!

[Published 1861]

LE REBELLE

Un Ange furieux fond du ciel comme un aigle,
Du mécréant saisit à plein poing les cheveux,
Et dit, le secouant: «Tu connaîtras la règle!
(Car je suis ton bon Ange, entends-tu?) Je le veux!

«Sache qu'il faut aimer, sans faire la grimace,
Le pauvre, le méchant, le tortu, l'hébété,
Pour que tu puisses faire à Jésus, quand il passe,
Un tapis triomphal avec ta charité.

«Tel est l'Amour! Avant que ton cœur ne se blase,
À la gloire de Dieu rallume ton extase;
C'est la Volupté vraie aux durables appas!»

Et l'Ange, châtiant autant, ma foi! qu'il aime,
De ses poings de géant torture l'anathème;
Mais le damné répond toujours: «Je ne veux pas!»

The Rebel

A furious Angel swoops like an eagle from the sky, grips the miscreant's hair in his fist, and says, shaking him: 'You will learn the rule! For I am your good Angel, do you hear? Such is my will. Know that you must love, without wincing, the poor, the wicked, the twisted, the stupid, so that you may make for Jesus, when he comes, a carpet of triumph with your charity.

'Such is Love! Before your heart becomes indifferent, rekindle your ecstasy in God's glory; that is the true voluptuousness, whose charms endure.'

And the Angel, chastising as much – heaven knows – as he loves, tortures the blasphemer with his gigantic fists. But the damned man always answers, 'No, I will not!'

[This poem was listed by Prarond among those written before 1844. If that is the case, why was it not included in *Les Fleurs du mal*, 1857 or 1861? Published in September 1861 it bears the mark of the poet's final, most powerful manner. Perhaps Prarond had confused it with *L'Impénitent*.]

L'AVERTISSEUR

TOUT homme digne de ce nom
A dans le cœur un Serpent jaune,
Installé comme sur un trône,
Qui, s'il dit: «Je veux!» répond: «Non!»

Plonge tes yeux dans les yeux fixes
Des Satyresses ou des Nixes,
La Dent dit: «Pense à ton devoir!»

Fais des enfants, plante des arbres,
Polis des vers, sculpte des marbres,
La Dent dit: «Vivras-tu ce soir?»

Quoi qu'il ébauche ou qu'il espère,
L'homme ne vit pas un moment
Sans subir l'avertissement
De l'insupportable Vipère.

The Warner

EVERY man worthy of the name has, in his heart, a yellow Serpent, set there as on a throne, and which, if he says 'I will!' replies: 'No!'

Plunge your eyes into the unmoving eyes of satyresses and nixies, and the Tooth says: 'Think of your duty!'

Whether you make children or plant trees, or polish verses, or sculpt marbles, the Tooth says: 'Will you still be alive, this night?'

Whatever he undertakes or hopes, man never lives a moment without enduring the insufferable Viper's warning.

[Published September 1861]

ÉPIGRAPHE POUR UN LIVRE CONDAMNÉ

LECTEUR paisible et bucolique,
Sobre et naïf homme de bien,
Jette ce livre saturnien,
Orgiaque et mélancolique.

Si tu n'as fait ta rhétorique
Chez Satan, le rusé doyen,
Jette! tu n'y comprendrais rien,
Ou tu me croirais hystérique.

Mais si, sans se laisser charmer,
Ton œil sait plonger dans les gouffres,
Lis-moi, pour apprendre à m'aimer;

Âme curieuse qui souffres
Et vas cherchant ton paradis,
Plains-moi ... Sinon je te maudis!

Epigraph for a Banned Book

PEACEFUL, bucolic reader; sober, simple decent-chap, throw away this saturnine, lustful, and melancholy book! Unless you learnt your rhetoric from that sly old pedant, Satan, throw it away! – you wouldn't understand a word of it, or you would think me hysterical.

But if, without letting itself be mesmerized, your eye is capable of plumbing the depths, then read me, so as to learn how to love me. Curious, suffering soul, wandering in search of your paradise, give me your sympathy: if not, I curse you!

[Probably written in 1861; published 1865]

RECUEILLEMENT

Sois sage, ô ma Douleur, et tiens-toi plus tranquille.
Tu réclamais le Soir; il descend; le voici:
Une atmosphère obscure enveloppe la ville,
Aux uns portant la paix, aux autres le souci.

Pendant que des mortels la multitude vile,
Sous le fouet du Plaisir, ce bourreau sans merci,
Va cueillir des remords dans la fête servile,
Ma Douleur, donne-moi la main; viens par ici,

Loin d'eux. Vois se pencher les défuntes Années,
Sur les balcons du ciel, en robes surannées;
Surgir du fond des eaux le Regret souriant;

Le Soleil moribond s'endormir sous une arche,
Et, comme un long linceul traînant à l'Orient,
Entends, ma chère, entends la douce Nuit qui marche.

Composure

Have patience, O my sorrow, and be still. You longed for evening, and look, it is falling now. A dusky atmosphere enfolds the city, to some men bringing peace, to others care. While the base herd of mortals, beneath the lash of pleasure, that pitiless torturer, sets out to reap remorse in slavish entertainment, my sorrow, give me your hand, come this way, far from them.

See where the bygone years are leaning from the balconies of heaven, in their faded robes of yesteryear; where Regret, with a smile on her lips, rises from the fountain's depths; where the dying sun falls asleep beneath an arch; and, like a long shroud drifting from the East, listen, my darling, O listen to the gentle night's approach.

[Published in November 1861, and no doubt written in that year, since it was not in 2nd edn of *Les Fleurs du mal*, February 1861. See the prose-poem *Le Crépuscule du soir*.]

LE CRÉPUSCULE DU SOIR

Le jour tombe. Un grand apaisement se fait dans les pauvres esprits fatigués du labeur de la journée; et leurs pensées prennent maintenant les couleurs tendres et indécises du crépuscule.

Cependant du haut de la montagne arrive à mon balcon, à travers les nues transparentes du soir, un grand hurlement, composé d'une foule de cris discordants, que l'espace transforme en une lugubre harmonie, comme celle de la marée qui monte ou d'une tempête qui s'éveille.

Quels sont les infortunés que le soir ne calme pas, et qui prennent, comme les hiboux, la venue de la nuit pour un signal de sabbat? Cette sinistre ululation nous arrive du noir hospice perché sur la montagne; et, le soir, en fumant et en contemplant le repos de l'immense vallée, hérissée de maisons dont chaque fenêtre dit: «C'est ici la paix maintenant; c'est ici la joie de la famille!» je puis, quand le vent souffle de là-haut, bercer ma pensée étonnée à cette imitation des harmonies de l'enfer …

Ô nuit! ô rafraîchissantes ténèbres! vous êtes pour moi le

Evening Twilight (extract)

The day is declining. A great sense of peace pervades those poor minds which are weary from the day's toil, and their thoughts now assume the tender and indefinite hues of twilight.

And yet, from the Montagne Sainte-Geneviève, through the transparent clouds of evening, there comes to my balcony a loud uproar made of a host of discordant cries, transformed by space into a baleful harmony like that of a rising tide or an awakening storm.

Who are those unfortunate ones whom evening does not calm, and who, like owls, take the arrival of night as a signal for pandemonium? The sinister howling comes to us from the gloomy hospital (Val-de-Grâce) perched on the hill-top, and, at evening, as I smoke and look down on the great valley's repose, bristling with homes of which every window says: 'Peace is here, now: here is family happiness!' – I am able, as the wind blows down, to soothe my thoughts, astonished as they are by that counterpart of hell's harmonies.

signal d'une fête intérieure, vous êtes la délivrance d'une angoisse! Dans la solitude des plaines, dans les labyrinthes pierreux d'une capitale, scintillement des étoiles, explosion des lanternes, vous êtes le feu d'artifice de la déesse Liberté!

Crépuscule, comme vous êtes doux et tendre! Les lueurs roses qui traînent encore à l'horizon comme l'agonie du jour sous l'oppression victorieuse de sa nuit, les feux des candélabres qui font des taches d'un rouge opaque sur les dernières gloires du couchant, les lourdes draperies qu'une main invisible attire des profondeurs de l'Orient, imitent tous les sentiments compliqués qui luttent dans le cœur de l'homme aux heures solennelles de la vie.

On dirait encore une de ces robes étranges de danseuses, où une gaze transparente et sombre laisse entrevoir les splendeurs amorties d'une jupe éclatante, comme sous le noir présent transperce le délicieux passé; et les étoiles vacillantes d'or et d'argent, dont elle est semée, représentent ces feux de la fantaisie qui ne s'allument bien que sous le deuil profond de la Nuit!

... O Night, O refreshing shadows! For me you are the signal for inner rejoicing, a deliverance from anguish. In the solitude of the flat suburbs, in the capital's labyrinths of stone, with your scintillation of stars and galaxies of streetlamps, you are the firework-display of the goddess Liberty!

O dusk, how gentle and tender you are! The rosy gleams that still linger on the horizon like the day's agony under the triumphant onslaught of the night, the candelabra-flames which make touches of opaque red on the final glories of the western sky, the heavy draperies drawn by an invisible hand from the depths of the East, reproduce all the complex feelings which conflict in men's hearts in the solemn moments of existence.

Or it suggests one of those dancer's strange costumes in which a dark, transparent gauze gives inklings of the dimmed splendours of a brightly-coloured skirt, just as the delicious Past breaks through the dark Present; and the shimmering stars of gold and silver, with which it is spangled, represent the will-o'-the-wisps of Fancy, which only brighten in the deep mourning of the Night.

[Published 1855]

[The last three paragraphs were added in 1864]

LE COUVERCLE

En quelque lieu qu'il aille, ou sur mer ou sur terre,
Sous un climat de flamme ou sous un soleil blanc,
Serviteur de Jésus, courtisan de Cythère,
Mendiant ténébreux ou Crésus rutilant,

Citadin, campagnard, vagabond, sédentaire,
Que son petit cerveau soit actif ou soit lent,
Partout l'homme subit la terreur du mystère,
Et ne regarde en haut qu'avec un œil tremblant.

En haut, le Ciel! ce mur de caveau qui l'étouffe,
Plafond illuminé par un opéra bouffe
Où chaque histrion foule un sol ensanglanté;

Terreur du libertin, espoir du fol ermite:
Le Ciel! couvercle noir de la grande marmite
Où bout l'imperceptible et vaste Humanité.

The Lid

Wherever he goes, whether on land or sea, under a blazing clime or under a polar sun, whether a servant of Jesus or one who courts Venus, a sullen beggar or a glittering Croesus, be he townsman, countryman, rolling-stone, or stay-at-home; whether his puny brain be quick or slow, everywhere Man endures the fear of mystery and only looks up above him with trembling eye.

Above, is the sky, that burial-vault wall which smothers him, a ceiling lit up by a comic-opera in which every actor treads a blood-drenched stage; the terror of the freethinker, the hope of the crazed hermit – the Sky, the black lid of the enormous cauldron wherein mankind boils, vast and insignificant.

[Published January 1862]

LE COUCHER DU SOLEIL ROMANTIQUE

QUE le soleil est beau quand tout frais il se lève,
Comme une explosion nous lançant son bonjour!
– Bienheureux celui-là qui peut avec amour
Saluer son coucher plus glorieux qu'un rêve!

Je me souviens! J'ai vu tout, fleur, source, sillon,
Se pâmer sous son œil comme un cœur qui palpite ...
– Courons vers l'horizon, il est tard, courons vite,
Pour attraper au moins un oblique rayon!

Mais je poursuis en vain le Dieu qui se retire;
L'irrésistible Nuit établit son empire,
Noire, humide, funeste et pleine de frissons;

Une odeur de tombeau dans les ténèbres nage,
Et mon pied peureux froisse, au bord du marécage,
Des crapauds imprévus et de froids limaçons.

The Sunset of Romanticism

HOW beautiful is the Sun when, all fresh, he rises up, bidding us good-day, like an explosion. Happy is he who can hail, with love, his decline more glorious than a dream!

I remember – I have seen everything, flower, spring, furrow, swoon beneath his eye like a throbbing heart. Let us run towards the horizon, it is late, we must run quickly to catch at least one slanting ray!

But in vain I pursue the withdrawing god; irresistible Night is establishing its sway, black and damp and dismal and full of shudders.

A smell of the grave floats in the shadows, and my faltering foot, on the edge of the swamp, bruises unexpected toads and cold slugs.

[Written in 1862. Far from being a condemnation of Romanticism (which Baudelaire once defined as 'a manner of feeling') this poem strikes a nostalgic note and is directed against the new movement. A note by Baudelaire on the proofs reads: 'It is obvious that by the "irresistible Night" M. Charles Baudelaire was seeking to characterize the present state of literature, and that the *unexpected toads* and *cold slugs* are writers who are not of his school.']

LE GOUFFRE

PASCAL avait son gouffre, avec lui se mouvant.
– Hélas! tout est abîme, – action, désir, rêve,
Parole! et sur mon poil qui tout droit se relève
Maintes fois de la Peur je sens passer le vent.

En haut, en bas, partout, la profondeur, la grève,
Le silence, l'espace affreux et captivant ...
Sur le fond de mes nuits Dieu de son doigt savant
Dessine un cauchemar multiforme et sans trêve.

J'ai peur du sommeil comme on a peur d'un grand trou,
Tout plein de vague horreur, menant on ne sait où;
Je ne vois qu'infini par toutes les fenêtres,

Et mon esprit, toujours du vertige hanté,
Jalouse du néant l'insensibilité.
– Ah! ne jamais sortir des Nombres et des Êtres!

The Pit

PASCAL had his bottomless pit, which went with him everywhere. Alas, all things are a gaping void – action, desire, dreams, words! and many a time I feel the gust of panic passing through my hair, making it stand on end.

High and low, all about, I find depth and desert, silence, a terrible, mesmerizing emptiness. Upon the backcloth of my nights, with cunning hand God draws a multitudinous, unrelenting nightmare.

I am afraid of sleep, as of some great pit brimmed with nameless horror, leading who knows where? – I can see nothing but Infinity through every window, and my mind, obsessed with falling through space, envies the insensibility of Nothingness. Ah, is there no escape from Numbers and Beings?

[Compare the note, towards the end of C.B.'s Journal, *My Heart Laid Bare* (LXXXVII): 'Both morally and physically I have always had the sensation of the pit (*gouffre*); not only the pit of sleep, but of action, dream, memory, desire, regret, remorse, beauty, number, etc. I have cultivated my hysteria with enjoyment and terror. Now, I constantly feel giddy, and today, 23 January 1862, I felt a strange warning; I felt pass over me the wind of the wing of imbecility.' This poem, together with *Plaintes d'un Icare*, was published in 1862, and probably written at that time or late in 1861.]

LA LUNE OFFENSÉE

Ô LUNE qu'adoraient discrètement nos pères,
Du haut des pays bleus où, radieux sérail,
Les astres vont te suivre en pimpant attirail,
Ma vieille Cynthia, lampe de nos repaires,

Vois-tu les amoureux, sur leurs grabats prospères,
De leur bouche en dormant montrer le frais émail?
Le poëte buter du front sur son travail?
Ou sous les gazons secs s'accoupler les vipères?

Sous ton domino jaune, et d'un pied clandestin,
Vas-tu, comme jadis, du soir jusqu'au matin,
Baiser d'Endymion les grâces surannées?

– «Je vois ta mère, enfant de ce siècle appauvri,
Qui vers son miroir penche un lourd amas d'années,
Et plâtre artistement le sein qui t'a nourri!»

The Shocked Moon

O MOON, whom our fathers worshipped prudently, from the height of the blue lands where the radiant harem of stars attend you in dainty attire; my old Cynthia, lanthorn of our dens,

can you see the lovers, on their thriving beds, revealing, in their slumber, the cool enamel of their mouths; the poet, bruising his brow at his task; or the snakes coupling under the dry grasses?

Under your yellow mantle, with furtive step, do you still, as in the past, from eve till morn, come down to kiss Endymion's faded charms?

'I can see your mother, O child of this impoverished century, who bends a heavy mass of years over her looking-glass, and artistically daubs the breast that suckled you.'

[Published 1862]

LES PLAINTES D'UN ICARE

LES amants des prostituées
Sont heureux, dispos et repus;
Quant à moi, mes bras sont rompus
Pour avoir étreint des nuées.

C'est grâce aux astres nonpareils,
Qui tout au fond du ciel flamboient,
Que mes yeux consumés ne voient
Que des souvenirs de soleils.

En vain j'ai voulu de l'espace
Trouver la fin et le milieu;
Sous je ne sais quel œil de feu
Je sens mon aile qui se casse;

Et brûlé par l'amour du beau,
Je n'aurai pas l'honneur sublime
De donner mon nom à l'abîme
Qui me servira de tombeau.

Laments of an Icarus

LOVERS of harlots are happy, cheerful, and satiated; but as for me, my arms are racked through embracing clouds. It is thanks to the incomparable stars which blaze in the sky's remotest depths, that my burnt-out eyes can see nought but memories of suns.

Vainly have I sought to discover the end and centre of space: beneath I know not what eye of fire I feel my wing dissolve, and, scorched by the love of beauty, I shall not have the sublime honour of giving my name to the bottomless pit which will serve me for a tomb.

[First published and probably written, in 1862; cf. *Le Gouffre*]

L'EXAMEN DE MINUIT

La pendule, sonnant minuit,
Ironiquement nous engage
À nous rappeler quel usage
Nous fîmes du jour qui s'enfuit:
– Aujourd'hui, date fatidique,
Vendredi, treize, nous avons,
Malgré tout ce que nous savons,
Mené le train d'un hérétique;

Nous avons blasphémé Jésus,
Des Dieux le plus incontestable!
Comme un parasite à la table
De quelque monstrueux Crésus,
Nous avons, pour plaire à la brute,
Digne vassale des Démons,
Insulté ce que nous aimons,
Et flatté ce qui nous rebute;

Contristé, servile bourreau,
Le faible qu'à tort on méprise;
Salué l'énorme Bêtise,
La Bêtise au front de taureau;

The Poet Examines his Conscience at Midnight

The clock, striking midnight, ironically summons us to recall what use we made of the now vanishing day. Today (an ill-starred date, Friday the Thirteenth), though we know better we behaved like a heretic. We blasphemed against Jesus, the most unquestionable of gods. Like a parasite at the table of some monstrous Croesus, a fit slave of the devils in hell, so as to toady to the brute we insulted what we love and praised what we loathe. We discomfited like a servile torturer the weak man who is unjustly looked down on; saluted enormous Stupidity – bull-browed Stupidity; kissed stupid

Baisé la stupide Matière
Avec grande dévotion,
Et de la putréfaction
Béni la blafarde lumière.

Enfin, nous avons, pour noyer
Le vertige dans le délire,
Nous, prêtre orgueilleux de la Lyre,
Dont la gloire est de déployer
L'ivresse des choses funèbres,
Bu sans soif et mangé sans faim! ...
– Vite soufflons la lampe, afin
De nous cacher dans les ténèbres!

À UNE HEURE DU MATIN

ENFIN! seul! On n'entend plus que le roulement de quelques fiacres attardés et éreintés. Pendant quelques heures, nous posséderons le silence, sinon le repos. Enfin! la tyrannie de la face humaine a disparu, et je ne souffrirai plus que par moi-même.

Enfin! il m'est donc permis de me délasser dans un bain de ténèbres! D'abord, un double tour à la serrure. Il me

Matter with great devotion, and blessed the sickly light of putrefaction. Finally, to drown our giddiness in delirium, we, the proud priest of the Lyre whose glory it is to disclose the rapture of sad things, drank without thirst and ate without hunger. Quick, let us blow out the lamp, so as to hide ourself in the dark!

[Compare *The End of the Day* and the prose-poem *At One o'clock in the Morning*. Published in February 1863]

At One o'clock in the Morning

ALONE, at last! Nothing can be heard but the clatter of a few belated, fagged-out cabs. For a few hours we'll have silence, if not rest. At last the tyranny of the human face has disappeared, and I'll suffer no more but from myself.

At last I'm allowed to relax in a bath of gloom! First, a double turn of the key in the lock: I have the feeling that this turn of the

semble que ce tour de clef augmentera ma solitude et fortifiera les barricades qui me séparent actuellement du monde.

Horrible vie! Horrible ville! Récapitulons la journée: avoir vu plusieurs hommes de lettres, dont l'un m'a demandé si l'on pouvait aller en Russie par voie de terre (il prenait sans doute la Russie pour une île); avoir disputé généreusement contre le directeur d'une revue, qui à chaque objection répondait: «C'est ici le parti des honnêtes gens», ce qui implique que tous les autres journaux sont rédigés par des coquins; avoir salué une vingtaine de personnes, dont quinze me sont inconnues; avoir distribué des poignées de main dans la même proportion, et cela sans avoir pris la précaution d'acheter des gants; être monté pour tuer le temps, pendant une averse, chez une sauteuse qui m'a prié de lui dessiner un costume de *Vénustre*; avoir fait ma cour à un directeur de théâtre, qui m'a dit en me congédiant: «Vous feriez peut-être bien de vous adresser à Z...; c'est le plus lourd, le plus sot et le plus célèbre de tous mes auteurs; avec lui vous pourriez peut-être aboutir à quelque

key will enlarge my solitude and strengthen the barriers that now isolate me from the world.

Horrible life and horrible city! Let's sum up the day: seen a few men of letters, one of whom asked me if you can go to Russia overland (no doubt he thought Russia was an island!); argued my head off with the editor of a review who answered every protest with: 'We stand for decent folk', which implies that all the other papers are scribbled by scoundrels; paid my compliments to a score of people, fifteen of them perfect strangers; gave the same number of handshakes without having taken the precaution of buying a pair of gloves; went up – to kill time during a shower – to call on a female dancer who asked me to make her a drawing of a 'Venustra' (Venus) costume; called on the boss of a theatre, who said as he showed me off the premises: 'You'd be well advised to see X... he's the dullest, silliest, and most famous of all my writers – you could

chose. Voyez-le, et puis nous verrons»; m'être vanté (pourquoi?) de plusieurs vilaines actions que je n'ai jamais commises, et avoir lâchement nié quelques autres méfaits que j'ai accomplis avec joie, délit de fanfaronnade, crime de respect humain; avoir refusé à un ami un service facile, et donné une recommandation à un parfait drôle; ouf! est-ce bien fini?

Mécontent de tous et mécontent de moi, je voudrais bien me racheter et m'enorgueillir un peu dans le silence et la solitude de la nuit. Âmes de ceux que j'ai aimés, âmes de ceux que j'ai chantés, fortifiez-moi, soutenez-moi, éloignez de moi le mensonge et les vapeurs corruptrices du monde; et vous, Seigneur mon Dieu! accordez-moi la grâce de produire quelques beaux vers qui me prouvent à moi-même que je ne suis pas la dernier des hommes, que je ne suis pas inférieur à ceux que je méprise.

no doubt go places with him. Try him, then we'll see.' Boasted (why on earth???) of a few dirty tricks I've never committed, and was cowardly enough to deny a few other lapses that gave me a thrill at the time – sin of showing off, offence against human decency – refused a friend a service that would have cost nothing, and gave a written testimonial to a perfect nitwit. Phew, is that the lot?

Dissatisfied with everyone, including myself, I would gladly redeem myself and retrieve my pride in the silence and loneliness of the night. O souls of those whom I have loved, O souls of those whom I have sung, strengthen me, bear me up, drive from me all falsehood and the world's corrupting vapours; and thou, O my Lord and my God, grant me the grace to produce a few lines of poetry which will prove to me that I am not the lowest of men, that I am not below those whom I despise!

[Published August 1862]

L'IMPRÉVU

I

HARPAGON qui veillait son père agonisant,
Se dit, rêveur, devant ces lèvres déjà blanches:
«Nous avons au grenier un nombre suffisant,
Ce me semble, de vieilles planches?»

Célimène roucoule et dit: «Mon cœur est bon,
Et naturellement, Dieu m'a faite très-belle.»
– Son cœur! cœur racorni, fumé comme un jambon,
Recuit à la flamme éternelle!

Un gazetier fumeux, qui se croit un flambeau,
Dit au pauvre, qu'il a noyé dans le ténèbres:
«Où donc l'aperçois-tu, ce créateur du Beau,
Ce redresseur que tu célèbres?»

Mieux que tous, je connais certain voluptueux
Qui bâille nuit et jour, et se lamente et pleure,
Répétant, l'impuissant et le fat: «Oui, je veux
Être vertueux, dans une heure!»

The Unforeseen

I

HARPAGON, watching over his dying father, said to himself as he mused over those already blanched lips: 'I suppose we have enough old planks in the loft?'

Célimène coos like a dove and says: 'I'm kind-hearted, and of course God made me very lovely.' – Her heart! – a shrivelled heart, smoked like a ham, cooks over again in the everlasting fire.

A dim-witted journalist who thinks he's a torch of light, says to the poor chap whom he's drowned in obscurity: 'Where, then, do you see him, this creator of beauty, this righter of wrongs whom you acclaim?'

Better than all, I know a certain sensualist who yawns night and day and laments and weeps, repeating, impotent fop that he is: 'Yes, I want to be good – but only in an hour's time!'

L'Horloge à son tour, dit à voix basse: «Il est mûr,
Le damné! J'avertis en vain la chair infecte.
L'homme est aveugle, sourd, fragile comme un mur
Qu'habite et que ronge un insecte!»

II

Et puis, quelqu'un paraît que tous avaient nié,
Et qui leur dit, railleur et fier: «Dans mon ciboire,
Vous avez, que je crois, assez communié
À la joyeuse Messe noire?

«Chacun de vous m'a fait un temple dans son cœur;
Vous avez, en secret, baisé ma fesse immonde!
Reconnaissez Satan à son rire vainqueur,
Énorme et laid comme le monde!

«Avez-vous donc pu croire, hypocrites surpris,
Qu'on se moque du maître, et qu'avec lui l'on triche,
Et qu'il soit naturel de recevoir deux prix,
D'aller au Ciel et d'être riche?

The clock, in its turn, says in an undertone: 'The doomed man is ripe. Vainly do I warn the vile flesh: man is blind, deaf, weak, like a wall infested and gnawed away by a beetle.'

II

And then Someone appears, one whom they had all denied, and who says to them, jeering and proud: 'I think you have taken communion often enough from my pyx, at the jolly Black Mass! Each of you has made me a temple in his heart, you have furtively kissed my loathsome rump. Now, recognize Satan by his triumphant laughter, as huge and ugly as the world! Could you really believe, unmasked hypocrites, that you can bamboozle the Master and play him false, and that it's natural to be given two prizes – to go to heaven, and be rich? The game must be worth while for the old

«Il faut que le gibier paye le vieux chasseur
Qui se morfond longtemps à l'affût de la proie.
Je vais vous emporter à travers l'épaisseur,
Compagnons de ma triste joie,

«À travers l'épaisseur de la terre et du roc,
À travers les amas confus de votre cendre,
Dans un palais aussi grand que moi, d'un seul bloc
Et qui n'est pas de pierre tendre;

«Car il est fait avec l'universel Péché,
Et contient mon orgueil, ma douleur et ma gloire!»

III

– Cependant, tout en haut de l'univers juché,
Un ange sonne la victoire

De ceux dont le cœur dit: «Que béni soit son fouet,
Seigneur! que la Douleur, ô Père, soit bénie!

sportsman, who has to cool his heels as he stalks his quarry! I am going to carry you off into the thickness, O cronies of my dismal joy – through the thickness of earth and rock, through the chaotic mass of your own ashes, into a palace as big as myself, all of a piece, not made of soft stone, for it is made of Universal Sin, and contains my pride, my sorrow, and my glory.'

III

And yet, set at the very pinnacle of the universe, an Angel acclaims the victory of those whose heart says: 'Blessed be thy lash, O Lord, blessed be suffering, O Father! My soul in thy hands is no idle toy,

Mon âme dans tes mains n'est pas un vain jouet,
    Et ta prudence est infinie.»

Le son de la trompette est si délicieux,
Dans ces soirs solennels de célestes vendanges,
Qu'il s'infiltre comme une extase dans tous ceux
    Dont elle chante les louanges.

and infinite is thy providence.' The sound of the trump is so delightful in those solemn evenings of heaven's harvests, that it filters, like an ecstasy, into all those whose praise it sings.

[Published in 1863, this poem is regarded as being a reply to Barbey d'Aurevilly (to whom it was dedicated), who had written in an article that the author of *Les Fleurs du mal* had only two choices remaining: to become a Christian or blow his brains out. Baudelaire's own note on the poem is: 'Here the author of *Les Fleurs du mal* is turning towards the eternal life. It had to end that way. Let us observe that, like all the newly-converted, he is very strict and very fanatical.']

Index of First Lines

INDEX OF FIRST LINES

Index of Titles

INDEX OF TITLES

Some other books published by Penguins are described on the following pages.

THE PENGUIN BOOK OF FRENCH VERSE

(This collection contains a plain prose translation of each poem)

VOLUME I

To the Fifteenth Century

EDITED BY BRIAN WOLEDGE

This volume covers the earliest six hundred years of French poetry. It contains an excellent selection of verse, much of it naturally anonymous, stretching from the *Chanson de Roland* to the work of François Villon.

VOLUME 2

The Sixteenth to the Eighteenth Century

EDITED BY GEOFFREY BRERETON

A selection covering nearly three hundred years of French poetry from the decline of the medieval influence to the beginnings of Romanticism, including French verse of the Renaissance.

VOLUME 3

The Nineteenth Century

EDITED BY ANTHONY HARTLEY

This century, which includes such names as Baudelaire, Hugo, Rimbaud, and Mallarmé, can rank with the greatest eras of world literature. The poems included have been chosen on their merits and not merely to illustrate historical development.

VOLUME 4

The Twentieth Century

EDITED BY ANTHONY HARTLEY

An introduction to this volume analyses the relationship between modern French verse and English and European literature, and the collection extends from the turn of the century to the present day. It includes Claudel, Valéry, Péguy, Aragon, and many others.

A SHORT HISTORY OF FRENCH LITERATURE

Geoffrey Brereton

This new, compact history deals in outline with the whole of French literature, from the *chansons de geste* to the theatre today. While the chief works of the Middle Ages are described briefly, the great writers since the beginnings of the Renaissance receive fuller treatment, and almost half the book is devoted to the nineteenth and twentieth centuries. Over eight hundred years of rich and varied writings are treated on a scale which makes clear the great general movements of thought and taste without neglecting the characteristic qualities of individual authors and their works. These are approached primarily as literature, to be read as the personal expressions of particularly interesting minds, but they are related to the social history of their time and, on occasion, to the literature of countries other than France. The book is intended for the general reader and for the student who wishes to take his bearings before specializing in any one particular field. Based on modern scholarship and reflecting modern critical opinion, it is a concisely informative as well as a companionable work.